Captured by Moonlight
~Twilight of the British Raj~
~ 2 ~

Captured by Moonlight
~Twilight of the British Raj~
~ 2 ~
Christine Lindsay

WhiteFire
Publishing

This is a work of fiction. All characters and events portrayed in this novel are either fictitious or used fictitiously.

CAPTURED BY MOONLIGHT

WhiteFire Publishing
13607 Bedford Rd NE
Cumberland, MD 21502

ISBN: 978-1-939023-00-1

This fictional story is dedicated to the memory of Pandita Ramabai,
a great Christian heroine, and to her work that continues today
at the Ramabai Mukti Mission in India,
where the redemptive love of Christ gives new life
to orphans and to forgotten and abused women

Christine Lindsay

"Buried with Him…that…even so we also should walk in newness of live."
~ Romans 6:4

1

Amritsar, Northern India, Late October, 1921

If the head woman from the temple looked in her direction, Laine Harkness wouldn't give two squashed mangoes for her life, or Eshana's. Laine could never be confused for an Indian, but with the tail end of this cotton sari covering half her face, and her brown eyes peeking over, she simply had to blend in. Still, any minute now that hatchet-faced female standing guard to the girls' quarters could let out a pulse-freezing yell.

A sudden blare of a conch shell from within the Hindu temple stretched Laine's nerves. She and Eshana must be mad to risk this exploit again. The principal matron at Laine's hospital would give her a severe reprimand if she ever found out. More likely sack her. If either she or Eshana had any sense at all, they'd turn around, go back to the mission, and mind their own business.

But a line from Wordsworth, one of Adam's favorites, ran through her mind...*little, nameless, unremembered acts of kindness and of love...*

Blast! She wouldn't call what she and Eshana were about to do little, but please let it be unremembered. Unnoticed would be better still.

Nudging Eshana in the side and closing her mind to the writhing creatures in the burlap bags they carried, she hissed into Eshana's ear. "Well off you go. You've got yours to dispose of, and I've got mine. Just please keep that guard distracted." Laine jutted her chin toward the obese head woman waddling around in a sari stained down the front with betel juice. Every once in a while she would take her long wooden club and rap on the doors of the hovels.

Eshana hurried through the narrow alleyway toward the guardian of the temple girls, carrying a burlap sack similar to Laine's.

On the opposite side of the bazaar, the globelike spires of a temple devoted to a Hindu goddess poked above nearby rooftops. Like a multi-tiered cake decorated in a variety of colored icings—pinks, blues, orange—the temple enticed like a sugary concoction.

But from there the loveliness ended. In these alleyways behind the temple, the pervasive scent of incense and stale flowers mixed with the reek of human misery. Girls who should still be playing with toys, and some a little older, chatted with one another. Many of the paint-chipped doors were closed, imprisoning within those adolescent girls forced into ritual marriages to a Hindu deity.

Laine flattened herself against a peeling plaster wall to watch Eshana shake out the contents of her sack at the base of a cluster of clay pots. Now she waved her hands about, talking in rapid Hindi to the older woman. *Good girl, Eshana, that's the ticket.* Laine's stomach writhed in rhythm to the creature in the bag she carried. She strengthened her grip at the top of the sack though the drawstring had been tightly pulled.

Sure enough the head woman stomped off with Eshana and began to clatter around the pots with her club, giving Laine the moment she waited for. Sixth door from the end on this side, Eshana had told her. Eshana had been visiting the inhabitants of this alley on a regular basis in an attempt to give them some sort of medical aid.

Laine hunched down at the correct threshold. A gap of five or so inches between the door and the mud floor of the girl's hovel afforded her the needed space.

The low voice of the so-called midwife seeped out. *Midwife, my eye.* Nothing more than witch doctors with their foolish notions that no water should be given to those giving birth and that the mothers be kept in dark rooms with filthy concoctions of ash smeared over them. Laine shut her mind to the atrocities of how they forced a baby out if it took too long to be delivered.

She kneeled at the bottom of the closed door. With a deep swallow and shudder, she slotted the top of the sack into the gap below the door. With her other hand she eased the drawstring, loosened the bag's opening, and jumped back to flatten against the wall.

Another shudder rippled through her as she waited. Nothing. Her gaze flitted from the ground to the flat rooftops of this rancid boil of a place. Where had the horrible, disgusting creatures gone? *Oh please don't come out at me.*

At last, screams from inside room number six shattered the sleepy deadness of the afternoon.

"Snake!" one woman screeched in Hindi.

Another cry pierced the air. "A cobra!"

They tumbled from the room, and with a gulp Laine slipped inside. "They're not poisonous. They're not poisonous," she repeated to bolster her flagging courage. But she had no time to worry where the rat snakes had wriggled off to.

She went still. There lay the girl.

So small for fourteen, lying on a heap of rags stained with water and blood. She peered at Laine with eyes soaked with pain. There was no time to waste. Laine picked up the girl and, cradling her in her arms, ran from the hovel. The young mother weighed no more than a ten-year-old. All skin and bones except for the mound that was a baby in her womb. The girl batted at Laine's arm as ineffectually as a wounded bird against a tiger.

Eshana, having heard the screams, scurried away from the women who were beating the bushes, searching through the earthen pots for the harmless snakes. Eshana ran ahead to help Laine lift the girl into the closed purdah cart they had hired. As soon as the three of them were in the cart, Eshana yelled, "Drive, *juldi, juldi*! Hurry."

Their Sikh driver flicked a whip, and his startled horse bolted down the cobblestoned bazaar. No one followed them as stalls full of wares, bolts of silk, fruits and vegetables, copper pots of steaming food, and a multitude of people flashed past in a blur of color.

Laine placed her fingers on the girl's pulse. "She's dehydrated. Feel her skin, her fingertips." She pulled back the girl's eyelids. "Eyes dull."

The patient pushed Laine's hands away and moaned.

"It's all right now, little one." Laine spoke in Hindi. Lifting the girl's wrist, she planted a kiss against the weakening pulse. "We're not going to hurt you."

The girl's gaze tracked from Eshana to Laine's while the purdah cart wound through the streets to the other side of Amritsar. Her eyelids drooped and closed by the time the cart stopped outside the narrow, four-story mission close to the Jallianwalla Bagh.

Mala and Tikah thrust the front doors open and carried out a cot. Within minutes they transported the patient into the surgery where they were met with the clean smell of carbolic soap. As Eshana and Laine washed their hands, Mala hooked the girl up to a saline drip while Tikah bathed her with a warm soapy cloth allowing them to see her pallid skin beneath its applied layer of ash. Laine pinned her nursing veil to her hair.

Eshana tightened the blood pressure cuff on the patient's arm. "Her pressure is dangerously low."

The girl fluttered her eyes open to see the sterile clinic and instruments. With a pleading look she tried to speak. Laine brushed the girl's hair from her forehead. "We only want to help you and your baby. Just tell me your name."

"Chandrabha," the girl choked out.

"All right then, I'm going to call you Chandra for short, and now I'm going to examine you. Don't be afraid."

Half an hour later, as the last of the afternoon sun faded, so too did Eshana's hope. Drenched in sweat and the girl's blood, she watched Laine step away from the examining table.

"No use, Eshana. The pelvis is too small. We have to get a doctor."

Eshana sank her head into her hand. "There is only Dr. Kaur. He is very kind, but I do not wish to involve him."

"If we don't involve him she'll die. If she does die, then we'll need him to record her death properly." Laine's matter-of-fact tone matched the steadiness in her gaze. "And you and I could go to jail."

Eshana gave a firm jut of her chin. "What of it? If Miriam still lived, she would do all she could for the life of this girl. I will go."

Tikah glanced up from bathing the girl's brow. "It will be well, my sister. Go, and bring the doctor. Mala and I will assist the nursing-*sahiba*."

Chandra gave a weak moan. The saline had rehydrated her body so that she had gained only enough strength to communicate her pain. There was no time to lose. Eshana rushed from the room and quickly changed into a clean garment. Whipping the end of her cotton sari over her head, she raced out of the mission. *Lord Yeshu, keep the temple woman from remembering my face. Do not let them come here to hurt the people of this house.*

Dr. Jai Kaur's office lay two streets away, and Eshana's thin-soled *chappals* pounded the cobblestones. She bumped into several people and pushed her way through the crowded bazaar. Her chest burned as she tried to catch her breath and opened the door to his clinic.

Patients sat cross-legged or hunched down against the walls waiting, but Jai Kaur shot her a glance as she stumbled into the room.

He left the patient he had been examining behind a curtain, strode toward Eshana, and towered over her. "What is it?"

"A girl in labor. She is dying." Eshana's hand crept to her throat to settle her breathing.

Jai turned away to wash his hands and spoke to someone behind another curtain. "Father, I will leave you to see the rest of the patients. I must attend an emergency birthing."

Hooks screeched along the metal rod as Jai's father, Dr. Kaur Senior, pushed aside the curtain. Beneath his red turban, the man's heavy-lidded gaze swept Eshana then rested on Jai. "Your responsibilities, my son, are with our own patients." He modulated his voice low for the sake of the people filling the room.

Jai met the older man's gaze. Like his father, in the custom of the Sikhs he had combed his un-cut black beard and rolled it beneath his chin. He had meticulously tied his royal blue turban around his head, adding several more inches to his imposing height. "Father, I have already ascertained that no one in this room is requiring emergency care. I will return as soon as this other life is out of danger. Is that not why you had me follow in your footsteps? To give aid to those who are suffering, no matter what their faith?"

The senior Dr. Kaur slashed a hand in the air. "Go then. But hurry back. It is most likely this woman is trying to save the life of another of those temple girls, who are no more than harlots. Disgusting, this *Devadasi,* a Hindu practice that is a terrible blight on India."

Eshana understood his Sikh revulsion for this particular Hindu custom, but felt that his distaste included her too. Jai did not waste another moment. He picked up his medical valise and strode from the clinic. She had to run to catch up with his long strides as he struck out for the mission.

Unlike her, Jai breathed normally in spite of his pace. "Is this patient a temple girl?"

"The suffering of this human being is no different than any other."

He stopped suddenly so that she had to turn back to face him. People filed past them in the bee-hive of a bazaar. "So it is true. I can see it in your eyes. You were never meant for subterfuge, Eshana." He picked up his pace again. "I have no qualms about helping anyone who needs my services. But you must take a care for yourself. I am worrying about you and the other women of your mission. It has been a year and a half since your founder, Miriam, died, with still no administrator to fill her place."

She pushed her chin out in a way her beloved Miriam would have recognized. "I have written to the mission headquarters. I see no reason why they should not consider me as administrator to carry on Miriam's work."

Jai must have seen something in the unbending set of her neck. He softened his tone. "The mission headquarters would do wisely to place you in that role. But do you not still desire to become a physician?"

Memories of sitting with Miriam at the top of the four-story house pulled at the strings of her heart. Many times they had sat mending clothing in the evenings while the houseful of orphans and patients slept. Many nights they had discussed Eshana's desire to become a doctor, and prayed for that. But Miriam had died. Eshana shook off the memories. "I cannot be leaving the mission to study medicine. Besides, the women of our house have learned much from Laine Harkness. And if we need a doctor you have been gracious to come to our aid."

His eyes as black as agates grew somber. "I cannot always come, Eshana. Someone in your mission needs to gain proper medical training."

"As I have said, I must keep the mission running." She turned her back to him, straight as a ruler, as her mother so long ago had taught her, and renewed her steps.

His swift paces caught up to her. "What will you do, Eshana, if the Hindu priests and certain high-caste people learn of what you are doing, that this is not the first untouchable female you have taken away, but the second? Your charitable work could come under scrutiny."

She let her gaze drop from his piercing one. Jai was right, of course. Miriam's mission could come under scrutiny. Did she have the right to place the mission—the children—in such danger? Or worse than scrutiny, what if one night a Hindu fanatic who believed her actions showed no respect for their religion entered the house as the children slept?

2

Laine could hardly wait for a soak in a hot tub. That and a decent cup of tea. She straightened up from washing her hands and arms under the tap in the surgery sink.

Her neck ached after assisting Jai Kaur in the Caesarean he had performed on Chandra. Shortly after she'd brought Chandra to the mission she'd known the baby would never take its first breath of life. Though that the mother—a child herself—lived was a miracle, the whole wretched situation bore down on Laine. She ran a hand around her neck to massage it. Unlike Eshana, she didn't believe she could change the world. But in the face of such suffering, one simply had to do their bit.

She needed to unwind these tired muscles though if she was going to be any good to her patients at the hospital tomorrow. More likely her neck screamed from the strain of kidnapping that poor girl this afternoon. She pursed her lips together to hold back a laugh. It wasn't the lead temple woman that had scared her. It was the terror of releasing those two snakes.

Another shiver slid like ice down her back. She hated snakes. Vile, despicable, malevolent things. She would never understand why God created them. If she ever got to Heaven she'd ask the good Lord about that. If the Lord let her through the pearly gates, which she sorely doubted. Not with her bad temper and irreverent manner of speaking. Her father had told her often enough her sauciness would bring her to a bad end. Good thing her parents had passed on and couldn't see her father's prediction coming true.

Jai Kaur had finished suturing the mother, while Tikah wrapped the poor little scrap of humanity in a white cloth and took the baby girl away. Laine held in a sigh. She'd learned early in The Great War to hide her pain when one of her patients died. And there'd been so many.

The doctor gave Chandra a shot of morphine for the pain she would have when she came out of her anesthetic. He sat waiting at the girl's bedside for this to happen, tapping her cheek and rubbing her hands. Eshana stood next to him, putting the final touches to the patient's bandages.

Laine listened to the two of them talking in low tones, and her ears perked.

Eshana had never shown the slightest interest in any man except Geoff Richards, and he filled the role of big brother in her life. She treated every other man who came to the mission simply as patients. The grown-up boys from the mission who returned home every once in a while to visit, she treated like brothers.

But today Eshana didn't bustle about the surgery, mildly ordering the other girls about, or setting things right the way she normally would. She, who never wasted a minute of any day that could be used to aid another, stood gazing up into the doctor's almost black eyes. Little Eshana was hanging on the words of this tall, slender Sikh as he gave instructions for the patient's care.

And his gaze frequently returned to Eshana's for much longer than necessary.

Laine didn't bother to hide her grin and sent a pointed glance to Eshana.

Not surprisingly, Eshana refused to acknowledge her. But when the patient gave a small moan, simultaneously as if they were two halves of the same person, Jai and Eshana turned to the girl. A moment later doctor and devoted nurse breathed the same breath of satisfaction at the girl's status.

Oh...my...goodness. Laine's laughter threatened to erupt. About time someone fell in love. Certainly never again for her. Once burned was enough in that department, thank you very much. It was the life of spinsterhood for her. But really, she ought to take up something a little safer these days to help out the populace. Slipping snakes under doors and kidnapping distressed temple girls was getting a bit risky. Perhaps instead she should take up knitting.

Jai readied himself to leave and nodded in Laine's direction. "It was good to work with you again, Matron. Although I desire to give you the same word of caution I gave to Eshana. As soon as this child is well you must return her to the temple. She is their property, and they are legally in their rights to have her back."

Laine removed the pins that attached her nursing veil to her hair and let her hand holding the veil flop to her side. "Where of course her syphilis will flare up, and she'll die in a few years. I thought you as a Sikh did not approve of girls from the untouchable class being used as Hindu temple prostitutes."

"As a Sikh I abhor the caste system and the way Hindus treat those lowest in their sight. But I am speaking of the danger in which you and Eshana place yourselves. If caught, the Hindus have every right to have you prosecuted. We can only hope the British courts will give you a mere slap on the wrist for interfering, but Eshana, being an Indian woman, would be punished severely for any such crimes."

He moved to the door of the surgery. "I beg of you...." His gaze dismissed Laine and sought Eshana's. "I beg of you to be taking my words to heart."

As if drawn by a magnet, Eshana went with him to the front of the house to see him out, and Laine trudged up the four flights of stairs to the room at the top. Miriam had been dead almost two years, and still the household referred to this floor as her room.

The glass-paneled doors stood open to let in the evening air. Scents from the city below invaded—spices, dust, the smoke from cooking fires carried on the breeze along with the fragrance of Miriam's roses and lilies on the balcony. The last wash of sunset outlined the shapes of the city, the minaret of a mosque, the *gopuram* of a Hindu temple, and the spires and domes of the Golden Temple of the Sikhs.

Inside, a smoking lamp in the corner lit portions of the room that glowed like warm marble. Miriam's single, rope-strung bed still took up the corner. And on a reed table next to the bed, her Bible written in Hindustani lay open where the girls gathered each morning and evening to read.

Eshana and the other young women used to be Miriam's girls, like the rest of the inhabitants of this house—poor children or newborn girls discarded by their families, cast-off child Hindu widows like Eshana. Or like Tikah the Muslim woman whom Eshana had brought to this house during the recent trouble between England and Afghanistan. They'd all found peace for their troubled hearts in this house. Even Abby Richards had.

But not Laine. No, definitely not her.

If she hurried though, she might make it to the going-away party for Abby and Geoff. Have a few laughs, throw off this millstone hanging about her heart.

She had planned on going home to the nurses' residence to change into party duds, but her no-nonsense tailored skirt and white shirt suited her mood better than a dancing frock. A cloudy mirror on Miriam's armoire afforded her a glimpse of her hair caught in a roll at the back of her neck. She patted the bobbed waves she'd worked so hard to shape out of her long, straight tresses. Well, that was as good as it was going to get.

But the grin she flashed at her reflection died. There would be no one at the party tonight to look at good old Laine Harkness as if he'd swallowed the moon and it shone out of his eyes, like Dr. Jai Kaur when he looked at Eshana.

Laine slung the strap of her nursing bag over her shoulder and took the stairs down to the main floor. At each landing the sound of splashing water, the squealing laughter of children, and a few sorrowful wails at having to go to bed filled the narrow house. Tikah and Mala, assisted by the older orphans, strode through the rooms lined with cots and dealt with each tiny mite.

One little tot darted out of a room and almost made it to the stairs before Laine nabbed her. It was the little girl who'd been born shortly before Miriam had died. They'd called her that deplorably long biblical name, Hadassah. At three she was a nimble little thing and wiggled to be released, until she realized who held her. The child's silk lashes fluttered as she laughed into Laine's face. "Where is Cam?" she asked in Hindi.

"With his mother. I'll be seeing him tonight."

"I want him to come and play cricket with me."

Tikah raced out, laughing herself, and whisked the giggling Hadassah from Laine to take her back to the room and finish preparing her for supper and bed.

No doubt Harmindar, in the kitchen with her crew of older children, had begun to cook the evening meal. Evidence of that came with the aroma of garlic, onions, and cardamom that wafted up the stairs.

Laine pushed through the doors to the surgery. Their patient slept in a room off to the side, while Eshana placed the instruments they'd used today into the autoclave for sterilization. She'd not heard Laine's entrance. A sigh escaped from her, but the shine in her eyes seemed at variance with that laden breath. No doubt she savored the doctor's visit.

Laine couldn't hold back her grin. "Are you coming to the party tonight? We won't see them for a year."

Eshana turned to scrub the examining table. "Geoff and Abby came this morning to say their good-byes. I would have gone tonight, but I cannot be leaving the burden of such an ill patient for the younger girls."

"What utter rot. In the last year and a half, Tikah with no official training has developed into a fine practical nurse. It's more likely you don't want to go because *he's* entrusted Chandra to *your* care."

Eshana's lowered eyelashes were her answer.

"Oh, my dear Eshana, do take a page from Abby's book. Fall in love. Get married and have twenty children. For my sake, please, let the man know you like him."

Eshana's eyes flickered wide. By her willowy shape she was as compliant as bamboo. Oh she'd bend all right, given enough pressure. But that glint of fire in her eyes proved that like a shaft of bamboo she'd snap right back, and the answering thwack would be decidedly painful for anyone who dared interfere with her charitable work.

Laine pretended to take a cautious step backward.

Eshana's laughter tinkled like the silver anklets at her feet. "You are speaking such foolishness. Dr. Kaur is a Sikh and would never marry anyone but a Sikh. I as a follower of Yeshu could not be happy unless I married a man who also loved Yeshu. But it is God's will for me to take care of Miriam's mission. There will be no such marital bliss for me as our friend Abby enjoys. So please give to Geoff and Abby my love, and especially to my young princeling, Cam."

Laine adjusted the strap of her shoulder bag. "In that regard we're united. There'll be no such bliss for me either." She held the surgery door ajar and let out a laugh. "I for one never wish to go through the torture of love again."

She left the mission and hailed a rickshaw. And if she ever did meet up again with the man who'd made her so gun-shy of romance, she'd give him a good, swift kick in the shins. It was the least he deserved.

3

The jigsaw puzzle of the old city of Amritsar fell behind. The *wallah* pulling Laine's rickshaw entered the clean and geometrically laid out British Civil Lines with its red-bricked and white-columned government buildings. As the rickshaw pulled up to the club, a recording of the Wang Wang Blues belted out. Lights blazed over the regimental club and flooded the lawn and flowerbeds.

Inside, people danced to the jazz tune. A few years ago nothing could have stopped her from sliding onto the dance floor and tripping the light fantastic. Nowadays she'd rather stride the hospital wards in a solid pair of sensible shoes.

She shouldered her way through the crowd of merry-makers. Off to the side on a table sat piles of food, ham sandwiches, chutney, roast mutton, salads, and trays of Indian sweets. British military men and their wives stood chatting, balancing plates and glasses in their hands. Abby wound her way toward her with a plate of food. Geoff stood by the display of regimental silver with a gaggle of officers in their khaki drill trousers and shirts and ties. Cam stood at Geoff's side as usual.

At five, Cam already showed the tall frame he'd inherited from his natural father, but Cam emulated the character of Geoff. How that boy adored his step-father.

As soon as the boy noticed her, he ran in her direction and wrapped his arms around her waist. "You came."

"You don't think for a minute I'd let you sail to the Orient without my good-bye kiss. By the way, Eshana sends you another kiss, so here it is." She kissed him twice on the cheek, and he fidgeted to be free. "And here's one from your little friend, Hadassah. I saw her tonight, and she was rather put out that you weren't there to play with her."

"Dassah is just a baby." He squirmed out of her arms, a sharp furrow between his brows. "Enough kissing, Laine. You're much more fun on the cricket pitch than acting like a girl."

"Oh but I am a girl, and I admit that I like kissing very, very much. You won't appreciate that fact about girls for a few years, but my dear young man, the day will come...."

Geoff's gaze swung around to stop on Laine and then connected with Abby's, a silent but pointed communication. The room suddenly felt too warm. Oh dear. He knew something. But then Geoff had a way of knowing everything.

She gave Cam another tight hug and straightened to send him back in the direction of his step-father. "Off you go, my lamb, help your dad keep the world safe and sound for the rest of us."

Abby reached her as Cam raced back to Geoff. She folded Laine's arm close and strolled with her to the veranda, away from the over-bright lights. Since her marriage to Geoff, Abby had bloomed, a veritable full-blown rose. Tonight Abby wore a chiffon sheath in pale green—its hemline swinging at mid calf—that clung to her shape and emphasized her radiance. Looking down at her own ensemble, Laine felt a twinge of regret at its dowdiness.

She and Abby found two empty cane chairs overlooking the garden, and Laine breathed in the roses.

"Get that in you." Abby gave her the plate. "If I know anything about you, you've been too busy to eat all day."

Laine tucked into the plate of sandwiches and curry puffs, and spoke with her mouth half full. "Bless you, luv, how'd you guess I'd be ready to eat the leg off a table?"

Abby signaled to a circulating waiter. "A pot of tea English style, please, and a pitcher of milk on the side." She settled back in her chair. "Believe it or not, Laine, news of your crimes may have preceded you here tonight, so beware."

Laine stopped chewing and swallowed, a lump of bread sticking in her throat. "Crimes?"

"That's what Geoff's in the corner nattering to the other officers about. Seems a delegation of Hindu priests and several high-caste lawyers dropped by the police station today. Caused quite a ruckus as they demanded the police start searching for the culprits who took a young woman from a Hindu temple."

Laine forced a laugh and took a sip of tea. "Why would Geoff associate me with such a thing?"

"Apparently these two women were described in amazing detail. The town is heating up, and there's enough trouble with Gandhi's non-cooperation movement as it is."

A long shadow fell over them from Geoff standing between them and the light inside the club. He strolled to the veranda railing and crossing his arms, leaned against it.

"Lieutenant Laine Harkness." Though he spoke in a quiet undertone, she didn't care for his unnerving emphasis on her rank. "Did you know that the head woman at a nearby temple recognized one of two female kidnappers today as a member of the Queen Alexandra Nursing Corp? The other woman, smaller in stature and clearly Indian, did not wear a kumkum dot on her forehead, and is not a Hindu. The police suspect she may be a Christian."

He arched a brow. "Don't give me that wide-eyed look of innocence. I know you too well. Guilt is written all over you. Really, Laine, instead of assisting Eshana in this hare-brained scheme you should have been talking her out of it. You're older than her and should know better."

"I hate to break this to you, Geoff, but Eshana is not a child. Though she's an angel of mercy, she's got more backbone in her than anyone I know. Besides, angels of mercy need to be tough as nails."

Geoff's brows arched higher. "So you admit it. Up to this moment I'd hoped and prayed my suspicions were wrong."

"I'm admitting nothing."

At that his brows creased together.

Abby placed a hand on Geoff's. "Darling, do stop brow-beating her. I'm certain this will all blow over. Go to the mission now. Give Eshana a good talking to. And give her another hug from me. Right now I want to spend some time alone with Laine."

At Abby's words Geoff's frown melted. "You're right, of course, as usual." A softness infused his eyes as he leaned down to grasp the arms of Abby's chair, to rest his lips against hers for a moment.

Only a moment, yet Laine choked on her breath at the love that flowed between them. She couldn't be happier for these two friends, but emptiness yawed inside her, and she reached for a thought. Any thought to fill her mind. The garden, the club...the mission today. Perhaps Geoff was right. She might have to scale down on these escapades with Eshana.

Geoff straightened and gave a weak smile to Abby and then to Laine. He gently squeezed Laine's shoulder as he left them. "Do be careful, old friend. You are as dear to us as Eshana and the rest of the inhabitants of Miriam's mission. Remember that."

Abby leaned back in her chair as Geoff made his way through the party inside. She swept Laine with a speculative gaze. "It's been said today's perpetrators used live snakes to create confusion. How on earth would two women have the pluck to do that, I wonder?"

Laine pulled a strand of hair toward her chin. "It's truly amazing what one can purchase in an Indian bazaar. It was a trick I learned from a boy I grew up with. If we wanted to sneak out of choir practice, Adam said there was nothing to empty a place quicker than a rat snake. It looks like a cobra. Did the trick all right. One sighting of the snake, the vicar cancelled choir practice, and Adam and I scampered off down to the marina in Madras to buy sweets and walk along the beach."

"Mmm, so that's how it was done. What are Eshana's plans for this girl you kidnapped?"

"Depends on the girl's recovery. We had to take the baby by surgery.... Dr. Kaur was brilliant. And, Abby, I'm sure our darling Eshana is smitten with him, and he with her."

"No!" Abby leaned forward. "Not Eshana. Well, I wonder." She tilted her head and studied Laine. "You got here late. I'd lined up a rather attractive man for you. Apparently he lives to dance. Still over there by the gramophone, putting on disk after disk of that Dixieland jazz you like."

Laine bit into a curry puff and licked a glob of cream from the corner of her mouth. "Good gracious, save me from well-meaning match-makers."

"Nonsense. You've told me for years you want a man."

"Abby, an intelligent lady like you...you shouldn't believe everything you hear."

"Oh, Laine, do stop bantering. It was Reese dying like that, wasn't it?" Abby lost her jovial tone. "Poor Reese, he'd made it through the war, and then to die in that stupid struggle with Afghanistan afterward. You and he really hit it off, didn't you?"

Laine gave the only response she could, a slight shrug. Something had started to bud between her and Reese. Love? Perhaps for him. Given time they probably would have made it to the altar. Dear, riotous, red-haired Reese. He'd made her laugh. Almost made her forget her first love. Then dash it all, Reese's plane had crashed in some desert in Waziristan. It had hurt dreadfully.

Abby's teasing voice tugged her back. "Is that your goal in life, like Eshana, to be a single woman nursing the sick? Somehow I never saw this missionary spirit in you."

"Missionary spirit, my eye." A rare sigh escaped her. "Abby, I'm going to miss you. A whole year of you and Geoff and the children off in Singapore. Why does Geoff have to be so indispensible to the powers-that-be that they have to send him to another political hot spot? As if India isn't hot enough already."

"Will you write me, Laine?" An unfamiliar fearful tone entered Abby's voice. "I'll need to hear from you."

"Of course, darling. You can't possibly think old Laine will abandon you. But lead on. Take me to that damp-bottomed little princess of yours."

She followed Abby into the club and down to the library where a pram took up a darkened corner. The pram jiggled, setting the toys and trinkets attached to the hood to jingle and clatter. In response, a soft coo issued from within, along with two woolen, booty-covered feet kicking and setting the toys to tinkle again. The little rascal was awake.

Abby leaned in and picked up Cam's nine-month-old sister, Miriam. After kissing the corn-silk hair, she passed the baby to Laine.

Squeezing the chubby arms and legs, Laine breathed in the talcum-powder scent and sweetness of baby skin. "Miri, why are you going so far away?" She sent an accusing glance at the child's mother.

Abby put up her hands. "Don't blame me. It's neither my desire nor Geoff's to go to China." She straightened Miri's nightgown down over her nappy. "It's only a year, and then we'll be home."

The baby snuggled closer, and a tight pain constricted Laine's chest. Abby and Geoff's offspring were the closest to a family of her own as she would ever get. But it was time to end this before she did something foolish and broke down in tears. At thirty, and the rate she was going, she was rapidly reaching the point of being too old to have the joys of children. Besides, who was there to marry? Thanks to *the war to end all wars*, there was an atrocious shortage of men.

Not that it mattered to a woman like her, who might find herself in jail come sun up.

4

There were exactly twenty-three paces from the office to the window at the end of the hallway, and back again to the office of the Principal Matron, Ada McFarlane, of the Queen Alexandra's Imperial Military Nursing Corp.

Matron couldn't possibly have found out about yesterday's abduction. It must be Geoff's over-protective lecture that made Laine see tigers in the closet. Still, something was up, otherwise she wouldn't feel as though a tribe of monkeys were using her stomach as a trampoline.

Laine rapped on the glass panel of Matron's door and received the command to enter. With a quick straightening of her gray-sleeved ward dress, white bib and apron, and a twitch of her nursing veil, Laine stepped into the room. She stood ram-rod still, waiting for her superior to look up from reading a letter.

At last Matron removed her spectacles. With a nod she indicated Laine take a chair in front of her desk. "This correspondence is from the district commissioner. The Hindu population is alleging that yesterday an Englishwoman with an Indian missionary abducted a girl from the women's quarters behind one of the Hindu temples."

Laine kept her hands from fidgeting. *Bluff it out, Laine, old girl, bluff it out, but for goodness sake don't try the wide-eyed look of innocence you'd tried on Geoff last night.*

"The description of one of the women fits you with startling accuracy, Lieutenant Harkness. This time it's more than a rumor, such as the incident three months ago when another girl was kidnapped from the same temple and no one has seen that child since."

Matron's raised hand halted Laine from speaking. "I don't have to explain to you how incidents like these create bad feeling between us and the Hindu population. I can turn a blind eye to a lot of nonsense, but I will not stand for anything that casts a bad name on the QAIMN."

"Of course not, Matron."

The look Ada sent across her desk would shrivel one of the younger nurses, but Laine raised her chin. Though perhaps it would be best to keep mum and listen.

Ada pushed her chair out from her desk and stood. Not a tall woman, but one whose starched confidence struck affection and a healthy dose of fear into the hearts of her staff. "Lieutenant Harkness, you are an excellent nurse. A decorated nurse. Not once have I had to lay a single fault at your door. But in reading over again the dispatches that accompanied the Royal Red Cross you were decorated with during the war, I am reminded that you are a brave woman. Not many could set up a dispensary for wounded infantrymen in a trench behind enemy lines until help arrived days later.

"It makes me ask myself—is this the same sort of insane gallantry that would sneak into the quarters of a Hindu temple and abduct not one, but two female occupants?" She quirked a brow. "Nothing to say? Well perhaps that shows wisdom on your part."

Ada turned to look out her window to the courtyard below. "So, I ask you, Lieutenant, can you tell me where you were between the hours of two and three yesterday afternoon?"

Laine gouged the skin at her thumbnail. If she told Matron she was at the mission, this would place Ada in the difficult spot of having to pass this information along to the police. But she simply couldn't lie. Any sort of lie would stick in her throat.

Outside the office, down the hall someone dropped a bedpan. The clock on the desk chimed half past.

Matron sat behind her desk and clasped her hands on top of her blotter. "I see."

Laine leaned forward and started to speak.

"No, Laine, don't. In the circumstances I wish to remain ignorant of your activities yesterday." Matron dropped her gaze. "If this situation is not resolved to the satisfaction of the Hindu population, then you have no other option. You will have to resign from the Corp."

Laine shifted in the chair. Matron's disappointment in her weighed like a stone on her chest, but she wouldn't cheapen her respect for Ada with excuses. "Yes, Matron."

"What's more, Lieutenant, I think it advisable you put considerable distance between you and this situation. Today. Why not go to Madras?

Going home to your roots may be just the ticket."

Laine swallowed past the lump in her throat. This grand woman who ran the hospital like a well-oiled locomotive knew she was guilty as charged and was still trying to protect her.

Matron picked up her fountain pen and began to write. "Friends of mine, a missionary doctor and his sister, are working with cholera vaccines in an out-of-the-way spot in the Madras Presidency. It's in the jungle, a fair distance from the nearest city, and they need a nurse who isn't afraid of rustic circumstances. It's temporary, but if this trouble with the local Hindus doesn't simmer down, your military career is over."

Matron cleared the roughness from her throat. "I'm writing Rory that you're on your way. And Laine, I understand the charity in your heart to help a child in such a horrific environment, but you must stop meddling in things you can do nothing about. That's all for now, Lieutenant. Dismissed."

"Thank you, Matron. It has been an honor to serve with you."

All sternness left Matron's face. "God-speed, Laine."

The office door and outer hallway ran awash with her blurred vision. Thank goodness the other sisters were busy on the wards, and she slipped into the office to retrieve her belongings before they noticed. One more good-bye and she'd crack. But this time she couldn't blame the good-bye on anyone but herself.

The smell of castor oil soap along with perfumes lingered in the hallway of the nurses' quarters. Her roommate Violet was on the wards, and Laine had the place to herself. Here in these rooms, she'd dreamed of a second chance at love with Reese, hoping he could help her forget her first love and the moonlit nights of Madras from before the war.

She shut the door behind her and leaned against it. The train for Bombay would leave soon, and if she and Eshana had really been spotted, then Eshana's life was in more danger than her own. It wouldn't take her long to pack, and she'd better get a move on. There was no time for regrets. Only the regret of removing her QAIMN cape for the last time.

She unclasped the scarlet cape from under her chin, drew it from her shoulders to fold and carefully place on the bed.

Half an hour later her bags were packed. All she needed were clothes to wear, a few of her medical books, and snapshots of days long gone. Lastly, she placed in her trunk the small case holding her Royal Red Cross medallion with its image of King George V engraved into the metal backing.

Her eye ran over the room and the things she was leaving behind for Violet, her gaze snagging on the leather-bound poetry journal that Adam had sent her when he studied for his First at Oxford. Next to this she had propped his copy of the Aeneid that he'd given her for her twenty-first birthday. She should have disposed of them years ago. All the same, she reached for the book. It fell open and her finger followed his favorite line from Virgil. *I recognize the signs of the old flame, of old desire.*

She snapped the book shut, stuffed it into her trunk and squeezed down the lid. She'd dispose of his poetry journals some day, but not today.

The narrow bazaars teemed. Someone lit a stream of firecrackers as the crowds prepared for the Hindu celebration *Diwali*, and the smoke teased Eshana's nose.

She made a mental note to buy more oil for the little clay lamps to set alight for the children at the mission. And sweets. *Jelabis* and *halva*. If only she could find some coconut *burfi* like they had in the south of India. That would delight the little ones, and perhaps bring a smile to young Chandra's eyes. Later she would have time for these purchases, but not now. She had to hurry back to the mission in time for Dr. Kaur's visit.

Eshana pushed her way through the crowd. Temple bells rang, copper pots clanged, along with the joyful din of people shouting and bargaining. The colors of the wares brought a shimmer to her within, a shimmer that resembled the ripples of light on a bolt of scarlet silk that a merchant unfurled. Red, the color of joy. Did she feel this way because of her anticipation of seeing Dr. Jai Kaur? If that were the case then she must stop this foolishness straightaway. There could never be anything between them other than their mutual respect.

Only one street from the mission, a hand gripped her around the elbow. She whirled to face who accosted her in the street.

The man looking down at her took her speech away. So many years had gone by. It could not be. Her Uncle Harish, Papa's brother. Her heart tore in two, and she dropped to the ground to touch his feet in respect. To see a member of her family after so long brought tears to her eyes.

He took a step back, and she rose to look upon his face. The last time she had seen his dark eyes, they had been filled with tears for her. Papa and Uncle had shaken her awake in the middle of the night. Uncle had removed the long string of pearls that at thirteen years old she had worn even to bed. His words from that night came back to her, "These wedding jewels must be given back to the groom's family."

Then Papa and Uncle had bundled her into a bullock cart and taken her from her home to another village, to abandon her like a shameful thing at an *ashram* for Hindu widows. She had not even been allowed to say good-bye to her mother.

Now Uncle Harish stared down at her in this busy Amritsar bazaar. Turmoil filled his gaze. What was he doing so far from their family home in Madras? His eyes widened as if he watched the dead come to life. "It is you, is it not? Eshana?"

She yearned to embrace him. "Yes, Uncle, it is I, your niece."

"We had thought you dead all these years. The women at the *ashram* informed us you had left one day. We had asked them this when your mother demanded news of you."

At the mention of her mother her heart leaped. *Amma* had demanded news of her?

Uncle's gaze took in her sari, not the coarse white cotton of a widow, but the exultant shade of mimosa yellow. Her hair ran in all its glory, a thick plait down to her waist.

He dropped his manacle hold around her elbow as if the touch of her stung his hand. "What is this vile thing you are doing, not dressed as a proper widow? You should be in the temple in constant prayers for your deceased husband, not prancing about the bazaar."

Eshana looked around her. This was not the place for such a discussion. She could not explain to him here that despair no longer shackled her, but that Christ had set her free. And Dr. Kaur would be waiting for her to discuss Chandra's case. If the unhappy past did not lie between her uncle and herself like an abscess, she could have invited him to the mission. But something held her back from telling him where she lived.

She placed tentative fingers on his arm, but he jerked a step back, his gaze wide with fear and yet with sadness. "Uncle, I cannot speak with you now. It is my dearest wish to explain to you the wondrous joy in my life. May I come to you tomorrow and tell you all?"

He shook his head, quivering. "I cannot be having you come to my place of business. Surely you would not wish such bad luck upon me." His face contorted with the jumble of emotions. "But for your mother's sake, I will meet you here tomorrow and I will listen."

His face hardened, just as it had that early dawn when she was thirteen years old and he and her father had left her at the *ashram*. His shoulders had heaved with his sobs then. But as he turned from her today his shoulders sat rigid as he stalked away.

She ran along the bazaar and at the corner turned to look behind. Uncle Harish stood not far off, his eyes following her. The look of his gaze did not hold the love he used to have for her, but something else, as if he held her in contempt. Or was it fear?

5

Jai Kaur looked up from examining Chandra, when Eshana burst into the clinic at the mission. She nodded to him while a wavering lamp of a smile lit her eyes. Yet something in her manner disturbed him. She breathed hard as if she had been running, and her gaze darted to the window.

He put up a hand to stroke his beard. "Is there someone you are expecting?"

"No." He had never before seen her so flustered, but she left the window and stood beside him. "Please, Doctor, tell me what you think of our patient."

He turned to view the girl from the temple who in a sleepy state paid them little attention. "You were wise to keep her on the intravenous fluid. As I have said before, you would make a fine physician, Eshana."

"As we have discussed many times, there is no opportunity for me to study to be a doctor." Though her answer came quietly, her eyes shone.

"Why not? I have heard there are several Christian hospitals training women to be doctors. Women practitioners are needed in our land when most women refuse to be treated by a male doctor."

"I am already knowing this. But with Miriam's dying words she meant for me to take her place in this mission. It is not only love for Miriam that is spurring me on, but love for my Lord."

Her eyes clouded, and he had no wish to bring back the sorrow of Miriam's death. He too remembered the horror of the Jallianwalla Bagh massacre.

Together he and Eshana examined the girl's sutures. He softened his voice for both the drowsy patient as well as Eshana's emotions. "I am familiar with your religion. I have read many of Sundar Singh's writings about this Christian god, Yeshu."

"I too have read much of Sundar's work." Her voice brightened. "He is a great, holy man of India, a Christian *sadhu*. What did you think of Sundar's experience when he was praying as a young Sikh man, 'if there be a God, reveal Thyself'?"

Jai had been about to answer, relishing the idea of discussing the differences of his Sikh theology versus her Christianity when Laine Harkness rushed into the room and strode toward Eshana.

Eshana's expression mirrored the strain on her English friend's face. "Something has happened."

"Didn't Geoff come by last night to talk to you?" The English nurse did not speak in her usual jocular manner.

"There was no need for Geoff to be concerned. No one knows Chandra is here, and as soon as she—"

"The police will most likely know any time now. I've been given the bad news. The authorities visited my matron at the hospital. Someone recognized me, but she's been good enough to send me away. I've got tickets for the train, but it won't be long before the police work out that I'm often here at the mission."

Jai pushed forward. "Are you saying they are looking for Eshana? Why have you put her in such a dangerous predicament? This is another instance of your British Raj mentality, do as you please and leave Indians to suffer the consequences."

Eshana placed her palms together and beseeched him. "Please, my friend. It was I who urged Laine to help me rescue the girl."

With effort he calmed his voice. "You must get the girl away. Better still take her back to the temple. If they find her here, your life will be forfeit."

The nurse spoke in that tone she no doubt used in the hospital wards. "Dr. Kaur, I assure you, I am not leaving Eshana."

The flame of anger within him lowered, though it still flickered. "Then you must hurry, before it is discovered Eshana was involved."

"Wait."

He turned at Eshana's cry.

"Wait," she repeated on a small breath. "I cannot be leaving this mission."

"You must go with the nursing matron. If it is discovered that you took the girl, they will be killing you."

Laine moved to the door and called out to the other girls who lived in the house. "Put together a quick bag with Eshana's belongings. She is leaving with me straightaway."

But Eshana stiffened. "I will not be leaving. On the night she died, Miriam told me to bring healing. It was me who Miriam trained to be midwife."

At her stricken look he softened his voice with reverence. "Eshana, you cannot bring healing to others if you are dead. Perhaps one day when it is safe you may return."

Laine spoke across the clinic room. "He's right, Eshana. We'd gotten away with it once, but the second time we were noticed. Come with me. The train leaves in an hour."

Comprehension made war with discontent on Eshana's face. "I cannot go. If Chandra is discovered here, the rest of this house will be in danger. Those who are frightened Hindu fanatics may easily decide it was Mala or Harmindar who stole the girl."

Laine met his eyes. "She's right."

He stroked his beard. "I will see that the patient is taken back to the Hindu temple—"

"No!" Eshana's voice rang out like the tolling of a temple bell. "She will suffer in their care. If she does survive, she will live a life of degradation." Her eyes pleaded. "Can you not take her to your clinic? You keep a handful of patients overnight."

Her voice rippled over him like the flutter of leaves in the breeze. Like India herself, a virtuous and nurturing female to be respected and revered.

"Eshana, the girl cannot stay at my clinic. My father would not be allowing this, and I have no dwelling of my own to care for her. I live with my family." But the fear in her eyes tore at his pious sounding words. "Surely you had a plan for Chandra when she became well. Tell me where you took the girl you rescued several months ago, and I will take our patient there."

"To Poona, the Ramabai Mukti Mission."

"But that is not far from Bombay. You must go by train with your friend. It is meant to be."

Eshana's brow wrinkled. "How can I take Chandra in her present condition?"

Laine cut in. "We'll take her with us, you and I, and care for her."

"In second class? How would that be possible?" But like the light of a small lamp, renewed hope shone from Eshana's eyes.

"There's a fellow I know with the railway," the English nurse added, though doubt lined her brow. "He's been begging to take me dancing for a year or more. I'm sure I can convince him to help us."

Jai released the full urgency in his voice. "Go. You must not be delaying."

Eshana's gaze latched on to his with a fierceness one would never expect in so gentle a woman, but she nodded and raced from the surgery.

While Eshana and the mission girls gathered a few belongings together, he and Laine prepared the patient for transport. He unhooked the intravenous drip, and Laine packed the instruments and medicines she would need. Thanks to the wisdom of *the God without form*, Laine had kept a *tonga* waiting outside. He took the patient in his arms and carried her outside as Eshana hurried down the stairs with the other girls following. The *tonga* provided enough room to lay the girl down on a mat.

He and Laine settled the patient and turned to Eshana. Long farewells would increase the danger to her, but still she embraced the three women who would remain at the mission. Mala and Harmindar had lived in this house for as long as he could remember. The Muslim woman, Tikah, wept in Eshana's arms as if she were saying good-bye to her own flesh and blood.

Eshana climbed into the conveyance, her gaze clinging to the women standing on the stoop of the tall, four-story house. When she had looked her fill, her gentle eyes turned to him.

He was a fool, but at the last minute he jumped to the seat at the front with the driver. It might be many months, perhaps never again, that he would see Eshana. He would at least make sure they arrived safely at the train station.

He looked around them at a few hostile glances in the crowded bazaar. *If* they arrived safely at the train station.

6

If Maurice, that vain peacock of a railroad administrator didn't agree to her request, then Laine would have to care for Chandra in second class. But if she could simper enough to make Maurice think she was madly in love with him, he might break protocol and allow the two Indian girls into first class. It would cost a pretty packet—all her savings.

She felt sorry for Eshana though. Miriam's mission had been her heart and soul. And Eshana wasn't pleased either at leaving the handsome Sikh doctor. Eshana had never been to the picture theater. She had no idea that Jai's flashing dark eyes, between his dark blue turban and black beard, held the same romantic mystique of Rudolph Valentino in the film *The Sheik*.

The patient stared up at Laine as their *tonga* rolled at a sedate pace. For the first time it struck Laine with horror. They'd never asked Chandra if she wanted to leave Amritsar.

The words to mention this hovered on her tongue when a shout reached them from the crowd in the bazaar. "It is those devils who seek to destroy caste. The ones who stole the dancing girl."

Jai ordered the driver to pick up speed. Their route to the train station wound too close to the Hindu temple for comfort. He sent another look over his shoulder at the men chasing their *tonga*, and urged the driver to go faster. At the crack of a whip the horse bolted to a gallop, and people began to jump out of the way, screaming and shaking fists.

Laine hung onto the cart with one hand, and Eshana did the same, while both of them tried to keep their patient from being jostled. If Laine still believed in prayer, now would be a good time to offer one up. But most likely, Eshana was praying hard enough for all of them.

Shouts grew to an uproar, and Laine's mouth went dry.

They passed the temple, but a group of people began to run after them, shouting, "Police! Stop!" The lead woman from the temple girls' quarters also dashed up the street. Her jiggling rolls of fat at the gap of her sari didn't seem to be slowing her down any.

Just as they turned the corner, their conveyance outran the angry knot of people following. Outside the redbrick station Laine yelled to the driver to stop.

Jai jumped from the front and picked up the girl while Laine and Eshana tugged down the luggage. Their Muslim driver didn't wait for payment but vanished into a swarm of *tongas* and rickshaws. He no more wanted to be questioned by the Hindu mob than Laine and Eshana did.

They ran under the brick archway, racing past the doors for the separate refreshment rooms for Europeans, Muslims, Hindus and women in purdah. Jai followed with the girl, and they darted past the offices, Station Master and Telegraph. Passengers from a branch line hurried across the footbridge. All the while steam pulsed from the locomotive of the Bombay Mail, a huge black metal animal with gold trimmings, straining to be unleashed.

Laine pushed open the door, District Traffic Superintendent's Office. A coolie-messenger jumped to his feet, and Jai followed her and Eshana inside, carrying their patient.

Maurice looked up in alarm as Laine wove her way through the desks of his staff. "Hide us, Maurice. Quickly. Order your men to say nothing. We're being followed."

"Laine Harkness, as I live and breathe—"

"Do as I say, Maurice. This instant."

Maurice's face blanched, but for once he showed some sense. Without a word he ushered them into his private office and shut the door. She could hear him in the main office ordering his staff to get to work and to keep their traps shut.

He returned a moment later and stared at them aghast. "Laine, old thing." He pushed a strand of hair heavy with pomade off his forehead. "What sort of shenanigan is this?"

Chandra's moan caught everyone's attention, and Jai laid her down on the string cot. Eshana joined him as he kneeled at the girl's side. The shouts of the crowd outside penetrated the thick walls of the station.

Laine worked up a smile. "Maurice, old thing..." She sidled close to him and injected a breathy tone into her voice. "I just had to come to you. For help. I knew you were the man for the job. So capable, so quick." *Et cetera, et cetera, et cetera.* She stuffed down her smarting conscience at this deception. “Oh do help me, Maurice. I’m in terrible trouble.”

The gaze he turned to her was not that of the simpleton she’d assumed he was. The light in his eyes flattened, and he shot a glance at Jai and Eshana caring for Chandra. Not the nicest of men, but as she’d said, he was quick to understand a situation. “So, Laine, it was you who riled up the Hindus. And you expect me to hide you, and that—” He waved a dismissive hand at the girl on the cot. “—that thing from the temple.”

“That thing as you call her is a human being.” She regretted the steel lacing her voice. She needed to butter him up, not add his anger to that of the rabble outside. “I’m sorry, Maurice. But she’s my patient, and I would no more abandon her than I would you if you were in pain.”

He stopped at that. “Laine, why can’t you enjoy a bit of fun instead of taking sides with the natives? For months I’ve asked you out, and you’ve cut me dead each time.”

She squeezed his upper arm. “I know, but in all honesty, I’ve not felt like dancing lately. It’s not you, Maurice...I suppose I’ve seen too much....”

“The war?”

“Yes, the war.”

He nodded on a sigh. He knew very well that even if all had been paradise she still wouldn’t have taken him on. But for whatever reason—his overblown pride probably—he let her off the hook. “I want to help you, Laine.” He frowned at the three Indians clustered in the corner. “But what the blazes do you expect me to do for you? And I assume this girl?”

A flash of people running past the window made all their heads shoot up. Collectively they held their breath. Maurice strode to the window and snapped the cane blinds shut. He pulled on the cords to open them a sliver and peered outside. “The police have arrived.”

“I need a first class compartment, private for myself and the two girls to Bombay.”

His brows rose. “Not asking for much are you, Laine? I’m afraid that’s impossible.”

The babble of voices outside rose in crescendo. She sank to a chair. “There must be something you can do.”

The gazes of Jai and the two girls followed Maurice as he paced the floor.

“All right, let me think.” Maurice shut the blinds. “You’re asking me to break the law, and I hope you realize I could lose my position as traffic superintendent if this ever got out. But I’ll take you in the staff carriage that's used for railroad business at the back of a goods train heading to Bombay." He started muttering to himself and left the office.

"Will he truly be helping us?" Eshana rose up from beside the cot.

Jai filled a glass of water from a pitcher on the desk and placed it against Chandra's lips. "Or is he fooling you, Matron, and plans to give you up to the police?"

Laine gave them a helpless shrug and kneeled on the floor to take Chandra's hand. "Do you want to come with Eshana and me? We can take you to a place of safety, and you'll never have to be a temple girl again."

Chandra's eyes brimmed, and Laine leaned over to catch her whisper, "Please...I am wanting to go to this place Eshana has been telling me of."

Maurice returned twenty minutes later, put a finger to his lips, and gestured for them to leave the office. Laine searched his face. Would he betray them? But as she stepped out of his office the empty spots at each desk filled her with hope. Through the windows outside, she saw that the crowd still eddied in search of them. She could only pray. But pray to whom or what?

Eshana followed her with Jai carrying Chandra. Maurice led them to a back room filled with crates and trunks. Double doors at the far end of the box room were closed, but from below the doors they could hear the hissing of the Bombay Mail.

"You and the other girl will have to change your clothes behind that partition." Maurice handed her two sets of men's grimy overalls and turbans to cover their hair.

Their disguises wouldn't bear much inspection, but it might be enough to get them through the jostling crowd. Minutes later when Eshana and she had changed, Maurice whispered to Jai to place Chandra into a long crate, with holes gouged here and there and filled with straw.

Eshana helped him lift the girl into the crate, whispering to her in Hindi, "Do not be afraid at this confinement, Chandra. It is only for a short time, and then you will be released, free to enjoy the good things God is preparing for you. Are you trusting me?"

The girl seemed to understand, and though her mouth trembled she remained quiet.

Maurice tacked the lid down with a few nails and signaled for Jai to help him lift it onto a cart, next to the one containing Laine's baggage. He kept his eyes on his watch. The minutes ticked by with only the steam outside to dull the ruckus of the angry crowd.

Maurice looked up. "You can't all go out at once. I'll start with Laine—"

"No, take the crate first and then Eshana."

He leveled a look at her. "You asked for my help, Laine old thing, and I'm doing it my way. If this scheme goes belly-up then I can at least get you away. You, not your little Indian chums. When I open the door, out you go and walk straight across the platform, down the length of the express. The goods train is at the very end. Up into the staff carriage, and then I'll send your friend. I'll follow with the crate. The man will have to take care of himself I'm afraid."

She turned to Eshana and Jai to apologize with a look for Maurice's lack of tact and to thank Jai for his help. But neither Eshana nor Jai appeared to notice her.

Over his hands, held as if in prayer, Jai inclined his turbaned head toward Eshana. "Though you are not Sikh, I know that you are a true woman of God. So I give you this Sikh blessing. May your devotion to the Lord be perpetual. May grace be showered upon you...and your sustenance be the perpetual divine singing of the Glories of the Lord."

In utter stillness, Eshana's gestures reflected those of Jai's. "You honor me, and I give you a blessing of my own and that of Paul, a follower of Christ. Since the day I heard of your love for the God without form, Jai, I do not cease to pray for you, and to desire that ye might be filled with the knowledge of His will in all wisdom and spiritual understanding."

The solemnity of their parting took Laine's breath away. Their demeanor suggested nothing more than respect. Yet she ached at the sight of them. Something about them touched the fringes of her mind—memories. A moonlit beach in Madras...cool, satin sand beneath her feet...and Adam asking her to be his wife.

"Laine," Maurice said through clenched teeth. "Now, if you please."

She veered from Jai and Eshana and, like a blind man, walked through the door into the painful sunshine that shut off her memories.

Masses of people pushed and shoved, exacerbated by those searching for them. Over the shouts of venders came that of Hindu devotees. She kept the collar of the railroad shirt turned up, and pulled the end of the turban across the lower half of her face. The reek of coal and oil filled her nose as she took steps toward the far end of the goods train. Steam billowed from beneath flanged wheels. Three more steps and she'd reach the vestibule of the last carriage.

A shout issued from behind, and her hand froze on the railing. But whoever shouted had run down the platform, mistaking someone else for her or Eshana. Up the two steps and she entered the carriage. She stared out the window and counted each of Eshana's footsteps as she followed.

A minute later Maurice rolled out the cart with the crate, and Eshana rushed to help him lift it into the carriage. Whistles blew and steam rose, obscuring the crowded platform as Maurice climbed into the carriage and slammed the door shut. With a jerk the train began to pull away from the station.

Laine remained by the window and caught a glimpse of Jai strolling out of the station. With only one glance at their carriage he hunched his shoulders in an attempt to blend in with the crowd. But people would recognize his tall frame and dark blue turban. Many would know him as Dr. Kaur Jr. Her insides twisted at the danger they'd left this good doctor in. As for themselves, were they running away from danger or running smack into it?

7

Dun-colored plains opened up as the train trundled southwest toward Bombay. Since the war ended Laine had grown used to these khaki-colored sands. Northern India's monsoons had ended in July, but the south's second set of steaming rains usually started at the end of October. She'd probably run into the south's pounding showers as soon as she arrived in the Madras Presidency with its lush jungles, white coasts, and emerald lagoons.

For now, warm air blew through the steel bars and mesh screens on the windows. A small electric fan whirled above their heads. Hardly first class, but it would do.

It had taken a few hours for Laine's nerves to stop jangling. Yet all had gone peacefully when their train chuffed into the next station, and the stations after that. No police with a contingent of Hindus waited for them like bees disturbed from their hive. Maurice had just left to go to the restaurant and bring them back some food.

Eshana held a cup of water to Chandra's lips. Thanks to the lucky stars—if there were any such thing—their patient's sutures looked good, and she'd been sitting up the past hour, chatting with Eshana. Her eyes glistened, no longer with fear but excitement. The excitement of a child. Poor little thing had never been on a train before. She'd probably never seen much but that hovel on the street behind the temple.

Maurice returned with a tray of chapattis, a dish of curried rice, and one of plain rice for their patient, as well as a container of hot tea and boiled water. "It's safe enough out there." He thrust his chin toward Eshana. "Next time she can get the food."

Laine sent him the scathing look she gave her nursing subordinates when their work wasn't up to snuff. "Her name is Eshana, and she is not a servant. I'll get our food at the next station if you're so adverse." She flicked a glance out the window. "Are you sure people aren't looking for us?"

"Relax, Laine, old thing. I checked with the telegraph office, and there's nothing to suggest anyone outside of Amritsar cares. After all, we're talking about the abduction of one little Indian chit, not the wife of the bleedin' viceroy." He swept a hand through his hair, but a greasy strand drooped over his brow. "Where did you say you're making this new start in your life, old thing? Bombay? Or farther south?"

Eshana's gaze bored into Laine's. Eshana didn't need to send her that silent warning. Laine had no desire to have Maurice looking her up. Though she couldn't afford to alienate him at this point. Bombay lay nine-hundred miles off, and the Madras Presidency another seven hundred from there. She summoned the sugary tone she'd used on him earlier, not liking the gleam in his eye. "I'm not sure where I'll hammer in the tent pegs, Maurice, old bean."

Though she must look anything but alluring, smudged and disheveled, he still advanced. "Come, Laine, don't play the tease. My but you're a stunner. Always were."

"Matron," Eshana's voice carried the exact note of concern Laine needed to extricate herself. "Our patient's sutures are not looking good."

Laine pushed past Maurice to Chandra. The girl's frightened eyes carried the knowledge of what went on between men and women behind closed doors. So disheartening to see in a child this age. A moment later Maurice left the carriage with a barely suppressed huff. The train left the station, and Laine could only assume he'd gone to another section of the goods train to plaster salve on his wounded pride.

Both Eshana and Chandra gave her a bemused look as the girl ate half a bowl of rice with Eshana's help. When Chandra had taken in all she could, Laine helped the patient to lie down. The girl dropped off to sleep almost as soon as she closed her eyes.

Together she and Eshana sat at the table by the window and watched the plains slip by. For the first time since this day had begun they had blessed silence to collect their thoughts. Soon the day softened to its short green twilight, and darkness came like the snuffing out of a lamp.

Eshana stood to switch on the electric light. "We have not yet spoken of where we will each be going once this train reaches Bombay. Will you be coming with me to the Ramabai Mukti Mission?" Eshana's tone held a wistfulness that Laine wasn't used to from her.

"No, I think it best you go on alone to the mission with Chandra."

"You are not coming with me?"

"I'm expected as soon as possible at this new position. Anyway, you won't need me, Eshana. By the time we get to Bombay, Chandra will be able to walk. I'll be buying your tickets to Poona of course. After that I hope you'll follow me to the Madras district."

They were entering the outskirts of a village, its cooking fires twinkling like fireflies, and the tang of wood smoke in the air. It took a moment to realize Eshana had not answered.

"What is it?" She turned to look into the young Indian woman's face. "You need somewhere to go till things simmer down, and this cholera research sounds interesting—"

"I cannot be going to the Madras Presidency." Panic poked through Eshana's voice.

"Oh come now. You can't return to Amritsar. Really, Eshana, do be sensible."

"I am sorry. I cannot be joining you there. As soon as Chandra is established at the Ramabai Mukti Mission, I *will* be returning to Amritsar."

Laine rubbed between her brows. She knew Eshana to have a will of iron, but never to be foolishly obstinate. But it wasn't just stubbornness. Eshana had never been evasive before.

Eshana opened her bedroll to make up her bunk. "We should be getting our rest now."

She had been effectively told to mind her own business. But over the next three days on this train she had to convince Eshana to be reasonable. In the bathroom Laine changed into her nightgown and brushed her teeth. She unrolled her bedding in the top bunk, and after switching off the light, climbed in. But sleep felt eons away.

Just when she thought Eshana had drifted off, her Indian-accented English floated upward over the rattle of the train, like the smoke of incense, delicate yet tenacious. "I admit I am most determined to go back to Amritsar, but that is not the only reason I cannot join you in the city of Madras. Or anywhere in that entire district." Eshana took a cleansing breath. "I have never told you that Madras was also my birthplace."

Laine bolted up and stared into the dark. "All this time you've known I came from there, you've never said a word. Does Abby know?"

"Not even Abby. I kept my secret because I do not wish to remember the time I was cast from my home for being a widow."

"I'm well aware of how a great many widows are mistreated in

Hinduism. But do you know for sure your family wouldn't want to see you? Gandhi is speaking out about that, as well as about other wrongs. Times are changing. Goodness, one of these days the Indian people may very well tell us Brits to get out."

Eshana's voice grew faint. "Perhaps things are changing in India. Until recently I had hoped to return one day to my childhood home, the Jasmine Palace. I desire with all my heart to see my family, most especially my mother. That was until...until this morning. No, I will be returning to Amritsar where I belong. That is God's will."

An unladylike snort escaped Laine. "Eshana, you're as obstinate as a thicket of bamboo."

"And you, my friend, remind me of prickly mimosa. Though it is fragrant, it curls inward upon itself when it is touched. I will confess to being persevering...or determined—"

"Persevering, my eye. The word you're looking for is stubborn."

Eshana's bedding muffled her giggle. "It is time for sleep, my mimosa friend."

The clatter of the train was the only sound after that, as well as Chandra's soft snore. Laine flumped over on her back and laid her arm across her eyes. *Mimosa, that curls up on itself when touched.* Ridiculous. So what if she didn't want her heart mangled like it had been? True, she didn't go out with men much. Though she pretended to want a man, each time they made serious advances, she did curl up inside. They soon left her alone, assuming she didn't care.

Two years ago she'd tried with Reese. She often wondered what would have happened if he hadn't died. Would she have made it to the altar, or sent him on his way too?

She raised up on an elbow, gave her pillow a swift but sound thrashing to soften it, and lay down. It was all Adam's fault. He'd ruined all other men for her. Blast him!

Only one more stop and they would reach Bombay on the coast of the Arabian Sea. Feeling braver than they had felt in days, the three women stepped down from the train. Eshana agreed that Laine should take Chandra for a stroll while she purchased their food. It must be as Maurice assured them. No one paid heed to the kidnapping of one girl of the untouchable class.

Eshana waved to Laine and Chandra down the platform that swam with passengers from all over India. Shorter dark-skinned Tamil people from the south milled around with those from the north with complexions like milky tea. Bengalis, Rajputs, Afghans, and tall Sikhs with black flashing eyes, turbans, and beards, reminded her of Jai. *Father in Heaven, it is my prayer that you return me home that I may assist him again.*

She reached the queue for the Hindu refreshment room when a man blocked her way. Uncle Harish. Her mind darted. Did he do business in cities beside Madras and Amritsar? Bombay? Because he must have left Amritsar on the Bombay Mail the day after they had left on the goods train. Her heart swayed one way and then the other. She did not stoop to touch his feet in respect. With all her soul she prayed Uncle would take no offense, but with the way he glowered at her this was not to be.

"What is this you are doing?" He nodded for her to leave the queue. He was her father's elder brother, and she obeyed. Once they were away from those desiring Hindu food his taut words matched the quivering of his jaw. "*Pavum*! What shameful thing is this? As a widow you should keep yourself out of the way."

"I am sorry, Uncle, I do not wish to offend anyone. But I no longer think of myself as something shameful."

He stepped back from her. "You should be living in an *ashram* for widows or in a temple. To add to your sins, you flaunt yourself with clothing not fit for a woman whose husband is dead." He winced as if her sari the color of eggplant caused him pain.

The longing to tell someone in her family of her joyful life would burst from her lungs if she held it in. All these years of her banishment since Papa and Uncle had left her at the *ashram* rushed upon her, an avalanche of Himalayan snows. Still, her gaze fell. "The Living God does not want me to live like dead carrion simply because the boy who was my husband died."

"You would cast shame on your relatives in such a way?" Tears blurred his eyes. "Think of your mother and father. Think of the parents of your husband. I beg you to stop defiling our caste in this way. Think of the bad luck you will bring to our households, our businesses."

His words crushed like spices ground by a stone pestle. Shaking her head, she backed away, but Uncle seized her by the elbow. "I must impress upon you to stop your sinful ways."

She squirmed, looking over her shoulder for a glimpse of Laine, while her uncle's grip remained a fetter of iron around her arm. Laine did not see her, her attention on helping Chandra to their train. Uncle followed her gaze and stopped on Laine and the young girl.

"Who are those females, and one of them an Englishwoman?" His gaze widened. "It could not be—the news and descriptions have been spread about Amritsar—an Indian woman of your age...and an English *memsahib*. You would not be so evil, surely?" His eyes grew black with comprehension. "It was *you* who stole the temple girl."

Eshana risked another glance at Laine and Chandra. Her uncle did not see them climb aboard the goods train. They were safe. She raised her gaze to her uncle, her insides quaking.

He began to drag her away. "You have given me no choice, Eshana. It is only right that you be given to the police who are searching for you in Amritsar."

"No, Uncle," she cried.

Tears shone like oil on his cheeks. "I cannot be letting you cause such disruption to our people. Though, I cannot leave you, the child of my brother, to the police. You will come with me to Madras. One of our relatives will have a place in their house to keep you from shaming us."

She tasted the salt of her own sorrow as she pulled at his fingers, hating to show him disrespect. But it could not be. She would not insult the free gift of God by going with her uncle and taking upon herself the dead existence of a Hindu widow.

Father God, help me! Gasping, she pulled, but to no avail.

A whistle blew. British passengers moved to the express train to board first class.

Lord, I have work to do. Let me...free myself. I must take Chandra...to freedom. She wrenched loose. And turned. She ran, not looking back when her uncle called out. In his voice she heard the piercing note of despair. He did not understand. But no one should be allowed to treat her less than what she was—a daughter of God, the light of His eyes.

She pushed through the wall of people to be swallowed up in the crowd rushing to the express. Crossing over the railway bridge she made it to the goods train, and turned to look over the platform where today's Bombay Mail waited. The last whistle for that train blew. Hundreds of Indian passengers ran to board, or climb to the top.

Most of the men wore white *dhotis* to their ankles and long white tunics, but still across the distance she made out her uncle. He climbed on a cart to peer over the crowd and called to someone in the crowd. Another man joined him on the cart to help him look over the crowded station.

Then her uncle turned. He started as his gaze found her.

He gripped the other man's arm and pointed across the rails to where she stood. Her train sat directly in front of him, and her purple sari would stand out vividly in the white sunlight.

Uncle's gaze followed along the goods train. He would surmise correctly that her train would take her to Bombay.

The shrill cry of the whistle announced the Mail was leaving. Uncle Harish hastened to board, leaving the other man to remain, keeping watch upon her train.

8

Under the wrought iron and glass ceiling of Victoria Station, thousands of passengers—English, Indian, and Anglo-Indian—departed and arrived each day.

Mercifully, Maurice, after a disgruntled good-bye, left Laine as soon as he'd escorted her from his train. Poor old bean, he hadn't even tried to insist on dinner and dancing for his troubles. But they'd made it to Bombay without the notice of anyone from Amritsar. Laine suspected he was right. Those outraged would soon forget about this one young, untouchable girl. Sadly, there were too many poor little souls from nearby villages to take her place.

Turning from the booth, Laine checked the tickets for Poona while Eshana waited with Chandra. She tucked her own ticket for the Madras Mail into her bag. No one would notice two Indian girls in this hive of humanity thrumming with passengers, vendors screeching, railroad staff barking orders, and blowing whistles. Eshana and Chandra would disappear into the tapestry of India, and no one would be the wiser.

Laine waded through the crowd to them. If only she could have convinced Eshana to stay put in Poona, but Eshana remained adamant that she would return to Amritsar as soon as she'd safely delivered Chandra to Ramabai's mission. Nor could she convince Eshana to come to Madras with her. Laine let out a huff. Obstinate little blighter. To think that Geoff blamed her for getting Eshana into trouble.

She had only minutes to talk to Eshana as the two of them settled Chandra in the carriage. "You should stay at this mission. Pandita Ramabai sounds a good deal like your Miriam."

"Ramabai is a wonderful woman. I would most dearly love to work in her compound and care for the widows and children, but I will not waver.

Nothing shall stop me from returning to Miriam's mission."

Laine straightened. "Please stay away for a while, a few weeks. Better still a few months. At least until Christmas or Holi. Let the situation simmer down in Amritsar before you return."

Eshana drew the end of her sari over her shoulder in a slow sweep. "A few weeks are all I can be promising."

"A few months then. Four."

"A few weeks."

She stuck out her hand as the last whistle blew. "A few weeks. Shake on it then. Now I must leave you. Take care of Chandra, and do write and let me know how you're doing. You have my address? Right, it's good-bye. No time for long drawn-out adieus."

Eshana only gave her a smile and leaned forward to embrace her.

She returned Eshana's hug, wiping the tiresome wetness from her cheeks. "All right. Cheerio. I imagine we'll catch up with each other soon anyway."

From the platform she waved to the two young Indian women staring out the window of the second-class compartment. She would have bought them first-class tickets, but of course that would never be allowed. At least they were off safe and sound.

She gestured to the porter with her luggage cart to follow her. After a quiet cup of tea, she'd find her own train, the Madras Mail.

The pony-pulled *jutka* rattled along the countryside of the Madras Presidency. Rust-red dirt flew up at Laine. She'd be a fine sight when she arrived with her hair, clothing, and every pore of skin stained with dust. After all this time it was good to be home. And good to be off the train, what with four days on the goods train and the last two on the Madras Mail.

On one side of the rutted track a rice paddy stretched out, a verdant green that almost hurt her eyes in the sunlight. Dotting the paddy, women's saris—saffron, crimson, vermillion, peacock blue—shimmered in the light like beads on a bangle. Seeing this beauty again, she admitted she shouldn't have let the painful memories stop her from coming back. Her roots to this southern land were as numerous and deep as those of the banyan tree.

Dr. Rory Johnson's clinic lay beyond the next village as the road took her deeper into mango and banana groves, and the jungle. The brightly painted *jutka* decorated with marigolds would get her there before dark, and her blood ran warmer with anticipation.

As twilight approached, a perimeter of white-painted stones led her to a series of huts. The *jutka* stopped outside a single-story white bungalow as the keens and screeches of thousands of birds came from the surrounding umbrella trees. A tall, thin man with a shock of silver hair came out the front door, stooping below the lintel so as not to bump his head.

He walked toward her. Close up, his square-ish face was quite handsome under that gray hair. "You're here at least. From Ada's telegram we thought you'd have been here days ago. I'm Rory Johnson."

She jumped down from the *jutka*. "Couldn't seem to manage the right connections, I'm afraid." No sense telling him about her lengthy journey on the goods train.

His grinning face looked at her askance. "What, the British-India railway not running on time? Must write a letter to the commissioner. But you're here now, looking hearty and hale."

She stood looking around her at his compound. "Those outbuildings, they're more than just clinic rooms?"

His smile took ten years off him. "That hut is for my laboratory. Those two for examining patients and performing surgery, though I prefer to send patients to the city hospitals."

"You don't restrict yourself to cholera research?"

"Oh my, no. I'm the only doctor for miles. Vellore has some wonderful hospitals, but often we can't get a patient there quickly enough. Those three other huts I keep for patients who need to stay overnight. And I can tell you, my sister who's been chief nurse and bottle washer is overjoyed you're here. You're an answer to our prayers."

Her feet drew her a few steps toward the huts. The desire to plunge into rudimentary nursing sang along her nerve endings.

"Oh no you don't." Rory's call pulled her back from tramping toward the outbuildings. The smile stamped on his face eased her fears that she'd overstepped her bounds. "I have strict orders from Ada to look after you. She says you're one of the finest nurses she's worked with. So come this way. There's plenty of time tomorrow to show you everything."

While clutching two of her cases, he ushered her toward the house. About to follow him, the words stenciled above the door stopped her. "I am the resurrection and the life: he that believeth in me, though he were dead, yet shall he live." She knew the Bible verse only too well, having memorized it during Sunday school. Mild consternation filled her. She'd had plenty of experience with white-washed teetotalers in her childhood.

Rory looked back at her as she stepped into the house. Its mud-brick walls, a foot and a half thick, would keep the place cool during the heat of the day. A ceiling cloth kept insects and other unpleasant visitors from dropping down on them from the thatched roof. Chintz-covered sofas and chairs were placed around a selection of teak tables. With the descent of night, a servant in a white *dhoti* and his hair oiled flat hurried to light paraffin lamps. Outside, the evening grew noisy with crickets and frogs.

Instantly, she felt at home. She had stayed away too long, and she shook off the odd sense of déjà vu she'd felt the last mile in the cart. It had to be the humid winds that unsettled her. The promise of the monsoons ran in her bloodstream, like the tide coming in wave by wave. With the promise of rain came a line of poetry from one of Adam's old letters. "And how am I to face the odds/ Of man's bedevilment and God's?"

Rory nodded her through the house, past a dining room and a gleaming mahogany table that sat empty, where alas no dinner was laid to the dismay of her rumbling tummy.

After lighting the lamps, the young servant bowed over his hands to her. "Praise the Lord."

"Meet Devaram." Rory pronounced over the small Tamil servant.

Devaram reached for her bags and in broken English added, "Welcome to Lavinia."

"Lavinia?" Laine spouted. "You named this place after a woman in Roman mythology."

A petite woman of about fifty, and shadowed by Rory's towering frame, strode toward Laine with a smile to match her brother's. "Lavinia is most definitely not our choosing. We're far too down to earth for Virgil. I'm Bella, by the way. If left to Rory and me, we'd probably have named the place *Great Expectations*."

As she spoke, Bella led them through to the back of the house. "Let's get you settled."

The bedroom, like the rest of the bungalow, was white-washed inside and out. Teak beams supported the ceiling, and a *punkah* hung from it, hardly moving the sluggish air. Mosquito netting draped over a bed with a rosewood headboard and a white cover.

Bella shooed Rory and Devaram out and turned to her. “I can’t tell you how glad I am you’re here. We’ve needed a nurse in these parts for so long, but I’m positively over-the-moon to have another woman to talk to.” She gave a minute tug to the cover on the bed, readjusted a pillow. “I’m sure you’d like a bath. If I’d known you were coming today, I’d have arranged to have the water heated. As it is you’ll have to do with cold.”

“That will be lovely.” Laine ran a hand along the smoothness of the rosewood headboard.

Bella hesitated only slightly. “Thing is, we expected you days ago and hadn’t prepared dinner, not knowing you would turn up today precisely. As we are invited to the big house tonight, Devaram can whip up something if you’d rather not attend. You must be tired. All the same we’d love you to come.”

Laine sighed with relief. So that’s all it was, a bit of concern over dinner arrangements, and not that Bella didn’t want her here. “The big house?”

“The patron of this little medical compound. He’s been doing marvelous things with his plantation. A forward thinking man in many ways. It was during a bad cholera epidemic a year ago that he brought Rory and me out here.”

“But I’d love to join you for dinner. I’m absolutely starving. Can you give me a few minutes to wash and change?” She ran a hand through her dust-covered hair.” I’m sure I look like I’ve had a henna rinse...all over.”

Bella clapped her hands. “I was hoping you’d say that because frankly the work here is too hard for a fainting daisy.”

“Have I passed the first test then?”

Bella’s eyes held a gleam of mischief. “I believe you have. Dinner isn’t until eight, so you’ve half an hour.”

The bath didn’t disappoint. Though it was the typical galvanized tub, Bella seemed to consider scented soaps from England a luxury she could not live without. Laine lathered her hair with shampoo perfumed by peony flowers and sank below the water to rinse it. Her hair would dry in no time, probably by the time she got to the big house.

She couldn’t help deepening her voice at what Bella called the plantation owner’s residence. “The big house indeed.”

In her room she found that Devaram had ironed the navy skirt and cream chiffon blouse she had shaken out before going into the bathroom. She dressed and sat on the bed ready to put her feet into her walking brogues, and let out a sniff of disdain. It was so humid. Might she not wear something lighter? Perhaps that pair of shoes with a delicate heel and straps that crisscrossed the top of her foot.

A feeling of weightlessness came over her when she stood. Her hips actually undulated. Like a woman's. First time in months she'd dressed to the nines, and she was out in the jungle with only a couple of middle-aged siblings to see her, and some grizzly plantation owner who likely soaked himself in whiskey each night. One of those Dutchmen of the old order, a remnant of Holland's colonies in India before the British Raj took over.

Rory and Bella waited for her outside, and Rory assisted Laine into the cart. He jumped up beside Bella and took the reins to the single pony as the moon made a poor attempt to break through the gathering clouds. But the densely matted groves blocked out what little light the moon did shed.

As the cart lumbered along the track, night-blooming flowers released their perfumes. It almost seemed as if their scents were drawing them deeper into the coconut, banana, and mango plantation. With the fragrances came a feeling of intense sadness.

She shook her head of the foolish notion. It was probably the coming of the rains she felt in her bones. More likely, she was in the need of a good meal.

A mile or so away, lights beckoned through the thick belt of trees, outlining an extensive home and outbuildings. The roar of a large cat shook the jungle, silencing the other grunts and snuffles of the surrounding forests. Incongruously, Rachmaninoff's *Second* concerto from a gramophone filtered out with its all-too-familiar composition. It wasn't the prowling predator stalking nearby that set her teeth on edge. The warm evening heavy with moisture altered the notes of the concerto, so that they echoed discordantly in her ears. That, and the unwanted memories the music dredged up.

A lemon grove surrounded the buildings that included a smattering of thatched huts. Rory stopped the cart and left the reins to a barefooted servant in a white fastened coat and trousers. Bella and Rory moved toward the house, and Laine strolled behind them to the sprawling two-story building, its deep veranda supported by thick white columns.

A dissonant series of bass notes from the piano jarred with the haunting and higher notes of violins. The heels of her shoes crunched on the path of crushed limestone, setting her off balance. Off-key.

Closer to the house, light penetrated the shadows of the garden. She halted at the edge of an aureole of light that splayed on the lawn at her feet. As the night air slipped over her skin, waves of scent upon scent wafted—lemon, frangipani, jasmine...mimosa.

Rory called out to someone, but Laine couldn't move.

It was a night for lovers. A night for the very first lovers when perhaps Eve had turned to her God-given husband.

With a hiss, the needle of the gramophone searched for its grove on the next recording, and a familiar line of poetry scratched through Laine's mind. *I recognize the signs of the old flame...of old desire.*

She shook herself mentally. How foolish to let this sensuous night stir up longings she'd tried to forget.

Thunder rolled as Rory turned to wait for Laine while Bella took the steps to a small pavilion of fretted marble, set a few yards from the main house. Their host presumably sat within. He stood, and the flaming torches on the lawn behind him threw his height and slender frame into sharp relief. The shape of his shoulders. The slight angle at which he bent his head as he listened to their chatter coming up the path.

"Rory and Bella," he called out in pleasure, "I should have sent the car to collect you. It's going to rain. Can't you feel it? Like Wordsworth wrote, 'How beautiful is the rain. After the dust and heat.'"

The tiger roared again out in the jungle. And Laine froze as Eve might have frozen when the first heartache had entered the world and everything had changed between Eve...and Eve's own Adam. Rory caught her gasp, his smile fading to a frown.

Still cloaked in darkness their host came down the steps of the pavilion, but he stopped suddenly. "I hadn't realized you brought company."

"It's the nurse we need," Rory said. "Remember, you and I talked about—"

"Of course." Their host's voice had gone a tad breathless. "It's just, Rory, we hadn't decided... You know how upsetting it is to..." He turned toward her, trying to make out her features in the gloom. In the dark his voice had turned warm again. "Never mind all that, we mustn't make the lady feel unwelcome."

As though she were cold, she shivered. His accent was that of an educated man, an accent molded by Oxford. Balliol College to be precise. A man who adored poetry—Wordsworth, AE Housman, Virgil—the only man in a million who would name his plantation after the Roman goddess, Lavinia. She should have known. He used to write so many of Virgil's verses to her in his letters, words that had set her aflame then with longing for him to return from college.

He took the remaining steps to the ground. His white shirt open at the neck and his gray flannel trousers, the garb of a man who never had cared for stiff formality. Light from the house and the torches sought out and found the lean planes of his face, the dark hair sweeping off his brow that when over-long curled at the base of his neck. The sensitive mouth curved in a welcoming smile for his uninvited guest.

She counted the stones at her feet, and looked up. It was not a dream. For there he stood.

His smile froze as her own when she stepped into the puddle of light on the path. She rallied up all the nonchalance she could. "Hello, fancy meeting you here, Adam."

9

The sight of Laine sent shock waves through Adam like that of a bullet wound. Seven years since the beginning of the war and the last time he'd seen her. She'd been wearing a pretty blue dress then, her dark hair windblown because she'd rushed to Madras Central Station to not miss seeing him off. He'd been in uniform, though he'd just joined up. They'd only had five minutes, and he'd kissed her good-bye. He remembered that. Though he'd prayed—prayed long and hard to forget.

"As I live and breathe, Laine." He regretted his futile attempt at humor.

She didn't move. Torchlight danced across her features and caught the sheen of her smooth hair. Flickering light touched the line of her mouth that he knew so well, set as tight as a clamshell to stop the trembling of her lips. She was as embarrassed, or was it as shocked as he was, after that wretched letter he'd sent when she was still in France?

He reached for the tone he'd used with his men when he'd held them as they were dying in the trenches, or later in the hospital as they'd suffered surgery after surgery. *No need to add to their pain. Speak with a trace of banter.* Ironically, the ability to banter he'd learned from Laine. "Must be quite a surprise to come across me out here in the sticks...Laine." To say her name out loud was more difficult than he'd imagined.

"You could say that." A hint of the girl he used to know came through her sharpening tone.

He tried again. "I must apologize. I'm afraid my last letter to you was rather...bad-mannered."

"Mmm. Bad-mannered? Yes, you could say that."

Though she didn't add a word out loud, the phrases, *horrendously cruel, unfeeling desertion of what they'd meant to each other*, clanged in his ears.

Bella's perplexed expression mirrored Rory's as they stood looking from him to Laine and then each other.

Strange, after all this time he still recognized that though Laine clasped her hands together like a schoolgirl and she spoke with that easy-going melody in her voice, she was seething. Confused, hurt, but seething as much as that tiger prowling the jungle two miles away. Her eyes, the color of tea, had always played traitor when she tried to hide her feelings. Now the girl whose humor used to ripple from her stood in the moonlight. Her face shone as pale as the petals of a lotus blossom...and as breathtakingly lovely.

He'd hurt her. Oh dear God, he'd hurt her.

Bella moved with swiftness to tuck Laine's arm in hers. With a hint of steel beneath her laughter, Bella turned to him and ordered. "It's obvious you two have a lot to catch up on. Don't you think, Adam, it would be a good idea to invite us in? We could all use a cold drink." She added, sotto voce, "And perhaps a dose of headache powder all round."

Rory, brilliant doctor he was, stood on the path, his expression as blank as blotting paper.

To his relief, Bella walked Laine steadily toward the house. Rory waited for him to precede him inside.

He motioned Rory on and turned to look behind. His gaze sought out the grounds where the gardens ended. All quiet out there. But he remained conscious every moment of the one staring down at them from the darkened room above.

Inside the house, the gramophone stopped playing Rachmaninoff's *Second*. One small mercy. Adam darted a glance at the dining room. The table had been set for three, but his house-servant, Ravi, who had seen Laine arrive, had set another place. Laine strolled with Rory and Bella into the drawing room, and he followed on unsteady legs. As if he were slightly drunk. He shook his head to clear it.

After plumping a cushion, Bella sat on the sofa. Rory leaned an elbow on the fireplace mantle. Wandering about the room, Laine studied the framed photographs he'd hung on the walls, the study of wildlife that had given him some comfort these past few years. She strolled to the small grand piano, one of the few luxuries from his old days he allowed himself.

Electricity fizzled inside him. To break the spell of unspoken questions, he opened the slats on the louvered doors to the veranda. He turned to watch Laine study his home, listened to the heels of her shoes clicking on the teak floors. Her gaze took in this old plantation home with its mahogany furnishings of decades gone by. Was she thinking this should have been hers?

Ravi poured glasses of lime juice and soda. With a cool drink in their hands, everyone seemed to take a sigh. All except Laine. She turned a page of sheet music at the piano. Rachmaninoff. He cringed. Why had he left out that piece of music, of all pieces?

She turned a smiling face to the rest of the room, but failed to meet his eyes. Her gaze went somewhere past his right shoulder. "So, Adam, how long have you lived here?"

Rory and Bella would have no idea the weight of her simple question, but the answer stuck in his throat. "I came here directly after being released from the army."

"Your mother never breathed a word, Adam. I thought you were at home in Madras near her." He heard the flat note in her chuckle. Saw her infinitesimal flinch. She ran her fingers along the piano lid. "Why, only two months ago I received a letter from Auntie—I mean, your mother. We correspond, but then we would, wouldn't we?"

Bella set her empty glass on a table. "You and Adam are related?"

Laine jumped in before he could. "My parents and Adam's...best of friends...since before I was born. Auntie Margaret and Adam were like family after my mother and father died. I was a miserable fifteen-year-old at the time." She rolled back her shoulders and bestowed a dazzling smile on the room that fooled everyone but him. There was more than a hint of challenge in the thrust of her chin. "In fact, I was thinking of visiting Auntie while I'm down here in the south."

He dredged up a light tone, which was becoming near impossible with each passing minute. "She'd love to see you, of course, but I'm afraid Mother isn't at home right now. On a bit of a holiday to Ooty with friends."

As he feared, that light of challenge in her eyes dimmed. A trace of dejection showed in the downward sweep of her lashes, but only until that chin of hers came up again, and renewed battle sparked in her eyes. "Well then, another time. And perhaps, Adam, we shouldn't offend your cook by dawdling any further. I'm fading from starvation as we speak."

Bella got to her feet. "Splendid idea, Laine. Lead on."

Adam gestured for the two women to go into the dining room.

With Bella at his right and Rory on his left, Laine sat directly across from him. Most nights he was happy to eat by a few paraffin lamps, but tonight Ravi used the chandelier. It hung from the teak beam in the ceiling, lifting all shadows from the room. He had a better chance to really see Laine now. And she him.

She shook out her napkin and laid it across her lap as Ravi served the mulligatawny soup. Color had returned to her face in two round spots of red on her cheeks. The color of anger and not just hurt, though you'd never know it from her laughter at Bella's comments. But then, Laine in her youth had gone out of her way for frivolity. She'd preferred a game of golf to a serious conversation. Loved a dart match over a discussion of good literature. Laine would never understand why he'd persuaded his mother to keep his whereabouts secret.

Silence thundered around the table. Or was that real thunder Laine heard? Had she seen a flash of lightning through the window? It had been nigh impossible to look Adam in the eye since that moment she first heard his voice. When he'd stepped into the light, and she knew for sure, the bandages of her barely healed world had been ripped off. She still felt the sting.

All this time she'd thought she wouldn't feel a thing if she ever did run into him. But the sight of his dark hair and lean face, that absentminded look of a scholar that use to delight her and drive her mad at the same time, was now not two feet away. She went dizzy. Times when he had read and read and read—seemingly unaware of her—until she'd tossed aside his book, and he'd laughed and drawn her onto his lap to kiss her in apology.

She wanted to storm out of his house, but she wasn't going to let him off the hook. That lamentably cold letter he'd sent her while she was still in France had been as vague as it had been cruel. But tonight, hearing that Auntie Margaret had...

She wanted answers.

Only by forcing herself to chat with Bella about trivial nonsense helped her get through the salad and fish course. Bella pretended to be interested in the larks of her fellow nurses in Amritsar and from when she'd worked in the military hospital in Colchester.

Rory's kind smiles across the table helped too. "You worked in Colchester?" He renewed his gaze with interest. "I imagine you patched up many a man who'd lost limbs. See much facial reconstruction?"

"A bit. I only worked there six months. Mostly I served at Étables in France."

"Was that where you earned your RRC?"

Adam's head shot up.

At the same time Bella piped in with, "My word, you've been decorated with the Royal Red Cross. Why, I'm sure any hospital in the British Empire would be happy to have you. Bless you, my darling girl, for coming to the back of beyond to help us with our poor villagers."

Laine took a sip of water, ignoring the pull of Adam's gaze. Though she didn't look at him, she was attuned to everything about him. His throat moved convulsively as he continued to recuperate from his earlier shock. She could smell the scent of alum on his clean-shaven face. Rubbing her fingertips together, she could almost feel that lock of hair that fell over his brow. Feel that ever-so-slight bump on the upper bridge of his nose from the smack of a hockey stick during a tournament when he was a boy.

Adam's voice jolted her out of her thoughts. "The RRC, well I must say I'm not at all surprised, Laine. You always were...amazing." He cleared the roughness from his voice. "The last I heard, you were at Étables. I passed through that hospital on my way back to England."

He'd been so close to where she'd been stationed and had not stopped to even speak with her. She trembled. She'd gone over it in her mind countless times. If he'd been well then, surely he would have found her, explained why he no longer wished to marry her.

She forced herself to study him with clinical interest through the next courses. He had not so much as a limp. His speech and ability to hold intelligent conversation—not to mention run a plantation—proved there was nothing wrong with him mentally. Even his face. Unscarred. Unmarked. Except for a touch of gray at his temples, he appeared as sound as he'd always been. Still though, she'd seen enough of the horrors to understand. Men whose faces had been half blown off, limbs gone, their memory lost, their minds shattered by shellshock.

She kept control of her voice. "Were you wounded, Adam? I did receive the news that you were missing in action."

He turned his startling blue gaze away from her. "Compared to many, you could say I got out with barely a scratch." Something in his buoyancy rang untrue.

Her fingernails dug into her palm. She still had no idea what had happened to him, only that first report that he'd been declared dead. Then months later his letter had arrived. She'd opened it, breathless with joy that they'd made a mistake—he was alive—only to read his baldly written note that he no longer wanted to marry her and wished God's blessing on the rest of her life. Bad manners? Yes, she could find a few other words to describe that letter, but not any she could speak aloud. Her mind spun. But Auntie Margaret?

For a long time she'd licked her wounds. If he'd wanted to marry someone else, he could have at least said so. But it was clear now there was no Mrs. Adam Brand. No womanly touches graced his home at all. At least she didn't have to suffer that humiliation.

"You were listed as dead, Adam. I know this because I checked." She was aware of Rory and Bella's shocked expressions.

A tinge of crimson mottled Adam's cheeks. "True. But in reality my company was merely cut off from our own lines for a number of weeks. We survived." He said this in the same vein as if he were discussing the weather, not as if he were a man who had wanted to spend the rest of his life with her.

"I see." So that was it. She still wasn't entitled to a better explanation.

They moved into the parlor for coffee. In a numb stupor she listened to the conversation shift to Adam's interest in the forestry works. She excused herself, needing to get outside even if the air was as sultry and unmoving as it was in the drawing room.

She strode through the house to the front door, across the wide veranda and down the steps. The garden's darkness reached out, a haven to quiet herself so that she would not cry. With her hands clenched at her sides she counted her breaths and stalked down the road along a high wall of bamboo that enclosed a group of huts, all the while fighting the trembling of her limbs.

She veered around once, thinking she heard the soft pad of footsteps behind her. Only the clammy winds moved the lemon trees, and she strode closer to the bamboo wall.

A flurry of movement behind the wall brought her up short. So too did a hiss of indrawn breath. Right now she didn't care if a Bengal tiger watched her through the gaps between the bamboo stocks. She leaned closer. In the darkness she couldn't see what hid between the barricade and back of one of the huts. But something breathed hard.

Running footsteps pounded on the road. "Come away, Laine, please."

Adam swung her around to face him. She could hardly see him in the dark. He breathed hard, but not surely from running a hundred feet from the veranda. "Please come back to the house. We were about to serve coffee."

They were alone, and that nervous tick to his jaw meant he knew she would jump on this chance. "A moment, Adam. You know what I'd like."

"All I can say is I'm sorry, again, Laine. I could have written you in a far more gentle manner, but somehow cut and dried seemed kindest at the time."

"What happened to you when you were missing? That's the root of everything, isn't it? Why you suddenly changed."

He ran a hand through his hair, letting it fall to his side with a slap. "It was all quite as I said at the table. You were over there. You know. At times it was hard to see where the lines were drawn in the mud. Where the Germans were, where my own men were. We were lost. Some of my platoon...hurt. Many died. What more can I say? We made it back."

"And you no longer wished to marry me."

He went silent for several heartbeats. His voice came out as soft as the moths fluttering in a trace of light. "I'm afraid that's correct, Laine."

His lack of explanation clawed at her last shred of composure, and she silently fought to win it back. He gestured for her to walk to the house. At one time he would have taken her arm to guide her in the dark. Most men would have. Strangers even. But apparently not the man who, when he was a boy, had been more of a brother than a friend. Or when he'd become a man who used to express his love for her with the passion of a poet. Now he walked far from her so that he wouldn't inadvertently touch her.

He glanced back at the walled-in huts. She knew him too well and recognized the poise he worked hard to strum up. "When did you transfer from Étables to Colchester, Laine?"

His lighthearted friendliness snapped her last strand of self-control. That was it! She stopped and glared at him with the fury of an offended water buffalo. "I was transferred to Colchester shortly after receiving the RRC, Adam. Which was shortly after receiving the news that you and your unit were missing in action. And then the news that you were dead. Then a number of weeks later, your charming letter arrived telling me that you were very much alive, but our wedding was off. You see, those in command thought I'd seen enough of the front and needed time to...grieve for you."

Even in the dark she was aware of his flinch. She didn't enjoy that but couldn't help her last jab at him. "We obviously just missed seeing each other. You must have been routed home to India around the time I was being sent back to France. Perhaps you were even on the same ship as the mail packet that returned your family engagement ring that I had been wearing."

He met her gaze but seemed unable to speak.

"I'm sorry, Adam. But it's not even that—Dear Jane letter and all—that has left me somewhat testy. It's that I've known you since I was a squalling, red-faced infant in a pram and you just learning to walk, and all these years have passed without receiving so much as a by-your-leave. If you didn't want to marry me, you could at least have treated me as the friend I had always been, and let me know how you were."

She gulped and shook her head. "And it's the fact that your mother... Auntie...must be in on this...this conspiracy to keep me in the dark."

He took her wrist with gentle fingers. "You mustn't blame Mother. I badgered her. She didn't want to—I alone am to blame, Laine, for...keeping you in the dark."

She rushed past him, swallowing the painful lump in her throat, and marched toward Rory and Bella who stood on the veranda. As she stomped forward, the rains landed in a sudden sheet of water. One moment the air had pressed against them, suffocating. Now the world disappeared as if she strode through a waterfall.

Adam reached the veranda a moment later. The strain in his voice showed as he focused on Rory and Bella. "Perhaps it's best we call it a night. I'll have Ravi drive you home."

He didn't look at her, but all four of them could distinguish that the change in his tone was for her. "Laine, the raw jungle is on our doorstep. It's best you don't go exploring the surroundings unaccompanied. Far too dangerous what with snakes, leopards, wild elephants, and tigers to name a few. So if you desire to visit the plantation...I must insist on—" He searched for words. "I must insist you send a note, and I'll make arrangements. I also ask that you respect the privacy of these outbuildings."

She stood frozen while the warm rain cascaded off the edge of the veranda, obscuring everything outside. She had no intention of visiting his blasted plantation or snooping in his barns anyway.

When a large black Daimler drove up, Rory stepped into the rain to open the back passenger door. Adam had the good sense to assist Bella into the car so that Laine could scramble in by herself. If he had so much as touched her she couldn't be held accountable for what she'd do to him.

In spite of the monsoons, her anger burned like a tin roof under the Indian sun. What a dolt she'd been when she'd thought him dead, to think that death, and death alone, had separated them.

10

Birds screeched and twittered as a wash of duck-egg green tinged the dawn sky. Laine waited for Bella and Rory on the veranda, twirling a scarlet hibiscus by its stem. The sun rose. And after last night's rains, steam lifted from the ground, and the trees and flowers were heavy with water.

Having dressed in her usual gray ward dress and white apron, she hoped she looked her efficient self. The pattern of sunlight and shade in the jungle drew her eye. Truth was, she still reeled from the shock of seeing Adam last night.

In a flurry of energy Bella came out of the house and crossed the compound to the cluster of thatched-roof huts that acted as a dispensary and wards. Earlier over breakfast Rory decided he'd show the laboratory to Laine before releasing her to work with Bella. Already a line of patients congregated outside the dispensary. Thirty or more Indian peasants waited with patience, their feet hardened by a lifetime of standing in the dust and eyes softened by millennia of suffering.

Rory headed toward his laboratory, and Laine plopped the blossom into a watering can and stood to join him. With a wave to his sister, he opened his laboratory and ushered Laine in. Sunlight angled through windows to a large room where counters lined the walls. Various tables filled the room littered with charts of cholera cases going back to the middle of last century. Laine strolled to bookcases jammed with annual yearbooks from the Indian Medical Service. On another table piles of rainfall reports were stacked.

Rory's pride in his laboratory showed. If he'd been a stout man, she would have expected him to pop a few buttons. "While it's still relatively cool I reserve the first hour or two in the morning for study. Bella can do as much for the patients as I can, even some minor surgery. I'll join her later, but I wanted to show you this first."

Laine brushed her hand along a table holding two microscopes, another table with Bunsen burners and boxes of slides. "Ada mentioned briefly that you are doing work with a cholera vaccine. Do you hope to find a better serum than Haffkine's?"

He sent her a mockery of a grin. "I don't flatter myself that I'll discover a better vaccine. It's my prayer, and Adam's of course, to ease the suffering of these villagers. There's a colony of untouchables a few miles away. We'll be going out in a day or so to finish the inoculations that Bella and I've been distributing for the past few months."

"How willing are the villagers to accept the inoculations?"

Rory's grin diminished. "The untouchables are so desperate they gladly accept a few *annas* to let us vaccinate them. It's the people of higher castes that remain wary. There's a Hindu holy man in the closest village who is constantly putting out rumors that we're trying to poison them, or take away their caste by injecting them with the serum. Especially lately, like the rest of India, we've had a few outbursts from the local people. Talk of running their own affairs instead of the British government. I don't care about politics. I only want the peasant to get medical treatment the same as any wealthy Indian in the cities."

She bent to adjust the lens on a microscope. "Considering the millions of people in this district alone, where on earth do you find the money to pay them a stipend?"

"Adam's worked out an arrangement with the Indian Medical Services, along with some of his own funds." At the mention of Adam, Rory glanced at her from under lowered brows. "About Adam...Bella and I don't know what to say—"

She straightened from looking through the lens. "I need to apologize for last night."

Nothing but kindness showed in his features. "Not in the least. I hope you and Adam were able to clear the air. These things do happen."

She moved a box of slides a few inches on the table. Last night after returning to the compound she'd barely slept. To think that Adam lived within one mile of her instead of eighty miles away in the city of Madras as she'd thought... "Rory, would you tell me if Adam had been injured during the war?"

His eyes glinted with speculation. "You heard what Adam said last night. He got out with only a few scars. Nothing to speak of."

"Yes, that's what he said. But there are so many...hidden injuries."

"You still care for him."

With a steady hand she smoothed the front of her apron, though her insides felt anything but steady. Part of her wanted to run off, but she refused to leave Rory and Bella in the lurch. She forced a laugh. "Any romance between Adam and I ended a long time ago. I'm concerned for him, as any old friend would be."

His gaze dwelt on her until a slow grin spread over his face. "Well in that case, I'm glad being near Adam and in effect being his employee won't cause you any discomfort. But you have nothing to worry about. Adam's war injuries left him with a few harmless scars. The Lord truly did look after him."

He was whole. She concentrated on keeping her slight smile in place as the roots of her hair tingled, and kept her tone as if they had been discussing any patient. "I'm so glad, but enough talk of Adam. Don't you think we should get started then? I've come to work."

Rory's mouth twitched. "My dear sister is absolutely right about you. She said you'd work like a Trojan no matter what the issue is between you and Adam. And on a personal level...I'm delighted. You're quite the breath of fresh air, Laine."

He turned a slight shade of pink, and thank goodness started to show her the rest of his laboratory, giving her time to shove Adam from her thoughts. With renewed interest she focused on each beaker, set of pincers, and autoclave, as if she'd never seen such things before.

He moved to a counter where he had been studying local water samples. "Adam's set us up with a generator. In the middle of nowhere we're able to run a small laundry and sterilize instruments. We take no chances with cholera being so rampant here. And records clearly show the disease peaks during the monsoons, usually seven to nine days after the first heavy rainfall."

She nodded. "Last night was your first significant shower from what I've heard."

He stared off into space. "The cholera microbe attacks a body quickly. Twenty-four hours or less, and a person can die."

A week passed, and Laine didn't know whether to be pleased or not that Adam hadn't set foot on the medical compound. This neglect on his part had been strongly voiced by Bella last evening over tea.

Most days it rained, but not today. The afternoon sun waned as Laine worked with Bella and Rory. Today the three of them had dealt with a number of conjunctivitis cases, the expected cases of ringworm, abscesses, various wounds, burns, and Rory set a broken radius in a young boy who had fallen from a tree while cutting down coconuts.

With a satisfying ache in her shoulders, Laine washed up in sterilized water. Her clean jodhpurs and fresh cotton blouse felt good after the nursing uniform that had been sticking to her like a second skin for most of the afternoon.

Bella called out from the parlor where she had her feet on an ottoman, reading *Anne of the Island*. "There's fresh tea and crumpets if you're in the mood. Dinner will be at seven. For the next while I'm too tired to move." With that Bella sank deeper into her chair and novel.

A shaft of sunlight pierced the cloud that would release its showers tonight. But it was dry enough for Laine to find a bicycle in one of the sheds and push off in the direction of Adam's plantation. The night of her arrival the tension between them had been as dense as the humidity trapped by the towering trees on either side of this road. If she was going to have any peace working here with him so close, she had to make things right.

She released a bitter laugh. If only she and Adam could revert to the feelings they'd had for each other as children. Before they'd grown up and he'd returned from Oxford...before he'd noticed she'd become a woman and she'd noticed he'd become a man.

A strain of music reached her as she got to the house. A gramophone played a not-so-polite ballad, one that had been popular in music halls in Britain before the war. Not Adam's high-brow taste. Nor would this naughty ballad suit the tastes of the average Indian.

She propped the bicycle against the pavilion where she'd first seen Adam. There was no reason for stealth, but all the same she lightly stepped up to the veranda. When she called out at the open door, no one answered, though the music stopped playing. There were no other noises, not even that of men working in the sheds or barn. Somewhere in the distance an elephant trumpeted. Must be one of Adam's elephants being ridden through the groves where no vehicle could go.

Well, she'd wait right here until he returned, and she planted her hands on her hips. The smallish village of huts surrounded by the bamboo wall caught her eye. She left the veranda and started off to the enclosed village. What could Adam be protecting in there? Gold-plated bananas and diamond-studded coconuts?

Ravi, who'd served dinner last week, ran up to her. "*Memsahib*, please come this way. Are you not knowing that no guests are allowed on the plantation grounds except by invitation?"

So it wasn't just her that Adam restricted from these grounds. She'd ignore that for now. "I've come to see Adam."

"Adam is not at home."

He made desperate gestures as if to sweep her away from the huts and to the front path where she'd left her bike. "When will he be back?"

"Perhaps in several days. None of the household are sure."

Household? What household? All she'd seen was Ravi. Now what? Get back on this bicycle and forget this whole stupid attempt to make up with Adam? Could she manage to ignore him for the next few months?

She softened her voice for Ravi. "I'll leave him a note, if you please."

The young servant threw a wide-eyed look over his shoulder, as if he were trying to locate something he'd lost. Together they walked back to the veranda and around the perimeter of the house. Potted palms dotted the airy space along with numerous cane chairs that would fit Adam's lanky frame. But how many chairs did one man need to sit on?

Below the veranda, flowerbeds ran riot with blossoms. Such a big house, and yet so empty. A stillness clothed the place that left her spellbound so that she jumped when Ravi spoke.

"*Memsahib*." He indicated a large teak Empire desk set against the veranda's balustrade and between two wide columns. The desk overlooked a lawn clipped as short as a bowling green and with the correct dimensions for cricket matches. Nothing could be more quintessentially British and Indian—like Adam himself. But the cricket oval gave off the same feeling as the house did—an empty stage, as if the players had strolled off and would soon return for another match. She glanced again at the number of cane chairs.

Behind the desk, louvered doors stood open to a darkly-paneled den. From the veranda she peered into this large room with windows from floor to ceiling, and bookcases jammed to overflowing. She went inside and touched a few of the spines—Virgil, of course, George MacDonald,

G.K. Chesterton for a few. The brass horn of a gramophone projected from the corner.

A soft cough issued from Ravi as he pulled a leaf of paper from the desk drawer outside on the veranda, and she scurried out of the den. He left her with a polite bow and rounded the corner of the house.

She sat at the desk overlooking Adam's private sports field and pulled the paper close, searching for something to write with. Her hand stopped, suspended over a fountain pen encased in silver and lapis blue. The pen she'd given him upon his receiving his First at Oxford. Her fingers curled around the pen, and she removed the cap as her thoughts came together as slowly as heavily burdened camels sauntering across a desert. He had kept the pen she had given him.

Using his pen she began to write:

Adam

I apologize for the way I spoke to you the other evening. But don't you think that two old friends like us could sit down for a chat, to meet in the days ahead with some sort of civility, for the sake of Bella and Rory as well as for you and me?

It's only common courtesy. After all, I am someone who has known you most of your life. I await your answer.

Laine

No one could accuse this note of anything other than an extension of the common courtesy she mentioned. But with no small trace of savagery she underscored the word someone a second time. She'd been much more than a mere *someone*. With more tenderness than she'd treated the notepaper, she replaced the cap on the pen and, setting it back where she'd found it, slid away from the desk. But she would not leave yet.

She stepped into the den.

A few personal items adorned the room, the shield from Balliol College hung on the wall, as well as his framed blues for cricket and field hockey, the items she expected. Similar photographs as those she'd seen last night lined these walls. This however was new. Wildlife, leopards, birds, tigers, as well as photos of this house and garden.

The mystery as to who the photographer might be was answered when her eye lighted on several sturdy-looking cameras sitting on a bureau in the corner. The lenses telescoped out like the unfolding of a fan from black or brown rectangular boxes. Here lay evidence of an Adam she didn't know. A new Adam perhaps? The man she used to know cared about the poetic recitations of long-lost civilizations and rhapsodized over Wordsworth.

She stopped at another series of photographs displayed on a table—Adam and his mother and father on holidays in the hill station of Ooty before his father died. A smattering of old friends from Adam's school days in Madras, his entire class at Balliol, and photos of him later with his two closest friends—his cousin, John Paten, and their mutual friend, Robert Bennett. If she remembered correctly, Robert had died in the war. Most of that year's student class had perished in the trenches. She'd not heard what had happened to John.

She picked up the photograph of Adam and John as they stood on the grassy quad at Balliol, both draped in their black student cloaks. John had grown up in England but visited India frequently in his youth. They'd been close in age, but looking at them in this picture, with their stunningly similar looks, they could have been brothers.

On the wall behind the table hung photographs of the Indian regiment Adam had served with during the war, rows of the rank and file in perfect precision.

But something didn't sit right. She felt it. Like a badly set bone.

A shot of hope had rushed through her when she'd seen that Adam had kept the fountain pen she'd given him. Hope for what, she couldn't say, when she'd already grieved the loss of any life with him. But now the lack of one single photograph of her struck her with its absence. Not one single photo of her! Even in a group. Not even to remember her as a friend.

She sucked back a breath and marched through the doors to the veranda. What a fool she was, wallowing like a love-sick chump. Men didn't keep photographs of the women they rejected.

At the desk she crumpled the note she'd left for Adam and threw it in the waste basket. She tramped along the veranda and down the steps. But her bike had been moved from where she'd left it.

Ravi appeared at her side a moment later. "I will see that you are driven home, *memsahib*, in the automobile along with your conveyance, as Adam has taken the truck. Have you not been told? There is a tiger on the prowl. Until this wounded marauder has been stopped we must all be taking cares."

She stared stupidly at the vacant space where her bike had been, as if it should suddenly materialize. This house, its gardens and cricket oval, hidden and silent behind folds of coconut palms, banana groves, and jungle...with its incessant wave upon wave of fragrance, must be turning her brain to mush. She shook her head to clear it.

Then it struck her. It wasn't the absence so much of her own picture that disturbed her. It was that—other than a photograph of his mother—Adam displayed no photos of women at all.

With all that had happened in the last week, a vicious man-eating tiger on the prowl only made perfect sense.

Clutching a loaded rifle to his chest, Adam sprinted along the narrow trail, Nandi behind him. Tall grass slapped at their thighs as they dropped off the trail to run adjacent to a spine of rock. For three days they'd hunted the female Bengal tiger. After she'd taken the life of a small child, a number of villagers had gone out after her, only to shoot the tigress with their ancient blunderbuss. But in failing to kill her they'd made her more dangerous than ever.

Nandi dropped behind the largest boulder, aiming his rifle in a slow sweeping motion over the area and whispering, "We should have seen her by now, my brother. The last sighting of her pugmarks in the dirt back there are fresh."

Adam's gaze tracked the tall vegetation, as high as a man's shoulder. The tiger out there could smell each bead of sweat that coursed down his back. She could be as close as ten feet to them, and they'd never see her until she moved.

Yet...he sensed she was near.

A breeze crooned through the trees, a flutelike sound that sang through Adam's bloodstream. As if he could smell her.

Adrenaline surged through him, his pulse a steady drumbeat to be near this noblest citizen of India. The same way he used to think he smelled the enemy's food cooking on the other side of no-man's land. They were just men, like him. How many of them had read the same books as he? How many of his enemy were poets, intellectuals, philanthropists, and men of God? How many of those men had he killed with a sniper's bullet?

He chambered a round while the bile rose in his throat. Why should this tigress die because she'd been wounded? Wounded men still lived. Though they may not want to.

From above came the caw of a myna bird. At the top of the tree Mitto crouched on a branch twenty feet above the ground. Again Mitto cupped his hands around his mouth to imitate the myna's call and pointed to the area west of where Nandi and Adam waited. The tigress must be close to the stream.

It was she who had been roaring in the jungle the night Laine arrived. He could not have known then that the roar of this predator had been a forewarning—that the life he'd worked so hard to bring peace to would be torn asunder by Laine's presence. Using his thumb and forefinger he pressed against the corners of his eyes to purge her from his thoughts.

Adam signaled to Mitto to climb down from the tree and follow him and Nandi into the thicket. An outcropping of rocks close to the streambed held a few caves. The three men trod through the vegetation toward the stream. Adam was acutely aware of his every footstep pressing into the grass. As aware as the tiger would be of their movements.

The recent rains had the stream gurgling over stones. With each successive rainfall, the tributaries and rivers would rise. He wiped the sweat from his brow. Following the rains and floods, a host of diseases would come. Laine would have to remain until this season ended, and then he and Rory could arrange for some other sort of help. Not a nurse. Certainly not a lovely young Englishwoman. Perhaps a male medic.

His gaze stopped at a thicket of bamboo about thirty yards off. His eyes passed the site. And returned.

The Bengal tiger raised her tawny, striped head above the saber tips of grass in front of the thicket. Her topaz eyes ringed with black looked straight through him. At the sight of her majesty, Adam's blood hummed bright through his veins. How beautiful she was.

She growled, her broad muzzle spread in a snarl. From this distance he could make out her yellow canines as long as his finger. She sniffed the air and blinked. He held back the desire to laugh out loud. Her feline strength overwhelmed him, epitomizing the India he loved...his and Laine's India. *Oh, Laine, why did you come here? Of all places?*

"My brother!" Nandi shouted, raising his rifle.

The tigress had sprung. Her muscular body bounded toward them through the grass, her taloned footpads eating up the distance between them.

Nandi yelled again, but Adam couldn't make out what he said with his pulse swooshing through his ears. The butt of his rifle dug into his shoulder, his finger remained steady on the trigger as he squinted down the barrel. He had the sights on the tiger, but he couldn't pull the trigger. No strength in his arms. He stood there...waiting, useless.

Nandi's rifle fire sent shockwaves through Adam as the tiger leaped to a pile of fallen logs and vaulted over them. She drove past them, a bullet of orange and black, disappearing into a patch of thick jungle.

The last echo from Nandi's rifle shot died away, and birdsong ate up the silence.

"*Pavum*! What are you thinking, my brother?" Nandi stared at him aghast. "You of all people could have bagged her in an instant." He swiped a hand across his mouth. "I am not able to speak with the amazement of this. And though I wounded her badly, my bullet did not find its mark."

Thankful for the excuse to sink to his haunches, Adam studied the ground where the tiger had leapt past them. With a shaking hand he touched the blood on the grass. The tiger had favored one side as she'd sped past, and he inwardly cursed himself. In her weakened condition—if she did survive—she was prey for another predator.

Now that the danger of the Bengal had been temporarily removed, monkeys crept out on tree branches and directed their belligerent white faces downward to investigate.

Adam moved to the stream to soak a handkerchief and wipe the back of his neck. He twisted the top off his canteen and gulped from it. He'd have to go out again tomorrow to look for the tiger. This time he wouldn't falter. He'd be doing her no favors if he did.

He pinched the crown of his slouch hat into shape, and a shrill growl, not much different than the screech of the monkeys, made him swerve around. Close to the undergrowth, a cub splashed in the stream. A male. The cub yowled again, and Adam signaled to Motti and Nandi to follow him. They could watch the cub from that rise over there.

In the shade of a spreading neem tree he removed a camera from his pack and focused on the young tiger. Photographing wildlife settled him far better than anything had since the end of the war. There was nothing so pure, so safe to the soul as nature. And thoughts of Laine dropped away. For an hour they waited and listened to the cub's mewling. But his mother's wounds must be keeping her from coming.

Mitto hunched forward, his gaze searching the thicket. "If the female does not come for her cub, what will you do, my brother? What of us, stuck in the jungle as it grows dark?"

Adam ran a hand around his stiff neck. "We've no choice. The mother is probably too weak to return, or she would have by now."

They gathered themselves and trudged down to the stream. The cub had fallen asleep close to a cave opening. Adam went deeper inside, and in its recesses found its sibling, but this cub was already dead, its ribs visible beneath its coat. Clearly the cub had died of hunger.

Slinging his rifle on his back, he picked up the little male, and they began their half-hour trek out to the road and the truck. The cub weighed no more than twenty pounds. About two months old he guessed, and as scrawny as his sibling. He couldn't leave it here for a hyena or python to make a quick meal of it.

Clouds captured an apricot sunset behind the trees as they climbed into the truck. Nandi took the wheel while Adam cradled the cub close to his chest, and an image of Laine strutted forward from his memories as brash and bold as she had always been.

It had been shortly before the war had started. He had come home from Oxford, and it was his first meeting with Laine in over three years. She had stood in his mother's garden, the dark green smoothness of mango leaves behind her. A filmy dress of blue lace molded to her figure and she'd been cradling an orange tabby. That night he'd asked her to marry him.

He gritted his teeth, fighting off this invasive reminder of what could never be. His love for Laine had been just one more casualty of the war.

11

To see Chandra, who only weeks ago had been suffering so much, now sitting in a classroom in the House of Salvation with girls her own age, brought tears to Eshana's eyes. Her heart poured out with thanksgiving to the Almighty.

As the girls recited their multiplication tables, Eshana slipped away, savoring the newfound delight she had seen in Chandra's eyes. This rescued girl had lost most of her childhood as a temple girl, but in this place the Lord would return to her the years the locusts had eaten. Here, Chandra could gain an education as high as a doctor or teacher, or if she did not show those aptitudes, she could receive training in weaving, or running a printing press.

Uma, one of the older inhabitants of the Ramabai Mukti Mission and who had served with Ramabai many years, strolled with Eshana. They stopped at the vegetable gardens, at the end of a long section of spinach. "Pandita Ramabai wishes to know how you are doing, Eshana."

Eshana adjusted the end of her sari over her shoulder. "Is Ramabai feeling better today?"

At the lack of a straight answer from her, Uma raised a brow. "She is well enough but is concerned for you. The young girl, Chandra, is doing well, is she not?"

"Chandra is doing very well." Eshana turned from Uma's penetrating gaze to look across the vegetable patches.

"And you, Eshana?"

"I am anxious to be returning to Amritsar. I have been away too long."

Uma gestured for Eshana to continue along the path to the flower gardens. "Yeshu commands us to not be anxious, though Ramabai and I understand your desire to go home to the mission you know so well.

But you must remember it is the Lord's work. He will see that His plans proceed." Uma stopped to pull a weed from the base of an oleander bush. "Ramabai asked me last evening if you have thought more of her suggestion."

"You mean learn to become a doctor?" Eshana dropped her gaze to the ground.

"From what you have told us, this was Miriam's hope for you. Yours too, at one time. Ah, I am seeing it in your face. You would like to become a doctor, but will not." She motioned for Eshana to sit with her on a bench shaded by a pink oleander the hue of Eshana's sari.

Uma drew in a breath of the blossoms. "While you have been here, Ramabai has had me observe you in the sick rooms. You are most gifted as a healer."

Eshana used her sandaled foot to press down the soil at the base of the oleander. During her teenage years she had adored Miriam and absorbed all of her medical knowledge in a practical sense. Miriam had brought in tutors to prepare her for college so that she might become a doctor. Then Miriam had died.

She looked into Uma's sorrowful eyes. "I respect and love Ramabai as dearly as I loved Miriam, but I am convinced that I must serve God by taking care of our mission in Amritsar."

Uma's fingers cupped Eshana's chin. "Rest assured, dear daughter, no matter where the Lord takes you, you will be in our prayers as you seek to serve the living God."

The following morning Eshana sought out Chandra before the girl could join her classmates. They said their good-byes while Chandra cried. Later in a shade-filled garden outside Ramabai's bedroom, Eshana dropped to the feet of that wonderful woman and felt her blessing upon her head. Ramabai, older now at sixty-three, had recently become frail with the loss of her own daughter.

Later at the train station, Eshana used the rupees Laine had left her to purchase her ticket to Amritsar via Bombay. The busy station at Poona pulsed with the great numbers of Indian people and a smattering of

English. She found a quiet place by a pillar to wait for her train to arrive and watched the people coming and going, a pastime that she rarely had the freedom to indulge—being always so busy—and smiled. God had made so many different kinds of people, and each was wonderfully made.

Her gaze, floating over the sea of people, stopped.

A face...she had seen that man before...from a distance.

Her spine went cold. Was it the man who her uncle had called to help him look for her that day in the train station not far from Bombay? Was this man a servant to her uncle?

A second later the man's face melted into the crowd. Her beating heart slowed as her train chuffed into the station, and she boarded quickly, looking around her. The man had not followed her. It could not have been the same man. She was being foolish to think so.

The short train journey in third class from Poona to Bombay went by in a haze, her thoughts chasing one another as the cinders that blew through the windows. She thrust the man's face from her mind and thought of the letter she had sent several days ago to Mala, Harmindar, and Tikah at the mission. She had not told them what day she should be arriving home. Her scattered thoughts flew to Laine as she changed trains at Victoria Station. For a moment she wished she could see once more the land of her birth. Though she missed the sultry south, she rushed through Victoria Station. When she found the correct track, she would board the train heading north.

Whistles blew and steam shrieked under the echoing glass roof. She had only the length of another five cars to walk along the platform to reach her carriage. The crowd, a wall too dense to penetrate, pushed and shoved, and held her immobile. Clutching her cloth bag, she strained to ease between the shoulders of two women. There, only one more carriage and—

A hand gripped her with terrible force, wrenching the shoulder of her blouse beneath her sari so that it tore.

She cried out, but trains squealing down the track stole her cry. The man who had searched the crowd for her with her uncle held her in his grip. It was the same man.

Another hand seized her by her upper arm.

Her bag fell from her fingers as she fought to free herself. The hands that held her were as unyielding as steel couplings connecting the trains while the press of people and the thud of elbows and knees jabbed into her. She struggled to see her other captor, but before she could the man she recognized from the crowd earlier held a cloth over her nose and mouth. A cloth smelling of almonds—a smell she knew from the clinic—chlora...

The clacking noise of a train woke her. Had she been dreaming? How far to Amritsar? Voices speaking in a mixture of Hindi and Tamil pulled her out of a gray stupor. Except she could not see. Only smell the aroma of rice, mustard, and turmeric, as people must be eating. She could hear people talking, though nothing other than the chatter of people traveling.

One of them—a child—whined, "How far to Madras, *Amma*?"

Madras!

Light pierced through the gauze that kept her blind. A covering over her face...pink...and silk. She thrust up her hand to pull the end of her sari from covering her. Someone beside her took her wrist and held it in an iron grip.

Yes, she remembered now.

The man she had first seen with her uncle on the Bombay Mail had taken her before she could board the train returning to Amritsar. On what train did she travel now? For she sat within a train carriage, of that she was sure. On the other side of her another person moved. She could hear only the sound of breathing. A man's breathing. Over her head, the captor she had not seen yet whispered in Tamil, the language used most in the Madras Presidency. "You should be putting her to sleep again, Duleep. Speedily, before the passengers notice."

It was her uncle who had spoken.

A sob escaped her.

He gathered her to his breast as if to comfort her, but there was no comfort in his manacle-hold. Uncle must have arranged for the man he called Duleep to follow her from that train station where he had first accosted her—perhaps even to Poona—to watch and wait for the very moment they could take her. Surrounded by friends in Poona they would not have attempted to steal her from there.

"My daughter, she is not well," Uncle said to whatever passengers filled this carriage.

From around her, various male and female voices murmured

condolences while Eshana struggled to free herself. Several females offered to take her from her uncle, to give her aid. But Uncle's hand came up and passed beneath the veil to cup her mouth, silencing her as he laughed. "It is most kind of you, but she will only cry if I do not hold her close."

Beside her, the other man moved quickly. Though she thrashed about, the almond scent again assaulted...and darkness approached...

Her face hurt from where she lay. No longer the train, but a solid floor of stone. And so weak. So weak...she could not lift her head.

Voices from far away talked. One was raised in anger—a woman's.

Eshana opened her eyes, her cheek still pressed against the floor. Her blurred vision took a moment to clear. The feet of three people stood in the corner. An oil lamp lit the room enabling her to see a man and a woman with Uncle Harish. Lamplight reflected off the intricate gold design on the woman's red sari and hurt Eshana's eyes.

Now she recognized the voice of the man. Her cousin, Kadhir, argued with Uncle Harish. "All these years Eshana has never been a burden to our family, and now you bring her to us. What are we to do with her?"

"I cannot be taking her back to her mother and father, or to her in-laws."

Eshana forced herself to stillness. A buzzing filled her head, the effect of chloroform, but she had heard correctly. Her uncle wanted her to remain here. Should she beg him to let her go? No. Remain quiet. She needed time to think. To see where they had brought her.

The woman—Kadhir's wife—moved and blocked Eshana's view of them. "For fear of bad luck you do not wish to keep our cousin under your own roof that you share with your brother. Yet you deem it acceptable that we should have this widow under our roof. This is an auspicious time in our lives. The astrologers have chosen this month as the marriage date for our daughter. It is not the time for us to be taking such a risk in our household."

"Your household?" Uncle Harish's voice cut across the woman's. "Remember, Lala, it is I who pay for this house so Kadhir may watch over our fields of hemp. Remember also, it is our family's fortunes that have produced such a prosperous match for your daughter." His voice softened. "I am understanding your aversion, but Eshana has not been acting as a good Hindu. If I leave her, she will only prance about the bazaars and not conduct herself with the sobriety of a widow."

Lala clutched at Uncle's arm. "Why not take her home to her mother? Her mother does not care for the old ways."

Amma. Eshana's heart expanded where she lay on the floor.

Uncle's voice took on an edge. "I have told my brother many times that he should make his wife submit. We as a family have always adhered to the old ways. Widows should be kept out of the road."

Lala whined. "Eshana is simply one small widow, and your house is big enough to keep her out of the way."

Uncle Harish strode across the floor. Eshana closed her eyes. He stood by an open door...or a window...that let in a wisp of moist night air resonating with the fragrance of banana flowers. The breeze revived her a little.

A sad resignation laced Uncle's speech. "Eshana's lack of respect for our ways goes much further than not living as a widow. Perhaps it is best you know. The police in Amritsar are hunting for her. She and an Englishwoman abducted a temple girl. I have confirmed this by a telegram. Though I have never used or cared for that aspect of our *Devadasi* custom, I will not allow Eshana to cast shame on Hindu traditions."

Eshana's head swam. If she and Laine had not taken Chandra from the temple perhaps her uncle would have let her remain in her chosen home. But she could never regret taking Chandra away to a life worth living.

Kadhir's voice floated down on her. "*Devadasi* is a perfectly good custom, Uncle, and very practical. If our menfolk do not use the temple girls to release their passions, they might be tempted to soil the daughters of good families." He heaved a sigh. "For this reason I agree that Eshana must stay out of sight. We will have an untouchable bring her food and water, so that her presence will not foul a servant of higher caste."

With her eyes clamped shut, Eshana heard Uncle move to stand above her. His voice broke. "But know this. I would not have you mistreat her. I have no daughter of my own, and when Eshana was a child she was the light of my eyes. I have wept for her these many years since the day the gods were unkind to her and the cholera took her husband."

A memory clear as water came to Eshana. What joy she had shared with her uncle and auntie each Holi when long ago they had thrown colored powders upon one another. They had all been pink and green and red and yellow when auntie had swung her in a dance, and uncle had whirled her into the air and let her soar in the safety of his hold.

He strode from the room, choking off his tears. "I am left with no choice."

Eshana bit her lip, her own loss echoing his. This segregation, this abandonment was not necessary when the true and living God was the Father of reconciliation.

Kadhir and Lala followed Uncle Harish from the room, taking the oil lamp with them, leaving the room in darkness.

Only when the door had been locked behind them did Eshana raise herself up, supporting her weight with her hands, her face wet with tears, her stomach listing. There would have been no sense in begging them to release her. She must discover a way to do that herself, but trembling overtook her. There was no time to mourn the loss of her family. How many days had it been since she had partaken of water or sustenance? How many days since she had left Poona? She dashed the tears from her face.

And where was this house? It was not the beautiful Jasmine Palace, the home of fountains and gardens where she had grown up in the city of Madras. All of her family, her father's brothers and sisters and many relatives, lived together in that great house. When Uncle had been talking to Lala, he had mentioned fields of hemp. If she could only remember... but the chloroform had made her mind a sticky mess of lentils. She remembered. Their family had lands some fifty or sixty miles from the city of Madras. Despair closed upon her as the thick door had, that locked her within this room.

No one would look for her here.

Tears threatened to overcome, but she clenched her fists and held them off. God had made her strong. She would not allow her faith in Him to weaken.

Tattered clouds across the moon cast an intricate pattern of white on the smooth floor. She looked up, feeling the caress of a rain-heavy breeze cupping her chin as Uma had only days ago.

Her head swooned, but she rose up to her knees and struggled to stand at what she now saw was a fretted window. She took hold of the scrollwork carved from sandstone. Air flowed freely through the decorative fretwork that was wide enough for her hand, but afforded no spaces large enough to squeeze her body through.

A narrow parapet lay directly outside her window. What light the moon gave allowed her to make out a tangled garden below, beyond that a river.

Lights twinkled along a larger wing. She was incarcerated in a section that jutted at right angles from the main house. Sandstone at the window left crumbling traces on her fingers. Clumps of stone had broken off into smaller pieces on the floor. Still, without a sharp tool, a large and heavy hammer, she could not break away enough of the fretwork to leave this room. Her throat ached with a renewed desire to cry.

"Stop this," she said aloud. "God will make a way out for you." This cell, though dark and holding only a string bed and a stool, at least stood high above the ground so that no predators could slip in to harm her. If her cousins were modern-thinking Indians perhaps she could convince them to let her go. If she remained calm and trusting, all would be well.

Footsteps rang on the hallway her cousins and uncle had left by. She sat on the string bed to await whoever came. Keys clanked to open the iron lock, and the wooden door, six inches thick, swung open. Two servants entered, one carrying a pitcher of water and a plate with a small ball of rice. The other held a basin of water and clothing over her arm.

And in her hand, scissors and a razor.

Eshana shrank into herself. The older female with the food and water hunched down on the floor to watch while the younger set down the clothing and basin. With a rough gesture, the younger woman pulled Eshana by the arm to sit on the stool. Eshana swayed but had no strength to withstand the servant. Using the scissors the woman cut off Eshana's plait that had grown to her waist. Eshana, as if outside herself, watched the braid drop to the floor. Dark swathes fluttered downward as the scissors removed the rest of her hair.

Tears dropped from her chin. *Have I been so vain, Lord, that You would want to punish me? Have I displeased You in mistaking my hair, the joy of my feminine crown, for pride?*

As the servant cut her hair she began to talk. "You are a widow and must spend your life praying for your husband's soul, that he may be reborn on a higher plain. Perhaps if you are very good you may be born a man in your next life."

The older one sitting on the floor cackled from a gaping mouth empty of teeth. "Or if you are very bad you could be born an insect, or worse, an untouchable like us."

The servant took the hot water and razor to Eshana's head. Eshana squeezed her eyes shut as the razor scraped over her scalp, stinging. When she was thirteen years old and Papa and Uncle had left her at the *ashram*, the widows living there had shorn her head too. At that time she had cried and wailed. She lifted a trembling hand to her scalp, smooth as marble. Now her tears fell thick and silent.

The servants took away her sari of oleander pink and left her with the course white cloth of a widow to cover her body.

Her soul cried out, *Yeshu, you have allowed me to be clothed in funeral clothes once more.*

12

"The newspapers are full of the troubles in the country." Jai's father thrust the morning paper away. He and Jai sat cross-legged on a carpet outside as sunlight filled the courtyard in the center of their home. A peepul tree shaded them where it sent an occasional leaf to float on the surface of a small, rectangular pool of water.

His father threw an orange peel to a parakeet that perched on a branch above their heads. "*Pah*! No matter how much Gandhi pleads, he will never be able to control the Hindus. And the Muslim people fear to follow his advice, thinking he will put Hindu interests before theirs. And what of us Sikhs left in the middle? There will be more violence to be sure."

Jai picked up the paper his father had discarded and read the article that distressed him. The Prince of Wales's visit had been greeted by demonstrations in Bombay, and each city on his itinerary. More bloodshed was to come. No matter how closely he looked into the hearts of people, he rarely found a soul that was without blemish. Even Eshana—he smiled to himself—had a willful streak in spite of her devotion to God and to suffering humanity.

His mother strolled from the house across the courtyard to them. Her eyes lit at the sight of his empty dish. He had devoured the fresh mango and breads cooked by her hand. She stood behind him and smoothed a tuck in his turban. "Well, have you decided?"

Both he and his father looked up at her, their brows furrowing.

She clapped her hands and frowned, setting the gauze of her veil to shimmer where it lay over her hair. "You have both forgotten. Oh to be burdened by such forgetful men. We have been invited to the house of Talib Ram at the end of the month." Her smile melted her frown. "So you can meet his daughter, my son."

Heat poured upward from the neckline of Jai's white *kurta* to his face. He avoided his father's gaze, but not before he caught *Appa*'s look of amusement change to one of anger.

His father took his mother's hand and drew her near. "Your mother and sisters have acted on your behalf. The daughter of Talib is a good woman and will make you a fine wife." His tone brooked no room for argument. "We will be accepting this invitation."

Jai uncurled his legs from his sitting position and stood. Both his parents implored him with their eyes. He adored them, and being their only son, he had been doubly adored by them and by his elder sisters. But the thought of marriage...to love and hold this woman they had chosen for him. Could he make this girl happy? Could she him?

The memory of Eshana dropped into his mind with the softness of a leaf falling on the surface of the water.

He sent a pleading glance to his mother. "I will meet this woman as you wish, but I cannot promise to marry her. If when we meet we are compatible, then I will honor you in abiding by your choice."

His father opened his mouth to speak, but his mother rushed in before him. She took Jai's arm. "This is all I can ask of you, comfort of my heart." She squeezed his arm, her eyes shining. "I have been praying for a wife for you since you were a babe in my arms, and I am sure *Waheguru*, wonderful, almighty God, will bring you to her. She will be beautiful and sweet and constantly singing the praises of God's name."

He smiled down into her beaming face, breathing in the scent of her jasmine perfume. "Yes, Mother, I believe *Waheguru* will answer your prayers."

His father kissed her good-bye, and together he and Jai left her at their home. The *tonga* ride into the city would not take long. They barreled under the stone archway into Amritsar and its labyrinth of bazaars, passing tailors, bangle-sellers, Jai's favorite shoe mender who patched *chappals* and British-made leather brogues, flower sellers stringing garlands of pungent marigolds.

A wheel of the conveyance hit a rock as they passed the fruit seller, jolting them and knocking over Jai's valise. Instruments fell out as well as some of the books Jai had been reading. His father assisted him in picking up the items.

After stowing his belongings and instruments in the valise, Jai glanced up to see Father inspecting one of the books by Sundar Singh that he had been studying. A hot flush that must be almost as deep as the red of his father's turban heated his face.

"What is this sacrilege you are reading? I know of this Sundar, a man of a good Sikh family who many years ago turned his back on what the gurus have taught us to follow the Christian god."

Father let his hands holding the book drop to his lap as the *tonga* driver continued to wind through the bazaars. His voice shook. "I do not care that Sundar Singh goes about in the yellow robes of a holy man. What he teaches is against our Sikh beliefs."

Jai could not tear his gaze from his father's rage-filled eyes. He swallowed through a thickened throat. "I am interested in this man. Though he is a Christian, he is filled with great knowledge and his devotion to the universal God is unsurpassed. He prayed one night for a vision of God's true *avatar*, and claims he saw the face of—"

"Do not say that name!"

His father lifted a shaking hand to smooth his beard as if he were ill. "Do not say that name. Our gurus teach us the names of God, and that is not one. I order you to stop reading this man's lies."

Jai slumped back against the seat. He looked out at the passing bazaars lined with stalls and businesses. His father had asked a fair thing of him—to stop reading the writings of Sundar Singh. For the love of his father he should do this. He bowed his head. He should do this.

His reading of these books was shaking the very pillars of his life, his faith, his family. He swept a glance at the rigid set of Father's mouth, the heavy eyelids that could not hide his fury. But surely what this Indian Christian wrote was strong enough to bear investigation. There must be instances where the Christian beliefs spoke the same as that of the Sikhs'. Then he could show Eshana that she could easily become a Sikh.

The aroma of cardamom and cloves, of sandalwood filled his senses as they rode through the busy alleyways. Buyers called out and thrust their wares forward. It had been more than a month since he had walked this street with Eshana as they had hurried to treat the girl, Chandra. According to the letter Eshana had sent over a week ago she should have returned to Amritsar by now. Perhaps he would find her there today. Although for her sake he wished she had remained in Poona.

Yet, even with her return, he held no hope of anything between them other than the respect of neighbors. But he would do as his father asked. He would cease his reading of Sundar Singh and marry the girl his parents and siblings chose for him.

They reached the street where their clinic was located, and the *tonga* drew up to the front door. His father jumped to the road, and Jai gathered his belongings, giving his father time to unlock the door.

A low moan issued from his father outside. Jai became aware of the hum of a crowd outside the *tonga*'s covering and rushed from the conveyance to stand at the side of the road. Occupants of the street milled about, gawking at their establishment. His gaze followed theirs to Father standing at the door of their clinic.

Broken glass from their front window lay shattered on the ground. Red paint slashed on the bricks of the building formed the words Haters of Hind. Defilers of Caste. Only the bars on the windows had hindered the culprits from making mischief within.

Father raised his hands and sliced the air. He didn't move for several minutes, paralyzed.

Jai took the key from his father's hand and unlocked the clinic. When he had opened it, he turned to help his father in, but *Appa* still stared at the front of his clinic with that pale, atrophied expression.

"Come, *Appa*. Come inside. I will make you tea and will set things right." Jai winced at the crunch of splintering glass beneath his shoes.

His father held on to Jai as if he had suddenly aged to a man far older than his fifty-two years, and sank to a chair. "I have lived in peaceful coexistence with Hindus and with Muslims for my lifetime." He raised his face to glare at Jai. "This is another instance of wrath from the local people because you helped that woman from the mission. Last week it was only rotten vegetables the Hindus had thrown, and that heap of animal dung on the front stoop. Now this. What will they do next, attack our home, attack us or a member of our family?"

Jai could not meet his father's eyes. He had been unable to tell him that a local Hindu priest and a fanatical set of temple devotees had sought him out as well, shaking their fists in his face and hurling insults at him as he walked through the city.

With a trembling hand Jai smoothed his mustache. It would be many years before the owners of the temple girl would forget. He had already expressed his sorrow to *Appa* on several occasions. Still, his head sank in renewed shame. Yet if Eshana ever asked him to rescue another such child, he knew he would do the same.

Father bolted to his feet to stir embers and add wood to the stove. "We must do all we can to befriend the Hindu people." He wrenched the book from the folds of his *kurta* where he had hidden it earlier. He tore the pages from the writings of Sundar Singh, crumpled them, and added them piece by piece to the growing blaze. "You are charmed by this woman from the mission. I am not blind, my son. She has tainted you with her beliefs, and now you must burn these lies from your mind."

Jai watched as pages from the book curled and disintegrated to ash.

The only souls Eshana had seen this past week were the untouchable servants who shaved her head and brought her food. Though the food they brought seemed to be whatever scraps they could retrieve from outside the kitchen.

At first they talked little, afraid she might mistreat them as people from higher castes often did. She gave them her most gentle smiles and speech, and gradually they warmed to her when they came to understand that she saw them as equals. No—she saw them as more than that, people of great worth, as Yeshu saw them.

Now the older woman, Shindu, would sit on her haunches on the floor and gossip each day, laughing her toothless laugh. As untouchables they were allowed only into the main house to remove the filth. For them it was a treat to sit in this high, cool room overlooking the farthest reaches of the garden, taking in the scent of flowers through the fretted window. No one could see them here to bother them.

Eshana's younger jailer, Vanji, also liked to sit with Eshana. She would listen entranced as Eshana told them of the land to the north, of the cities she had seen by traveling on a train, of the mission that Miriam had begun, and of what Ramabai was doing for women in Poona.

They did not stay long each day. The few *annas* they received for their work fed their own children.

After Shindu and Vanji left today, Eshana picked up the banana leaf that held a few bites of rice, a trace of spices, and bowed her head. She mouthed silent words of praise to the Lord God. Though all desire for this little food left her, like the Apostle Paul she tried to count this persecution as joy. For most of the days she succeeded.

A heavy breeze drew her to the window. Birds swooped on the wind that rolled the clouds like a woman rolling a bundle of clothing. Those clouds heavy with warm rain inched closer. She grasped the stone scrollwork and leaned her head against it. Not far from the house lay the river. But what river? The Palar or one of its tributaries?

She drew in deeply of the breeze. "When will you send an angel to unlock my prison door as you did for Peter?"

Her only answer was His continued silence.

She raised her head to listen to a rustle on the parapet. Had the rains begun already? But she could see nothing below her window.

The rustle came again from directly below the sill. A dark head moved, and Eshana jerked backward. A second later ebony tresses plaited with marigolds tilted back to reveal a tiny face, and Eshana's heart eased. Wide, almond-shaped eyes ringed with kohl absorbed most of the little girl's face. The child stared in at her and laughed, only to duck down again to where she had been hiding on her knees. How could this little one have climbed up here to this narrow rampart?

The child tired of ducking out of Eshana's sight, and her eyes grew sober as she peered past Eshana to the room behind. Her mouth, which had been open with laughter, became a tight rosebud of concern. "What are you doing in there? Come out and play."

"I cannot."

"Why?"

"The door is locked, and—"

"I will get my *appa* to open the door and let you out."

"No." This child could be the daughter of her cousin and his wife, Lala. If the girl told her parents to let Eshana out, they might scold her and keep her from climbing this parapet again. Though the child might not be able to help her escape, she could be of help.

The child peered closer at her. "Why is your head shaved?"

"It is only for a short time. Do you not think it amusing?"

The little girl pursed her lips to one side. "Yes, it is funny, but still I do not like it."

Eshana stood on her toes and tried to see beyond the balustrade to the ground below. "How did you get up here?"

"There is a staircase over there. Many of the steps are broken, but I can climb it. What is your name?"

"Eshana. And you, little one beyond the price of rubies, what is yours?"

The little girl giggled. "My name is Ruchi." She twirled a strand of pearls and stuck them into her mouth, sucking on them as if they were sweets. "I am to be married soon. This was a present from the family of my husband."

A stone formed in the bottom of Eshana's stomach. This little girl was as imprisoned as she was in this room. Would Ruchi's parents be kind? Choose a good man for their daughter? Or would they—bound by tradition—bind their daughter to people who may not love her? She forced a smile. "You are such a pretty bride. When will your wedding be?"

"In eight days."

"And will you go to your husband's home after your wedding, Ruchi?"

"Not for a long while yet. My *amma* made *appa* insist on keeping me with them until I am older."

Eshana closed her eyes briefly. *Oh thank you, Father, for this mercy.* "I was married when I was not much older than you. I was seven upon my wedding day."

"Did you have many jewels to wear?" The child shook her bangles for the sheer enjoyment of hearing the jingle.

"Oh yes, a string of pearls like you have. And gold bangles with rubies."

"You like rubies?" The child's bright eyes and bejeweled ears missed nothing.

Eshana's chuckle bubbled up inside her. "I do like rubies, and I also had emerald earrings, and my *amma* strung pearls through my hair with jasmine and marigolds."

Ruchi's eyes grew wide. With her heart-shaped face, her kohl-darkened eyes gave her the appearance of a tiny owl. "Did you have many sweets to eat?"

"Lime sherbet, my favorite."

The child grew bored with their conversation. "Why do you not come out? I want to play in the garden, especially if it rains. I like to dance in the rain."

"I told you I cannot. The door is locked. But it is best that you do not tell anyone. It is a secret."

"A secret? Why? Who are you?"

Eshana hunkered down to Ruchi's height, and peered at her through the fretted stonework. "I am a secret princess." She had used this story many times to help women and girls comprehend their value to God. Perhaps that was the problem. Clearly she had thought too highly of herself, and God sought to remind her to act humbly by allowing her to be imprisoned.

Still though, she used the familiar word picture with Ruchi.

Just as she had thought, Ruchi's owl-eyes grew wider.

Eshana deepened her voice with drama. "Your *amma* and *appa* have been given the task of keeping me here, but if you would like to be my friend, I will be yours. You could visit me, and I will tell you stories."

"If you are a secret princess then where is your father, the rajah?"

"You are a very intelligent girl." Eshana leaned back to gain a visual measure of her little friend, but dipped her head, finding it hard to bring out the words. All week her heavenly Father had been silent, and at this moment she did not feel the truth of the story she used to tell.

"My f-f-father..." she stuttered. "My father is the greatest Rajah of all rajahs." Somehow saying the words by rote strengthened something inside her, and her words took on new energy. "He is the Rajah over all. Lord of Lords." A small joy spurted in her heart like the colored water at the time of Holi, and the words practically sang from her. "His son's name is Yeshu."

"Will he come here?"

Tears pricked at the back of Eshana's eyes. Since she had been locked in this room she had struggled to feel God's presence. But this small sacrifice of praise had been the key to unlock the door that barred her from Him. "Yes," she said on a wisp of breath. "Yeshu is here." She glanced over at the clouds. "But you, beloved beyond the price of rubies, must go down the steps before you are noticed."

"Can I visit you tomorrow?"

"Oh yes, come, please."

Ruchi clapped her hands and ran from Eshana along the parapet. Eshana sank beneath the window, her back to the stone wall. A moment later Ruchi returned, clattering along the rampart, giggled through to Eshana while clasping her small knees, and then ran laughing down the steps again. Eshana's heart followed the pitter patter of the child's footsteps and jingle of her jewelry down to the garden and then silence.

She turned at an angle to look over her shoulder to the building clouds outside. *I will sing your praises, Lord. Though you have dressed me in funeral clothes, I will sing your praises with joy.*

13

Rust-red mud churned beneath the truck tires as Adam steered clear of villagers who were leading flocks of goats along the road. In the truck bed behind the cab, Rory hunched down with the crates of supplies they would need for this last inoculation at the untouchables' colony. The silver-haired physician had insisted the ladies ride up front with Adam, and it had taken him and Rory several minutes back at the compound to convince Laine to sit in the cab.

A smile came unbidden to Adam's lips. Nothing had changed about Laine. The woman was still as obstinate in her kindness as she'd ever been. No doubt today she would inject hilarity into the work they had to do, but the small shot of happiness seeped out of him. She'd always been able to draw him out, make him laugh when he would have preferred to be quiet and study. It wasn't going to be easy to guard his heart against the sweep of her personality.

For the umpteenth time he shook his head. Why couldn't Laine have taken a job in the hospital in Madras or any large city in British India? She would fit right into the social whirl. He remembered with mortification the number of times she'd dragged him out on a floor to dance that Ragtime stuff she liked. He never could catch the rhythm that came so easily to her, and his face flooded with heat at another memory when she'd led him in that Brazilian tango to the song *Down in Zanzibar*.

She sat quietly in the cab with him and Bella now. He could smell her fragrance, something light, floral. He shook his head and focused on his driving to push away the memories her scent evoked. She'd be far happier in a big city. Not here in the jungle. That's all he'd ever wanted for her. To be happy.

And for his men to be happy, if they could.

They reached the village of Cholajure, closest to the compound. At the start of this village, women washed clothes in a pond, while buffalo stood knee deep in the water. From the narrow alleyways between mud-brick huts, villagers watched the truck go past. Children ran out to laugh and wave, like they always did when he passed, but he caught a few disgruntled looks from the elders as they sat around the village tree.

Adam wiped his brow against his shoulder to remove a trace of sweat. Something was up. Only last week the elders had waved with as much friendliness as the children did. But even out here, far from the nearest city, news of the non-cooperation movement reached, and tensions ran high.

He swung the truck to the left to follow the road that would take them to the colony. Various Christian missions did what they could, but each time Adam came to the colony, the abuse these people suffered from higher castes kicked him in the gut. Though the villages they had just passed were poor, most of the inhabitants had a hut of mud-brick walls and thatched roofs while these *Harigan,* the children of God as Gandhi called them, existed in makeshift hovels if they were lucky.

He threw a quick look at Laine, her expression soft with compassion. She'd always been that way. Never could stand to see anyone or anything suffer.

A few minutes later they reached the colony, and he parked the truck beneath a large umbrella tree. Children dashed at them from all corners of the community before he could pull the brake.

Rory jumped down from the back and began pulling off bunches of bananas from the man-size cluster Adam had lopped off his plants that morning. Laine stood with Rory to disperse the fruit. With a laugh, Bella joined them, but a band of children swarmed Adam, hanging on to his waist and keeping him from helping Rory.

One little fellow he'd spent some time with on their last trip clung to him, until Adam lifted him into his arms. The children jumped up and down, grins splitting their faces as they waited—albeit impatiently—for what they knew his pockets contained.

"All right, if we can have some order here," he yelled out in Tamil. "Make a straight line, and I'll give you each a sweet so no one misses out." It always amazed him how quickly the toffees disappeared, but by the time he had given out all he'd brought, so too had the bananas and coconuts.

Adam didn't know whether to be relieved or not that Laine avoided him. She took her cues from Rory and struggled to haul a wooden sawhorse from the back of the truck while Bella lifted out a crate of medical supplies. Laine had always been an athletic girl, but the sawhorse was a cumbersome item. He reached the back of the truck in time to help her lift it to the ground.

She sent him a look that would wither the confidence of most men. "I am perfectly capable of lifting down a sawhorse. Bella could use your assistance."

"I'm well aware how capable you are, Laine, but many hands make light work. Besides, Rory has already assisted Bella with the crates."

Today was the first time he'd seen her since she'd arrived several weeks ago. That first night he'd been dumbstruck and had spoken like a pompous dandy. Ravi had told him of her visit a week later, and he'd found her crumpled note in the wastebasket. For days the flattened note sat on his desk until he'd thrown it away as she'd wanted. And now this trip, the last of a series of inoculations was throwing them together, and the desire to berate her—about anything—grew.

Together they carried the sawhorses and boards to the shade under an umbrella tree and assembled them into long tables. He'd seen Laine use a hammer and nails before when they were children, helping him build a tree house. What surprised him today was her tight-lipped silence. Laine had never before let him have the last word. When everything had been set up, she tucked a strand of hair under her nursing veil and donned a white apron over her ward dress.

They were ready for Reverend Schmidt of the Lutheran mission to bring them the last group of people to be inoculated.

A moment later, the reverend walked toward them with a clipboard and a stream of people. By then there was no time to wonder about Laine. Pastor Schmidt checked off the patients while Bella cleansed the arms with alcohol. Rory and Laine shared the task of preparing the syringes and injecting the serum, while he at the very last gave the patients their stipend of a few coins.

The sun glowed like a pale disc behind the growing clouds as the afternoon passed. His blood surged in rhythm with the monsoons that had set the boundaries of his life. Indian rains were warm and sumptuous—powerful—unlike the cold drizzle in England.

Yet each spring during his years at Oxford, England's showers had dampened his black student cloak as he, Robert, and John hurried across the Fellows' Garden to sessions. Those days with his fellow students and professors had been some of the happiest of his life. Wordsworth had captured the joy of those college years best. "A host of golden daffodils; beside the lake, beneath the trees."

His classmates remained in his memory, as that. Not as vibrant young men with warm blood flowing through their veins—but that of mounded graves with daffodils for their covers. All but two of his class were dead, their names forever inscribed on a bronze plaque in those hallowed halls of learning. His best friend Robert had died at the Battle of the Somme. His cousin John might as well have.

He glanced up to catch Laine's gaze on him. Her brow puckered as she packed up instruments and unused serum, but he turned away. His memories of her belonged to his youth, and so they should remain there. Buried. These days his allegiance belonged elsewhere.

Laine lost count of the roadside temples they passed on the way back. Each small alter to the elephant-headed god Ganesh, Rama, Krishna, and a host of others, held the remains of offerings, broken coconuts, decayed flowers, food the birds had stolen.

Bella's chatter filled the silence inside the truck. For once in her life, speech eluded Laine. The Adam she used to know would have noticed this and cajoled her out of any doldrums. But not this new Adam, though he looked the same—his long legs in khaki drill trousers, desert boots, his shirt open at the neck to show the mahogany of his tan that only emphasized the intense blueness of his eyes.

She flicked a glance at him. His hands gripped the steering wheel as if his life depended on it, showing the corded muscle of his forearms. Arms that used to hold her. She remembered the strength of them.

And the strength of his mind, how he'd helped her through her schoolwork evening after evening as she grew up. If it hadn't been for Adam's academic bullying, she doubted she'd be the nurse she was today. On the other hand, it had never taken much for her to pull him out of whatever text or poem enraptured him and make him laugh.

Now, the scowl between his brows scored deeper, and he slowed the truck as they entered the village of Cholarjure on the way back to the compound.

Bella sat up straighter. "What is it?"

Adam nodded toward a group of men blocking the road. Some held clubs and a few balanced rocks in their hands. Adam ran a hand down his chin, but he stopped the truck. "Stay here please, ladies."

He glanced at Rory in the back. Together they got out and walked toward the group of men. Laine felt Bella stiffen beside her as the older woman leaned forward to stare through the windshield.

"Has there been trouble here?" Laine asked.

"A bit, here and there. Normally these villages have been cordial. Whatever the problem is, I just hope Adam can get through to them."

Laine clenched and unclenched the side of her skirt into a bunch. "Adam? Wouldn't it be better to listen to Rory? He's the doctor."

"It's Adam who has a way with the villagers. He knows a number of dialects. The villagers also know that he shares his plantation profits with his workers. He's done a lot for each village, digging new wells when needed."

She followed Bella's gaze. They couldn't hear what was said. Though Rory spoke, the village men looked to Adam. The dark faces surrounding Adam and Rory remained closed though. If anything, the muscles in the villagers' arms grew more defined, their hands tightening around their rocks.

But they waited. Poised. Until an emaciated man wearing only a loincloth sauntered up to the group which parted to allow him entrance. His hair was long and matted, yellow and red paste painted his forehead, and ash smeared his body. A wandering *sadhu*.

The *sadhu* pierced Adam with a look and shouted for all to hear, "You children of the devil have come from the colony of the untouchables. We do not care what you do with the untouchables, but you will not put your poison inside our people to destroy our higher castes. We cannot tolerate such pollution from your touch and your venom."

A good number of the village men, young and old, mirrored the fury of the *sadhu*, but here and there Laine picked out those where confusion mingled with remorse, and no small amount of fear. None of them took their eyes off the *sadhu*.

Laine grasped the door handle.

"More than this," the *sadhu* added. "Your British Raj knows that India is too many for you. If we revolt, we will overpower you. This is why you think to trick us and kill us with the cholera."

One of the elderly men lifted a hand in supplication to the *sadhu.* "Swami, I am assuring you that we in this village have not taken the British medicine. Yet the cholera has come. Two of our people are sick."

Rory and Adam spoke together. "Show me the sick."

"Let us help them."

The small statured *sadhu* stalked to within an inch of Rory and thrust out his bare chest where his holy thread crossed from his left shoulder to under his right arm. "Cease your words. The cholera comes each year as it always has. If our people become unwell, they should pray to the goddess Oladevi. Or let the cholera take them, and they will proceed on the wheel of life."

A number of the younger villagers raised their arms as if to throw their missiles at Adam and Rory, until the older man plucked at the arm of another. "Do not do this." He turned to the *sadhu*. "Swami, as a teacher of the Vedas, no doubt you are ready to remind our young men that we must never do harm to any living thing. Surely these Englishers deserve as much mercy."

The knot of men around the *sadhu* stood almost motionless while the Hindu holy man took his time. He shrugged. "Yes, I was about to remind these men of that tenet." He sauntered off in the direction he'd first come, but over his shoulder he threw the words, "Let these defilers of caste go unharmed as is right, but do not let them pollute you with their poisons."

Laine released her breath the same time as Bella. One by one stones were dropped, although a few villagers continued to clutch theirs. Eventually these rocks fell to the ground too as women came out of their huts, and the entire village watched the holy man wander down to the pond. He sat beneath a tree and dangled his feet in the water as if bored by the entire proceeding.

A few men escaped to their huts and stayed close to their wives and children. Slowly, the village took back its normal rhythm. Women returned to washing clothes in the pond while others went back to watering buffalo. Children darted out like a swarm of butterflies. But a handful of older men, village elders, remained stock still surrounded by the small mountain of rocks that had been discarded.

The *sadhu* seemed to have lost interest, although Laine doubted that. She had the feeling he was shamming, but Adam took the moment and with a friendly gesture invited the reduced group of men to join him under the village tree by the well. Without giving them a chance to disagree, Adam walked to the roots of the wide-spreading tree and hunched down. With a smile he waved the village elders to encircle him.

Bella blew a breath through tight lips. "Good for you, Adam."

The old man who had stopped the violence was the first to walk over and squat on his haunches next to Adam. Rory cupped the shoulder of the headman and with deference led him toward Adam. As if a pebble disturbed the surface of water, the group shifted and disbanded to ripple toward the tree.

Laine resumed breathing as Adam began to talk, though she couldn't hear what he said. As the elders asked questions, Adam took a stick and drew on the dusty ground. Rory interjected here and there. A good half hour passed until the expressions on the villagers' faces lightened. One or two still glowered, but the old man walked Adam and Rory back to the truck.

Rory hopped into the back, and Adam jumped into the driver's seat. He waved to the old man, started the engine, and said, "*Poytu varukirehn*, good-bye," in Tamil as he drove out of the village.

Bella pulled at his sleeve. "Well? Will they let us treat the sick?"

"Not yet. The only thing we have going for us is we never inoculated anyone in this village, and the elders are keenly aware of this. Rory explained to them what to do for those who've come down with the cholera, and we reassured them we are always available to help."

"We can only pray they'll trust us eventually." Bella's nostrils flared. "That old *sadhu* certainly has them in his grip."

Adam reached out to gently squeeze Bella's hand. "The villagers are starting to realize that medical care is not his area of expertise, and they want the same sort of aid as the wealthy receive in the cities, and what they deserve. It's only a matter of time."

Laine threw a glance his way. A smile crossed Adam's face for Bella, that easy grin he'd given to the children at the colony today when he'd handed out sweets and to the elders as he'd sat around the village tree.

His gaze—a lightning flash of warm blue—met hers, but he looked away.

Adam was as kind-hearted as he'd ever been. And he could smile. She glanced away to the slender betel nut trees lining the road. He just couldn't smile for her.

Dusk was falling as the truck rumbled into the compound, the noise of its engines hardly bothered the cacophony of birds. Adam helped Rory unload the crates, giving Laine a moment to convince Bella to take a long cool bath while she stored everything away. As soon as the truck had been emptied, Adam roared up the road to his plantation. Laine could almost taste the words on her tongue. *Go, go Adam, and stay away...from me.*

Frogs and crickets serenaded as evening shrouded the compound. The usual scream from a hyena, or a leopard chuffing added to the song of the surrounding jungle.

Devaram had boiled more water for Laine to have a soak in the tub where she used the peony-scented soap. In her room, after dusting herself with talcum she slipped a sleeveless sheath of pale blue linen over her head and re-tied the bow at the dropped waist. Feeling decadent, she didn't bother with stockings and slid her bare feet into a pair of canvas plimsolls. She brushed her hair, but decided against putting it up, and let it fall down her back.

Over dinner of cold ham and salads they discussed the need for a treatment center if the number of cholera cases rose. Frustration tempered their conversation, but their hands had been tied by the *sadhu* in helping the village of Cholarjure.

Afterward, she left Rory and Bella ensconced in their favorite chairs in the parlor. It didn't take long for Bella to become entrenched in her novel. Rory was reading the latest medical journals that had arrived in that day's mail, but he glanced up at her.

He looked from the journal to her. "Would you like to sit on the veranda or take an evening stroll? I'd be happy to keep you company." His face wore an expression she hadn't seen in him before, and a slow flush stained his cheeks.

"Don't be silly, Rory. Enjoy your journal. I've got my own letters."

Two letters had arrived for her. She curled up in a chair and read the first one from Ada who gave her the bad news that the Hindu people in Amritsar had not forgotten the theft of Chandra as easily as they had hoped.

Her second letter was from Abby and Geoff. They'd addressed it to her former nurses' residence, and Violet had forwarded it here. Abby filled her letter with her typical exuberance and admitted she might enjoy Geoff's posting in Shanghai more than she'd first thought. The children were fine, and Laine blew out a puff of sadness at missing them. Abby finished her letter with a complaint that she had yet to hear from Eshana. According to Abby, neither had Harmindar or Mala at the mission since the last letter saying she was on her way to Amritsar. But that was weeks ago.

Laine's hand holding the letter dropped to her lap. Surely Eshana must be home by now. But what a foolish girl—she could have come here and given the people of Amritsar time to forget the incident of Chandra.

A nightjar began its churring song. Laine moved to the writing desk in the corner when Adam knocked and entered the bungalow. The three occupants looked up, all with varying responses. Rory slanted a grin in Adam's direction, and Bella sent him a sleepy smile before returning to her novel. Laine rallied a look of mild interest that she hoped camouflaged her peevishness. She'd looked forward to the evening away from the mixed feelings Adam stirred in her.

He must have noticed the strain in her attempted smile. A flush blazed across his cheeks as deep as the glow on Rory's a while ago. "I don't mean to disturb your evening, Bella and Rory, but I have a patient for Laine to see."

Rory half rose from his chair. "You don't mean—"

"No...no, of course not," Adam rushed to answer. "Just something I'd like to show Laine."

Rory sat back relieved. But relieved over what? Laine caught the look that passed between the two men. Then Rory's expression changed as he started toward the door. "Let's see it then, whatever it is. Come on, Laine."

Bella made a pretense of a cough and tapped her brother's hand. "Ten minutes ago you told me you were too exhausted to finish reading. Let Adam show Laine this new patient, and I'll make you a cup of cocoa."

The last thing Laine wanted was to be left alone with Adam. But here he was asking her to look at...something. Rory wasn't pleased about it either.

She summoned up the same wicked smile for Adam she'd used on Maurice, hoping it expressed her full aversion. "Well, Adam, old bean, I'm not interested in coming up to your studio to take a look at your etchings. Isn't that the old ploy men use to entice proper young ladies into doing something naughty?"

Adam's smile softened his lean face. "I assure you, my intentions are honorable. I have something I know will interest you. My way of apologizing for being such a poor host since you've been here."

Without casting a glance at Rory and Bella, she followed Adam outside. The cork tree at the end of the veranda threw off its delicate fragrance where Adam surprised her by going no farther. She waited for him to explain, when close to her ankles came a noise like that of a squeaky door. A leather lead had been tied to the pillar. And over the edge of the veranda in the roots of the bougainvillea, two round eyes glowed. A rusty yowl came from the bushes again.

Adam reached down to pluck into his arms a tiger cub, no bigger than a lapdog. Her fingers itched to touch the tawny fur and the cub's rounded, black-tipped ears. Light from the bungalow showed the cub's eyes were still the blue of babyhood. She didn't have to say a word.

Adam understood her indecipherable cry and placed the warm, strong little body into her arms. "His mother is the tigress we've been hunting. I couldn't leave the little chap to fend for himself."

"Of course not."

"I've set him up nicely in the barn on the plantation." His voice took on an embarrassed tone. "Well, he stays in the barn part of the day, but I must confess he prefers to sleep in my room some nights." He coughed. "In my bed, I'm afraid."

Adam swiped his hair off his brow, and she had a sudden image of him when he'd made that boyish gesture at twelve years old. For a moment he looked as vulnerable and as strong as he'd been then, just before his shoulders had grown wider and his height had sprouted. Before his beard had started to grow. Her fingers itched to touch his smoothly shaven jaw that no longer looked like that of a boy's.

"Do you want to feed him?" he asked.

"Yes," she said on a breath and sat on the veranda swing, holding the cub and letting it gnaw and suckle on her thumb.

Adam went to the truck and returned a moment later with a baby's bottle. "I made up a solution of goat's milk, horse colostrum, and rice water. He's been doing well on it. But I think he'll soon be ready for meat."

The cub wiggled to take the bottle from her, but scratched her arm in the process. She yelped, and Adam raised her arm to examine the scratch. "I'll get you some antiseptic."

"I'll take care of it later." She couldn't take her eyes off the beautiful creature lying on its back on her lap, suckling from the bottle like any human child and gazing at her with sapphire eyes.

Neither she nor Adam spoke as the cub drained the bottle. And like a human child, it fell asleep in her arms.

"I brought him to show you, Laine, because I truly am sorry for how I treated you."

The pain inflicted by his apology dragged her mind from the tiger cub. She ran her hand over the cub's warm sides to steady her breathing. "Was there someone else?"

He sat in perfect stillness and then folded his arms only to unfold them a moment later. "I'd rather not talk about the reasons. I just...well I just wanted to tell you that the past is past. While you're here I agree that we must act cordially." His voice wavered. "But I am not the same person I was eight years ago."

His lack of explanation brought a haze of red to her vision. "You are not the only one altered by time, Adam. So I wish you would stop assuming that I'm longing for a return of your affections."

Her outburst disturbed the cub, but she petted its head while it searched for her thumb. Suckling on her hand again, the cub returned to sleep. Holding the small tiger soothed her ravaged feelings, and she gave in to the peacefulness of its steady, pulsating sides.

Adam went so very quiet for a long moment. "How right you are." He ran a hand around the back of his neck. "I was never one for putting things into words properly."

"What utter rot. You've got a way with words like few others, Adam." She stroked the cub's muzzle. It was true Adam could write an essay or give a speech like no one else, but he did get stuck when it really mattered. Good gracious, the night he'd asked her to marry him, he'd shown her the ring, gave her a lopsided smile, and said, "Well? Shall we?"

"I only hope we can move ahead as friends now." He cleared his throat and nodded toward the cub. "Since the war ended I kept expecting to hear the news through Mother that you'd swept at least a dozen men off their feet."

"You assumed I'd spend the rest of my life flitting from one social occasion to the other, I imagine."

"Of course not. That's not what I meant, Laine. I'd hoped that by now you would have settled down and were married with several children. You'd make a wonderful mother."

She refused to wince for him. The remembered feel of Abby's baby Miri in her arms. Cam's hugs. The memory of their soft little bodies crowded in. But she laughed off the desires they stirred. "What! Marriage and children? Certainly not for me. Nursing is my life, and I wouldn't trade that for a husband and loads of nappies."

He stared off into the dark jungle, his fist clenching as it rested on his knee. "You're a wonderful nurse, Laine. That's no surprise to me. But I'd wanted more for you out of life than a career. You were meant for...so much more."

She stood, cradled the tiger cub close and kissed it on the top of its velvet head before handing it to Adam. She'd had enough of this. His apology carried more barbs than a direct insult. She would join Bella and Rory.

Adam could go drown himself for all she cared.

14

From her window high above the far end of the garden, Eshana watched heavy clouds bruise the sky. Twilight approached, but the rains held off. From this distance she could see the servants. All day long they cleaned and swept the courtyard, stringing garland upon garland of jasmine and marigolds over the crenellated rooftop, doorways, and arches, to the main section of the house. No one came near her except for Ruchi. It was as well the little girl did, as the servants were too busy with the wedding preparations and had not come at all for two days.

As soon as Eshana told Ruchi that she was hungry, the child had left her and returned later with a selection of cakes and sweets rolled up in the end of her sari. By the time she had run from the kitchens and huffed up the stone steps to the rampart, the food had mashed together. But Eshana savored each mouthful, and laughed as the child entertained her with a report on the flurry of activity inside the house.

"The servants are squatting in the kitchen, chopping mountains of vegetables, scooping out coconuts, and cutting chickens. And *Amma* is shrieking like a hyena at all of them. Poor *Appa* has been sent to town to buy more and more flowers, and my aunties and uncles are arriving, and everyone is getting in the way."

"Where are Vanji and Shindu?"

"They are sweeping the courtyard. Auntie Kaveri does not want a speck of dust to soil my day."

"Will your *amma* or auntie not be looking for you?"

Ruchi shrugged. "They will not need me until it grows dusk. Then they will bathe me and dress me and put more flowers in my hair. It is only the first of many days' festivities. But look." She thrust her hands through the fretwork and held out her palms, turning her hands over to show the backs. Newly painted henna designs ran up each wrist, an intricate twist of flowers and birds. "And this." She puffed out a breath as she raised first one foot and then the other to show Eshana the designs adorning the tops of her feet and ankles.

While Ruchi balanced on one foot and supported herself by bracing against the stonework, Eshana drew in one tiny foot and kissed the top of it. "You will be very beautiful, gem of my heart."

"I have brought more chalk." Ruchi's interest flitted with the swiftness of a magpie to another subject. "Draw on your floor and tell me my favorite story." The child came every day for stories, some of ancient India and others from the Bible.

Eshana smiled, knowing which story held Ruchi's fascination, but she widened her eyes in mock confusion. "Which story is your favorite?"

"Yeshu at the wedding of Cana." The child clapped her hands. "We should ask Yeshu to come to my wedding. *Amma* would only be crying and squealing if we do not have enough food for our guests, and Yeshu could make some more. Does he know how to make *dal payasam* with cashews on the top?" She rubbed her tummy and grinned.

Eshana softened her voice. "I am sure that Yeshu can help with that. Why do we not speak with Him now?"

This time it was the child's turn to widen her eyes. "He is here?" She peered inside the room. "I do not see his statue."

"You cannot see Him, my beloved, because He resides in Heaven with Almighty God. He does not reside in something made of stone or wood, but His living spirit is here, as if He were standing in front of you. Come, let us pray to Him to keep your wedding free of calamity."

Eshana knelt at the window and placed her palms together. Ruchi copied her movements on the opposite side of the stonework as Eshana began to pray. "Father in Heaven, I approach you in the name of your Son, Yeshu, and ask you to bless us with your visitation upon Ruchi's wedding festivities. And Father, I pray that you will bless her with a husband who will love her and care for her all her days..." She choked on a sob with the last few words, "that she will never be mistreated."

Ruchi poked a finger through the fretwork to capture a tear clinging to Eshana's cheek. "Why are you crying?"

"I want you to be very happy, little one beyond the price of rubies."

The child dropped her chin to her chest. "If you come to my wedding I will be happy."

Eshana reached out to caress the little face. Pulling her hand inside again, she kissed her fingertips that had touched Ruchi. "No, my beloved, you must not disclose our secret. I have been thinking. After your wedding when all has been fulfilled, and you and your parents have received their hearts' desire, then I will ask them to release me."

"They will be happy that all has gone well with my wedding." The little one nodded with the wisdom of an old woman, the marigolds in her hair bobbing.

Music began to play, tom-toms beat, flutes and harmoniums whined, someone strummed a *veena*. A band of mauve fringed the sky, and beyond the gates of the garden Eshana could make out a number of flaming torches coming toward the house.

Ruchi jumped up and, holding onto the parapet, bounced with excitement. "It has begun. My wedding is here."

The music grew louder as it approached the house, and the voices of a large group of people rose on the air like a gaggle of geese. Ruchi's relatives and friends had arrived. The drums continued to beat as the crowd paraded under the archway and inside the house.

Someone called out from the garden for the child. Ruchi ducked down below the parapet. "It is my auntie," she said in a tragic whisper. "They have been looking for me. She will want to wash me again."

Laughter bubbled from the depths of Eshana's heart. "Then hurry, my princess, you have stayed too long. When you can, come and tell me all of your auspicious day. I will be praying to Yeshu that your heart will sing and dance with joy."

The little one reached through the window, caressed Eshana's cheek, her small fingers trailing down to Eshana's chin. She stood to leave, but before she did she kissed her own fingertips that had touched Eshana, and dashed away.

Eshana sank down with her back to the wall, listening to the child's footsteps grow faint, and remembering her own wedding day. She had barely seen the boy who was her husband. If he had lived, what would he have looked like?

The picture of Jai Kaur came to her mind as she had last seen him at the train station. His tall frame had stood before her, and he had bowed his head. She saw his dark eyes as they had been that day, lit from within by ardor for the God he sought. If only the Lord would free her. Imprisoned as she was, she would never be able to help Jai in his search.

15

Laine examined a pregnant woman in the hut designated as the purdah ward, but it wasn't the eighteen-year-old Tamil girl lying on the string cot that held her thoughts. It was the bluish-tinged faces, hands, and feet of cholera patients. For the past week the village nearest to them kept their distance, but fifty-seven people from the surrounding area had brought their sick.

She helped the young pregnant girl into the purdah cart with the warning, "Your baby is developing well, it won't be long now, but do boil your water. Never drink it straight from the well or river."

The girl bowed to her with her palms together and promised to be careful.

Now that she'd helped Bella with the dispensary's daily run of ailments, Laine hurried to Rory in the ward he'd sectioned off for the cholera. Together this past week they'd set up an area around this largest of huts to control infection. They had enough cholera beds for the moment. Adam had sent over a number of wooden cots that his plantation workers had constructed.

At first Rory had taken tissue and fluid samples from those patients who had died to study them under his microscope, but the days had become too full for research. Too full for much of anything except work. They were thankful though they'd been able to bring thirty-eight of the patients through the illness by intravenous fluids and later, when they could manage it, oral rehydration.

Rory looked up when she entered the ward. Above his cotton mask his eyes crinkled with a smile, but he looked down again at the woman he was attending.

Laine donned a clean apron and mask and hurried to assist Vishnu, one of Adam's men who he'd assigned to help with the sick. Motti and Satish along with Vishnu made up the dayshift, and three more of Adam's men would presently come on duty for the night.

She knew Adam shared his plantation with a number of Indian men, but it surprised her that they were maimed when she first saw them the day they strolled onto the compound. How foolish of Adam to hide his men in that walled-in enclosure. It didn't take long from their conversation to piece together that they'd served in the war. But Satish's lack of a right shoulder and arm didn't slow him down any, nor did Vishnu's badly scarred face and eye patch, or the fact Motti bore burn scars over most of his body.

Vishnu was supporting a patient, a man who writhed over the side of his cot in pain. As Vishnu cleaned and settled the patient, she listened to the heartbeat. Slow and irregular. The man's eyes rolled wildly, his lips drawn thin and dry, and his hands curled in pain.

At her instruction Vishnu adjusted the saline drip as she palpated the patient's leg muscles. Already, the man didn't seem as blue as he had been. But you could never tell with cholera, just as you thought they were getting better you could lose them. Motti and Satish rushed from cot to cot and saw to patients' needs. Rory, frowning, leaned over to examine a middle-aged man.

Laine cupped her current patient's shoulder, and for a moment his gaze connected with hers, until another spasm attacked him. Her heart tightened, watching him suffer. But she nipped the sentimentality in the bud. These people needed her training and experience. Later, alone in her room, she could afford to indulge her pity.

After she soothed the patient she caught Vishnu's eyes upon her and his nod of approval. Strange how affirmation from this Indian man had the same bolstering effect on her as the trust Ada McFarlane used to endow her with—the instant trust she'd received from Bella and Rory. But apparently would never receive from Adam with his heightened sense of privacy.

Bleary-eyed, Laine moved from cot to cot and to the mats on the hard mud floor. The afternoon had brought another twenty patients. Sweat beaded on her brow. She mopped it with her sleeve cover. Between Rory, herself, and the nursing dayshift of Indian men from the plantation, they'd lost only one patient so far today—an elderly woman.

Her nose stung with the germ-killing reek of perchloride of mercury when she left the cholera ward hours later. It had been a long week. A long day. She tore off her mask, dropped her soiled nursing gown and apron into the bin for laundering, and scrubbed with a cake of lye soap inside the newly constructed washing hut. Another of Adam's projects he'd recently arranged.

The wash was as good as a rest, and she left the hut wearing a clean set of clothes when her gaze stopped on two men walking in the distance through the betel nut trees.

With their backs to her they carried a mat away with the latest of the cholera victims. She'd hardly gotten a glimpse at these plantation workers who came silently into the compound before dawn or after nightfall to take the deceased down to the Hindu burning *ghats* along the river. There, the victims' families would arrange funerals. The urgency of cholera had thrust some of Adam's workers out of the plantation groves, but these men assigned to take away the dead, as shy and secretive as deer, avoided the main population even more than the temporary nursing staff at the compound.

Laine came out of the area fenced off for cholera to find Vishnu filling the hand-washing basin with sterilized water. As the sun touched trees and vegetation, steam wafted from the ground, and she drew in a whiff of damp earth and saturated flowers. But she was none-too-happy about this evening's plans. Adam had sent a note to the bungalow, inviting Rory, Bella, and her to the big house for dinner. He had guests, his note explained, buyers of his produce.

This sudden lifting of Adam's curtain of secrecy unnerved her, and she glanced back to where she'd seen the two plantation workers carrying the mat through the betel nut trees. The jungle had swallowed all sight of them.

She smiled at Vishnu who waited for her. "Are you sure the men of the nightshift will be able to manage while we're out at dinner? I'd be happy to stay."

"Oh no, Matron, all is arranged. I was a corpsman in my army days, and Adam has asked me to stay longer this evening so that you, the doctor, and his sister may have this refreshment. We will do very well here with these patients, as I am used to treating my brothers."

"Your brothers, Vishnu?"

He set the empty water can down, and didn't appear to have heard her.

"Your brothers?" she gently repeated.

He looked over his shoulder to the spot in the betel leaf grove where she had been looking. "Only the men of our plantation. We have worked together for so long, we are brothers, *memsahib*."

Vishnu was as tight-lipped about the running of the plantation as Mitto had been when she'd tried to wangle a few explanations out of him earlier. They spoke openly of their produce, their frustrations of soil, pests, the transport of their wares to far-flung countries, but it was understood—and strangely Rory supported this—that Bella and Laine were not allowed on the plantation grounds unless invited. And tonight, Adam had flung open the door.

It wasn't right of her to keep Vishnu stewing on the coals though. She touched his hand. "You're a marvel, really. Wonderful with the patients. I wanted to let you know that, since you take on the risk of treating the sick with so little thought to yourself."

The smile that came from the good side of his face tugged at her heart. "I am most pleased, Matron, to be of service. This is something my brothers..." He looked at the ground. "What is life unless we can use it to bring health and joy to others? I learned kindness as a child at my mother's knee, but I did not know what it meant for a man to give up his life for another, the greatest act of love, until I met..." He looked off to the plantation again.

"Met whom, Vishnu?"

He turned away, busying himself with the water can.

She reached for his arm to have him look at her. "Vishnu, who are you speaking of? Who gave up his life for another? Someone who died during the war?"

He patted her hand. "Yes, yes, that is it of course, my friend who died from the war. Now you must prepare for this evening's merriment. I know Adam has made many, many arrangements that all will be just so."

Laine trudged across the compound to the bungalow. She liked Vishnu, but he remained as reticent as Adam, as if the plantation was a cloistered enclave of monks.

Rory exchanged glances with Laine as she came in the bungalow. "I'm giving you fair warning, Laine, beware. Bella's wound as tight as a child's top. She's been digging through closets and trunks for the last hour searching for what little evening wear we own."

Laine released a mock yawn. "Here I was thinking it was only a boring dinner. There once was a buffet for a few buyers of bananas...from Bombay. Oh dear, I never could put a limerick together."

Bella looked at them askance. "How terribly droll the two of you are. Other than our weekly supper with Adam, this is the first time he's entertained on even the smallest scale. So do hurry up." She bent close to Laine to sniff. "And do something to get rid of that aroma of disinfectant. It's quite off-putting."

With a wink at Rory, Laine stomped to rigid military attention and gave Bella a salute. "Yes, sir! Right away, sir!"

Bella's brow couldn't arch much higher. "You can be as amusing as you like when we get to the dinner party."

If it had not meant so much to Bella, Laine would have taken delight in declining Adam's invitation, but she scurried to her room. Perhaps if she doused herself with a quart of violet eau de cologne she might pass muster.

A sheath of white voile overlaid the satin under-dress that clung to Laine's shape. She stared blankly in the armoire mirror. The sheer material cinched in a knot at a dropped waist, gracing her right hip, with a sash falling to her hem. The whole garment ended one shocking inch below her knees. She'd bought the dress last year on a whim but had never worn it. After bringing it home from the shop, her brief interest in it had faded.

She joined Rory and Bella in the front room, and they both turned to her with widening eyes.

Bella took her by the arm. "My darling girl, you are breathtaking in that frock." She pulled on her elbow-length gloves as if they were going to Windsor Castle. "Now, let's be going."

Rory gave her a drop-jawed stare. "Laine, you shimmer like a moonbeam."

Her face grew warm. She disliked vanity in people, but it was nice to think she hadn't lost the ability to make an entrance.

Adam had sent his car for them. The shiny black Daimler waited outside the bungalow with Nandi, the tall Indian man from the north. This driver stood by the car with the bearing of a soldier in a spotless *kurta* and *dhoti*, and a turban in the shape of a paper boat on his head. Most people were calling them Gandhi caps these days.

He placed his palms together. "Not only will it rain this evening, but the female tiger we hunt has yet to be captured. We fear she is prowling nearby, for we have seen more of her pugmarks."

During the short ride the darkened groves outside the car window drew Laine's attention, lit here and there with the reflective eyes of creatures. As if Adam's home suddenly grew out of the dark, there stood the white columns of the house lit from within and from torches on the lawn. At least this time she knew what she was in for. But at her first opportunity, she'd sneak out to the barn and visit the cub.

A gramophone recording gave a passionate rendition of one of Tchaikovsky's concertos. She'd have preferred that impolite music hall ballad she'd heard the day she left the note, but thankfully Adam wasn't playing Rachmaninoff. In the distance lightning sizzled with a violet hue. It had to be only the pressure of the newest storm that stirred her blood. Because she didn't care that she was about to enter Adam's home again.

At the front door, Ravi bowed over his fingertips that were set in a perfect cone of greeting. He led them through the hallway to the front parlor where a number of men stood around in evening clothes and drinking aperitifs. Rory introduced the three of them and started getting the names of the buyers. As Laine had expected, they were merely fruit representatives from Bombay and Calcutta. But to Bella it was Christmas and Easter and Holi rolled into one.

Laine accepted a drink from Ravi, who glided throughout the room holding a silver tray as if he were a waiter at the Connemara Hotel in Madras.

Footsteps rang on the teak floor behind her, and her spine tingled. Without him saying a word, she knew Adam stood in the doorway. He moved past her and shook hands with his guests. His white dinner jacket emphasized his dark tan and the lock of hair that never would stay combed back from his forehead. He clapped Rory on the shoulder, kissed Bella's upturned cheek, and turned to stare at her.

The blue of his eyes deepened to the lapis color of the pen she'd given him. Oh that was nonsense. Now she was imagining things.

But a muscle ticked along his jaw as he reached to shake her hand. "Ah, Laine, met everyone? Good then. Splendid. You, ah...you look quite—" He swallowed. "—quite lovely...as always."

He turned from her as if he'd done his bit as host and could get on with the rest of the evening without having to say another blessed syllable to her. She released the breath she hadn't realized she'd been holding. With the hard part out of the way, she could surely survive dinner by talking to his guests, his male guests. Not one single woman graced his table other than her and Bella.

Ravi motioned to Adam, and dinner was announced. With a joviality she'd not seen in Adam since the old days, he ushered his guests into the dining room. The chandelier dazzled above, and a breeze heavy with the coming rains played with the candle flames that were interspersed between bowls of floating orchids.

One of the buyers—Edwin somebody—held out a chair for her. As soon as Ravi served the beef broth seasoned with cumin and red chilies, she kept up a steady flow of conversation with the men at the end of the table. Across from her, Rory's eyes twinkled as they talked through the salad greens, fish course, and roasted chicken with coconut chutney.

But over the voices of others, Adam's baritone at the far end of the table resonated within her of conversations from long ago.

Like the night he'd returned to India when he'd first come home from Oxford. She'd been waiting for him in his mother's garden when she heard his footsteps on the patio. She had dropped Marmalade, his mother's tabby, and run to Adam. In the moonlight he'd taken her down to the Madras Marina, and they'd walked along the promenade listening to the breakers crash upon the shore. He had whirled her in his arms, and with a few stuttering words slipped his family ring on her left hand.

"You've recently come from Amritsar, Miss Harkness?" Edwin at her left jolted her from her memories. "What do you think of Gandhi's desire to have a memorial built?"

She hadn't noticed that dinner had ended and Ravi served apple custard and toffees. She glanced at Edwin. "A memorial?"

"The one Gandhi's proposing should be erected for those killed in that policing measure, the one in the Jallianwalla Bagh."

The Calcutta buyer addressed Edwin. "It's a shame the way General Dyer has been maligned for taking the stand he did."

Adam quietly cut across the discussion, his voice a hard edge. "No one has been able to obtain an accurate number of how many Indian people were mown down by General Dyer's guns that day. Some reports say three hundred, other reports claim the number is much higher, closer to six hundred."

Laine carefully set her water goblet on the table, unable to tear her gaze from Adam's cold expression. He'd never been a verbose man, but his visage spoke more powerfully than any editorial on the massacre. As if six hundred people gunned down in a crowd needed debate anyway. "I knew one of the victims, an Indian woman by the name of Miriam. So I'm afraid I must agree with what Gandhi has said. 'The Battle of Plassey laid the foundation of the British Empire in India, but the massacre in Amritsar has shaken it.' If that is the case, we have no one to blame but ourselves."

For the space of a heartbeat she glanced at Adam, only to be held immobile by his fathomless gaze. Her throat suddenly dry, she lifted her glass to her lips and turned from him as conversation erupted around the table.

"Horrible business," one of the other buyers said. "Have you heard how the Indian population treated the arrival of the Prince of Wales in Bombay?"

Edwin threw his napkin beside his plate. "Foolish people. What do they want? Take India back to the dark ages? That's what would happen if we left. Hindus would fight with Muslims, Muslims with Hindus. India would revert to the age of despotism where Maharajahs ruled their small princely states with the scimitar. Where no white man would see behind the peacock veil, that sort of thing?"

Adam rose at the end of the table. "You've been reading too many novels, Edwin. I believe Ravi is ready to serve coffee in the drawing room." He gestured for all to precede him. "Shall we?"

He seemed the calm, polite host, but a nerve flickered at his temple. Was he angry with his guests? The recent political upheavals? Every so often he would check with Ravi, and she had the feeling they were not talking about how to serve the after-dinner beverages.

She caught Adam's gaze as he stood by the piano sipping his coffee. Why did he send her these long searching gazes all evening when he'd made plain his lack of feeling for her? She had a good mind to stick her nose in the air and put him in his place as she'd done with the likes of Maurice.

In another corner of the room, Rory chatted with a buyer about the latest cricket test match. Another of Adam's guests had found the ear of Bella, who appeared enthralled with more news of the Prince of Wales's unsuccessful visit.

Edwin set his cup on the mahogany table and leaned back against the sofa. "Nothing will ever come of all this chatter about India separating from the Empire. Besides, most of us in this room were born in India, attended grammar school in India. Had an Indian *ayah* to raise us. My ancestors like yours, Adam, have lived in this country since the days we British first started trading here. Where are we to go if Gandhi chucks us out?"

Silence thundered around the room while the real thing clapped over the house and shook the foundations. Lightning flashed. In the same instant the electricity shut off.

"No need to panic." Adam's voice floated through the darkness. "Ravi and I will have lamps lit in a moment."

Someone struck a sulfur match and set flame to the wick of an oil lamp. Ravi returned with more lanterns, and conversation took up a new topic, led by Adam on the price of fruit going to England and the United States. It was as good a time as any for her to slip out and see the cub.

Laine eased herself off the sofa and moved to stand by the wall. No one noticed. Though the flickering lamplight made it hard to tell. She sidled along the wall, and in the foyer picked up a lamp by its metal handle and ran down the veranda steps.

16

A trimmed lawn and a road separated the house and the barn that sat about fifty yards to the right. Beyond that were the elephant stalls. Laine's footsteps crunched on the pebbled road when the familiar animal yowl like that of a broken door hinge reached her, and she quickened her pace. She didn't know where in the barn Adam kept the cub. Lifting the lantern high she took tentative steps. At the far end Adam's few horses nickered. Then the cub mewed, and she headed in the right direction.

"Yes, my darling, I'm coming." After the weariness of the day and tension of the evening, the anticipation of seeing the small tiger brought a chuckle from her.

Her laughter must have startled the animal, for it scuffled in the dark corner. She made her way toward the straw-filled pen. The cub stretched upwards, balancing his weight on his paws against the side of the stall. His tawny muzzle spread in a comical snarl as he yowled again.

She unlatched the gate and stepped inside, hanging the lantern on a hook. Crouching down she took hold of the warm body and cuddled it. "Are you hungry?" From her sequined bag she pulled the rice biscuits they gave out to the children who came to the dispensary. "Oh, you do like that," she cooed as the cub gobbled the biscuits and snuffled his nose, searching her hands for more.

The cub let out his rusty rumble at the same time something rustled in the darkened corner outside the pen. The horses hadn't made that noise, and she'd heard no other animal sounds within the barn. And it was definitely in the barn.

She stood to lift the lantern. "Is someone there?"

Another shuffling noise, as if someone or something backed away from the light.

An icy trickle snaked down her spine. The mother tiger? She went as still as death.

An odd slurping noise came from the dark not eight feet from her, and she inched forward. But an all-too-human moan told her it was not the tiger.

"Are you quite all right? I'm sorry I startled you." She took another few steps closer.

A man cried out in slurred English and barged past her. "You ssss...s... ouldn't be here. No wo...woomen 'llowed. Tha's...rule." As he stumbled past, the light from her lantern illumined his face—a flattish sort of face with glasses, startling white and a sharp nose.

He ran from her, and as he did he let out an awful sob, so deep it sounded almost animal, sending a chill along her arms. She turned to follow him out of the barn to see Adam standing at the foot of the veranda. As if he'd been looking for her.

His head jerked up when the man from the barn charged past and disappeared behind the bamboo wall that hid the small private village.

Adam went still and, for too long a moment, studied her. He began to walk across the lawn to her as thunder clapped overhead and lightening split the sky. She couldn't move. The closer he came the more she recognized that vulnerable set to his mouth. His eyes dark with emotion riveted on her.

It was the moment she used to dream about—Adam coming back to her.

She shook her head to clear it of the illusion. It was only the pounding of piano keys from the gramophone playing, the press of the coming storm, tonight's tension around the table. Adam was not coming back to her.

At last he reached her, the area around his eyes tight as if caught in a permanent flinch.

He raised his hand as though to touch her face, then let his hand drop to grip her by the upper arm and pull her close. "Laine," he said her name as if testing it for the first time in his life, but his voice contained all the softness he used to reserve for her. "I asked you to respect the privacy of this plantation. To stay away from the outbuildings."

His words lashed and left welts on what was left of her heart.

She thought she'd prepared herself, but still. "Oh, I see you received the bulletin that I'm an anarchist. It's true. I left a trail of burning buildings from Delhi to Calcutta." She shook off his hand and rubbed her arm where he'd gripped her.

"Life isn't a lark, Laine, as I'm sure you're well aware—"

"Of course not. It's full of pain and suffering. Who was that man? He's obviously in need of care." She looked toward the thatched rooftops on the other side of the wall. There had to be a hundred reasons for that man's slurred speech and terror.

He made a helpless gesture. "Laine, leave well enough alone."

She took half a step in the direction of the thatched-roof huts, but he gripped her wrist. "Laine, please."

"Well, I never could let well enough alone, could I?" she croaked. "Not while people suffer. And he's suffering, isn't he, Adam? While you and I stand about chatting in our remarkably good health."

He truly winced this time. His horses snorted and whinnied, and they both turned to see what had disturbed the animals. A few seconds later thunder shook the ground, and before they could get their bearings the rains landed all at once like a heavy curtain dropping on a stage. She could just make out the tiger cub's howling as rains drummed on the roof loud enough to drown out conversation, had there been any.

She and Adam glared at each other as the monsoon hurtled in a frenzy on the roof.

Her fists curled at her sides.

His throat moved as he swallowed. "I think it best you return to the house. I'm sure Bella and Rory are missing you. In the future—"

She finished for him, "Yes in the future, stay off your property."

He looked at her as if she'd struck him. "Laine, I meant only that you let me know ahead of time, and I'd be happy to...escort you."

"Of course your property is not open to the public, especially women. It's common knowledge that you share the profits with your workers, and some of them are soldiers who served with you in the war. I'm not stupid, Adam. I can see they are men that have been brutally wounded. So you've set up for yourself a rather exclusive boys' club. Cricket pitch and all."

She ran from him, across the lawn to the veranda. The rains had soaked her to the skin by the time her feet landed on the steps, in déjà vu of the first night she'd been here, as if someone rewound the gramophone and played the same song over and over and over again.

From the barn doorway Adam watched her go. How could something that had died hurt so much? Yet Laine's words had sliced deep. Both of them were in perfect health, while...

Since he'd come to live on the plantation, not one woman had disturbed the peace. Without a great deal of explanation Bella accepted the residents of this enterprise preferred their privacy. Adam, except for a few of the Indian men, was the only one who represented them to the outside world.

"My brother," a voice called to him from the dark.

"What is it, Ranjit?"

The tall Sikh hobbled out of the rain to stand under the barn's overhang. "Come my brother, your guests are retiring for the night, and even as we speak Nandi is whisking the girl away with the doctor and his sister. And I am needing your help with John *sahib*. The young woman has distressed him, and he is weeping and gnashing. I cannot control his anguish, nor get him back to the house quietly so your guests will not notice. Only you can soothe him."

Adam watched the headlamps of the Daimler as it drove away from the house, removing Laine's provocative presence.

He stepped out into the warm deluge, not bothering to take a dash for cover. The rains would do their work like nothing else could. He simply stood there, letting the rain pound him like a furious massage, working out Laine's words, letting them wash out of him into the puddles forming at his feet. She didn't know how accusing her words had been.

He *had* narrowed his world to exclude the beauty and sweetness of women. Like the men who lived here, he too had found a meager comfort in their absence. Like a starving man with no money removes himself from outside a bakery, to stop himself from going mad over what he could never have.

At last he looked up to see Ranjit waiting for him with an umbrella. A good lot an umbrella would do now. But he slicked back his streaming hair and turned to follow Ranjit to the huts. Only in the company of these men, seeing their disfigurements every day, their faces that embodied the horrors of war, did he experience some peace. Those who died, and those who merely lived out their days in a death-like existence, deserved never to be forgotten.

And while he was remembering them, how could he seek out the sweetness of a woman? Hold a woman, kiss the woman he loved, when they could not?

Rains fell like the floods of Noah, their drops bouncing on the parapet outside her window. With her throat parched, Eshana held her cup out through the stone fretwork to catch what water she could. Ruchi's wedding music had played most of the night. Festivities would start again on the new day, keeping all servants, even the lowest of the low, busy. They had yet to remember to bring her food or drink. The few drops of rain she collected did not slake her thirst.

As the hours passed, and night grew close to dawn, part of the blessing Jai had bestowed upon her in Amritsar rang in her mind. *May your devotion to the Lord be perpetual...and your sustenance be the perpetual divine singing of the Glories of the Lord.* Her stomach cramped with hunger. Those few sweets Ruchi had brought had not filled her after two days of nothing. But her thirst was harder to bear.

She raised her hands palm upward, beseeching. "I have much work to do. Why do you lock me away when I could be working for your Kingdom?"

Her self-pity shamed her. Jai's Sikh blessing also shamed her. She knew the One who was the water of life, Yeshu. Yet she had not been satisfied with singing His praises no matter what her circumstances. She would change that now.

Holding onto the window base she lifted herself to her feet as the first rays of light erased the shadows. Tom-toms beat from the house below, cymbals chimed, and other instruments created a sweet dervish. She began to dance, holding her feet, hands, and fingers in the delicate gestures of ancient India, though the words that poured from her mouth were those of a psalm, "As the hart panteth after the water brooks, so panteth my soul after thee, O God."

The house grew quiet as dawn broke, and Eshana continued to dance and sing. Her heart grew lighter with her worship, when over the hiss of rain came the patter of Ruchi's feet running along the parapet.

Ruchi stuck her tiny face into the largest space in the stonework and giggled.

Eshana rushed to her. “Are you married yet, gem of my heart?”

“No, I will see my husband tomorrow. Tonight has been only the start of many things. Priests prayed many prayers and made me stand for a long time while they passed a brass tray over my head, many, many... many times.” She yawned while the rain plastered her hair to her head, and pelted the flowers entwined in her tresses. “*Amma* thinks I am in my room asleep.”

“Go, my princess, go to your house and to your sleep before you catch cold.”

In the growing light Eshana could see Ruchi’s rosebud of a mouth turn to a pout. “No. I heard you singing. Were you dancing? I want to dance too. I did not get to dance tonight, only the women did in *Amma*’s quarters.”

Eshana laughed at the child’s impudence. “If you will promise to go to bed, we will dance one dance.”

The morning lightened, and she led Ruchi in the steps she had danced by herself earlier. The little one laughed as the rains fell in sheets of silver silk over her.

When the dance ended she took hold of Ruchi’s hands. “Now go, but first put this cup out to catch the rain. Tomorrow will you come and bring it to me?”

The little one left her, and at last Eshana lay upon her cot to sleep. Her physical reality may be incarnated within these stone walls, but her spiritual reality was that of a princess of God, close to the right hand of the Almighty, where the Son of God sat, Yeshu.

She was not sure how much longer it would be before she was united with God in Heaven. Perhaps she would waste away in this prison, but she still had so much she wished to accomplish here on earth.

17

Rory came to a halt at the foot of the cot where Laine injected a boy of fifteen with morphia. The boy had been brought in last night and dehydrated within an hour. He'd been hooked up to nine-percent saline all night, and she had a great deal of hope that he would be one of those who made it. With roughly twenty new cases a day, a good thirty percent of those died within forty-eight hours.

Rory's grave eyes looked at her over his mask. "Well, it's hit all the local villages."

Her arms suddenly felt like lead. She glanced around the over-crowded ward, to the recovering patients lying on woven mats outside under the hut's overhang. "We're going to need a larger treatment center."

"Adam's already working on that. His men will have tents set up by this afternoon. He's also sending more of his men to act as nursing staff."

"More men, how many actually work for him?"

"Only nineteen left from the original platoon." Perhaps if Rory had been less distracted he might have been less forthcoming. He didn't seem aware he'd leaked out the first snippet of information about Adam's workforce she'd heard in the entire time she'd been here.

He cast his gaze over his shoulder as he gathered his thoughts. "At the moment, Adam wants to drive out to the village of Cholarjure. Bella and Adam's men can take care of things here while we do that. I'd like you to come with us for the sake of the women."

The village seemed eerily quiet as Adam drove the truck through its narrow, dusty lane flanked by betel nut trees. A number of faces stared out of darkened doorways. Elderly men crouched at the thresholds and glared at them. Only a few weeks ago the pond had been filled with chattering women washing and banging clothes on rocks. Today a smattering of buffalo stood knee deep in the water, but only a few women worked the rice paddies in the distance.

Where on earth were the children? A couple of boys were climbing a coconut tree to chop down the fruit. One girl in a pathetically soiled sari stood staring at them, holding an earthen water jar at her hip. Laine's searching gaze found a small group of children sitting listlessly beneath a soft-needled casuarina tree. No longer did they resemble butterflies swarming over the village, giggling and laughing.

Adam parked the truck, and a few children wandered over to him. Some of their former exuberance returned as they reached out hands in the hope of a sweet. They didn't have the fear their elders did for these British infidels who had been roused by the local holy man. And thinking of the *sadhu*, there he was.

He sat cross-legged outside a hut on a string bed, throwing flower petals on a fire. He didn't speak to them as he watched the petals burn to ash. Though he never looked their way, not even a hooded glance, she felt his attention was entirely focused on their arrival. Only when they had passed him did she feel his gaze come upon them. She shivered as Rory, Adam, and herself reached the hut of the village headman.

The old man who'd acted as their advocate several weeks ago walked toward them with measured dignity. "All the household of our village leader are ill, as is he. His wife died yesterday, and we sprinkled her ashes upon the river. We have done the same for many in the village."

Adam didn't hesitate. He stooped to enter the thatch-roofed hut.

Laine and Rory followed. Coming in from the sun her eyes rebelled at the dim room. All the shutters were closed, but her nose told her all too well how bad the situation was. She pulled the cotton mask up to cover the lower half of her face, as did Rory.

Adam didn't acknowledge the stench, but dropped to the mat where the headman lay. "*Sahib*, let us help you and your children."

The compassion in Adam's voice brought a phantom pain to her heart, like that of a lost limb. She brushed it away and bent to take the pulse of a girl who lay on a grass mat, then the pulse of a boy not much older than

Cam. Both children's heartbeats were weak, their skin the telltale color of the rapid loss of bodily fluids.

Their father was too weak to answer Adam, but his sunken eyes spoke for him.

Adam looked up at Rory. "Right, that's it. We load them in the truck bed. God-willing if we can save at least one or two of this family the rest of the village may follow suit." He and Rory began to lift the headman when a shadow at the door cut off what little light there had been.

The *sadhu* stood at the threshold. "Do not touch him. I have made *puja* and brought what they need." He opened his hand that contained several balls of rolled ash. He moved toward the headman and prepared to place the ball of ash into the headman's mouth when Rory stopped him.

Laine stood with the little boy in her arms while the holy man thrust out his bony chest as he had weeks ago.

Adam stepped closer to the *sadhu*. "Swami, no one is stopping you from performing *puja* for your people. Go, pray for them, but leave medicine to those who know how to treat the body. Your Indian doctors, faithful Hindus, would tell you the same." He motioned to Rory to help him pick up the headman.

The old man beseeched the *sadhu*. "I have heard this is true, Swami. Perhaps the gods have smiled upon us and sent these doctors to help."

Adam didn't wait for the *sadhu*'s permission. He and Rory carried the headman out of the hut and to the truck. Laine followed with the boy, and Rory hurried back for the little girl.

Before jumping into the driver's seat, Adam turned to the old man and the *sadhu*. "If you truly care for your people, gather the sick and bring them to the compound. We can't promise to save everyone, but we can give them a better chance of surviving than leaving them in their huts to die. If you can't do that, then at least give them coconut water to drink. It's more pure than the well water and has other benefits."

Laine and Rory sat with the patients. By the time they made it back to the compound, ten or more canvas tents dotted the red earth that had dried in the last few hours of sun.

In their absence, Adam's men had built two more temporary outhouses and rigged up an additional fresh water tank. Devaram sat at a table at the front of the compound with a surgical mask covering his face, writing down the particulars of patients from a long line of waiting family members. Ravi assisted the next person to one of the tents. He too wore a mask. In fact as Laine glanced around, a number of Adam's people—ten or more Indian men she had yet to meet—were assisting Bella in the center that was in the full swing of operation.

A tall Sikh man supported himself with a crutch over to Adam.

"An update, Ranjit?" Adam asked the Sikh as he motioned to Vishnu to help him lower the village headman to a cot. They began to carry the patient into the treatment tent while others came to take the children as well.

Bella ducked out of the tent and hurried over to them. Her mask gusted with a breath. "Glad you're all back, with this new lot that's arrived. And, Rory, a message came. The Indian Medical Services says we may be in for an epidemic. One thing for certain, things will get much worse before they get better. So wash up. There'll be no time to pray on your knees—we'll have to beseech the Lord while we work."

Before any of them had a chance to do her bidding, a series of bullock carts rumbled into the compound. The elderly man from Cholarjure had brought their sick.

Laine squeezed her eyes shut with relief. When she opened them, her chest went warm with pride. Adam brushed past her, his arms extended in welcome to the villagers.

Eshana had not come. Each day Jai had checked, and each day he had come away with the news that there was still no additional letter from Eshana. He hurried to the narrow, four-story house on Bazar Lakar Mandi, his valise clutched in his hand. The young women of this mission had not called for him, but there was always someone in the house who could use the ministrations of a doctor. He swept past the shoppers who examined figs and dates and bartered with a fruit seller, along the bazaar to stop outside the mission door.

Harmindar gave him entrance.

Before she had a chance to speak he asked her, "Is there any news?"

"We have received no letter."

Now that he was here he had no wish to hide his true intent. "I am becoming worried."

"As are we, doctor. Will you come up the stairs? We have been praying."

He followed her up the four flights to the room jutting over the *bagh* below. December's cooling air came across the balcony and through the glass-paneled doors.

The other two women were kneeling at the cot. He had disturbed their prayers, but they rose from their knees as he entered. Harmindar joined Mala and Tikah and gestured for him to sit on the brightly colored woolen rug. All three sets of features were pinched with worry, but Harmindar spoke for them.

"We wrote a letter to the Ramabai Mukti Mission for more information and received this letter today." She held the missive out to him. "They are saying that before she left Poona, Eshana wished to return to us with much haste. They too fear that if she has not come home, then something has happened to our beloved sister."

Mala raised her clasped hands to her chin. "If Eshana were well she would have sent us news."

He read the letter's contents. The writer, a woman by the name of Uma, expressed alarm over Eshana's disappearance. *Disappearance.* The word struck cold into his heart.

The husky voice of Tikah brought his head up. "What can we do, doctor? The police will not listen to us, being only women and widows at that."

He read the letter again, noting the day she had left Poona for Bombay. She must have disappeared somewhere between Bombay and here. Or had she even made it to Bombay?

Disquiet thrummed through his veins. He could sit still no longer and jumped to his feet. The three women before him could take care of all manner of ailments, feed their eighty or so children and patients, but they were helpless to find Eshana. "Write to your English friends who have sway with the government. See if that cavalry major—"

"Geoff," Mala and Harmindar chimed together.

"Perhaps he can be of assistance. The nursing *sahiba*, Laine Harkness, have you not written to her? Perhaps she has word of Eshana. If you have her address I will send a telegram today. Unless you have someone who is ill I will leave you to start my inquiries." He was about to take the stairs when Harmindar stopped him.

"There is more that you must hear, doctor. We have received word at last—a new administrator is being sent from Calcutta to head up our mission. Should we not wait for this woman, a Dr. Victoria Owens? She is from England."

Jai released a sigh. After all this time, two years almost since Miriam had died in the massacre, those in charge of this charitable house had chosen an Englishwoman over Eshana. "When is Dr. Owens to be arriving?"

"Next week," Harmindar answered.

"We cannot wait for her. I will return as soon as I have learned anything."

He clamored down the stairs and out of the house. Surely the transcendent and immortal, universal God would care about Eshana. The crowds in the bazaar hindered his movement, and he pushed through them. His father would be angry with him for taking so long away from their practice, but first he must check with the police in case Eshana had returned to Amritsar and they had arrested her. If that was not the case, then he must send a telegram to Eshana's nursing friend.

Two days later his father pounded the desk in their clinic, shaking the glass beakers. One slim tube rolled off the desk and splintered on the floor. "What is this foolishness you speak? Let the police be looking after this woman. What is she to you that you should care?"

Jai held the older man's gaze. The anger in his father's eyes would have made him quake in days gone by. But no longer. Though he loved and honored his father, he could not stand by and do nothing to help Eshana. Expecting his father's rage, he had waited until the last of their patients had left before telling him of his decision.

"I went to the police station two days ago. They have no word of her. Nor are they concerned. I have also received this telegram today—her nursing friend in the Madras Presidency has had no word of her either."

"What do you expect to do? Search the length of Hind for this Christian?"

"I will go to Bombay and Poona where she was last seen to learn what I can."

His father's fists clenched white on top of the desk. "Your regard for this woman is outside the bounds of neighborly respect. As your father I command you to throw away your feelings for her. They are rubbish. Rubbish! By following after this woman you are putting yourself in danger of turning your back on your Sikh beliefs. And know this, my son, if you take up these Christian ideas you have been toying with...you will no longer be my son."

Jai backed away as if slapped. "I have not turned my back on our beliefs. It is only my desire to help a peer. Can I be any less compassionate than the man you brought me up to be?"

Tears glistened in Father's eyes. "I did raise you to be compassionate." His gaze traveled to the wood stove. "But I have seen changes in you. I am afraid the writings of Sundar Singh have tainted you. And you would never have picked up those writings if you had not spent so much time with the mission woman."

"I will never turn my back on God. But I will search for this young woman who may need my help. I ask for your blessing, but if I do not receive it, I will go nonetheless."

His father rested his forehead in his hand. At last he waved him away. "I cannot be giving you my blessing, for in my heart I know you will betray me. I have seen the signs this past year. I have seen the signs." He raised his face, his eyes red with tears. "If you turn your back on the words of the *Guru Granth Sahib*, you are no longer...you are no longer one of us."

Appa's words resonated in Jai's mind as he turned away. *No longer one of us*. How could he bear it if his father's predictions came to pass?

18

The words in Jai Kaur's second telegram burned in Laine's mind as the sun beat through the canvas tent. She mopped her brow as she adjusted the saline drip for a man from Cholajure. According to his family he was thirty-three, but at the moment he looked a wizened old man of seventy.

Still, though the suffering surrounded her, it was Eshana's face she kept seeing. If only Geoff were here, he'd find Eshana, but Geoff—blast it—had gone off to the Far East. Now Jai was on his way to Poona. She couldn't just leave the search in Jai's hands, but where could she possibly start to look, especially stuck here in the jungle in the middle of a cholera outbreak?

Rory and Bella had been equally concerned when she'd shared the telegrams with them. When Rory came into the examination tent, she trotted over to him, removing the cloth mask from her face.

"You need a rest, Laine. You've worked the past twelve hours."

"I'm all right, and you worry too much about me. What I want to do is go into town. I've got to at least talk to the police."

"I hate to be a wet blanket, but I don't think the local police will be able to help you locate your friend."

"All the same, I'd like to try. I'll take the bicycle or, better still, the bullock cart."

He drew closer. "Don't be silly, you're far too tired, and it's ten miles to the nearest town."

She found she didn't mind his nearness, a look of surprise stamped on his face as if he'd just discovered a new disease or better yet the cure for one.

"Laine, I know I've told you already, but Bella and I...well *I* am delighted you're here."

Rory wasn't the type to move fast, but for the first time since Reese passing, the idea of a nice man in her life didn't make her want to kick someone in the shins—thanks to Adam. Though Rory was a good twenty years older, she found herself taking a step toward his tall, angular frame that stooped over her. He tucked her arm into his and drew her out into the sunshine. A breeze stirred the cork tree by the veranda, releasing its perfume.

"Laine," he whispered as they strolled toward the tree, "I must ask—I hope you'll forgive the impertinence—you're sure your prior relationship with Adam is a thing of the past? At a time like this, your worry over your friend, I want to be a support to you, but..."

The engine of Adam's truck backfired as it barreled a ways up the road. Laine shut her eyes briefly to the bad timing she'd come to recently associate with the owner of that vehicle. In a surge of frustration she leaned up to kiss Rory's cheek. "I can assure you the last nail has been hammered into that coffin. And I very much want your support."

"It's just that as Adam's my friend and yours, I wouldn't want to make either of you uncomfortable if I...if we...if you and me..."

She had to rescue the poor lamb before he suffered a stroke on her account. He was out of his element with an available woman. And she was available—even with her recent worry over Eshana, she was available. That thought stood out as vibrant as the scarlet hibiscus brushing against the white-washed bungalow in the sunlight. Something had changed in her since coming here.

Taking hold of his arm she grinned up at him. "Tell me, Rory, dedicated missionary that you are, how do you feel about dancing? Or more importantly, how do you reconcile your devotion to your Christian ideals by rubbing shoulders in close environs with a sinner such as me?"

She squashed down the twinge of guilt as Eshana's accusation rang in her ears. *You are like mimosa, Laine, that curls up on itself when touched.* What if she found herself unable to go through with this lighthearted promise that bantered between her and Rory? Might she be leading him up the garden path, only to balk at the door of the wedding chapel?

His eyes lit. "Laine, while you've been here I've come to recognize your cheeky wit is an attempt to cover up a genuinely pure heart. In spite of your struggle over spiritual things, I know deep down you still believe in Christ." Rory's brows lifted at the look of surprise she sent him. "Yes, I'm aware of your confusion over faith, but I want you to know that I think you're the most wonderful woman I've ever met. I'd trust you with anything. Wholeheartedly, my dear."

She couldn't move.

Adam's truck ground to a stop outside the treatment center. He and two of his men jumped down from the cab, and the two Indian men began to pull down crates and haul them into the hut where they kept the medical supplies.

With a quick glance at Adam, she noted under her breath, "Trust me with anything, Rory? Perhaps there are others who would not." She squeezed his arm. "I adore you. I'm not sure where that will go, but for now let's see where it does lead. At the moment I can't think of much more than finding Eshana."

Adam strolled toward them, and whatever Rory would have said flew off as if snatched by the sparrows flirting in the surrounding trees.

With a squeeze of her hand, Rory freed Laine's arm from his. As Adam drew closer, his features registered not so much as a quiver, but she had seen his gaze land on hers and Rory's joined arms before they'd separated.

"I was able to get everything on your list, Rory," Adam said as he reached them. "Except the extra saline you requested. The local Medical Services can't give you any from their stock. Looks like I'll have to go as far afield as Vellore or Madras for what you'll need."

Their need of medical supplies wiped all other thoughts from Rory's expression. "We've enough for two weeks providing the number of cases remains relatively steady. Let's not fear the worst at this point."

The growing need of saline warred with her worry over Eshana. Surely she was all right and had simply not written. But here, if they ran out of saline the number of cholera deaths would rise. Was that what had happened to Eshana? Had she contracted the disease and fallen unnoticed somewhere?

Rory stroked his chin. "We'll see how things go next week, if the number of patients drops off." He turned to consider Laine for a long moment. "Adam, Laine has a problem and she was going to ride into town. I've just stopped her from doing that."

"What problem?" Adam's brow furrowed.

Common courtesy won over her desire to ignore him. "A friend of mine's gone missing. Right off the map. I thought the local police might be able to help. But perhaps if you know some of the local civil servants you could get someone to listen to me."

"When did she disappear?"

"Eshana was last seen in Poona on November eighteen. A friend—a doctor friend—has gone there to see what he can discover."

"I don't suppose she's just enjoying herself somewhere?"

"Not Eshana. No one is more meticulous, and she was passionate to return to the mission in Amritsar. No word from her is not a good sign I tell you."

His glance lifted from her to the trees. "Well I'm afraid Rory's right. For one thing, the local police won't be interested in something that's happened in Bombay, hundreds of miles away. Secondly, what's one more Indian woman but a grain of sand on the seashore—"

"Just one more Indian woman!" Heat flickered up the back of her neck.

His eyes flew back to her, his seemingly benign expression shattered. "Laine, let me finish. Good gracious, I don't mean to say that your friend isn't important." He glanced toward his plantation as if he could find the words he sought in that dense mat of jungle, and swept a hand across his brow.

The air clung close. With the oppressive midday heat the birds had grown quiet. Rory didn't look at her but at Adam, his expression heavy. With the compassion of a doctor...with a suffering patient. *Adam?* Rory had said Adam was perfectly healthy. But she'd seen what shellshock did to a man. Adam showed no outward signs. No tremors. Right now he simply looked like a man...a young man...a boy from long ago, the boy she knew, lost and alone.

But in seconds he shored up his feelings and began to speak in that kind but matter-of-fact tone she would use with her patients. "The police have no way of searching several provinces between here and Bombay for one woman who in their opinion is of low status."

Anger spilled from her, not only from her frustration over Eshana but for Adam himself. "If you expect me to sit on my thumbs and do nothing, then you don't know me at all. I'll take the cart into town and talk to the police myself."

For a moment she glimpsed a fragment of that broken Adam again. "I do want to help you find your friend, Laine. Give me all the information about Eshana you have. Every tidbit of information. Where she came from, who she knows, her family? I'll see what I can find out."

For all the world she'd love to tell him she didn't need his help. Her foot tingled with the desire to connect with his shin. But she gave him a firm nod of agreement, unable to trust herself to speak with any politeness to him. There was Eshana to think of. *Dear God where is Eshana?*

19

Father's parting words resounded in Jai's mind as the train sped toward Poona. Yesterday, as he asked innumerable venders and porters in Bombay if they had seen a woman of Eshana's description, his father's voice had reverberated like an echo in the cavernous station. How could he search the length of Hind for one Indian woman? There had been little hope from the start that anyone would remember her out of the millions that passed through this cauldron of India.

He could only hope the Ramabai Mukti Mission had some small piece of news that may put him in the right path. Perhaps the child, Chandra, knew something. He had sent telegrams to the Amritsar mission of his plans, as well as one to Laine.

His train pulled in to the Poona Station, and he acquired a *tonga* to take him to the Christian mission outside the city. Dust covered Jai by the time he reached his destination. As he waited by a pool of water outside the main building, he brushed the worst of the dust from him, and cooled himself by washing his face and hands.

An elderly but spry Indian woman came toward him wearing a light-colored sari. "Dr. Kaur, we have been expecting you. I am Uma, and was one of the last to speak with Eshana. Come, you must have refreshment, and we will tell you all we know."

He followed this lady to a shaded courtyard surrounded by gardens. On the way Uma called out to a young woman to have Chandra brought from class. An oleander bush shaded a stone bench where he sat, but even in the coolness he had a difficult time stopping his knee from jerking in anticipation.

"Please partake of this mango juice, Dr. Kaur, as we wait for Chandra." Uma held out a tray with a cup and a plate of fruit and chapattis.

The drink quenched his thirst, and he glanced up as a young girl ran toward him. Her pigtails bounced on her back, and he didn't recognize the girl dressed in a clean pinafore until she spoke. "Dr. Kaur, it is I, Chandra."

He looked up at her, dazed. In spite of his worries over Eshana, delight filled him. How different Chandra appeared from the first time he had seen her.

"Doctor, I am in school, and only the joy of seeing you could pull me from my arithmetic which I love so very much. Are you not pleased?"

His smile came easily. "I am without speech." He tore his eyes from Chandra and glanced around him at the great number of women and children going about their business. This place, the House of Salvation, did similar work as Miriam's mission, but on a much grander scale. Schools and gardens, many brick buildings were home to the inhabitants.

He met the older woman's gaze. "Is Ramabai taking visitors? I would like to meet this great woman of India who has done so much for our country."

Though Uma's smile remained placid, her eyes shone with pride in Ramabai's accomplishments. "She has indeed done many things to bless the women and children of India, too many to count. I myself have been most happy working in the *Sharada Sadan* for discarded Hindu widows. And soon Chandra will live in the *Kripa Sadan* for girls who have been misused as she has been. There are different types of suffering, and therefore require different types of rehabilitation and education."

Her smile faded. "But Ramabai is unwell. She has asked me to convey to you her deepest concerns over Eshana."

"Do you have any idea where Eshana might have gone?"

"The train master in Poona confirmed that she did travel to Bombay. After that we were unable to discover any trace of her."

He rubbed his knee that continued to jerk with nervous energy and turned to Chandra. "Did Eshana say anything of where she might go if not to Amritsar?"

Chandra's brow puckered. "There was no place in the world Eshana wanted to be other than her mission. The last words she said were that she must be on her way home, and would write a letter to me as soon as she arrived."

His knee went still as the disappointment found its way inside. Where could he search for Eshana next? In his soul he knew she was in danger or gravely injured.

Uma pulled the girl close as Chandra began to cry. "My dear child, we have seen far too many miracles of answered prayer to become disheartened. Not a sparrow falls from a tree that Yeshu does not see."

The girl continued to sob and then straightened to wipe her eyes. "I know that Eshana wanted to go nowhere else in the world than Amritsar. She did not even wish to go home to Madras with the way her uncle had treated her."

Jai did not lift his gaze from the ground. "Madras? Her uncle? What do you know of these things, Chandra?"

Uma caressed the girl's cheek. "Come, my child, what is this you are speaking of?"

Chandra took a gulping breath. "After we arrived here, I teased Eshana one day for forgetting to bring us food on the last day we traveled by train to Bombay. She told me she had not forgotten our food, but that her uncle had found her at the last station and had hindered her. She wanted me to know that I should never accept the mistreatment of anyone, not even a relative."

Jai raised his gaze to Chandra, hoping this trickle of information would not be like a stream coming to nothing in a dry *nullah*. He leaned forward. "Tell us all you know of Eshana's uncle."

"Her uncle was angry that she did not live as a Hindu widow." The girl's eyes went wide. "I forgot. All this time I had known but I forgot. This uncle had shaken Eshana and tried to abduct her, but she had been able to free herself. Then we had come to Poona, and I was so happy here...I forgot."

Jai strove to keep his voice calm. "Did Eshana tell you where this uncle lived?"

Chandra clasped her hands together in her lap. "She said that she came from Madras close to the sea, that her family lived in a great house." The girl's brow seamed. "She called the house a name...a pretty name." She looked away from him, and started to cry. "I had not paid attention like I should."

Uma held her closer. "It is all right, my daughter. You have told us much that we did not know."

The desire to leap up and catch the first train to Madras rushed through Jai's veins, but as in the extraction of debris from a wound, he needed to move slowly. He gentled his voice. "Is there anything more you can remember about Eshana's uncle or family?"

The girl stooped to pick up a stone, a pretty stone though worthless. She rolled it between her fingers. "Gems...Eshana's uncle is a dealer in gems."

Jai's heart soared and then plummeted. There had to be hundreds of gem dealers in Madras.

Chandra had been whisked back to her classroom, and Uma promised Jai that if the girl remembered more they would send him a telegram. He promised to keep them informed about his whereabouts. He planned next to travel to Madras, even if he had to search out all the gem sellers in that great city. If only he had their family name, but Eshana had never spoken of her family.

Uma walked with him to the gate and his waiting *tonga*. "From your dress it is evident that you are a Sikh, Dr. Kaur. Yet you search for a lowly Christian woman. This is most unusual."

Heat engulfed his face. "I...am most concerned for her well-being, having had the honor of treating many patients at the mission with Eshana assisting me. She would make a fine physician."

"We have also seen this in Eshana, and have added to our prayers our desire to see her become a doctor." Uma tilted her head at him. "Eshana is also devoted to Yeshu. I am suspecting that she has told you of her Lord."

"She has, but I have also read the writings of Sundar Singh."

Uma's eyes shone. "Like our own Ramabai, Sundar is a great Indian Christian. He walks over Hind in the yellow robes of a holy man, a true *sadhu*." A smile played at the corners of her mouth. "Sundar is known for saying that a true Christian is like sandalwood, which imparts its fragrance to the axe which cuts it, without doing any harm in return. Would you not agree, Dr. Kaur, that is an apt description of our friend, Eshana?"

He smiled in return. "No truer words could ever be spoken. It is the fragrance of Eshana's holiness that urges me to see that she is safe."

Uma continued to walk by his side. "If you are aware of a whiff of holiness in Eshana, then I must correct you. It is not her holiness but the sweetness of Yeshu that fills your senses. It is the spirit of Christ that lights Eshana from within. I would encourage you, doctor, that on your travels you continue to read the writings of Sundar Singh to understand your friend."

He stopped by the waiting *tonga*. "With sadness I must confess I have...

lost my copy of Sundar's words."

"Then, doctor, wait but one moment." She rushed into one of the brick buildings and returned momentarily, a book clutched in her hands. "Please take my own copy. Like yourself, Sundar was born a Sikh. Like you I believe, when he was a young man he desired above all else to have a vision of the Almighty God. Please forgive the notations I have marked in the margins."

He thanked her and bowed over his hands to her. "You have blessed me with kindness."

She watched him climb into the *tonga*. "We will be praying for your search, that Eshana will be soon found. Also, Dr. Kaur, I will be praying that your desire to see the Lord with your own eyes will be fulfilled."

A tremor rippled through him as the *tonga* pulled along the road. It was clear Uma of this Christian mission desired to see him converted to her faith. This did not offend him. He had long known of Eshana's desire for the same thing, just as he had wished she would become a Sikh.

What sent an arrow of fear into his heart was the sensation that he was being unceasingly pursued by someone other than these gentle women. Someone far greater. His mind balked at this. It could not be the universal God who sought him...who urged him to read the writings of this yellow-robed *sadhu* by the name of Sundar.

Yet what if it was? If the true *avatar* of God was Yeshu, he would have no choice but to surrender. And he would lose all. His family. His culture. His home.

20

Ruchi's wedding week would be over today. A week of celebration and only once Eshana had seen the child. If it had not been for the lowly servant, Vanji, remembering Eshana at last and bringing her food yesterday, she would have fainted. Her stomach hurt with hunger still, but she was well.

She must take no chances though. The servants would not bother to boil the water she drank as most likely they never thought to boil their own. The need to at least strain her water was of great importance now that the rains had started to diminish. The cholera was not carried on the air, but it swam in the river mud and floods caused by the monsoons.

Eshana's hunger pangs fled at the sound of Ruchi's bare feet pattering up the crumbling staircase. The little one ran along the parapet to the accompaniment of doves cooing and mina birds squawking.

They grasped hands through the stonework. "I have missed you, gem of my heart."

Ruchi's sari, the blue of a bird's egg, fluttered in the warm breeze. Rosebuds were woven through her hair along with pearls. "Oh I have been busy, very, very busy. So many people wanted to pat my head and tell me stories." Her eyes grew round. "Eshana, Yeshu answered our prayer. We did not run out of food, and *Amma* was most happy. There are some who have eaten so much they are ill today."

Eshana jutted her chin up. "How are these people ill? Is it a fever, or does their stomach hurt?"

"It is a fever to be sure, and their stomachs."

"Ruchi, my princess, you must stay away from those who are ill. Do you remember what I told you, to have the cooks boil your water?" It may only be as Ruchi thought, stomach ailments when people had eaten too much rich food. *Please, Lord, let it be this.*

"Yes, yes, I remember." The child pouted. "But I am telling you, this sickness is only from the guests eating too many sweets. It was as we had prayed—there was plenty of *payasam* with cashews on top and coconut *burfi*."

Eshana reached out and pinched Ruchi's nose. "You are most wise, but all the same do as I ask. And will you be doing something for me? The servants took away my good *sari*. Do you know where there is an old ream of silk that no one wears any longer?"

"Are you getting tired of your widow sari?"

"I need silk to cleanse my drinking water."

"How can you clean water with silk when it is water that is used to clean silk?"

"Bring me a sari, and I will show you. But let us talk of more wonderful things. Did you meet your groom?"

Ruchi pursed her small pink mouth to one side. "He does not play any of the games I like. He stuck his nose in the air, so I did not bother with him. I am glad I do not have to see this bothersome boy until I am a little older."

"How old will you be when you go to live with your husband's family?"

"*Appa* says I can go when I turn ten."

Eshana's chest went tight. Ten was too young to fully become a wife.

"That is a long time away." Ruchi did not notice her sudden quiet. "But soon you must come out of there, Eshana. *Amma* and *Appa* are happy that my wedding is done, they will be happy to listen to you. I am getting bored talking to you through this window." She stamped her foot.

Eshana could not help but laugh at the small bundle of fury, shaking her bangles and jewels so that she tinkled and clattered like a wind chime.

"I am especially bored that my husband's relatives will be leaving today. I should go down and say my good-byes. If I did not want to leave my *amma* I would like to go to Madras with them and to the Jasmine Palace."

Eshana's heart ceased to beat. *The Jasmine...*

She let the child prattle, and lifted her hand to smooth her throat. "Ruchi, tell me about your groom, his name and his family."

"Chadi is the son of my father's cousin Mohana, but she is one of the people who has become sick and..."

Mohana. Eshana placed the back of her hand against her mouth. Mohana was the name of her mother's younger sister, her young and pretty aunt who lived in the Jasmine Palace...with *amma* and her own *appa*.

Ruchi's attention had been taken up by something below, beyond the garden. "Oh, I must go, Eshana. My relatives are leaving."

Eshana reached through and took Ruchi's hand. "Wait but a moment. Tell me, dearest one, did Mohana's sister, your auntie Sumitra and her husband Ganan, attend your wedding?"

Ruchi's eyes sparkled. "Uncle Ganan is one of my favorites. He told me stories, and Auntie Sumitra held me on her lap and sang to me. Somehow my wedding made her sad, and I saw her wiping tears away when she cuddled me."

A roaring filled Eshana's ears. *Amma...Appa* had been here. She squeezed her eyes shut. *Amma, oh Amma, were you crying for me?*

"Uncle Harish will be staying here for a few days—I do not like him as much—not the way I like Auntie Sumitra. But I must leave you, Eshana, to say good-bye to my relatives."

Eshana made her voice small when she wanted to cry out. "Ganan and Sumitra are still here?"

"They are getting into the *jutka* to go to the train. Mohana must be well enough to travel."

The child peered at her through the stonework. "Are you ill, Eshana? You have gone very quiet and pale, like Mohana did this morning." She looked closer and traced her finger along Eshana's cheek. "You are looking like one of those skinny holy men."

"I am well, gem of my heart." But she was not well. Her heart and mind raced. She could not breathe. *Oh dear Father in Heaven...help me to succeed in this.*

"Ruchi, go to Auntie Sumitra. No one else. Tell her that Eshana is here and bring her to me. Tell her that her daughter Eshana is here. Her child is here. Hurry before they leave." She could not keep the tears from falling.

The child stared at her and blinked. "Auntie Sumitra is your *amma*?"

"Yes, beloved, now go. Hurry. Please. I would have had you go sooner had I known that Sumitra was here."

Ruchi looked over the rampart. "They are coming out of the house and climbing into *jutkas* to be taken to the station."

She ran down the steps, and Eshana counted each patter of her feet, and then the quiet as Ruchi's footfalls faded. Though she could not see, she heard the child calling out as she raced through the garden below toward the courtyard. "Auntie Sumitra, Auntie Sumitra!"

The faces of those gathering by the *jutkas* were too far away to see clearly.

A cluster of people got in, and then it pulled away from the house. Too late.

Eshana's fingertips gripped the stonework and she strained on her toes to shout over the grounds. "*Amma*, it is Eshana."

Her cries disturbed the birds. The minas berated her, the doves flew off in a flurry, and parrots and parakeets screeched, drowning out her sobs. She raised her voice to its loudest and shrieked, "*Amma*! It is I, Eshana." But even she could not hear her own voice over the shrieking birds.

Was her mother one of those women sitting in the *jutka*? Did she wear the yellow sari or was she the woman in magenta? But not one woman turned to look back at this crumbling old wing. Eshana could make out the small figure of a child from this distance—Ruchi in her blue sari—being picked up in the arms of a man. And *Amma* was gone.

Eshana sank to the floor with her back to the stone wall. She buried her head in her arms and, shrinking into herself, wept. *Amma* had been so close, and God had allowed *Amma* to go before knowing she was here.

Grief engulfed her. Once she had known the Lord's comfort, but not now. Truly, He had abandoned her.

The train neared Vellore. Only another ninety miles and Jai would reach the city of Madras. The first thing he would do when he arrived would be to send a telegram to the nursing-*sahiba*, Laine. His thoughts tumbled and made the headache that had plagued him for the past hour worsen. He stood, and a wave of dizziness overtook him as he pulled from his bag the book Uma had given him. He had been reading the writings of Sundar Singh, The Yellow *Sadhu*, since he had left Poona, and this had distracted him from worrying over Eshana.

As he turned the pages he flexed his hands to rid them of the cramping in his fingers.

Sundar could not only recite the entire *Guru Granth Sahib*, the holy book of the Sikhs, but many of the Hindu scriptures as well, and the Qurán and Hadis of Islam. Yet from the night of Sundar's vision he had filled his life walking all of India and into Tibet to say that Yeshu was the fulfillment of all his desires to know God.

The Yellow *Sadhu* had his vision a few years after the loss of his mother and brother. As a young man, after washing himself of his sins one evening he had been in despair. He had vowed before God that he would throw himself under the morning train that would pass his village unless the all-pervading, incomprehensible, universal spirit did not appear to him as an *avatar*.

Another wave of dizziness blurred Jai's vision. He rubbed his eyes and read on.

That night as Sundar had prayed, a glowing globe of fire filled his room, and within that fire he had seen the face of Yeshu, the foreign god. Only the day before, Sundar had set the foreigner's Bible on fire. At first Sundar could not accept the vision, but in time he had taken on the role of ascetic preacher and shared with all who would listen that the hunger for God—in the scriptures of Hindus, Sikhs, Muslims—was fulfilled in the God-man, Yeshu.

The pain in Jai's head grew worse, and the tips of his fingers cramped again. Like Sundar, from his mother's knee he had grown aware of the One who had created all. But Jai doubted God would send him a personal vision like he had sent to Sundar. Still, a silent prayer moved through his mind. *If thou art hearing the request of my heart, show me if this vision that Sundar had was real. Show me if Yeshu is the true Master. The truth, oh Lord. Show me the truth.*

As the train neared Vellore, a sharp pain drove through his stomach. Another passenger pushed past him on the way to the toilet, but a stench sullied the air. The man had not made it in time and had soiled himself.

Another pain sliced through Jai's abdomen, and he took his own pulse. It beat slowly. A trickle of disquiet ran through his heart. Thinking back on his symptoms, the headache, the cramping in his fingers, the unwelcome truth bore down on him. He had drunk no un-boiled water, only tea from the vendors that walked the train. Had they carried a drop of water containing the crescent-shaped microbe on their hands as they had served him?

The heat of his fever chilled and burned. He stood and wavered on his feet, the muscles in his thighs trembling. He must get off this train. Madras was too far. There were hospitals in Vellore.

The train slowed. He must get off the train...here.

21

Sitting on the veranda swing close to the hibiscus, Laine tore open Abby's letter. Morning light filtered through the umbrella trees surrounding the complex. From here she could keep an eye on the treatment center. Thank God, or Rory's prayers, that with their stringent control over germs, no one from the compound or plantation had become sick. Christmas had come and gone with barely a ripple.

She had time to herself for once and clutched the pages of Abby's letter, saving the letter from Jai for last.

Abby and Geoff were desperate with worry over Eshana. Geoff would telegram a number of men he knew in the Indian Civil Service to look into Eshana's disappearance, but there was little he could do from Singapore. Except pray of course.

Laine blew out a small breath. Yes, pray of course, that was always Geoff's answer to everything. Abby's now too.

She read to the second page, and her heart lifted. Abby was going to have another baby. How delighted they must be. Abby had always wanted hordes of children running amok in the garden, and the buttons on Geoff's khaki drill uniform must be popping off.

And Miri had taken her first steps!

How she would have loved to have seen that cherub taking her first tottering strides like a drunken sailor. But this family, hers by friendship only, were too far away to savor. Abby signed off, sending all their love and reminding Laine that they included her in their daily prayers. She'd also sent one of Cam's drawings of all of them—Eshana, Miriam, Abby, Geoff, the orphans—standing outside the mission. There was even Dassah as Cam referred to two-year-old Hadassah.

A hot wind gusted as she stuffed Abby's letter in the pocket of her nursing apron and opened Jai's. He had visited the mission in Poona and was on his way to Madras.

As she read about Eshana's uncle, she stood, her hand holding the letter flopped to her side. Why on earth had Eshana kept this to herself? If she ever found her she'd give Eshana a piece of her mind. And a good shaking.

Rory stepped up the veranda stairs. "Bad news?"

She slumped down again onto the swing. "If there's one thing that frosts my morning mango, it's when people like my friend go about this world silently—and if I understand my Sunday school education correctly—bearing a burden that, if they'd only tell others, could be lightened by the sharing."

Rory sat next to her, a strange look coming over his face as he glanced toward the road to the plantation. "A great many people do that." He extended his arm to lay it along the back of the swing, his hand close to her shoulder. "Perhaps you too are guilty of that."

"Me!"

"You've shared your worry for Eshana with us. We will do what we can, but is it not time you shared your burden for your friend with the Lord?"

Her instinct, the one she'd had for years—to ignore the whole issue of faith—rose up. Didn't all roads lead to the same place? But stubborn, determined Eshana, who'd left her Hindu faith for Christ, had gone missing. And Laine wanted to pray for her, but to whom? A Hindu god? The Allah of Islam? Or God the Father, God the Son, and God the Holy Spirit, the Three in One?

Rory took her hand in his. "What's in your letter that upsets you?"

The warmth of his hand gave her comfort, a comfort she could easily fall back on like a hammock draped between two trees. "It's from Jai Kaur. But by the postage date of this letter he should have arrived in Madras days ago. He should have telegrammed by now. I'm worried, Rory. First Eshana, and now Jai."

"Then you'll have to go to Madras and see him. He sent you the name of the hotel he was going to stay at?"

"Well, yes, he did. But, Rory, I can't possibly leave you and Bella at a time like this. I won't hear of it."

He removed his spectacles. "Your friend needs you. Bella and I, along with Adam's men, can handle whatever comes. And as Adam is going to Madras for the supplies, he'll take you in the truck. I only wish I could go with you."

"Rory, I can't leave the treatment center now of all times."

She moved to stand, but he stopped her. "I insist, Laine. Take a few days and look for your friends."

Her sigh came out on a whoosh. She looked forward to going to Madras with Adam as much as chewing on a sour lemon, but she squeezed Rory's hand. "Thank you, Rory. You are a dear."

His eyes warmed, and he raised her hand to kiss it. "Remember what a dear I truly am and come back to us...to me."

She gave him a heartfelt smile. They had so much in common, camaraderie, but the look in Rory's gaze spelled out far more than camaraderie. His mouth turned up in a half smile as he dipped his head toward her. His lips softened to touch hers. The energy and sweetness took her by surprise.

She took his kind, dear face in her hands and matched his kiss, passion for passion. Perhaps one day she could have her own little Miri?

The note from Rory before breakfast asked Adam if he would take Laine to Madras. Adam hadn't planned on visiting Prince Udayan this trip, but with his mother away it made sense for him to stay at the palace. Sitting at his desk overlooking the cricket green, the idea took hold. If anyone knew anybody in Madras, it was Udayan, the youngest son of the deposed Rajah of the former princely state Sangmajure. Maybe he could help Laine.

But as Adam readied himself to collect Laine from the compound, Ranjit begged a moment of his time. Adam sent Nandi in the truck to bring Laine to the plantation while he drew in the scents of the garden's damp earth and dripping flora after this morning's short rain.

Ranjit stumped up the veranda stairs, supporting himself on his crutch. Adam waited, knowing better than to help his Indian friend. The war had robbed this tall Sikh of much more than was visible, but dignity still etched the man's sharply defined features.

Adam waited for the conversation to start as the two of them sat in cane chairs and surveyed the cricket oval where even Ranjit had played as best he could. Adam didn't have to worry about any adverse reactions on the Sikh man's part when Laine would arrive in the truck. Ranjit's fear of society never stemmed from what a British *memsahib* would think of him, and these past few weeks Ranjit had mentioned how he admired the young English nurse at the compound.

"We have been together many years, *sahib*," Ranjit began.

Adam kept his gaze riveted on the cricket pitch. "Why do you call me *sahib* when we have called each other brother for so long?"

"Today is an auspicious day, and I call you *sahib* because I wish to honor you, and thank you."

Adam shifted uneasily in his chair. "We became family, Ranjit. What more is to be said?"

The Sikh drew in the humid air. "Yes, what else could we do in the trenches when one of us died but hold each other as siblings? However, the war has been ended these three years, and today I wish to tell you that I am well enough to leave this sanctuary."

"Leave?" Adam's throat went tight. "What about your nightmares? What about...?"

Ranjit lifted his gaze to the top of the veranda's white column. "The horrors continue to torment me, as I know they torment you. But I no longer wish to cower under my cot. I have been corresponding with my wife this past year. Her letters say she does not care that I am...but a shell of a man."

It took all Adam's strength to hold back his wince, but some pinching of his features must have shown.

Ranjit's brow arched in understanding. "I would never have considered returning to her, until this outbreak of cholera thrust us from our hiding. In helping these villagers I have regained my courage."

"You never lacked courage, Ranjit."

"Ah, but I have been unwilling to accept what war has done to me. These villagers do not care if I have less of my limbs than when I was born. When I bring them water, or see to their dignity after they have been ill, they look upon me with gratitude."

Ranjit's eyes shimmered. "This has given me courage to go home. I long to see the smile in my wife's eyes. I am believing that in her embrace I will experience a faint memory of what we shared before the war, though it will not be the full flower of what we used to enjoy."

The truck drove onto the grounds, and Ranjit went quiet. After parking the vehicle, Nandi waved to Adam and strode off to the elephant lines. Laine remained inside the truck like a scolded child. And she would, wouldn't she, after his brusque orders to stay off his grounds? His face burned with mortification of how he'd spoken to her that night. She deserved so much better. Deserved someone to love her. Someone like Rory.

And Rory deserved Laine.

Pain nicked deep inside. It was the best thing, really. He'd seen how Rory had looked at Laine from the first night she'd been here. But then a man would have to be blind to not see Laine...and want her.

It would mean he'd have to convince Rory to take up his medical missionary work in another place far from here, and find another single doctor to replace him. Not an easy task. But the sacrifice of losing Rory and Bella would be worth it...if it made Laine happy.

Sunlight winked through the clouds, and a couple of parakeets squabbled in a nearby lemon tree when Laine got out of the truck. She glanced over at him, and he read her mind. Of course she wanted to see the cub. Thank goodness he'd made arrangements for that already. All the inhabitants of the plantation—at least those who wished to remain unseen—he'd advised to stay out of sight. The rest were already working on the wards at the compound, a few still managed the plantation.

Without moving from his chair he nodded in the direction of the barn, and as though they were twelve and fourteen again, she knew what he meant. He too felt lighter and younger.

With a flash of a smile she sauntered toward the barn. She was incorrigible, and he felt his lips curve in a smile. But they weren't fourteen and twelve. His smile dimmed. He just hoped Ravi would be able to keep John on the far side of the plantation so he'd not notice a woman was here.

He turned his attention to Ranjit. "With this latest crop we had planned on going to Madras to have your leg measured for your prosthesis. It's your turn."

"I will not leave until the danger of this cholera outbreak is passed."

"Then if this is your wish, you must take your portion of our earnings and have your prosthesis fitted to you in the north? There are good military hospitals in the Punjab."

"Thank you, *sahib*."

He cupped Ranjit's shoulder. "My brother, don't thank me." His voice broke. "I will miss you, my brother...more than words can say."

Ranjit glanced to the grass matting on the veranda floor. "As I will miss you." With the aid of his crutch, Ranjit stood with surprising agility and wiped his eyes. "I am thinking, my brother, that more than myself will be wanting to return to their families. You should prepare yourself, because one by one I believe the men will leave. Vishnu and Nandi and I were speaking of this last evening."

Ranjit's gaze slid away from Adam to the truck where Laine had darted from, and to the barn where she had disappeared inside. "Perhaps you too should consider that the arms of a loving wife may help you forget your sorrows."

Adam tugged the brim of his hat down to deflect the sun's rays from his eyes. "Some of the men may leave, but it will be a long time before they will. And some will never be able to face the outside world. Most of all, John. But I am glad for you, Ranjit, that you're returning to your wife. She will delight your heart, and you will bring her joy."

They embraced, and Ranjit hobbled toward the huts while Adam slipped into the den. He patted his pockets to ensure he had everything for the trip, counted the money he'd left on the desk. Having all that he would need, he was about to leave the den when a glance at the pictures lining the walls stopped him.

Most days he hardly ever looked at them, well used to the symmetry they created in this room. A symmetry he'd worked hard to create in his day-to-day life. A symmetry that the woman visiting the tiger cub in the barn was spinning into disarray.

He pulled open a desk drawer and reached into its depths. The silver-framed photograph still lay where he'd hidden it years ago, and he brought it out to hold close to the window. Sunlight fell on Laine's features, that cloud of dark hair. Throughout the war a smaller version of this picture had been tucked inside his woolen tunic as he'd trod the duckboards in the trenches, and when he'd gone out on that last patrol.

When he'd returned from England he had thrust the photograph into the drawer. Foolish now to keep her picture hidden when the warm, flesh and blood, intoxicating woman had invaded his self-made refuge. He slipped the photograph back into the drawer, feeling again the ache that never would heal.

But the den wouldn't let him leave yet. Pictures on the walls drew him. Too many of the men in these photographs were gone, their lives snuffed out by German bullets and artillery. But what, dear Lord, had they done to the enemy? How many men's lives had he destroyed with his ability as a sniper? A wave of weakness swept over him at all that had been lost. All of those he must have killed.

He lifted the photograph of him and John standing on the quad at Balliol.

And then there was Clarice.

Clarice, the girl who used to love John. Clarice who had promised to be John's wife. And Clarice who shrieked in terror when she saw John at the end of the war. The sobbing man that Adam had carried back to the convalescent home for officers was a different man from his lighthearted cousin before the war. Not studious in the least like himself, John used to be almost fey in his enjoyment of life.

With a shaking hand he replaced the photograph of himself and John into its place of prominence on the desk and left the den.

Each time he knew he would see Laine he needed to strengthen his resolve. He took his time crossing the lawn. Before he entered the barn he braced himself with the adage that had helped him through the war and after. "Greater love hath no man than this, that a man lay down his life for his friends."

He found Laine with the cub in the dimly lit pen. She was crouched down, and the tiger lolled about on the floor, exposing his stomach to her. His large, ungainly paws batted the air. The cub's playful growls harmonized with Laine's cooing as she petted and rubbed his rounded head and broad nose. At the sight of them, the wave of dizziness hit Adam again. How extraordinarily lovely she was.

When the tiger heard Adam approach, he let out his rusty rumble and jumped up to the side of the pen to scour the wooden planks with his claws.

Adam rubbed the cub's velvet head in an attempt to slow his galloping nerves with the nearness of Laine. Her fragrance. Pulling the cub's sturdy orange and black-tipped ears helped somewhat. Laine sat with her back to the wall of the pen, straw sticking to her white shirt and navy skirt, and in her hair. A look of euphoria gleamed from her eyes as she watched the tiger, while Adam's insides did a slow tumble.

"So you found Hector," he said when he found his voice.

"Hector?" The distaste on her face was almost as comical as that of the cub's. "What sort of a bally name is Hector for a tiger?" Her lips parted. "Ah...of course, Hector from Virgil's poem. Hector the protector of Troy. Yes, I suppose Hector would do for him."

Silence fell, broken only by the cub's growls and the horses munching on oats. He leaned on the half door. "You would have named him something else?"

"Certainly. Samba or Baboo. He is an Indian tiger, is he not?"

The desire to laugh swelled inside him, but it didn't erupt. All the same, he recognized the teasing note that he used to reserve for her alone. "You always did have a knack for the ridiculous. Come on out of there and tidy yourself up. You have straw sticking out of your hair, and if we want to reach Madras before dark, we should get going."

She stood, but Hector seized his opportunity, and before Adam could alert Laine, the cub stalked her from behind. His eyes grew large as he rested his weight on his hind end and made a mad, flying leap at Laine, knocking her off balance so that she fell forward onto a pile of straw with a thump.

Adam flung the door of the pen open and offered his hand. She let out a low moan, but ignored his offer of help. She had to be hurt. But the moan turned to a chortle. As she lifted her face he recognized the crinkles at the corners of her eyes, and her mouth spread in a smile. A smile that squeezed his heart.

Laughter bubbled from her. She ran her fingers through her loosened hair, and he supported her back as she stood.

"Are you hurt, Laine? Anything sprained?"

She slapped dust from her skirt. "Not at all. He's far too young to do any serious damage, even if he does think he's Shere Khan from the *Jungle Book*."

"True, but don't tell Hector that, it will only hurt his feelings."

"I wouldn't dream of insulting him, I assure you." She grimaced slightly, her chuckle fading to nothing as she looked past him, over his shoulder at the barn wall where nothing but a few tools hung.

He continued to support her back. "Are you sure you're not hurt, Laine?" His own voice suddenly lacked any strength, his fingers remembering the small of her back through her blouse. How many times had he placed his hand there to guide her into church, a dinner party, onto the dance floor?

She looked about to speak, but whatever it was, she left unsaid, preferring to stare at the dusty wooden wall. He couldn't move his hand from her back. The only movement between them was the tiger cub prowling at their feet, sensuously entwining his body between them and around their legs, mewling for their attention.

"I'm fine, Adam," Laine said at last and raised her gaze to meet his.

Warm brown eyes thickly fringed with dark lashes stole the breath from him. His fingers quivered with the desire to trace the line of her cheek. That pert nose. Touch those lips that smiled more often than not.

But John would be back from the other side of the plantation within the hour. John could face down an enemy soldier, a king cobra, a host of other predators, but the sight of a beautiful woman like Laine would send him into a tailspin.

His hand dropped to his side, and he sputtered, "We should be going. It's a long drive to Madras."

Hating the coolness in his tone, he turned away from that sherry-brown gaze that used to enchant him. He didn't want this kind of enchantment. He mustn't want it. He'd made a promise. And he'd keep that promise even if it killed him.

22

They reached the spacious city of Madras, a mixture of classical, Victorian, and Indian architecture, just as twilight began to gray.

Laine could almost feel Adam's relief when he drove the truck onto the grounds of Prince Udayan's palace. She and Adam had hardly spoken during the trip. He had set the mood for the journey when he'd reverted to that frosty tone of his back at the plantation this morning. For a moment there in the barn she'd thought he'd drummed up the audacity to kiss her. And then nothing. He'd given her the cold shoulder again as if she were chopped mutton.

Well, if he was going to play this game of Ping-Pong with her emotions, then she'd have to do a better job of protecting her heart. She wasn't made of iron.

Adam must have been to his friend's home before. Even his interest brightened and lifted the gloom that permeated the truck cab. As the sun set, the turrets and central dome of the prince's home appeared like a cutaway against a lilac sky, and she let out a small gasp of pleasure. Along the drive of crushed coral, fountains splashed from white marble spouts, linked by narrow canals. She sat up straighter as the drive led to a mansion only slightly larger than Buckingham Palace.

She no longer cared that they'd simmered in silenced for the entire afternoon and blurted out, "Your friend the prince has quite the little cottage to call home, and overlooking the Bay of Bengal to add to its simple charms."

A smile softened his mouth. "Yes, Udee—that's what we called him while we were all at Oxford—Udee has an undeniably beautiful home."

"Yes, Udee, I remember the name now. From your letters."

A shade of their former coolness settled between them, but only for a moment, and Adam broke the silence. "This mansion is a mere summer house compared to the sandstone bastion belonging to Udee's father. Now you could fit a couple of soccer fields into his father's palace, tucked away within the ranges of the Western Ghats." A fleeting grin crossed his face. "But the old Maharajah likes having his youngest son close to the pulse of commerce in Madras, and not living at home with the rest of the extensive family. A very non-Indian idea."

"Very non-Indian indeed. I take it your friend Udee has a way with money."

"Has the Midas touch, that one. Since the time his father sent him to Eton and then to Oxford, Udee's dabbled in business—automobile stocks, rubber plantations, and a raft of other products that aided the war effort. He's done well for the family's royal coffers."

Adam stopped the truck at the arched front of the palace. As soon as he helped her out, a rather dapper Indian man in his early thirties, wearing an impeccable gray tweed suit and an Eton tie, ran down the marble stairs. A small mob of servants in Indian livery followed him.

He extended one hand to grasp Adam's, and the other to clap him on the back. "By jove, old chap, about time you got here. It's been simply ages." A staccato of crisp vowels tripped off the man's tongue.

If she closed her eyes she could imagine him as British upper crust. He was also the right age to be a classmate of Adam's. This had to be Udee.

With a chuckle Adam grasped Udee's hand. "I thought I'd take you up on that open-ended invitation. Well to be frank, I have a favor to ask."

"What? You're not here to catalogue my library like you did last time you visited?" Udee's gaze left Adam and traveled to her, and the laughter in his eyes heated to molten black. "Adam, you absolute rotter, you never breathed a word in any of your letters that you'd rejoined the human race." He advanced toward Laine, joined his palms and bowed.

"Don't go rushing your fences, dear chap," Adam admonished. "This lady is in need of that favor. Udee meet Laine Harkness. Laine meet Udee."

Laine returned the prince's greeting by bowing over her own hands. "Your Royal Highness."

"Laine Harkness?" Udee's brows rose. "*The* Laine Harkness?"

Adam sent him a scowl. "May we go inside, Udee?"

With a wicked smile the prince ushered them through a threshold three feet deep with Hindu gods engraved on brass doors. "Certainly, old son, I'm sure you could do with tea."

"I could absolutely kill for a cup," she said with more gusto than she felt, not knowing what to make of Adam's scowl when Udee had recognized her. It seemed the prince knew something of her and Adam's past. She felt her own brows draw together. Maybe Udee knew even more than she did, such as why Adam ended their engagement.

Udee sent Adam another laden glance as they trailed along to a reception room big enough for a small army. She arched her neck to take in a domed ceiling encrusted with colored tiles and semi-precious stones, where a mosaic of a blue-faced Krishna playing his flute and dancing with maidens filled the ceiling. Two marble staircases with brass railings curved inward from the two wings and converged in the foyer where another marble and gold fountain splashed.

Their host sent a number of servants off with instructions and led her and Adam through to an intimate sitting room that faced the bay. Kashmiri carpets covered the floor, and open French doors offered a glimpse of a white balustrade that projected over the beach. From there infiltrated the sound of pounding surf and rattling palm fronds.

"They say some nasty weather's brewing out on the Indian Ocean. I must say, Adam, you certainly pick your times for a visit." Udee relaxed on a settee of red velvet, but his arched brow and the tapping of one finger gave evidence as to how avid he was for Adam to explain. The glances he shot at her showed only too clearly what sparked his curiosity. Her.

Adam rubbed a hand over his jaw. "How bad do they expect this storm to be?"

"Too early to say, really." Again, Udee flashed an all-too-knowing smile that earned another glower from Adam.

A servant brought in a tray of tea, milk, and sugar, English style.

Udee inclined his head toward Laine, his arm draped along the back of the settee. "As my wife is resting, would you be mother and pour?"

She picked up the heavy silver teapot as requested. Might as well put her hands to use, to ease the tension of unspoken conversation the two men seemed to be having. Or more accurately, the questions brimming from Udee's eyes and Adam's refusal to budge and answer them.

"After tea you'll need time to refresh yourselves," Udee continued. "The servants are making up a room for you, Laine, in the north wing. At dinner you'll meet my wife, but for now I'd like to hear what's brought you and Adam to Madras. Only something of considerable magnitude would drag him away from his plantation and taking care of—"

"It's Laine's friend," Adam interjected far too quickly.

He began to lay out for Udee what Laine had shared with him about Eshana, and all the necessary details. As he did, whatever lightheartedness Laine had been feeling upon entering the mansion dissolved.

Udee leaned forward to take his cup from her and stir sugar into it. A frown replaced his mischievous expression. "I'll get some people on that straightaway. If they are a wealthy family of gem dealers it shouldn't take too long to find them, but if they're sellers of cut-rate stones then we'll have a harder time."

Laine glanced from Adam to Udee. "Eshana once said that she grew up in a beautiful house. She called it...the Jasmine Palace."

The deepening frown on Udee's face didn't elicit much hope. "Madras is a large city, and we Indians tend to name our houses. I know of several Jasmine Palaces. But do leave it with me." He quirked a brow at Adam, his good humor instantly restored. "And you, old son, I assume it's per the usual, with your mother out of town you'll want to stay in my lowly beach bungalow instead of the house?"

Adam nodded. "If I may. I suppose this storm won't hit during the short time we'll be here."

"They don't expect it to." Udee grinned. "Don't suppose you have time for a spot of cricket tomorrow?"

Adam chuckled. "We have medical supplies to pick up, and then we must pursue whatever your line of inquiry opens. Sorry, old friend. No time to play."

She was still savoring the sound of Adam's chuckle when Udee said, "Quite right. Quite right. Playacting at Sherlock Holmes will have to satisfy me. And while you're here, I want you and Laine to take advantage of my home. Treat it as yours since we're practically blood brothers."

Adam attempted to interrupt, but Udee rushed to speak over him. "Did he tell you that story, Laine? Adam's family and mine go quite far back. Shortly after the eighteen fifty-seven uprising, his grandfather, a civil servant, did his best to convince England not to take over our state, but it was no good, and we were absorbed into British India. My ancestor wanted to reward him for services rendered as we of the following generations live out our lives in deposed splendor."

"The land was enough of a reward, Udee." Adam seemed to have difficulty controlling his grin, and she found herself grateful to the charming Indian man for doing what she and others seemed incapable of—making Adam smile.

She looked up into Adam's face with wonder. "I knew your grandfather was in the civil service, but never knew about the plantation."

Udee clapped Adam on the back. "Well, my ancestor had his way of thanking your ancestor, old boy. But I'll really never be able to pay you a big enough reward for your friendship. Who else was there to talk to at Oxford about cricket test matches going on in Bombay or Allahabad? Or convince the school cook to add spice to my meals when I was suffering from homesickness? So I insist you enjoy yourselves tomorrow."

The prince's mobile smile glimmered like quicksilver. "I know it's many years since you enjoyed Madras, Adam, but one can surely make time to take a lady to lunch at the Connemara Hotel."

Laine turned away to study the brocade on the arm of the settee as if her life depended on it. She'd rather wear a hair shirt and eat wild locusts than go to the Connemara for lunch with Adam.

Laine had brought only one dress, the one she'd worn the night Adam had so rudely ordered her from his barn. He never had explained who lurked in the shadows, and Rory had remained mum on the subject as well. But her dress of white voile would have to do no matter how elegantly the prince's wife would be attired. She fussed with the sash at the dropped waist of her frock.

The room issued to her had given her a surprise when she'd first entered it. Not Indian at all, but as English as a manor in Sussex with a rosewood four-poster bed and chintz-covered chairs with matching drapes. Charming, yes, but somehow disappointing. She'd hoped to sleep in something more Indian. The lovely young servant who'd helped her with her dressing and hair was a delight though. She'd brushed Laine's hair to a gloss and wound it into perfectly bobbed waves.

Laine's heels clicked on the marble stairs that curved downward to the reception hall, feeling the eyes of a host of servants. Above the wide, spiraling staircase and fountain hung a chandelier of gold and crystal. Now this was Indian, breathtaking in its extravagance.

In the equally elaborate dining room, reams of sheer draperies hung from marble pillars. Low satin divans created a sensuous backdrop, and lamps lit the room, shining off the deeply polished table.

Udee's wife stood beside him, and Laine felt a twinge of awe. These two people in their finery could have stepped out of an Indian court from a much earlier century. Udee had replaced his English style suit with a long, high-buttoned coat of white silk and black trousers. A neat, smallish turban perched jauntily on his head.

His wife, whom he introduced as Innila, wore a silk *sari* of turmeric yellow with gold thread and emeralds swirling along its border. She had tucked the end of her *sari* into the back of her blue-black hair with a silver comb. Below the hem, her bare feet were ornamented with gold and emerald toe rings. Against this stunning display of the regal East, Laine felt almost dowdy in her best frock that had been the pink of fashion in London, Paris, and Bombay.

But though these two looked like they'd stepped out of India's ancient past, their confident smiles carried traces of the modern world.

Adam stood by the windows listening to the surf. He had dressed once again in dark slacks and white dinner jacket, his bow-tie only slightly askew. For a moment she wished she could take his arm, but she wasn't sure if it was because two pairs made up this foursome, or if in the company of Udee and his wife, she felt so terribly commonplace.

Adam's eyes lifted to hers, and he sent her a half smile. A cool breeze blew in from the bay, but she went warm. His gaze shot from her dress to her hair, and her breath hitched at the darkening appraisal in his blue eyes. But then his face flushed to match the heat in hers, and he glanced away, pretending great interest in the roiling waves outside.

Innila took Laine by the arm, and they crossed to the windows, not two feet from Adam, and she strove to settle her pulse. She was not going to have a repeat of this morning in the barn, imagining a warmth from him that was no longer there. The flame he'd held for her had died years ago.

From this side of the house Laine could see a long, covered walkway, its roof supported by pillars that led to a small pavilion acting as vanguard against the waves.

Innila's voice broke through the tumult of her thoughts. "It is a lovely spot to sit and enjoy the rising sun, but too dangerous with these waters to venture there tonight."

They turned to their places at table, and Adam held out a chair for Innila. Udee did the same for Laine. Four silver *thalises* were set on the table. When they were served, Laine's nerves calmed somewhat and she began to eat of the *patchadis* and *sambars, rasams* and curds.

Udee offered Laine a dish of raisins. "My wife and I are quite modern, as I'm sure you've noticed. It's not that we do not worship in our Hindu ways, but I think that Gandhi chap is a man we should listen to. Much of India's old traditions are only that, traditions, and many of them should be thrown out with the new India."

Adam quirked a brow and smiled. "At long last you've switched your interests from polo to politics. I'm pleased to hear it."

Udee leaned forward, urged on by Adam's encouragement. "Well, there is one thing on which I disagree with Gandhi. You can rest assured I'm not one of those Indians bellowing for independence. I'd like us to remain under English rule, but with better treatment for our people. The British have given us so much, taking us out of centuries of warring principalities and uniting us under one king."

"And making India one strong country." Innila peeled an orange with long tapered fingers.

Adam inclined his head toward Innila. "Yes, India is now one strong country, and if the Indian people ever do decide on independence, your numbers are so great you could very well simply ask us British to go home."

"Don't be ridiculous, Adam," Udee interjected. "You—go home? To where? India is your home."

Adam's eyes held Udee's. "There's the rub, old friend, I love India, her people, the scents and rhythms of this land." His glance traveled to reach Laine's. "Without India, I don't know where home is." He didn't remove his gaze from hers—a gaze that for once didn't have all the answers.

At the periphery of her vision a servant poured water into a glass. Udee said something she couldn't catch. Innila spoke, drawing Adam's focus reluctantly from her. But the heat that Adam's questioning gaze had brought her—like sun-drenched silk against her skin—enveloped her.

The shining moment couldn't last. She shook her head slightly as reality returned. He didn't need her. Didn't even trust her on his plantation, never mind with what was going on in his life. She'd imagined that bewildering thirty seconds just now, because his features were once again set in that studious look as he listened to Innila. A lock of hair fell over his forehead. He wasn't aware of it—just like the old days—too intent on who he listened to, or what he was reading.

Udee's wife concentrated on the piece of fruit with the grace of a queen.

"In my opinion the day of Indian independence will surely come."

Laine glanced up at this. "Do you wish for that?"

"The issue is not what I wish, but what I believe India will decide upon." She sent a pointed glance at Udee. "I, too, am pleased that my husband has taken an interest in politics, as I have for a long time been listening to Gandhi and the Indian Congress. With Udee's years in England, it has taken him a long time to be willing to listen to those who are speaking on behalf of our people. But if independence is desired, then India will need her educated men—like my husband—to help the people keep cool heads."

She rose then. "Come, let us retire to the drawing room, away from this talk of discord that always seems to plague the best intentions."

The four of them strolled to another parlor, this one away from the sound of frothing surf. A servant distributed hot tea while Laine pressed a handkerchief to the back of her neck. The air felt like soup. She held back a smile as Innila's toes curled for heat into the fur of a tiger skin on the floor.

She didn't want to ask who had bagged this tiger, but Adam must have read her mind, again. "Udee killed this when he was a young man with his father." His tone held an apology. "A sort of manhood right. I haven't shot a tiger since before the war."

Laine set her teacup on a nearby brass table. "What about Hector's mother?" Poor baby, how was the little cub doing tonight in that barn full of shuffling noises and shadows?

"I didn't shoot Hector's mother. Didn't have the stomach. Nandi managed to get a shot into her, and I can only hope she died quietly somewhere because if she hasn't, she's a danger."

Udee's head popped up. "What's this, a wounded tiger in your neck of the woods? I should polish off the old Enfield and come out your way. But a wounded tiger isn't much sport."

"She must be got rid of speedily. I've been out for days at a time hunting her, but she's eluded us."

"If anyone could bag that tiger it would be you, Adam. Jolly good shooting you did for the sniper division during the war. Your cousin, John, was a fine sniper as well, as I remember. Got several medals for that, didn't he?"

Udee didn't notice the flush rising up Adam's face and continued talking as he lolled against a low-slung divan. Innila went to the corner where a long stringed instrument made of wood, an Indian *veena*, stood against the wall. Innila lifted the *veena* and sank down to the Kashmiri carpet at

Udee's feet. The long neck of the instrument rested on her left shoulder, and the wooden body on her lap. She began to pluck the strings and play a composition that resonated with the pulse of India.

Udee cast a glance of pleasure at his wife while the three of them listened to the haunting sounds that took them back hundreds of years.

A while later Udee began to speak in a low tone as if the music pulled him back to memories within his own lifetime. He reminisced about his and Adam's school days—how they outdid each other in pranks and bested each other on the cricket pitch.

A chuckle reverberated from Udee. "Adam, do you remember what we used to call your cousin—old beetroot John. He was a ripping cricketer, but how he blushed over everything. Remember how ghastly red he went the day he had to give an oral paper on *A Shropshire Lad*. How'd that bit go that we all had to memorize... 'Into my heart on air that kills, from yon far country blows—'"

"'What are those blue remembered hills,'" Adam took up the poem, startling Laine, but not Udee, who sat back to listen, all laughter drained from him.

"'What spires, what farms are those?'" Adam's voice shook, but gained new strength in the next stanza. "'That is the land of lost content, I see it shining plain. The happy highways where I went...and cannot come again.'"

Adam went silent with a faraway look in his eyes. Like Udee, he was not in this room, but somewhere in the past with their classmates. A tenderness softened the grim look she'd become used to these past weeks. A tenderness that spoke of love.

Her heart contracted as Adam's voice lightened. "The lads were marvelous, weren't they?" His voice broke. "But they're gone now."

Udee's tone drifted along with Adam's. "Some of them came back... ghosts...barely alive, and broken beyond all repair. It's not the men with lost limbs that disturb me so much. A great deal can be done with a false leg or arm. Most of those soldiers get on with their lives. It's those who lost their faces." He shuddered. "Even with reconstructive surgery they're still frightful. No wonder they create their own communities to hide away from others."

The air in the room became too close for comfort.

Udee didn't notice Adam grow pale under his tan. Or perhaps Udee mistook Adam's grief to match his own for the men they used to know.

Tears glinted in Udee's eyes. "On my latest trip to England I saw these blue benches, the blue paint indicating that the man sitting on those benches would be distressing to look at." He broke off when he caught something in Adam's rigid stare and white face. Udee ducked his head. "Right, totally unsuitable discussion for the ladies." When he glanced up at Adam, his gaze held a silent appeal.

Laine sat wooden. While she no longer loved Adam, jealously sliced through her. It might have hurt less if he'd turned from her to another woman, but she could never compete with his love for his friends, his classmates who had been wounded or died in the trenches. And that he'd never trusted her to share that heartache.

23

How many hours had passed? Days? Since leaving the train all had been lost in a vortex of sickness. Jai vaguely remembered falling to the platform. People shrank from him as he'd stumbled toward the station. Their hands had thrust him away, and he remembered the shame of losing control of all bodily function.

He'd found his way outside again to the platform...and fallen.

Then the brisk voice of a woman—in a language...an accent—not Indian. A jolting ride in a cart, and a place that smelt of disinfectant... Some kind of hospital. People lying in cots near him. People with streaks of blue and purple on their skin. Their eyes rolling back wild into their sockets. Their features sharpened to strange masks.

His own body writhing in pain. He remembered his hands—they too had turned that telling shade of blue. The wrinkling of his fingers.

The clang of a tin kidney basin—he recognized that as it fell to a solid floor. And clean sheets. A clean smell of soap. He had no strength to lift his hand to see the color. No doubt his blood type O had predisposed him to the sickness. But sleep covered him. A dark cloak of reprieve. If God so willed, he would survive the villainy of this illness that had struck him.

Jai awoke. This time his eyes remained open. How much time had passed? He became aware of each ache. It was not the pain that had knifed him in two, that had sucked all moisture from his body and expelled it with violence. The bruising pain he felt now was that of a body that had been emptied of all. Each muscle wrenched. A small pinch on his arm intrigued him.

This time he had the strength to withdraw his arm from beneath the sheet. The terrible blue had gone from the skin, and his hand had returned to a shade closer to normal. And the pinching on his arm came from an area where he had been attached to an intravenous drip.

"So, you're awake," a woman said to him in English but with an American accent. "Do you speak Tamil or Hindi?"

"Hindi. But I am comfortable speaking in English." His throat throbbed from the exertion of the past day...days? "How long?"

"Two days. You collapsed outside the Vellore train station. I was getting off the Madras Mail the same time as you, and you practically landed at my feet. I could have taken you to the government hospital which would have been closer, but after reading the paperwork in your valise to determine who you were, I discovered you are a doctor. I preferred to have my staff treat you."

The woman sat on a chair by his bed, and he could see her more clearly. A woman—not young but not old—he could not tell the age of women who were not Indian. She smiled down at him from a kind face framed with white hair.

"Your staff?" He moved his head to look across a room that contained only a few beds.

"You're in The Mary Tabor Schell Hospital, and nearby, our medical school for women. I'm Dr. Ida—Dr. Ida Scudder. You're not in the main wards with our female patients, naturally." Her tone became brisk as she stood to leave. "We'll chat later. I'll have one of the nurses bring you an oral solution to help you regain your strength. In the meantime, rest. You've beaten the cholera, Dr. Kaur."

He glanced at a bureau as Dr. Ida left the room. There sat his medical valise. Somehow in his struggle to get off the train he had kept hold of one of his bags. The other had been lost. Eventually someone would have taken mercy on him at the train station and transported him to the government hospital. But as he took in the cleanliness and order of this place, gratitude filled him. This lady doctor with the white hair fascinated him. So too did this medical school for Indian women.

After punching his pillow into shape, Adam gave up on sleep and left the bed. It was almost dawn anyway, and surf assaulted the beach. He opened the bamboo shutter. Rising winds rattled the palms, making them sound like sabers clashing, and played havoc with the bungalow's thatched roof. He might as well get dressed.

He worked his way against the wind as waves pounded the beach. Sand hissed as the surf ebbed. He hadn't bothered with shoes and walked barefoot along the hard-packed shore, the tang of salt on his lips.

The pillared walkway from the house to the beach lay ahead. Silver light on the horizon lifted the marble pavilion out of the night. Yet the gray dawn brought out the greenness of the trees and grass, reds and purples of flowers, the white sand, painting everything a deeper hue.

A single figure in jodhpurs and shirt stood within the pavilion that jutted out on the rocks like the prow of a ship.

A woman stared out at the bay and the clouds that shrouded the rising sun.

Laine leaned against the pillar farthest out so that waves splashed upwards and soaked her. Was she a woman or a child? She had the best of both. As a child she'd always acted the bossy little woman that he'd found endearing. When he'd returned from Oxford and found she'd become a woman, he held her child-like enjoyment of everything under the sun equally endearing.

But the Laine standing in that pavilion was not a girl. She was a woman who'd seen as many atrocities as he had in the trenches. The tide had turned. And he fought against it. *Dear God, help me fight against it.*

He started to veer away when she saw him. A friend would raise their arm and hail the other. Neither of them did. If they couldn't be lovers, married, then they couldn't be friends. From childhood on they'd been meant for each other, two parts of one whole, and friendship could never fill the gap. He'd always known this, though she had not.

Laine took the steps down to the beach. Though he was standing, the sense of falling came over him.

The sky beyond her showed that strange color of clouds amassing above the ocean. Clouds with that greenish tint that meant a cyclone was on its way.

Her dark hair lay tousled on her shoulders. Her feet, bare. Those tea-colored eyes reflected the hunger of the growing clouds behind her. A wave crashed on the shore, sending up a spray while a kingfisher flitted out, flashing the blue of its wings. And a current of his former passion for her sluiced through him.

She stopped two feet from him, and they stared at each other, the moment stretching out forever until she lifted her hand in a helpless gesture of defeat. Her small indication of unhappiness crushed his heart.

He must be mad, but he took a step toward her and reached for her shoulders, and the next thing he knew she was in his arms.

She clung to him. For a moment he resisted. His mind clanged to stop this madness. But there was no resistance in Laine, only the warmth of a woman who always gave all. In a heartbeat they sought each other's mouths, and he lost himself, a man parched with thirst savoring the sweetness of her lips. How could he have lived so long without...

She moaned against his mouth as his hand moved to the small of her back, and he drew her closer. Her hands wound their way along his shoulders, her fingers in his hair.

The ground beneath his feet became unsteady, and he lost all sensation of the world around him. All but Laine. Intoxicating Laine who drowned out his every thought, every shred of reason.

Their kisses turned slower, he felt her lips against his unshaven cheek and jaw, and he found her mouth again.

The oncoming tide swirled at their feet and ankles, soaking their trousers.

Dear God! What am I doing? He pulled his lips from hers and stared at the foam-flecked surf as it retreated.

She resisted as he removed her from him as gently as he could. Her face remained soft with the answering passion to his as the space between them grew.

He shook his head as he dropped his hands, and heard the quiver in his voice. "I'm sorry. I'm sorry, Laine. I shouldn't have..."

Even in the gray dawn, the horrible pain of rejection robbed her face of all color. Her gaze fell, and those long dark lashes hid her eyes from him. She wouldn't cry. Not Laine. But he knew her too well, and the pain in her shuttered eyes kicked him in the gut. He stood rigid, waiting for her to slap him as she should.

Her throat moved as she swallowed with difficulty. "You're right, Adam, you shouldn't have done that. Nor I." Her words came out full-throated. Raw. "Because nothing has changed, has it?" Her gaze lifted to his.

"Nothing has changed. I'm—"

"Don't say you're sorry again. I couldn't bear it. In fact, it's best we both pretend this never happened. It didn't happen. Do you understand? It just didn't." She turned from him and walked back the way she'd come. Not in a flurry of emotion, but with precise steps as if she were made of glass and would break with any jarring movement.

He didn't follow her. Just stared at nothing and raised a trembling hand to his brow. He turned and, without the ability to see, retraced his steps to the bungalow. He slumped into a chair on the veranda and threw his head back to stare at the thatched ceiling. His mind struggled to make sense. Somehow he had to get through this time in Madras with her. Get them both back to the compound. Maybe there they could pretend that interlude never happened, this interlude of...madness...and an emotion he dared not name.

Because as she had said, nothing had changed. He would always hunger for Laine, but nothing had changed.

No fishermen were out on the sea later that morning. Laine watched the skies. She and Adam had left Udee's palace early this morning after that... episode on the beach, to get on with the task at hand. She fought to put the image of Adam and her, and the wretched sensations, out of her mind.

Few travelers ventured out on the trams that rattled down the center of the road to the harbor. The rain had started again, and this time with a vengeance. At least the pounding of the showers drowned the silence between them.

The first part of the morning he waited for her in the truck as she darted into each hotel in Madras to see if a Dr. Jai Kaur had registered, but with no success. Later she and Adam hardly spoke while at the Indian Medical Services they purchased crates of saline and various other medicines. Under the arch of the covered entrance, she turned away as Adam stored the supplies in the bed of the truck and covered the crates with tarp, securing them tightly with rope. Neither one of them wanted to look at each other and silently ask, *now what*?

"Do you think Udee is back yet with any news?" she managed at last to get out.

"I wouldn't expect so." He glanced at his wristwatch. "Can you think of anywhere else we can look for this doctor?"

She shook her head, and he held the door open for her to get inside the truck.

Once inside himself, his fingers drummed on the steering wheel. "Well we can't sit here all day." He pushed the starter button. "Look, I'm famished. I don't suppose you'd care for tea at the Connemara? There's nothing we can do until Udee gets back, and God-willing with some news of Eshana."

There were innumerable restaurants in a city the size of Madras, even with a storm on the way, and the only eatery he could suggest was the Connemara. But her heart squeezed tight, and all she could clip out was a blistering, "Fine."

The uneasy silence descended as he drove through Madras. Outside the colonial white façade of the Connemara's portico Adam placed his truck in the charge of the hotel valet. They found their way to the dining room overlooking an English garden, and again that sense of déjà vu hammered at her. They used to come here every Sunday afternoon for tea before the war.

Few patrons had come out today, but tables were arranged the same as they'd been on her last outing with Adam, white linen cloths, sparkling crystal and china. The chasm of the last eight years hadn't happened. But it had. In a few days it would be 1922. She shook her head. The last eight years *had* passed, and the man at her side wasn't smiling like he'd done back then. A muscle ticked high on his jaw.

Ceiling fans whirred above, moving the sultry air as their waiter seated them. They ordered sandwiches, cream cakes, and a pot of tea, and avoided looking at each other.

A small quartet played. One or two couples danced on the floor, and she wished with all her heart that it was Rory sitting across from her. Kind, older Rory, who didn't turn her inside out with longing, and who certainly didn't treat her the way Adam did.

He'd said he was famished. Yet after fiddling with half a sandwich for twenty minutes, he shifted his cup to one side, and she bolted to her feet, saying she needed to freshen up in the water closet before they returned to the palace. The humid air pressed against her, and she dampened a cloth under the cold water faucet to dab her neck and face, tidied her hair. She had to get out of this hotel, out of Madras. She couldn't bear another moment here with him.

When she returned, he stared out at the garden which was being beaten by rain. Something about the way he sat, his entire person mesmerized by the patch of red roses outside stopped her from moving forward.

Monsoon rain streamed down on the garden, a silver-blue silk crushing the roses and scattering their scarlet petals in a small river of water. Then she caught the notes of a song from before the war.

Adam turned to her. The creases from his nose to his mouth or on his brow had deepened slightly over the past eight years. Yet a tremulous quality touched his mouth, and with it the promise of his smile that used to make her ache. His eyes captured hers with the old yearning.

Behind her, a murmur of voices broke in, but she couldn't move as Adam's gaze imprisoned her. His eyes roamed her face, her hair, her mouth. For all the world, she could swear he still loved her. Why then...? When his eyes met hers, the Adam she used to know, that scholarly, sensitive man was there. As if there'd been no war. As if no time had passed. As if he'd just come home from Oxford, and there was no one else in the world—

A swirl of wind outside, a shudder of thunder, and a moment later the electricity shut off. A disconcerted mutter of people rushed from their chairs, wandering between them, severing the gaze they shared.

She thought she heard Udee's voice and looked around, listening to the chatter of the musicians and waiters. The few other patrons gathered their belongings. And Udee's voice lifted above the rest.

He stood at the entrance to the dining room and strode toward them. "I've got good news. I've found Eshana's family. But we'd better hurry. There is a cyclone developing out on the Indian Ocean. I say, old chap, we're in for a bit of a thin time."

24

Laine could hardly hear what Udee had to report over the rain beating on the car roof. Udee's driver drove his Rolls Royce along the Poonamalle High Road and turned in at a pair of brass gates. Servants battling with umbrellas labored to close the gates behind them.

They drove through a grove of palms and tamarinds thrashing in the monsoon. Though not as big as Udee's palace, the sweeping sandstone home that sat in the center of expansive grounds certainly qualified as a mansion. Even in the rain, Laine caught sight of peacocks taking shelter beneath the trees.

So this was Eshana's childhood home. Little Eshana—who thought nothing of cleaning up after a person had been sick, or would scrub floors and mend clothes until she dropped into her string bed at night for a few hours sleep—had been born and raised in a wealthy Indian home.

Udee chattered in his Eton-accented English. "Of course I've been a fool to not remember this particular Harish. He and his brother are two of the biggest gem dealers in Madras. His brother, Ganan, is the father of your friend Eshana. I dropped by their home this afternoon and asked him and his wife if they would see you."

"Have you spoken to Harish?" Adam asked.

"No, he's away at another of their homes where the family recently celebrated a wedding. Ganan and his wife, Sumitra, have just returned from there."

Udee's driver stopped outside a wide set of stone steps that led up to a door of carved teak. More servants with umbrellas rushed down to escort them inside. A small man came toward them, bowing over his hands, and Udee introduced them to Ganan, Eshana's father.

Laine studied him. He had the same inquisitive eyes and expressive winged brows as Eshana. He appeared a kind, intelligent man as he ushered them into a large drawing room. A woman in a pale yellow sari stood by a brazier of smoking incense. She shared Eshana's heart-shaped face.

Sumitra rushed to her and gripped her hands. "Prince Udayan has told us that you know our daughter. Is this so? Please be telling me."

Laine's heart went out to her. "Eshana is one of my dearest friends."

Eshana's mother wilted within herself, and in muffled tones she cried, "Then tell me where she is that I may go to her and bring her home."

"We were hoping to find Eshana here...with you." All day long she'd tried to convince herself that Eshana was safe and sound with people who cared for her.

Sumitra's features pinched. "What is this you are saying? We have not seen her for these ten years."

"Yes, what is this you are saying?" Ganan strode forward, took his wife's hand and tenderly led her to a rug strewn with cushions for her to sit upon. "His Royal Highness has told us you know of our daughter."

Laine recognized the holding back of his emotions. This was no harsh man, only a man grief-stricken over his daughter. "I saw Eshana last in Bombay." She glanced around to Udee.

The prince stepped forward. Udee may have been dressed in the garb of an Englishman this afternoon, but his demeanor was all Indian as he couched his questions with a slight bow over his hands. "It would be most beneficial if we could speak to your brother, Harish."

"My brother?" Ganan wrinkled his brow. "As I told you already he is remaining in the house of one of our relatives, not far from the town of Velanapur. If you wished to speak to him, you could find him there, although by now I am sure he has begun his pilgrimage and is on his way to the temples in Tanjore."

"Did Harish mention that he had spoken to your daughter recently?"

Ganan threw Udee a dark look. "If my brother had been having speech with Eshana, he would have told us."

Laine searched for the right words to avoid offense. "It has been brought to my attention that your brother may very well have had an encounter with Laine at a railway stop not far from Bombay. It's been said that he wanted her to come home to Madras."

A cry emanated from Sumitra. "Is this true? Is Harish arranging for Eshana to come home?" She clutched her husband's hand. "My prayers have been answered."

Ganan looked down at his wife and at Laine again. “Many years ago I made a grave mistake. When our daughter became a widow we adhered to the old traditions and took her away.” His voice cracked. “I should not have done this thing. After several months my wife made me see the error of my ways. But by the time we had gone back to the *ashram* to bring Eshana home, she had gone.”

A single tear trailed down his cheek. “Please tell us of our daughter. Where she has lived all this time, and why you are searching for her as if she has become lost once more?”

Adam had to admit that Laine, though gentle with the parents of her friend, had the foresight to not stay overly long. She told them all she knew, stressed the importance of starting a search for Eshana and that they would continue to do the same. By the time they left the house the winds had risen—at his guess, somewhere around thirty miles per hour—and were continuing to rise.

The rain slatted against Udee’s Rolls Royce as they drove to the hotel to pick up Adam’s truck. The time for long good-byes had passed. Udee needed to get back to secure his own home. And Adam could delay no longer.

He squeezed Udee’s hand. “I promise I’ll visit again soon during more clement weather.”

Udee returned the iron grip. “So you should. I shall be expecting you. And do pass on my regards to John. Tell him...” His voice became husky. “Well, pass on my regards.”

“He’ll be glad to hear from you.” He turned toward his truck and to Laine, who waited inside.

“And, Adam...”

He turned back to Udee. His friend’s pointed glance at Laine sitting inside the truck and his grin took Adam back to those days on the cricket pitch at Balliol. Udee didn’t need to speak for Adam to know what he meant. He released a sigh and lowered his voice. “No, Udee, I cannot turn back the tide.”

“Are you sure?” Udee’s eyes lost their laughter. “When I saw the two of you back at the hotel, I wondered."

"Quite sure, old chap. Laine and I have long since gone our separate ways. Now I'd best get inland before this storm hits, and you go home to your palace and batten down the hatches."

Even at this distance from the main house Eshana could hear the uproar. Rains had begun to fall again. This time at a terrible rate. The river which had become full last week now threatened to crest. Vanji and Shindu had brought her a pail of water and a *chapatti*, their brows lined with concern.

"Listen to that Lala." Vanji scowled. "Her wailing and weeping can be heard in the next village. She is having the servants move all carpets and *divans* from the bottom floor to the one above for fear of floods."

"What of the poor?" Shindu spat out. "Already snakes and rats have been thrust from their holes by the rising waters, and the village is overrun. People like Lala care more for their riches than the life of one such as me. Now the old woman of the house is dying, if she is not dead already."

Eshana's chin jutted upward. "Of what old woman do you speak?"

Shindu's toothless mouth moved as if she wished to spit. "Lala's mother. The little one is with her."

"Ruchi? What are the grandmother's symptoms?"

"She is sick." Vanji shrugged. "When Lala is not ordering the servants to save her treasures she is at the temple praying to Ganesh. People such as us are not allowed near the old woman to pollute her."

"Send the little one to me."

"Lala has ordered the child to remain near the grandmother's side."

Eshana waved her hand. "Lala will be too busy to notice. I must talk to Ruchi. And do not send Ruchi to the parapet outside. The steps are treacherous with this rain. Bring her to me within this room."

Vanji's brows arched high. "If I bring the child to you, you will promise not to flee? Though they never ask for you from moon to moon, it would mean more than our lives if you run off."

"I vow to you that I will not flee. But I must talk to the little one."

The day had almost passed, and Eshana feared Vanji had been prevented from doing as she had asked. No one had come near Eshana's prison, and the wailing from the main part of the household wrapped cold fingers around her heart. She curled upon the cot and listened to the rising trills of grief in the distance.

At last the key rasped in the iron lock, and the door swung open to reveal Ruchi on the threshold and Vanji behind. Shindu waited outside.

The tiny girl ran to Eshana, and Eshana fell to her knees to embrace her. Ruchi wrapped her arms around Eshana's neck as if she would never let go. "Grandmother is dead." The child's sobs shuddered against Eshana's course white sari.

Vanji sat cross-legged on the floor. "It is true, as is the custom, the family conducted the funeral pyre immediately. We were unable to come to you because the old woman died. Now they are gathering her ashes, and Lala is most upset that they cannot leave to sprinkle her remains upon the Ganges, but must wait for the rivers to cease rising."

Eshana sat on the stool and held Ruchi on her lap, crooning to the child and rocking her in her arms. "My precious pearl, my heart is darkened by your sadness."

Ruchi sobbed. "Grandmother always gave me my favorite sweets."

"Yes, my love?" Eshana cradled the child as a fresh wave of sorrow overtook. "Cry, heart of my heart. I am here to catch your tears."

She waited a long time until the hiccupping sobs ceased.

"Tell me of the grandmother's sickness," she asked of Vanji.

"As untouchables we were not allowed close, only to clean the soiled floors and take away all that is unclean. But I could see the blue of her skin, the purging and spasms."

"Cholera," Eshana said beneath her breath, and Ruchi stirred to cry again.

"Gem of my eyes," she said, lifting the child's chin, "you must tell the cooks in the kitchen that you will not drink any water that is not boiled. It is to keep the sickness from you. And there is something I wish to show you. It is like a game, only it is not a game."

Ruchi's owl-face looked up at her, the kohl from her eyes smudged by her tears.

"Come," Eshana whispered. The child slid off her lap, and Eshana led her to the new pail of water Shindu had brought. She pulled from the cot the length of old silk Ruchi had given her weeks ago. "Do you remember this, gem of my eyes?"

The child nodded as she hunkered down beside Eshana.

"See, the silk is old but it is clean. I fold it over, once, twice...four... and now seven times." She took the second pail that she had insisted Vanji provide her with, and set the folded silk across the top of the empty container, and began to slowly pour today's water through the silk into it.

With the child's grief temporarily set aside, her small brow creased. "Why are you making the old sari wet?"

"A sari can do much more than clothe us, my precious gem. In this instance the sari becomes a filter to clean the water. Now remember, if the cooks do not boil your water, strain it as you have seen me do."

Vanji's eyes caught Eshana's and brightened with understanding. "When I am allowed near the child I will remind her of this."

"You and Shindu must drink clean water too." Eshana cuddled Ruchi, smoothing the tousled plaits and kissing the salt-stained cheeks. "My treasure, you must go before it is discovered you are here."

Ruchi rested her head against Eshana's breast and placed her thumb in her mouth. Eshana rocked the little one. "I wish I could hold you and catch your tears for all tomorrows, but you must return to your mother and maids before they notice you are gone."

The child did not fuss when Vanji lifted her from Eshana's lap but stared with longing at Eshana as she was carried from the room.

Eshana sat and waited in the stillness. A half hour later, as she expected, the trilling of mourning echoed along the hallways of the abandoned wing. The sound of clapping hands resonated with the increasing vibrations of her heart. She sat forward on the edge of the cot and gripped it with tight fingers. The women of the house approached. Lala shouted out for the women to remain at the end of the hallway, far from Eshana's cell.

The door opened, and torchlight from the hallway framed Lala alone. She wore the white of mourning as Eshana did. Her hair streamed unbound and wild about her shoulders. Her face shone wet with tears. In one hand she held a torch, and in the other a clump of twigs, the same sort of broom the lower castes like Vanji and Shindu would bend over with to sweep the courtyard. She strode toward Eshana while from the far reaches of the hallway the women continued to shriek and wail and clap their hands.

Lala's eyes glittered like broken glass. "Do you know what I am doing, my cousin?" Her voice grated with the hoarseness of recent tears.

Eshana feared to answer, lest Lala truly did not wish her to speak.

Lala leaned closer, her face a mask of misery. "My mother has gone the way of all people." She swallowed. "This I could accept. Sickness comes. But because of the rising waters my husband fears the roads will flood, and he refuses to take her ashes to Benares on the Mother Ganges. I tell you this—there will be no rest for my soul until my mother's ashes are scattered on the sacred river. One drop of those waters would cleanse many lifetimes of sins."

"Lala, my eyes are darkened by the death of your mother—"

"Silence!" Lala stood over Eshana, her arm raised. The light of her torch flickered on the stone walls behind her.

Eshana shrank back and swept her gaze to Lala's feet.

"Do not dare to offer condolences, cousin of my husband. Our priest has said there is evil in our house that has caused these misfortunes. Others are falling sick as well. He has ordered me to go through the house with a broom and sweep it free of evil spirits. Everyone in the house is to clap their hands and yell to rid us of this evil goddess who brings bad luck. Yet I know that this will avail no good because *you* remain here."

She flicked the twig broom against Eshana's face.

Her skin broke. A welt like fire burned and brought stinging tears.

Eshana remained still, taking in the pain, the hatred directed at her. She would not return evil for evil. She would not. She would not. Like Christ commanded her, she must return love instead.

Light of my eyes...whosoever shall smite thee on thy right cheek, turn to him the other also....

She felt His compassion fill her as she stood and faced Lala, noting the quivering of her cousin's mouth, the fear that seized her. "You do not need to do this evil thing. Let me go free, Lala, and you will bring blessing upon your home. You know my mother visited this house not one week ago. You saw how tenderly she treated Ruchi. Do you not realize that my mother loves me as dearly as you love Ruchi?"

Lala backed away. "It is because I love Ruchi that I cannot let you free. Uncle says you are wicked and go against our ways." Her cousin trembled and raised the twig broom as if to strike Eshana again. Her fear for her child made her as dangerous as a mother tiger.

She inched closer to Lala. "Why do you fear for Ruchi? Are you not pleased with her wedding?"

Lala dropped her hand holding the twigs. "Many things can go wrong. Look at what the gods did to you, Eshana. Only a few years after your wedding, before you even went to the house of your in-laws, your husband died because of the sins you committed in a former life."

"My husband died of cholera. A disease."

"It does not matter how the gods took his life. As much as I do not want you in my house, I cannot have your presence taint the lives of other Hindus of high caste outside these walls. I must protect my daughter's life by pleasing our gods."

"Trying to appease idols of stone by keeping me locked away will not keep Ruchi safe. Only the loving God Almighty can do this."

Lala did not seem to hear her. "I do not wish to act without mercy, cousin." Her voice grew soft. "I will give you two days to pray that the rivers do not overflow, and I will allow you to stay in this room. But if the rivers do not drop, and we are still unable to travel to the Ganges to scatter my mother's ashes, I will have no choice. I will see that your eyes are put out and that you are left at the brothel behind the local temple. Once you are given to the deities in this way, no doubt my house will be blessed."

Lala turned and left. The door clanged shut, and unearthly silence filled the cell. Slumping to her knees, Eshana prayed in sobs. *Father, oh Father, I am not afraid to meet You, my Maker. To die is gain. But to be blinded and shamed is so much worse than death.*

25

Rain pelted the truck. Adam wiped at the moisture inside the windscreen and passed the cloth to Laine for her side. He'd tied canvas to the side of the truck that was open to the elements, but he could barely see through this torrent. The first few hours of driving had gone reasonably well, but the last hour they'd moved at ten miles an hour. And Lavinia lay another twenty miles away.

At the start of the trip he'd thought they would make it back to the plantation safely with time to spare. At this rate he and Laine wouldn't make it back before dark.

"Dark," he muttered under his breath as another mile passed. It was as black as kohl already, the wind screeched, and trees flanking the road creaked. At least they'd made it far enough inland to avoid the surge from the sea, and so far the canvas tarps he'd tied to the crates in back stayed secure. He pulled aside the rigged-up canvas from his side window and glanced upward. If the wind rose much more, they'd have to pull off the road and wait it out. In a high gale these trees hedging the road would dance and bow like living creatures, and his truck would be tossed about like a child's toy.

"We're not going to make it in time," Laine echoed his thoughts.

"No, but I want to keep going a little longer, to find shelter."

"We should have left earlier." Her voice held a note of apology.

"How could we have left sooner? We went to Madras to find out about your friend. Sadly, we didn't receive the news you'd hoped for. But you mustn't give up."

This sudden spurt of conversation struck him as odd after their hours of silence, but talking about her friend brought them some sense of camaraderie.

She seemed as relieved as him, and her voice rang with its usual confidence. "If it weren't for this storm we could go to the house of that relative where Harish was staying. Isn't that town, Velanapur, near here?"

"About ten miles north. But Eshana wouldn't be there. Remember, her mother and father visited that house recently."

"True, but we could talk to this Harish. Put a bit of pressure on him to tell us if he knows of her whereabouts."

"That is if Harish has done anything with Eshana—we don't know that for sure." His tone came out harsher than he intended, but he didn't want her hoping for something that would only disappoint her. He softened his voice. "The girl, Chandra, that supplied this information, she's just a girl and may have got it all wrong. And Ganan said that Harish is most likely gone south on his pilgrimage. As soon as this storm ends he'll catch up with Harish in Tanjore."

Laine mulled this over. "If Harish has done anything to Eshana, Ganan will have his guts for garters. I suppose it's better we leave the search for Eshana in the hands of her mother and father."

The wistfulness in her voice tugged at something inside him. "You must keep your friend in your prayers."

She let out a soft snort. "I haven't prayed in years. Well, I did a few years back when a little boy I care for, Cam, had been kidnapped. But, really, who do we pray to?" She didn't seem aware that she shared her thoughts with him. Perhaps she was tired. "I mean you and me, Adam? Are we English? Do we pray to the God of England? Or as domiciled English living in India should we be praying to a multitude of Hindu gods?"

"I've had the same questions over the years. There are many beautiful elements to the various faiths. But during the war one element about Christ stood out for me in the trenches as I saw men dying...getting terribly wounded...in their attempt to save one another, as if they were imitating something holy. 'Greater love hath no man than this, that a man lay down his life for his friends.' These words stop me in my tracks from turning to other beliefs. No other god but Jesus laid down His life for others. And that speaks truth to me."

He kept his eyes on the road. But would she guess what those words "that a man lay down his life for his friends" had meant to his life?

A quarter of a mile passed, and she didn't speak. Then, "Adam," she said just above a whisper, "what happened during the war?"

Her softly voiced question stole his breath. She had a right to know.

If he'd married her before he'd left for the war, she would have been his first priority. But he hadn't married her, and afterward...he couldn't. He couldn't abandon John. Not after what John had suffered, and Laine in her vivacious, carefree ways wouldn't understand his need to identify with his brothers in their shadow of life. Or his promise to John.

His silence churned up his insides. But the explanation she wanted—deserved—couldn't be loosened from his tongue.

"I'm still not to be trusted," she said with a white face.

He gripped the steering wheel tighter. Of course he trusted her. Would trust her with his life. But what happened to John—his cousin—he couldn't explain. No one except Rory had ever questioned him on his decision before. Rory had grudgingly accepted his reasoning. But Laine would not. If he even tried to explain, she'd point out...she'd point out the deficiencies in his thinking....

A sudden wind scouring over the truck broke the painful hush, thrusting the truck to the side of the road. The whole vehicle shuddered with each gust, and he could no longer hold it steady.

"It's no use, Laine, we've got to find shelter. This wind is rising. There's a town about two miles ahead and has several large stone buildings that'll be safe to take refuge in."

"At the pace we're going we won't reach that town for another hour."

The wind howled and shoved at the truck. A tree loomed ahead. To fight the winds, he struggled with the steering wheel. The storm almost won as it grabbed the truck, thrusting it off the road with a will of its own. He managed to brake and swing back onto the main track, narrowly avoiding the tree.

"Perhaps you're right," he said, out of breath as if he'd been running, "we won't make it to the town ahead. I saw a derelict building back there." Though he shouted, the screaming wind swallowed his words. "Keep your eyes open for any sign of habitation."

A crack-like thunder broke, so close it sent a ripple of shock through him.

But it wasn't thunder. A black shape danced for a moment before the truck and then fell with a thud, sending a jolt through the earth. Adrenaline pumped through his veins as he pressed the brake to the floorboards and reached out to hold Laine's shoulder, bracing her for impact. The brakes squealed, but they were hardly audible in the gale. The truck stopped mere inches from the fallen tree. The truck's headlamps bored a thin tunnel of light through the downpour, showing the giant snake of a tree trunk across the road and it's leafy head buried in the grass at the roadside.

He glanced over to see Laine. Her brisk nod assured him before he jumped out of the car to investigate. Water with floating debris swirled about his ankles when he stepped down. Rain stung his face and wind slashed at him. Laine followed, but in their slow fight against the wind they trudged like mountain climbers in a blizzard. In the beam of the car's headlamps they battled their way forward. Water streamed from his hair.

It wasn't an entire tree that had landed across the road, but as good as. The thick branch of a peepul tree—twenty inches in diameter—had landed squarely across the road. He studied the blocked way. While Laine was an athletic girl, she didn't have the strength to help him shift it. Perhaps if he used some of the boards in the back of the truck the two of them could leverage the bough far enough to the side to drive past.

First he needed to see how far this branch extended across the road. If there was any way to drive around it. An embankment dropped a few feet at the side of the track, and he battled against the storm to make his way there. He positioned his feet to brace himself in the thick grass where the leafy branches of the bough had landed, and strained to see beyond where the headlamps couldn't reach. Just how much tree blocked them?

It was still hard to see, as if he'd just come up out of a pool of water. He trod further into the grass and dislodged a rock with his foot.

Searing hot pain jabbed into his calf.

He cried out. Light from the headlamps reflected two pinpoints of light. A snake scuttled off into the bush, and Laine started to rush in his direction.

"Wait, Laine. Don't come any closer."

"What is it?" she shouted over the gale.

"A snake." He clenched his fists and bit down on his lip with the throbbing in his leg. "Ruddy thing bit me. The tree must have disturbed its nest, or perhaps it was me plodding along in my size ten boots that threatened it. Blast, I should have known better." He looked back at her. "Stay where you are. I don't know if there's more than one."

He studied the ground in the dim light. Unable to see any sign of movement, he shivered. The blasted reptile had gone, and there didn't seem to be others. All he'd been able to see in that quick flash was that it was green.

Laine, heedless of his warning, joined him. "Where is the wound?"

"I told you to stay where you were."

"Is it your leg?"

"My calf."

She slipped her shoulder under his arm and swung her arm around his back. "Stay calm. Do you hear me? No panic. Lean on me. Put as little weight on that leg as possible. I want to get you onto the truck box."

He put his weight on her shoulders, and she walked him back to the vehicle.

"Balance yourself against that," she said. "I'm going to hop up there, and if you push with your arms then I'll pull. I've got to get you lying down."

"I can make it up."

"Sorry, me luv, but I'm giving you a hand anyway." She spoke in a fake Cockney accent, no doubt the one she used to cajole many a soldier into treatment or help them withstand the terror of dying.

She hauled him up as she said she would, and without a word had him sitting and then lying down, covered with a blanket that the rain quickly soaked.

Her hair dripped and hung down as a curtain to frame her face as she pulled off his boot and ripped the bottom of his trouser leg up to his thigh. She bent to examine the punctures at the side of his left calf and then left him to go to the cab. A moment later she returned with her medical bag. "You know the routine, no panic."

"I know, and I assure you, Matron, I'm doing my best."

"No talking. Save your strength. That's the ticket."

He watched Laine screw open the wooden cylinder of the snake-bite kit and remove the lancet. He did know the routine only far too well. She had to clean the wound and hope the crystals did the trick. After that, unless he could get to a dispensary or hospital, they could only pray the snake hadn't injected a fatal amount of venom into him.

"What kind of snake was it?" she asked in her nursing voice, a no-nonsense tone counterbalanced with the jovial Cockney.

"Not sure. There are two types of green snake in this area. If it was the least venomous, the whip snake, I'll be sick for a few days but live."

"And the other?"

"The bamboo pit viper. I think you should know...if it was the viper... the outcome is...less optimistic, I'm afraid."

She stopped momentarily. So momentarily only someone who knew her as well as he did would notice. But she resumed her brisk composure and took the lancet in her hand with the container of potassium permanganate on the floor at her side. "Nothing to be afraid of, you're my patient now, and I don't allow morbid talk on my ward. As I'm sure you're aware, this will hurt. So lie back, soldier. Grit your teeth. And think of England."

In spite of the hot pain clawing at his leg, he choked on a chuckle. It might be the last time he'd laugh. If he was going to die, then he couldn't think of a better way. One last chuckle with Laine. How many men had laughed in their pain and fallen in love with her as she'd treated them in the trenches? How many men died looking up into her delightful face?

She didn't hesitate but applied the knife to his skin. He ground his teeth as she made an incision in the shape of a cross. His vision went red as livid flames seared his nerve endings. His fist pounded the truck's wooden floor.

"Relax that fist. It's over now." Her gentle intonation brought him through the haze of agony.

A metallic taste entered his mouth. He inwardly cursed. The venom must have reached his bloodstream already. *Dear God in Heaven.* Pain washed over him poker hot as Laine packed the crystals into the wound and proceeded to bandage his calf. The throbbing in his leg took over all thought.

Laine slapped his cheek.

He must have blacked out.

"Adam, stay awake. Stay calm. I'm going to drive down the road to that derelict building. There was an old wall. I'm sure it can provide some protection from this wind until I can find a better place to take you."

As he came too, the storm had risen a notch and tore with a shriek at the canvas covering the crated bottles of saline.

The headlamps lit the twisted and convoluted towers and façade of an ancient ruin. Laine drove the truck off the road and across a series of ruts and a shallow ditch where the engine groaned as the vehicle became mired in mud. Adam lay in the back getting drenched. She reversed and jolted forward, praying under her breath that she could get him into some kind of shelter.

"If you don't cooperate," she threatened the vehicle, "it'll be instant annihilation for you. Now come on. Out of the mud, you wretched..."

The truck bounced up from the ditch and onto flatter ground. "Ah, that's better, laddie," she soothed the vehicle.

She parked behind a shielding wall of the ruin which might protect it from the ravages of wind. In this dark she had no idea how far to the nearest village. She snatched the one remaining dry blanket from the first-aid box inside the cab, along with an oil lamp, and dashed up the steps and inside the ruin with her medical bag.

Beneath the stone gaze of an ancient Hindu ruler, she ran along a hallway that led to a maze of rooms, and found a small one that would protect them. Stamping her feet she prayed no snakes and rats had also sought sanctuary within these dry walls. Upholding the lamp, she swung a quick glance around. Tree roots poked between pillars and sculptures set in stone relief around the perimeter of the room. The roof that had held during hundreds of years would surely withstand this storm. The place appeared dry and clean. Nothing rustled or slithered.

Back at the truck bed, Adam lay immobile. As immobile as the thousands of casualties she'd seen in the trenches. Wind roared past her ears. Her heart became as still as Adam...and stopped. *Dear God...*

Then his hand moved, and her pulse started again.

"Up you come, old bean," she ordered as if he were a patient arguing over an unwanted sponge bath. His khaki shirt flapped outside his drill trousers as she helped him rise and held the sodden blanket around him to keep off the worst of the howling downpour. She hated having to move him. It would be so much better to have him remain prone so the venom couldn't travel quickly through his body.

Inside the ruin, she guided him over flagstones smoothed by generations of bare feet. He leaned on her like a child half asleep and unaware of her through the hallways and carved stone walls to the small haven she'd chosen. He sank to the floor, and she folded the dry blanket to prop beneath him to keep his heart higher than the leg. Outside, the storm wailed, but here they were dry and safe. The three-foot-thick walls that protected them had lost their former glory of marble and jewels centuries ago.

She returned to the truck and loosened a corner of tarp to remove a crate of saline. Good thing she knew about knots, and secured the tarp before racing into the ruin with the crate. Dripping wet, she set out her medical supplies, although there was precious little more she could do for Adam. Without knowing what type of snake, and without an injection of anti-venom, they had no option but to wait.

The coming night would tell. She cleansed his arm with alcohol and hooked the intravenous bottle onto a tree branch that protruded into the room. After she placed the thermometer under his arm, she had a quick look at his leg, a frightening purple color. His calf had already swollen to twice its size.

"I may have to face the music if it was the viper that bit me," he croaked. He looked in her direction, but his glassy eyes weren't focusing.

She adjusted the drip going into his arm. "Not if I have anything to say. You think you're the first man I've brought back from the brink of death?"

"Hardly, what with you winning the bleedin' Royal Red Cross."

"Enough larking around." She felt his forehead. "How are you feeling?"

"A taste like Hades in my mouth. Though I see you've lit the lamp...I can't quite make you out. Dizzy."

She slipped the thermometer out and read it. "I won't lie to you. You've got a fever, but we can hope that if it was the viper it didn't have time to inject a full dose of venom."

"Quite right. Let's hope it was only the whip snake." He closed his eyes, and tremors shook him with violence.

She wrapped her blood-pressure cuff around his arm and used her stethoscope to take his pressure. It was high. From the anxiety of the moment, she hoped. As was her own. Sweat beaded on his brow, and he drew deeply on his breath. If he went into respiratory failure or paralysis there was nothing she could do. Nothing. Nothing but keep him as calm as possible, and hope the saline and the crystals would help. *Dear God... if you're there.*

She stood and paced, shoving her wet hair away from her face. When he groaned she dropped to her knees and took him in her arms to warm him. His tremors grew worse. His breath more rapid.

"Laine..."

"I'm here. Stay quiet."

"Must talk. If I don't make it."

"Do shut up, of course you'll make it."

"All's taken care of. My plantation...my men will continue... Rory knows what to do."

"Fine, now lie still."

"You...sorry..." He lay quiet for some minutes. "Laine...Rory's a good man. I'm glad you two found each other...."

She spoke through gritted teeth. "Stop talking. That's an order."

The wind vibrated like a cello through the ruin. Outside it picked up stones and hurled uprooted trees against the outside walls. Within her, her mind and heart roared as loudly. *Do not take him. Don't let him die on me twice. I don't know who you are anymore, God, but I pray to you now. Just let him live, and I'll be content with that. Just let him live.*

Careful not to move him, she draped her body along his to give him warmth and held him, feeling each jerk of his muscles as his body convulsed.

The lamp flickered wildly with the wind, and time passed.

It seemed they were watched by the life-size sculptures in sandstone around the room. The marble and gold that used to adorn this small chamber had been replaced over time with moss and twigs. It had to be the ancient room of one of the king's lowly concubines. Not as flagrantly erotic as many Indian sculptures, this room held a touching sweetness. The king strolled with his arm around the girl. Her mouth raised to his. His mouth lowered to take hers.

Her tears fell hot and stung her face. She caressed Adam's cheek. His burning skin felt clammy to her touch, and he didn't waken.

After taking his pulse again and checking that he still breathed, she cried softly. So often in their youth she had laid her head on his slender and finely muscled shoulder. After they'd become engaged she would kiss the spot where the strong column of his neck began. But so much time had passed, and now she was his nurse. Only his nurse.

She lifted her head and dried her tears. *Pluck up, old girl.* Though he rasped, at least he still breathed. Outside, the wind continued to shriek, battering the ruins. Its shrieking drowned out all sound, and she watched Adam's chest rise and fall.

Breathe. Breathe. Help him breathe.

A shudder heaved through Adam, and he rolled over to retch. She rubbed his back and wiped his mouth with a cloth.

Hours passed. Adam's fever reached frightening heights close to midnight, and then again somewhere around three.

By the watch on her wrist, nine hours had passed since they'd come to the ruin. Propping herself against the wall, she pulled her knees up and sank her head into her hands. She sobbed like she had when she'd received the telegram in Étables, telling her he'd been killed in action. A blast of the storm echoed as loudly as the artillery on the front had that day. A prayer rose again inside her. *I'm not sure of your name, but please...*

And then she sobbed for the letter that had come. She sobbed for all that had been between them and that had died.

She reached for the canteen and brought it to Adam to quench his thirst.

He drank with the greed of a little child as she supported his back, and he lay down again. For a moment his gaze connected with hers, and then he closed his eyes. But she was cold now too, and lay beside him. With her hand on the breadth of his shoulder she would feel his slightest move and be ready.

Laine woke to the dull moan of the winds outside. Its screeches had subsided. Her watch said just after six. In a few hours they might be able to leave this ruin and seek help. There had to be a village close by. If a road could be cleared she could get Adam to the nearest hospital.

He hadn't moved since the last time she'd checked him. His skin felt warm to her touch. His breathing remained labored and his heart rate still too slow. His leg was still too swollen and bruised to look at. But she'd have to leave him.

With effort she lifted herself up. She kept her gaze resolutely forward. The wind forcing its way through the corridors had abated considerably from what it had been when they'd first come here last evening.

A pearl-gray sky met her as she came out of the ruin. Branches and boughs lay scattered on the ground. But under the stone arch the truck had been untouched except for twigs and vegetation that were snagged in the bed. The ropes securing the canvas tarp remained as tight as when she'd reattached them. Packed as the bottles were in straw, they had survived the storm. And the rain had stopped.

Around the ruin, several large trees had been uprooted, creating hills where the roots had been thrust from the ground. Flotsam from nearby villages littered the roads. Clay pots, mattresses of reeds, a few sticks of wooden furniture spread a trail of humanity over all. But a warm December breeze chased away the last scraps of monsoon cloud.

As she reached the truck, voices stopped her. A group of village men hailed her in Tamil. "*Memsahib*, are you not knowing that the rivers have risen? The floods will not allow your vehicle to be going down the road.

It is washed away."

Laine slumped a hip against the vehicle, her hands dropping to her sides in defeat. With the roads washed away, she'd not be able to get Adam to a hospital. There was only her to keep him alive.

26

Silence draped over all. From her cell, Eshana could see the river escape its banks. Water covered the grassy meadow, creating a shallow swamp. As the cyclone had roared like a tiger, rain had slashed through the open fretted window and the crumbling sections of roof to scatter puddles across her prison floor.

But the household noises that Eshana had grown accustomed to had ceased.

Dawn had come an hour ago. By this time of day the chatter of servants below should equal that of birds squawking in the trees. The clatter and ping of brass pots from the kitchen should carry over the air. She should have heard the Hindu priest ring his bell as the family made their morning *puja* in their private temple.

But not even the wailing of mourning for Lala's mother disturbed the breezes. Only a warm wind blowing over the tops of palms and betel nut trees reached Eshana. That gentle current of air stroked her face as her stomach cramped. For the past two days no one had come to bring her water or food. And there had been no sign of the child.

She turned from the window and sank to her knees by the cot. As she had watched the river rise, she had expected Lala to return and fulfill the threat she had uttered. But no one had come.

Eshana lifted her head to listen. Strained to listen. And sniffed the air. No wood smoke. Cooking fires did not burn in the kitchen. Had the family left for their pilgrimage to the River Ganges in spite of the flooding? Had they thought to leave instructions for her well-being? Vanji, surely Vanji had not forgotten her?

Sunlight poured in from the east and warmed the stone floor where she sat, her upper body sprawled on the cot to pray. The garden below steamed as the sun rose higher and turned the world below into shades of emerald, jade, and leaves the color of limes. Blossoms burst forth, scarlet, yellows, orange, and pinks. Upon the wafting steam ascended the perfume of lilies, jasmine and roses.

This room, so similar to that of Miriam's at home in the mission, rose high in this abandoned wing. It overlooked a vast area—not the Golden Temple of the Sikhs and the city of Amritsar—but this fertile valley on the bank of the River Palar. Unlike Miriam's room, this cell did not contain a Bible. It had been too long since she had held God's Word in her hands, but she comforted herself by the biblical accounts she had learned in years past and laid her head on her arm.

If she were to die here, she could rest in that joy. To go home to be with Yeshu was far better than life on this earth. Though her heart still ached with the desire to accomplish much work for Him. Work she had loved in Miriam's mission. Had she loved that work more than Him? Was that why...?

A whisper, like that of a foot brushing against stone, pulled her from her thoughts. It came from outside. Ruchi!

She jumped to her feet and swooned but crossed to the window and clung to the sill. "Ruchi. Are you there?"

Only a palm frond had landed on the parapet, and the wind pushed it so that it scratched across the stonework. It had not been the patter of Ruchi's tiny feet running up the broken steps.

"Ruchi," she whispered, dropping her chin to her chest and squeezing her eyes shut. "Come to me, little one. Someone...Vanji...someone..."

The heat of the morning sun embraced her. With her head heavy, she opened her eyes to look at her feet poking out below the hem of her widow's garment. She lifted her arms to study her funeral clothing. For two months she had worn this cloth and been buried in this tomb.

Her words rang as if wrung from her chest. "I wanted only to serve you, Yeshu, with my life. I wanted to live my life...for you. Be holy...for you. Yet you keep me in this prison where I can do nothing." She bowed her head again. "I have tried to count this persecution as joy, to be like Joseph when he was in prison. Like Peter...Paul." Her speech weakened to a breath. "But I am failing, Lord. I am failing."

Have you come to the last of your days, light of my eyes?

She glanced up, the tingle of life running along her arms. Had she heard His small and still voice within her ear? Her heart? Fingertips of a breeze touched her cheek, her brow, her chin.

"My Lord? Speak, for I am listening."

Beloved, are you ready to die, as I died? Are you ready to cease striving, cease fretting? Are you ready to say as I had said, 'Not my will, but Thine, heavenly Father'?

The rising sun had reached midway up the sky so that she could stare straight into its all-consuming countenance.

Come, light of my eyes, be one with the Father and with me. You have believed. You have been buried with me. Now walk with me in newness of life, for I am the resurrection.

The sun blazed upon her, and her coarse sari whitened in the brilliance. Softened in the brilliance. She held out her arms, and sunlight flooded her, seeping into her soul. "Not my will...but thine. I die to myself, my plans, my aspirations. Yeshu, live your life through me."

Laughter eddied through her and met with her current of tears. Renewed strength took hold of her body, and she set her arms, her hands, and her feet in the ancient ways of Indian dance. She tapped her feet and let her hands open and shut like those of lotus blossoms in worship of the Son of God.

The memory of Chandra came to her in that moment, of the day she and Laine had laid the young girl in the wooden crate before they had hammered down the nails and boarded the Bombay Mail. Her own words to Chandra came back to her. "Do not be afraid at this confinement. It is only for a short time, and then you will be released, and free to enjoy all the good things God is preparing for you."

Eshana whirled in her dance and released a joyous cry. "My precious Lord, I trust in your love. Thy will be done."

A scratch like that of the palm frond on stone stopped her in her dance.

She looked out to the parapet. The soft noise came again. But not from outside.

The door.

The grating of a key in the lock invaded the quiet joy of her cell. Had Lala returned to make good on her threat?

She turned to the door and rolled back her shoulders. The warm sun ran like a hand along her spine.

I am here, light of my eyes, do not fear. I am the resurrection...and the life.

With the strength of her Savior she would accept with joy whatever He allowed in her life...or did not allow.

The key rasped again in the lock and clicked. The door popped open an inch, yet no one entered. Only a whisper of noise came from the passageway.

She took tentative steps and peeked through the sliver of space, but where she expected to see an adult face there was nothing. Her gaze lowered, and there stood the child. So small. Backed against the wall of the passageway, her hands splayed against the stones. But fear pinched the normally laughing little face.

"Ruchi. Gem of my heart, what has frightened you?"

The little one strove to speak. "The man...with the shiny face. He brought me...to you."

"What man?" Eshana looked down the hallway. "Is it he who has frightened you?"

The child shook her head, and her untidy plaits swung against her cheek. No one had arranged her hair or had seen to her dressing.

Eshana hunched down to embrace Ruchi. "Then what has struck your heart with such fear?"

The little girl began to cry. "Everyone is sick. *Amma* and *Appa*. Everyone. I was afraid, until Yeshu came to me and brought me to you. Only when He held my hand I was not afraid."

Eshana lifted the child and held her as she strode down the unlit hallway. When they came to the end, Ruchi pointed to the left. The rough floors of the abandoned wing changed to the smooth stone of the new, and she found their way outside to a vast courtyard surrounded by pillars upholding a shading roof. This part of the house had not been visible to her on the opposite side overlooking the river. Thank the Lord, the building sat upon high ground, and the river had not crept too close.

Clay urns as high as her waist, overflowing with lilies and roses, filled the courtyard. Splashes of yellow and pink blossoms and birds that scolded and sang were the only signs of life. Early morning sun angled beneath the sculptured pillars as they crossed the courtyard.

Ruchi hiccupped, the only human sound echoing in the unsettling quiet.

Eshana raced toward the area where the kitchen must surely be. She rounded a corner of the house and stopped.

Under the thatched roof of an open-aired storage area three people lay, and Ruchi buried her face in Eshana's shoulder. By the poorer cloth these people wore they had to be servants. Their eyes and cheeks were sunken, their noses sharp, their cheekbones gaunt. One appeared already dead of the cholera. The other two feebly thrashed their arms and legs about, but from the shortness of their breath they, too, were close to dying.

She clutched Ruchi to her chest to shield her, but there was no need. The little one had squeezed shut her darkly fringed eyes.

"It is all right, my gem, do not be afraid. I will find a place in the house where you will not see such things. Is there anyone sick in the room where you sleep?"

The child shook her head.

"I will take you there, my precious one. Then I will help these who are suffering."

Inside the wing where the family lived, she found the hallways lined with a dozen or more sick. Her heart grew heavy. *I will come back to you*, she promised them silently as she wound her way to the kitchen.

The large cooking kitchen loomed ahead with a thatched roof. Outside on a shaded veranda, five more people slumped against the house. One man in a soiled *dhoti* tried in vain to help the woman lying next to him. He held a cup of water to her lips, but the woman could not take it and curled in pain and moaned. Another groan came from the other side of the veranda. And then another, while most lay far too still.

In the house proper, the elegant rooms above were much like the Jasmine Palace she had grown up in. Smooth floors felt cool against her bare feet. Silk draperies hung from pillars, and cushions graced the floors or low divans. But these riches and comforts were of no use in the face of such illness.

With Ruchi's directions she found the child's room. Thank Yeshu, no one had entered the bedchamber. Sunlight streamed through the window and illumined the painted walls that held birds and animals—tigers and jaguars, peacocks and mynas—from the jungle. Painted blossoms danced throughout the room, and mosquito netting draped the little one's small rosewood bed.

"Stay here, my gem, until I return." She kissed the soft brow. "I will shortly bring food for you and me, and clean water to bathe you. Do not leave this room, and cry out if someone enters."

Ruchi nodded and sat down upon the floor in a patch of sunlight. The pinched look to the tiny owl face lessened as Eshana handed her a box of beads to play with. Eshana looked back at her from the threshold. Lines still furrowed the little brow.

Downstairs once more, Eshana found a clean sari hanging over the veranda to dry. She swept it off and quickly changed, tearing off a piece from the end to tie around her nose and mouth. She hurried back to the kitchen. *Dearest Yeshu, send help. There are so many.*

She swooned again and leaned against the wall. When she could open her eyes, her gaze landed on a mound of coconuts sitting on a shelf in the kitchen. She raced to chop one open and drink of the liquid inside, eat of its meat.

With a return of some strength she went outside. The well sat away from the house, and river water lapped against its stone lip. Eshana splashed through the puddle and filled pail after pail. Back in the kitchen the fire started easily, and she soon had several brass pots of water boiling. When the smallest urn of water boiled, she poured this into a bowl and some into a cup to return to Rutchi along with the chopped coconut. She found the child where she had left her, as if Ruchi feared to leave her patch of sunlight. Ruchi took the coconut and drank of the milk inside and began to nibble at the chopped meat while Eshana bathed her and ate more of the coconut as well.

The water had cooled enough to drink by the time she had Ruchi dressed in a clean sari and her hair brushed into one loose plait.

"I cannot stay, my little gem. I must go down and help the others. Stay here, my love."

Again Ruchi nodded and yawned. Eshana smiled at the yawn. The little girl would fall asleep soon, and she left her with reluctance. The people below were in such need, and she took the stairs.

In the kitchen, Eshana reached for crushed sugarcane and added handfuls to the sterilized water. The salt must be nearby, and...

A footstep rang on the stoop, and she whirled to see who entered the kitchen. "Vanji!"

"You have been released." The young untouchable woman ran to embrace her. "I could not come to you, Eshana. Many in our village have been unwell, and I stayed to help and to protect my children. I did as you said, I boiled our water, and my little ones have remained untouched by the sickness."

Eshana returned Vanji's embrace. "Praise Almighty God. I am thankful you are well. But help me. Cover your face like I have done. Wash your hands in this urn that we will use for cleansing ourselves. This one we will take outside to wash the sick. And these pots we will use for drinking water. Start boiling more, and we will add sugar, salt, and coconut milk to give to those who can receive it."

Vanji did what she was asked as Eshana stood and turned to the rest of the sick. They must be servants, for she did not see Lala, her cousin Kadhir, or her uncle. Ruchi's parents had to be upstairs in the family quarters, at a distance from the child's room. Already Vanji moved from person to person and tried to give them the prepared drink.

Eshana placed a hand on her shoulder. "I must go up to the family and see how they fare. But first let us move the dead from those still living."

They found Shindu close to the river, her body curled in a fetal position and cold. Eshana brushed the first of her tears away for the old woman who had been kind to her. Vanji, too, took this death harder than the sixteen other bodies they had removed from the house. But there was no time to dwell on Shindu's death.

Movement at the corner of her eye startled her. Three men and a woman came out of the huts that were servants' living quarters. They had wrapped long strips of cloth around their nose and mouth, and trod with care toward her. One of the men raised his hands in supplication. "We were afraid, and have been hiding. But we will help you now. Show us what to do."

Eshana left them in Vanji's capable hands, and she immediately set these servants to boiling more water, burning soiled clothes, and making more of the mineral-infused brew for the sick to drink. These higher-caste servants, who would never have let an untouchable like Vanji near them before or enter this part of the house, took their orders from her now, leaving Eshana free.

It was time to see to Ruchi's parents. Eshana left the temporary clinic and took two of the healthy servants with her.

They found a man lying on a hallway floor. One of the servants with her let out a cry and rushed to him. From the sacred thread that crossed his bare chest, she assumed he must be the house priest. Perhaps he had come to say *puja* with the family. A cushion that he had been sitting on was near a small brass plate with ashes within it. Eshana left the priest with the servants and carried on to what appeared a large and airy chamber at the far end of the hallway.

Kadhir, her strong and slender cousin, lay curled upon a soiled bed. Lala, who must have been trying to aid him, had slumped to the floor as the sickness had overcome her. Eshana rushed to them and touched first Lala's head and then Kadhir's. Lala's skin burned hot and dry. Kadhir—blue and pinched, his fingertips had shriveled to resemble those of a washerwoman. He trembled and could not catch his breath. Her heart crushed in upon itself. She had come in time only to hear the death rattle as his lungs shrieked for oxygen.

She slipped to his side and took his hand. "Kadhir." Though her cousin had tried to bring harm to her, the perfume of Yeshu's forgiveness seeped from her heart. "Kadhir, if you can hear me, go in peace. Call out with your heart to the son of the Living God, Yeshu. He is merciful."

Lala lifted her head, her eyes glazed in an attempt to focus on her husband. Her hand fluttered toward Kadhir with the strength of a newly hatched bird.

His labored breathing ceased with a terrible suddenness. The room grew quiet but for a breeze that riffled the silk curtains, and Eshana remembered him as a boy. Long before she had become a widow, Kadhir had been a playmate in the Jasmine Palace. She touched his hand one last time and wept within for him. There was no more to be done for her cousin, except care for his widow and child.

The servants came into the room, and she ordered them to take Lala into a clean room and lay her upon a string bed. As she had seen to Ruchi, she bathed Lala and gave her sips of the prepared water.

In the west, a rim of gold outlined the hills that lay dark in silhouette. Daylight had come to an end. Eshana had left this room throughout the day to oversee Vanji and the other servants. But Vanji needed little direction after Eshana showed her what to do but once. All the servants, high caste and low, observed Vanji's instructions. She had them boiling clothes, boiling water, cleaning the sick, and helping them to drink. But still the cholera made victims of half the household.

For brief spaces of time Eshana went to see that Ruchi remained well. As she had expected, the little one had fallen asleep for most of the day.

Lala felt cooler to her touch. For the last hour she had kept the coconut milk down but was still too weak to awaken for long.

Eshana took a few moments to wash and drink some of the sterilized water and eat one of the chapattis that had been made. She insisted Vanji do the same and made her way to the staircase that would take her up again to Lala's room and Ruchi's.

The servant she had left with them rushed down the steps, his black eyes grave. "*Memsahib*, come. The child is ill. Ill unto death, I am swearing."

Eshana raced up the steps with Vanji following on her heels. *Oh dear Yeshu, not the little one.*

The hallway seemed so long as she ran to the chamber where she had left Ruchi sleeping, and from where she could now hear the sounds of pitiful retching.

27

"Dr. Jai Kaur, what a joy to see you looking so well." Dr. Ida beamed up at him when she came to stand at his side in the dispensary.

Jai returned her smile and continued to examine the ten-year-old lad who had come to the Mary Tabor Schell Hospital with his mother that morning. Ida must have completed her surgeries scheduled for that day, along with the medical practitioners she was currently training.

He told the boy in Hindi to stick out his tongue so he could get a good look at the child's throat. He then switched to English so the boy would not understand. "How is the child's mother?"

"We were able to remove the entire tumor. I have great hope for her." A gleam of Dr. Ida's indomitable spirit shone through her eyes.

During the past week, he had been astounded at what this woman from the United States had accomplished. If only Eshana were here to see this hospital compound of the Union Medical School, these new buildings, doctors' and nurses' bungalows, students bungalows, all to care for the needs of Indian women. Patients healing on cool verandas surrounded by gardens splashed with marigolds and poinsettias did his own heart good. Yes, when he found Eshana...

He let his hand drop from the lad's shoulder. If he found her...surely he must find her, and he would show her this place. He lifted his hands again to palpate the boy's neck glands.

For here, Indian women of all faiths came for training. In time, Dr. Ida hoped the government would give her teaching hospital the authority to grant the status of medical doctors. But for now these women took two years to become practitioners. They could do much with that level of education.

He tweaked the little boy's nose. This lad was healthy, but if not for this teaching hospital, his Muslim mother probably would not have come for the surgery she so desperately needed. She would not have allowed a male doctor to have touched more than her hands as she sat behind a purdah curtain. But she had allowed Dr. Ida and the female doctors to help her.

Dr. Ida settled into a chair in the corner of the examining room. "Have you made your plans?"

Jai lifted the boy down and sent him to his father who waited outside. "I leave tomorrow on the train."

"To search for your colleague?"

"Yes, I sent a telegram to the English nurse who is a friend of Eshana's, but strangely have not heard back from her. I am contemplating whether it is prudent to continue on to Madras as originally planned, or seek out this nursing friend."

"You'll make the right decision. You've got a good head on your shoulders, Dr. Kaur. But whenever you can, please come back and see us. And when you do find your friend, I'd love to meet her. If she's half the physician you say she is, she'd make a wonderful practitioner."

She readied herself to leave the examination room.

"Dr. Ida, you have been a follower of Christ for many years."

"Most of my life."

He struggled to find the words. "Have you ever had a vision of Christ, to know if he is the true Master?"

Her bright blue eyes studied him. "I have felt Him speaking to me many times, though not in an audible manner. When I was a young woman, three times in one night, husbands came to our house looking for a doctor to help their wives through childbirth. Each of those three men would not allow my father to treat their women. I fear those women died when perhaps they could have been saved by medical care. That night I knew the Lord was calling me to become a doctor."

He turned away. "Because you are such a devout Christian and have done so much for Indian women, I had hoped you would have seen the face of Yeshu, as Sundar Singh had."

"Dr. Kaur, look back at your journey. Perhaps Yeshu has been clearly speaking to you, and you have not comprehended...yet."

She held out her hand to shake his. "My dear new friend, I will be praying for you, that you will find the answers you seek. Come back as soon as you can." Her blue eyes twinkled. "And Dr. Kaur, the Vellore Government Hospital is always looking for physicians of quality such as yourself."

He returned her smile. If he truly could find Eshana, and if she indeed began to study here, it would be a great joy to work nearby in the government hospital. But this was not to be. As soon as he knew she was safe, he must return to his father and their practice in Amritsar.

Had the storm passed? At times Adam felt the quiet. At times the noise raged. The eye of the storm? The winds—were they winds? Or did his blood pound through his temples? Yet, outside, the sound had decreased to a whine. How many people had died?

Was that why he couldn't breathe? Could not move? And the pain...

Too weak.

Was he dying?

Each time his fever burned, Laine came with a cold cloth and a sip of water.

Last night he'd had a moment or two of consciousness. He lay on a mat of woven reeds in the headman's hut...of a village. On a floor of hard-packed dirt. Today—the third day, wasn't it, since the snake had bitten him. As soon as he got back to the plantation he would send a gift to thank the village for their kindness. Too kind...these people.

For now...he gave in to Laine's ministrations. He closed his eyes in weakness and felt the blessed cool touch of her fingers grazing his cheek.

Surely he had responsibilities? Others who needed him? John?

But here he lay on this mat. And Laine. "*Agnosco veteris vestigia flammae*" in the Latin... "I recognize the signs of the old flame...of old desire."

The memory of Laine's kisses warmed him when the tremors shook. Until the memory of John pushed out those memories. And filled his mind.

He cried out with the remembered shot that ricocheted through his head. One shot among so many. He would have surely died if John had not pushed him out of the way, and he had fallen to the mud-coated duckboards at the bottom of the trench. The artillery had roared. Then he'd seen John, who had possessed a face so similar to his own. The lower half of his cousin's jaw had been blown away. A gaping mass of torn flesh.

Tattered tissue where once had been a mouth, a jawline.

"John!"

Laine's arms soothed him. Her hands touched his brow. *Laine.*

If only she could go back thirty-eight hours and stop Adam before he'd walked into the grass. Laine swept her hair off her shoulder and wound it into an untidy knot. For most of those hours she'd held Adam's head on her lap and leaned against the mud-brick wall of the hut. The people of this village had been more than generous since they'd found them at the ruins yesterday morning.

She wouldn't have left Adam at all, except early today the headman asked her to look at one of their young men who was ill. It had been too late. The man died while she'd watched helplessly. She'd known it was too late even as she hooked him up to the saline, and as the people of this village watched her with astonished eyes.

"Is this how you are saving people from the cholera?" The headman gingerly touched the tubing as she unhooked it from the patient's arm.

"But I couldn't save him."

His glance encompassed his village. "Not this one, but can you be taking care of the rest of our sick? Perhaps others are stronger and will mend."

She thought for a moment. There was Adam to think of as well as these sick villagers. She had to keep Adam from being infected with the cholera microbe. "I'll teach you what to do then."

After instructing several of the villagers to set up a makeshift treatment area with clean water, she hung bottles of saline on the tree branches and showed them how to keep the drips steady. Between then and now she'd trekked back and forth between Adam and these patients. She'd lost a few, but the saline brought a good many back from the brink. In preparation for those who would be over the hump by tomorrow, she had already instructed the women on cooking the salted rice water for rehydrating the patients, explaining to them that it should have the taste of tears.

She left the women and walked back to the hut. Much of the day had passed, and she nearly tripped over her feet as she hurried to Adam. He'd been alone for the past twenty minutes. For her, that was far too long. His breath had continued to rasp. His heart rate had stayed too slow. And his calf remained that virulent purple, but had it started to diminish in size? And every once in a while he'd regained consciousness. For a moment or two. But it gave her hope. Wild, insane hope upon hope.

Pigeons cooed in a nearby banyan tree, and the clean, stringent fragrance of the basil plant, sacred to the Hindus, met her at the door of the headman's hut. The dim light inside the shuttered room confused her for a moment until her eyes adjusted and sought out where Adam lay.

His gaze, lucid and inquiring, latched onto hers, and her heart thumped.

"I think I'll live," he croaked.

"Of course you will." She turned away, not wanting to expose the relief that must be showing on her face.

"You sound as if you never doubted."

"Never doubted for a moment." She couldn't let on that he was still far from out of the woods, but confidence was half the battle.

"I know I certainly doubted. In fact..." The newfound strength to his voice tapered to nothing. "Where are we?"

"In a village a quarter of a mile from the ruins we stayed in."

"I thought so. We should get going. I've wasted enough time acting the invalid."

She swept around to face him with her hand on her hip. "Oh my yes, you should jump to your feet and drive us back to the plantation. While you're at it, why not try running the world? Really, Adam, you make my blood boil. We're not going anywhere. The roads have been washed out by the cyclone."

He gave her a smile from the old days. "Quite right. I'm sorry that I, ahem...make your blood boil." His voice turned serious. "But we've got to get back to Lavinia. The people in the villages along the river will need help with the flooding. Sandbags..." He tried to rise up on an elbow but slumped down again prone.

"If I were going to take you anywhere it would be a hospital."

"As a medical professional you should know there's nothing a hospital can do for me now. If it had been the more fatal viper I'd be a cold corpse. I'll be better within the next day or so. And my men—"

"The workers on your plantation are reliable—of those I've met. I'm sure they'll take care of things in your absence."

His brows met in the middle. "What about the saline? We must get that back to Rory."

She pushed out a hard breath. "I'm fully aware of that too. But Rory and Bella will do the best they can. At the moment the saline is saving the lives of this village. So what do you say to me unplugging your arm from your own personal vintage, and getting some rice broth down you?"

She couldn't get away from Adam's keen gaze fast enough. Outside she leaned against the side of the truck and allowed the relief to flow unhindered. She'd cried the night he'd been bitten by the snake—a sobbing mass of incoherent prayer. Now, all she could manage was wordless thanks. Adam's chances of living grew stronger with each hour.

The sun had set a while ago, and the sky turned a pale green, setting the stage for the thousands of birds that sang and screeched in the trees. She threw her shoulders back and lifted her face to let the peacefulness of the twilight purge her from all anxiety and heartache of the last few days. No, not just days, but the heartache of the past three years. The early moon rising above the treetops softened the protective layer she'd built around her heart. She loved him. She always had, and she always would. That he still lived would satisfy her for the rest of her days.

Adam tried to sit up again when she returned to the hut with some of the salted rice water for the cholera patients. It would do him good too.

"What have you learned? Can we leave yet?" he asked.

His ridiculous statement didn't deserve an answer. "As soon as the rivers go down." She clipped it out in her best nurse's tone. "For now you're still my patient, and I'm still your nurse."

Keeping her face impassive, she put the cup of broth to his lips. At least with something in his mouth he would be unable to babble about his plantation for the next five minutes.

After a few sips, with the briefest of touches he pushed the cup away and placed his hand on her arm. A tingle of electricity jolted through her. It took all her strength to stiffened her lips into a half smile and lift her brows to convey only mild interest.

"I am a heel, Laine. I may have been out of it for a while, but there were moments when I knew very well how you cared for me. It's most humbling. Thank you." In the dim light his eyes burned darkly, but they'd done nothing to warm up those cool, polite words.

Her throat ached with the desire to cry again. For once she wanted to be the one to be comforted. To have him hold her. To stop her trembling with his arms around her. But that was stupid. Stupid. Stupid.

He'd made his feelings abundantly clear when he'd thought he was on his deathbed. Nothing would make him happier than if she were to marry Rory.

28

A tattered cloud sailed in front of a crescent moon as Eshana prayed. All that she knew to do did nothing to help the child. For the whole of the night Eshana had trickled fluid into the little mouth, only to have it purged from the small body. Ruchi's fingertips now looked like her father's had before he died, the shriveled fingertips of a washerwoman.

The little one moaned. Eshana sat on the floor, cradling her, and touching her lips to the child's brow. She squeezed her eyes shut—Ruchi's fever was so high—and she set to bathing her again.

Then the girl's mouth stirred as Eshana dribbled more of the water and coconut milk mixture into her mouth. After a few swallows, Ruchi's owl eyes opened and fixed on Eshana. "I saw him...I saw him. Yeshu...has a shiny face." She fell asleep again, her head on Eshana's lap.

Lala groaned in the cot beside them. Eshana had brought Ruchi and her mother together in the same room, while Vanji and the other servants saw to the rest of the household.

"I must take her to the temple," Lala whimpered. "There will be priests who can pray for her."

"Rest, my cousin. Your child needs a hospital, but the servants say the closest is many miles away." Her chin slumped to her chest. Weakness plagued her, and tears came too easily. Was there something she had missed because of her weariness? Something to help the child? Uncle Harish had taken the automobile for his pilgrimage to the temples in Tanjore. A bullock cart would take hours to get Ruchi to a dispensary, and she had no knowledge of how the flooding had damaged the roads. Had the river receded? She could not bear for the little one to die on the road. *Yeshu, Yeshu, what am I to do?*

Lala tried to rise up on her cot. "I will take her to the house temple myself. I am Brahmin. I will make *puja* for her as there is no priest."

"Rest, Lala." Tears stung behind Eshana's eyes.

Too feeble to resist, her cousin complied. She lay back and closed her eyes, not noticing Vanji hurry into the room, carrying a brass urn of salted rice water and clean linens. Vangi finished her task and turned to the door when Lala's eyes fluttered open. She shrieked and curled into a ball at the far end of the string cot.

"What is it, Lala? Has the sickness returned?" Eshana set the child aside to see what had caused this distress.

Lala moaned and pointed at Vanji. "She...her...what is this low-caste filth doing in my private rooms?"

Such hatred brought a pain to Eshana's heart, but she held in the chiding remark she longed to give to Lala.

Vanji back away. "I have brought only rice water for the child. I mean no harm."

Eshana reached up and took hold of Lala's hand. "It is Vanji who has provided what we have needed this day to save your household. It is Vanji who has been making the solutions for the sick to drink, and what I have been feeding to Ruchi all night. What does it matter now, when I who you consider as polluting as Vanji, have been caring for you this day?"

Her cousin fell back on the cot and sobbed. "It is your fault, Eshana. What our uncle said is true. Even with the disgrace of your shorn head and widow's garment you have taught rebellion to the lower castes, and we will die because of your wicked pollution."

Eshana held her tongue. In her weakened condition, Lala did not know that she too had become a widow.

At the threshold to the room, Vanji fell to her knees. "Is this true, Eshana? Have I made matters worse by my touch? Am I hastening the little one's death?"

Eshana rushed to speak. "You could have stayed in your village and cared for your own loved ones. Though Lala does not comprehend, you have been her greatest blessing this day, and mine. God has used you, Vanji." The untouchable woman swayed on her knees, and Eshana felt her own weariness engulf her. "Yeshu, Yeshu, if only there was a hospital nearby?"

She felt Vanji's touch.

"Eshana, you ask your god to tell you where there is a hospital?"

Eshana raised her head. She had not realized she had prayed aloud.

"Yes, a hospital where there are medicines that might save Ruchi."

"I know of nothing like that, but one of the servants has been to a village not ten miles from here. An English nurse has been helping the villagers by sticking a needle into their arm attached to a bottle of medicine."

A quiver ran along Eshana's arms. "An English nurse? What village are we close to?" She tried to remember the postal address Laine had given her, that slip of paper that had long since been lost when her uncle captured her in Bombay. "Is this nurse still within that village? Who saw her?"

She held Ruchi close to her heart as Vanji ran for the servant who had seen the Englishwoman. Within moments she returned with one of the men.

"Tell me of this nurse," Eshana asked of him. "What does she look like?"

His brow wrinkled. "She is English."

"What color is her hair?"

"Dark, like yours or mine."

He could tell her no more. It mattered not. Did this nurse remain in this village? *Could it be, Yeshu? Is Laine this nurse they speak of?*

The conviction tolled in her heart. *Get up, take the child in the cart and to this nurse.*

Eshana commanded that bullocks be harnessed. For the first time she noticed the birds welcomed the day. Dawn had begun to gray and define the lines of house and garden.

She had almost left the bedchamber with Ruchi in her arms and looked back at Lala who had fallen asleep again. As a widow now too, Lala no longer had power over Eshana. But what if their uncle returned? Would he subject Lala to what he had subjected Eshana? She could not allow this.

At her request two of the male servants lifted Lala and brought her.

Vanji helped Eshana settle Lala and Ruchi in the cart, along with jugs of salted rice water, water for washing, and clean linens. A servant jumped into the driver's seat.

"I would go with you, heart of my heart." Vanji kissed Eshana's hand. "You have become a sister to me."

Eshana clasped Vanji close. "As you are to me. But you are needed in this house until this illness has passed. I will see you again, if it be the will of God."

A thread of rose lay along the horizon as the cart lumbered away from what had been her prison these past two months. *Yeshu, Son of God, I am trusting in You. Wherever You lead, there is life.*

Cooking fires sent blue smoke up through the betel nut trees when a jumble of voices reached Laine outside the headman's hut. A moment later a group of villagers rushed upon her.

"The flooding is receding, *memsahib*. We are clearing the road as we speak."

The next hour dragged, but with the help of two young men she tucked Adam onto a makeshift gurney, and had him installed in the passenger side of the truck.

He glowered and muttered something about feeling as helpful as a lady's parasol in a cyclone.

She let that go with no retort and got behind the wheel. Though Adam seemed a little better, his fever returned intermittently.

He'd been so much easier to care for when he was comatose. She could hardly wait to be rid of him. That was a lie though. She'd savored every moment she'd bathed his forehead and held him until his tremors eased. When he'd cried out for his cousin John and sobbed against her, she'd held him tighter until his weeping stopped. Poor John must not have made it home from the trenches.

But this morning Adam gave no sign of the nightmares that had gripped him these past few nights. He sat beside her, a lump of wounded male ego, while she pushed the starter button and released the clutch. Two of the younger village lads hunched in the back with the crates. They had relatives in the next village and so had volunteered to come with them to help her clear the road of debris. With any luck the truck would make it to Lavinia within two or three hours.

Laine pressed her foot to the gas pedal.

The sun warmed the wet jungle and dried the road hard after the rains, but Eshana's hope had dwindled to a paltry string ready to break. For an hour this cart had plodded along the rutted track, and there was still much ground to cover before they reached the village that Lala's servant had spoken of. *Please, Lord, let the nurse be there still.* Ruchi lay against her, her small arms and legs convulsing in pain. She struggled to breathe, and Eshana wept.

From her prison she had prayed to be freed, and the child had been God's instrument, but at such an expense. To lose this child shattered all prospects of joy. Eshana's arms grew weary. With so little to eat these past two months, and no rest since she left her cell, she too had weakened. Hot tears blinded her, and her vision of the jungle and the track that wound through it swam together.

A cloud of red dust billowed ahead, coming in their direction. Eshana's eye caught the glint of sunlight flashing on metal, and her heart thundered like that of the recent monsoons.

From its speed it must be an automobile or truck. She could hear its engine, an alien sound soaked up by the dense groves. If the driver of the vehicle had any mercy in his heart, he would take her and the child in minutes to the village or nearest dispensary. It would be only minutes.

She shouted for the bullock driver to stop, and jumped down. With infinite care she took the child in her arms and began to run down the road to the fast-approaching vehicle, crying out, "Stop! Help us, please."

Her legs felt meager as sticks, and she stumbled once but held Ruchi close. She would not drop the little one. She would not drop the little one. Though she was faint, the spirit of Christ within her grew strong. He would enable her to do all things. Her body, though frail, became as resilient as bamboo. The breath in her lungs scorched with the effort, but her arms around the child strengthened. And as she ran, the size of her strides increased.

At Laine's side, Adam had fallen asleep already. His head slumped against her arm as she drove down the road. That he'd survived was a miracle. She was convinced it had been the bamboo viper, the more poisonous reptile that had got him. In Rory's care he would come back to full strength, and she pressed on the gasoline pedal still more, sending up a cloud of red dust behind them. Her eyes were on the track when a speck—a person—on the road grew larger as the truck barreled ahead.

The villages and roadways had been quiet as a morgue since the cyclone, and now there ran a figure. Running down the middle of the road. There was no room to pass. The woman bolted toward them...carrying what looked like a child.

Laine mashed her foot to the brake. The vehicle's brakes squealed, and she prayed the crates of straw in the back would protect the bottled saline. When the truck jerked to a stop she sent a quick glance to confirm the two village boys were unharmed. Adam had awakened and threw a glare as to why she'd almost thrown him through the windshield with her chaotic driving. If he were well enough he'd demand control of the wheel. Well let him try. She'd soon sort him out.

The woman, the cause of this near accident continued to run at them full tilt. She reached the front fender on Adam's side. Through the settling dust, Laine could see the woman hunched over, breathing hard, and still holding a pathetic child in her arms that had no doubt died from the cholera. The signs were all too horribly clear as the little head with dark braids fell back over the arms of the woman who held her. Laine winced at this young mother's grief.

Unable to speak, the woman raised her head, heaving for breath, and stared through the dust-coated windscreen at her and Adam.

Laine opened the door and jumped to the road. Adam, too, hopped down on his side, and to her annoyance hobbled to the woman. Why couldn't he just have remained in the truck, away from possible contamination and let her do her job? But the least she could do was comfort the woman, and see how far her own cholera symptoms had developed. From the look of her she would soon follow her child in death. A torn sari covered her rail-thin body, and her head was shorn. The young woman's eyes, set in deep wells, spoke of the loss of minerals and fluids Laine had been seeing in patients since the outbreak began.

Even in his weakened condition Adam gently took the child from her arms as Laine rounded the front of the truck. The woman's gaze met hers, and she gasped, clapping her hand to her mouth. She fell to the dirt, crying and rocking on her knees. "Praise be to Yeshu. Praise be to Yeshu."

The sun beat down on Laine's head, striking her dumb. The woman had spoken in English. Her voice...and those hands raised in prayer as she kneeled on the ground...

The woman lifted her head. Tears rained down her tired face as she whispered, "Like Joseph of old, others planned evil against me, but, Laine, as it says in Joseph's account, 'God meant it unto good...to bring to pass... as it is this day...to save much people alive.'"

"Eshana?" Laine took hold of the thin arms and stooped shoulders, and lifted her, holding her close. "Is it really you?"

"Yes my friend, but there is no time. My little cousin! She is dying. Do what you can for her." Eshana pulled Laine toward Adam and the child he held. "See, she still has breath."

No words were needed. Adam limped to the back of the truck that the two young boys had already vacated and laid the child on the canvas tarp. Laine grabbed her medical valise from the cab and jumped into the back, pulling out a crate of supplies as she did. Before she could stop her, Eshana had climbed up as well.

"What are your symptoms?" she asked Eshana. "Do you have the cholera?"

"I am only anemic, but I will tell you all later." She sat and placed the child's head on her lap.

"Then get a cloth out of my bag and alcohol. Clean her arm. I've got nine percent saline here. And say a prayer, Eshana, that we're in time to rehydrate this little scrap. There's certainly not much left of her, is there? We can't jostle her around in the truck to get her back to the compound."

Eshana dipped her head in answer.

In an instant it became what it had always been in Amritsar when they'd worked as a team over a poor villager or poverty-stricken woman in the city. Quick as two blinks they had the small patient hooked up to a drip. As Laine adjusted the rate of flow, she became aware of a bullock cart that stopped near the truck and a woman calling out in a reedy voice. "Does my Ruchi live?"

"It is too soon to tell, Lala," Eshana called back.

Eshana made movements as if to jump from the truck to attend this Lala, but Laine stopped her. "You're in no great shape yourself. I assume she's the mother—is she stable?"

"She had the sickness, but is on the mend and taking fluids orally."

"Then stay where you are, and I'll see to her soon. First we need to stabilize the child."

Laine shook out the thermometer and slipped it under the tiny arm. Minutes later she checked the temperature and sighed. Either the child would die soon, or the God who worked miracles would work another one. But she was beginning to believe in miracles, having seen two with her own eyes in the space of twelve hours, for one of those miracles sat beside her holding Ruchi on her lap.

But what on earth had happened to Eshana? She looked starved, and Laine didn't dare ask why her lovely head of hair had been shaved. As soon as she could though, she'd get to the bottom of it.

As for the other miracle—Adam shuffled around the area with renewed strength, organizing the young Indian men to set up a makeshift camp.

For the past three hours as Laine cared for the little girl and her mother, Adam had overseen the building of a temporary shelter of woven palm leaves. Laine could see the drain this had on him—his white face and slow movements—but still he carried on. A quick glance at his torn trouser leg assured her the swelling had not increased but actually looked a tad better.

While the men from the village and the servant from Lala's house hauled water from a nearby stream, Adam built a fire. Soon after, they had water boiling and rice cooking for those who could eat.

But Eshana was right. With a day or two more of fluids, Lala should completely recover.

Laine let out a soft snort of disapproval. Eshana was as bad as Adam. She too had the strength of a fledgling deer yet she fussed over Ruchi and Lala. It had taken a stern directive from her to make Eshana take food and drink and get some sleep under the woven shelter. Eshana had obeyed, but after only an hour and a half, she rose again to see to Lala's needs. Laine's harrumph did no good.

A lump formed in Laine's throat. *Dear Lord in Heaven, if You truly did bring her back to us, then all I can say is thank you. I...I don't know what else to say.* With an impatient hand she wiped the annoying wetness from her cheek.

A moment later Adam joined her under the shade of the peepul tree where she'd just finished cleaning Ruchi and changing the soiled sari. The little girl who meant so much to Eshana lay curled on a canvas tarp, asleep from exhaustion from a recent bout of purging.

"Will she live?" he asked.

Laine touched the dry, sunken cheek that should be plump and petal soft. "There's no logical sense for why this child is still breathing." She met Adam's eyes. They both knew that with such wretched signs of dehydration the small body couldn't possibly make it. And there had to be a cap on how many miracles God allowed per day. Because it would take an out-and-out miracle for this child to survive.

"The next few hours will tell, I suppose." He rested his back against the tree trunk and lifted one of Ruchi's plaits then laid it gently down on her shoulder. "Poor little thing. There's nothing to do but wait and pray."

"Do I detect a note of exasperation in your voice? About the praying and waiting."

"I daresay you do." He pulled at some long blades of grass nearby. "But believe me, Laine, that exasperation is directed entirely at myself. These past few days have shown me how utterly useless I am at times. The world goes on. People survive...or not, totally independent of whether I'm doing my utmost or I'm incapacitated."

She angled her head at him. "Does this have anything to do with what happened to John? You can't continue to blame yourself for his death." Although she knew his frustration. Didn't she feel the same over waiting for this child to die? The last hours of watching Ruchi fade had dissolved that belief that a third miracle was on its way.

His hand that had been pulling the grass stopped. It took a moment for him to find his voice. "Why do you bring up John?"

"You cried out his name over and over in your sleep."

He looked away as he swallowed with difficulty.

When she and Adam were young and in love they'd finished each other's sentences, but since finding him at the plantation, she could not even broach such a sensitive issue as this with him. They were not much more than strangers now. Still, she'd blundered in anyway. "How did John die? He is dead, isn't he?"

He winced. A breeze disturbed the tall grasses.

"I'm sorry, Adam. I understand how you feel."

He rested his forehead in his hand to massage it. "I don't think you can, Laine."

Her tone raised a notch. "Oh, Adam, how foolish can you be? Of course I can. Did I not weep for you when I thought you were dead?"

His gaze turned dark with wounds. What pain did he still carry from the war that kept him as dead and buried as his cousin? Why couldn't he let go of his cousin's ghost?

If Adam would have decided at last to give her a straightforward answer she would never know. The little girl began to writhe in pain, and Laine turned to the child's needs. It was senseless trying to comfort him. The sooner they could get back to the compound and put some distance between them the easier they both would feel.

Eshana, hearing Ruchi's groaning, rushed to her and held the little one as the child's body shuddered with sickness. "Can you not give her opium to ease her pain?"

"She's too tiny. I can't risk it."

Ruchi took their entire attention, and tired as they were they worked in tandem, washing the small body, massaging her aching legs and arms, checking her saline drip over and over again, and when the child was able to, placing a few drops of salted rice water into her mouth.

Eshana began to pray out loud, "'No evil will befall you. Nor will any plague come near your tent.'"

Laine mouthed the familiar psalm she'd learned in Sunday school so long ago. "'For He will give His angels charge concerning you...'"

As another hour passed and then two, Adam paced. He did what he could, precious little at that. After a short rest Eshana had regained her strength and with expertise as proficient as Laine's, she treated the small patient. The others in their group remained well and stayed away from the area beneath the peepul where they cared for the two cholera victims.

All day long he'd worried over the residents of the plantation, and most especially John. There was nothing he could do...but leave them in Rory's hands...and God's. If it weren't for the nagging worry over John though, he would have felt complete freedom to be here and assist in whatever way he could. Enjoy working at Laine's side.

The afternoon sun blazed down with relentless fire. They could have been back at the plantation by now, and Laine could have been resting in Rory and Bella's cool bungalow. He flicked another glance at her. White with weariness, shadows bruised the area under her eyes. She'd be sick soon too if she didn't lie down.

He rummaged through the truck to find a clean tarp. "Laine." He moved to her silently on the grass. "Come, Eshana can care for the patients while you take a short rest."

Eshana looked up. "Yes, Laine, Adam is right. Rest."

The expected argument didn't come. Laine let him take her hands and pull her up from where she sat under the tree. She leaned against him for a moment, and the desire soared through him to sweep her up into his arms and carry her to a shaded spot beneath a scarlet hibiscus that used to be her favorite flower.

"Only a half hour," she said. "Don't let me sleep longer."

He spread the canvas on the grass in the shade, and she held his hand for support as she lowered herself. Moments after she lay prone she fell into a deep sleep, and he sat with his back against a nearby tree to watch over her.

Birds grew quiet with the heat of the day. He must have fallen asleep as well, and opened his eyes halfway. A pair of dragon butterflies flitted close to the hibiscus where Laine still slept. Her dark lashes cast a smudge of shadow across her cheeks. He watched as with each breath her ribcage rose and lowered, and one of her hands lay under her breast.

Eshana cried out, startling him and Laine. She rose with a jump, and raced over to where the young Indian woman sobbed, holding the child.

His chest went tight.

Laine too started to cry, but then she whirled to him, her face wet, but her wide smile gleaming.

The child's brown eyes opened. "Eshana?" she murmured, "*Amma*?"

Laine ran to him and threw her arms around his neck and laughed. "She's going to be all right. Oh, Adam, she's going to be all right." She left him to return to Eshana and Ruchi, and sank to her knees to examine the child. "She's not entirely out of the woods. But it's worth the risk of taking her back to the compound now."

He couldn't take his eyes off Laine. Far from elegant in her grass-stained jodhpurs and white blouse smudged with red dust, her hair a tousled mass of dark silk, she took the child's temperature and blood pressure, grinning the whole time. She was breathtaking, achingly beautiful.

The little girl stirred as Eshana lifted a cup to her lips. Her mouth, a small pink rosebud, moved as she swallowed the rice water. She no longer looked like an old woman with sunken eyes and gaunt cheeks, but a child who had her whole life in front of her.

His gaze swung back to Laine. She too had her whole life in front of her, and it was time he stopped getting in the way.

29

Laine drove the truck into the compound and jumped down as soon as she shut off the engine. Several of Adam's men saw him propped in the back surrounded by crates and charged at him with excited greetings in Hindi and Tamil. Rory and Bella dashed out of separate cholera tents and sprinted toward them.

The men who'd acted as nursing staff hurried from various corners of the compound. They swarmed Adam, thumping his back and embracing him while others helped Lala and Ruchi from the cab.

Laine reached for Rory's hand, holding it between them as they drew together. Behind them she could hear Adam explain to his men what had kept them away. She could also hear the effort it took for him to speak in that jocular fashion. The energy he'd expended today must be fading fast. But for a few minutes the compound had the atmosphere of a circus. She expected dancing bears wearing pink tutus to come out of the tents any minute.

Rory's blush rose up his forehead above his mask, and he pulled it away, only to clasp her hands in his again. "Laine, my dear, I can't tell you how wonderful it is you're home. I can't imagine ever being without you again. We...I needed you."

Rory's uncomplicated warmth rolled much of the strain of the last week off her shoulders, and she leaned toward him. "We're here to stay. How've you managed?"

She caught Adam from the corner of her eye as Bella piped in, "We managed just fine but were worried sick over you and Adam. The number of cholera cases may have reached its plateau, so we think we're on the downward trend." She gasped as Adam limped closer with his torn trouser leg showing the bruised swelling of his calf. "What on earth happened to you?"

His eyes locked on Rory and Laine and their clasped hands. "Snake bite. Maybe a bamboo viper. But obviously not a fatal dose." He attempted a smile. "Laine saw me through a tight spot."

"Good gracious!" Rory let go of Laine and took Adam by the shoulders. "Right, I want you in the examination hut. A shot of anti-venom won't hurt at this stage."

That was exactly what she would have ordered and mentally blessed Rory.

Adam had gone awfully pale though. "I'm quite all right," he assured Rory. "Laine was a marvel. Had me hooked up to those infernal bottles and badgered me until I shook off the poison." But his wry grin directed at Rory didn't last.

"Well of course she's a marvel." Rory's smiling face included all standing.

Adam held his gaze. "You saw that right away, which goes to show your amazing good sense."

An odd look passed between them as Rory's hand fell from Adam's shoulders. "I don't know about that, but I told you…ages ago she'd be an amazing help to…to all of us on the plantation."

"I never doubted it." Adam laughed.

Laine's ears perked. Was she the only one who heard the hollow sound in his chuckle?

A stiffness came over Rory. He put out a hand to take Adam's elbow. "You're looking tired, my friend. I think—"

"In fact, Rory, she's a veritable inspiration, as you and Bella are." Adam's tone softened. "All I can say is I'm thankful Laine was there when I needed her help, but I'm glad to have brought her back…to you."

At the slight intonation Adam placed on the word, *you*, what little energy she had left, evaporated. All color left her surroundings. Rory's brow furrowed, but Bella seemed unaware of what had just been handed over. Herself…to a good man…from Adam. Reality dashed like a bucket of cold water in the face.

Bella bustled forward. "Adam, you'll do as the doctor orders." She touched his forehead. "Yes, a fever, as I thought. And a high one. That's why you're talking such blather."

Rory, after appearing to have nothing to say, came to life. "Bella, you see to Eshana and Laine, and these new patients. I'll see to Adam."

"I'll leave you all then," Adam continued, but it was Laine he looked at. "You're in the best of hands." He tried again to smile and failed. His gaze slid away. He should feel ashamed, fever withstanding. Passing her off to Rory as if she were a package of toffees. Did he think she was his to hand off?

Bella's sharp voice cut through. "You're going no farther today, Adam, than that hut over there." She gave a nod, and Ranjit and Nandi took Adam by the arm and led him to the examination hut. Rory followed.

Bella turned to the rest of their motley group. "Laine, you're going immediately to bed. And these lambs you've brought—"

Eshana spoke up. "I wish to remain with Ruchi."

"Nonsense, Eshana, you may care for Ruchi and her mother in the hut we've assigned for mothers and children, but not until I've had a chance to examine you. Goodness, you are in need of a meal, aren't you?"

Laine's hands hung useless. His men had taken Adam into the hut, but she refrained from looking back and strode to the bungalow. She'd not deluded herself at any time. He didn't want her. But his fever had removed any polite inhibitions from his ramblings and underlined that fact only too well. The night she thought he was dying she'd told herself she'd be happy knowing that at least he lived. That should content her. Would content her. And if it gave Rory a modicum of happiness to have her in his life... well then...why not?

Why not indeed, Adam Brand? She was tired of being hurt and lonely. So very, very tired.

Eshana had not thought she could slumber so long and so often. The first day they had come to the compound the doctor's sister had examined her.

Bella had clucked her tongue over Eshana's shaved scalp, pursed her lips at her thinness. "You're undernourished and it's a good thing you got out when you did." But though Bella gave her a clean bill of health, she would not allow her to work until she had eaten for three days of a special diet to build her strength. Bella had also set up a cot in Laine's room for her to sleep.

The day after their first night of rest Laine had been full of a thousand questions, and sitting on the cool veranda they spent morning to evening sharing the months they had been apart.

She expected Laine to tease her about her shaved head. But a subdued Laine sat beside her on the swing. With gentle fingers she touched the tufts of Eshana's hair that stuck out here and there like a brush. "It's not long enough to be one of those bobbed hairdos, but you may start a new trend, and shaved heads could become the pink of fashion. Besides, it will grow. Hair always does."

Eshana held back her laugh. "I am not concerned. More importantly, do you have word on Adam's condition this morning?"

Her friend froze but a fraction before answering. "Rory says he's much better. Back up at his own place...so I've been told." Having measured out her words, Laine's gaze darted from the treetops to the canvas tents to the ground.

"You have not gone to see this for yourself?"

"I'm sure he needs his rest. And knowing Adam, he wouldn't be pleased with my intrusion."

A throng of noisy birds in the trees cloaked the silence that fell between them.

She tilted her head at Laine. "I do not know Adam...as you know him. But do you not think that his eyes are as blue as the deepest sapphire in the feather of a peacock? And though his smile holds much kindness, there lingers behind it...a terrible sadness?"

Laine sputtered and stood. "Oh, my dear girl, I see where you're going with this. His eyes like lapis blue or nonsense like that. It breaks my heart what you went through these past months, because it must have addled your thinking. You...Eshana? Noticing the color of a man's eyes? Next you'll be singing the praises of his fine stature...his...his..." She slapped imagined dust from her trousers. "You've got it all wrong. If I have any romantic interest it's Rory."

"The doctor?" *The older doctor?* This she had not noticed whenever she had seen the doctor and Laine together. There was no...*none of that feeling that flowed between a man and a woman.* She had felt it once...at the train station in Amritsar.

"Yes, the doctor, Eshana. And why not?" Two spots of rose tinged Laine's cheeks.

"There is no reason why you should not consider such a man as your spouse. If this is your wish, then I am most happy for you. Has he spoken of this to you?"

Laine grew quiet. "He's mentioned it. Last night. Here on this veranda while you were in the back room snoring to beat the band. Nothing formal...just that I consider him."

"And your answer?"

"I told Rory that I thought he and I stood an excellent chance at rubbing along together. Two peas in a pod as it were." Her smile dazzled. "So what do you say to that, Eshana? To think that months ago back in Amritsar I was as committed to spinsterhood as you. How do you feel about being a bridesmaid at my wedding?"

Her friend's words about Dr. Rory sounded zealous indeed, but they did not match the passion in her eyes when she spoke of the plantation owner.

Eshana glanced over at the treatment center, to the men from the plantation who were most helpful, to the doctor's sister bustling to and fro, and to the doctor himself. Her thoughts flew home to Amritsar and the clinic. To her loved ones there. To her own commitment to spinsterhood.

Laine stirred at her side and reached across to take Eshana's hand. "Eshana, there's something I must tell you. I waited until now, till I felt you were a bit stronger."

She shut her eyes in preparation for what Laine would say. Somehow she had felt in her heart that there was more to this particular valley of testing. Lifting her gaze to Laine, she saw her friend's brow lined with concern.

"It's Dr. Kaur, it's about Jai, Eshana. He's been searching for you as I have. His last telegram said he was on his way to Madras. That was three weeks ago, and I've heard nothing since. Of course the cyclone has hampered communication—"

"Yes, the lines must be down." Eshana's heart began to race. "That must be it." She heard Laine continue to talk about Jai, but her friend's words did not penetrate. Was Jai as lost as she had been? Was he ill and lying beneath a hedge to die like so many of the cholera?

The following day Eshana woke to find that Laine had returned to work. For the first time in many years Eshana had not awakened before the dawn. For most of the night she had stared into the dark, praying for

Jai, and had fallen asleep only before sunrise.

After a restful breakfast that Bella insisted she eat, and then a restful lunch, and after writing letters to Mala, Harmindar and Tikah in Amritsar, to Abby and Geoff in Singapore, and to the women of the Ramabai Mukti Mission in Poona, she yearned to put her hands to labor. Her concern for Jai threatened to overwhelm her, and she grasped hold of the arms of her chair to push herself up. This respite had been long enough.

The temporary treatment center hummed with clean efficiency as she entered the hut set aside for mothers and children. Men from Adam's plantation moved here and there, caring for patients. Bella had told her last night that by the festival of *Pongal* they hoped this outbreak would have come to its end.

Lala sat on the cot next to Ruchi and accused her with her eyes. "I cannot be sitting here any longer, weeping for my husband. I wish to return to my house."

Eshana looked down at Ruchi who still slept. "It is a matter of Ruchi regaining her strength." She met Lala's gaze. "But, my cousin, now you are a widow, how can you be sure that you will not be mistreated as I have been mistreated?"

Her cousin had the grace to lower her head, but found no peace in sitting in front of Eshana and took a few steps away. "For the sake of my child, surely Uncle will treat me..."

"Better than he treated me, his niece by blood?"

Lala pulled her arms around herself as if to protect against assault. "I have been considering, perhaps it is best Ruchi and I go to Auntie Sumitra in Madras. Your mother was most clear on her opinions at Ruchi's wedding. She is believing that we must treat our widows with love, not shut them away, and allow the young widows to marry again. Gandhi has great pity on..." She tried to meet Eshana's eyes, but could not. "He has great pity on child widows."

Eshana viewed Lala. How differently her cousin was thinking now that it was she who would be wearing the widow's course white *sari*. She stood and lifted Lala's chin. "I am pleased that you will not submit to any cruelty. Hold your head up and feel the honor it is to be a woman of Hind. And what is more, Lala, be kind to your daughter. Protect her. Do not send her to her husband until she is old enough."

"But he is a good husband. He is not an elderly man, but a boy only a few years older than Ruchi."

"Still, Lala, do not push these children into the physical union of marriage too soon. Let Ruchi's body grow to be able to bear the fruits of such a union, I beg you."

"*Pavum!* What is this foolishness? Do you think that because you have helped us through the sickness we must listen to you and change all of our traditions?"

Eshana looked away. This arguing against Hindu tradition was like beating her fists against a stone ruin.

Her silence must have disturbed Lala. She sat down in a hurry before Eshana. "Well, then, what is it you think I should do, if you are so full of wisdom?"

"I am only asking that you let Ruchi remain with you until she is fifteen or sixteen." *Dear Yeshu, give me patience.*

"Sixteen—that old?" She must have seen the tightening of Eshana's mouth. "Very well then. I will keep her with me until she is fifteen."

The breath left Eshana's chest in a great sigh. "Thank you, my cousin. I can rest easy for your daughter now."

But Lala had enough of this new understanding, and her whine returned. "When can I return to my house? I am tired of this poor cotton wrap I have been given and desire my *saris* of silk. I have no jewels with me. Not even a glass bangle."

"It is too soon to move Ruchi. Besides, the body of your husband has already been burned, and his ashes will wait to be spread."

Her cousin's eyes widened. "As soon as Uncle Harish hears of Kadhir's death he will cut short his pilgrimage and return to our house. He will not wait for me, but will travel to the Ganges to sprinkle my husband's ashes." Lala's voice broke. "I doubt he will bother to take the ashes of my mother along with him."

"Lala," Eshana said with softness, "let you and me remain here a while yet, and I will pray for the Lord Yeshu to guide us."

Ruchi took that moment to awaken. When she saw her mother and then Eshana her smile shimmered like light upon still waters. She did not look like the little married princess she had been in December, but a six-year-old child. Eshana made a funny face, and Ruchi's eyes crinkled with laughter, until she plopped her thumb in her mouth.

"You are well enough, gem of my heart, to move into the house where I am staying with my friends."

Ruchi's eyes grew round. "You mean that little house over there?"

Eshana's laughter pealed from her. "Yes, my precious ruby, it is not as grand as your home, but it is where your *amma* and I will be for a while, and there you will find love."

She lifted Ruchi, and together the three of them walked out into the sunshine. Eshana led them to the bungalow, and in the bathroom filled the galvanized tub with warm water, scenting it with the bath salts that Laine had set aside. After the child had been scrubbed and dried, scented and dressed in a clean *sari* that Adam had sent over for Ruchi, they went outside to the veranda.

Purple bougainvillea traveled up the walls and mingled with a fragrant cork tree. Ruchi had grown tired with the simple exercise of bathing and dressing, and Lala took her in her arms as they rocked on the veranda swing. Eshana too found all she wanted was to sit and rest in this moment. The Lord had His eyes on each of her loved ones in Amritsar. He knew where Jai was. And He knew tomorrow's plans.

Groves of mango moved in the breeze, and the warm air tugged gently on the silk strands that had escaped Ruchi's plaits. Eshana's heart sang in ceaseless praise for God's mercy. And though her heart was tugged back to the children at Miriam's mission—young Zakir, Ameera, Hadassah, and so many others—she would let the Lord choose her path.

Thy will be done, Yeshu. Whatever gives you the greatest joy is my desire, but please cover each one with your protection.

The creak of a pony-pulled *jutka* coming down the road into the compound drew her attention. A man left the back of the conveyance and came forward to pay the driver. He carried a valise, and after the *jutka* turned back the way it had come, the man walked to the tables in front of the cholera center.

Then he turned to face the veranda. An Indian man, tall, with a straight back and a strong chin and...

The breath left Eshana as the man looked in their direction.

A royal blue turban had covered his hair the last time she had seen him. His combed beard then had been rolled neatly beneath his chin. But the man who walked toward her now had recently cut his hair. Raven black hair ended just above the collar of his English shirt which was tucked into gray flannel trousers. His clean-shaven face showed his lean features and kind mouth that hailed, "Hello, I am Dr. Jai Kaur, I am looking for a nursing-*sahiba*, Laine Harkness."

Eshana put a shaking hand to her head. God had answered her prayers.

Oh dear Father in Heaven, he is alive and well, thank you.

Her joy bubbled forth until her fingers touched the stubble of her hair, a cruel, ugly bristle.

30

There had been no one at the table to the entrance of the treatment center. Jai looked around him at the number of tents and huts. Not the growing hospital that Dr. Scudder had built in Vellore, or the considerable compound of the Ramabai Mukti Mission, but a sizable dispensary set in the thick of a jungle. Though he could see no sign of Laine.

Two women and a child seemed to beckon to Jai from a bungalow on the outskirts of the compound, and he strolled toward them. They had to be recovering patients from their lethargy, and the thinner of the women had recently had her head shaved. The closer he got he could see the hollow to her cheeks, and her eyes widen as she shrank from him.

He introduced himself in Hindi and asked if she knew of Laine Harkness. Instead of answering she hurried down the veranda to go within the bungalow but stopped at the door.

A wave of pity washed over him. "Are you unwell?" He took the first veranda step.

Still facing the door she shook her head. The woman sitting on the swing with the child in her lap sent him an imperious glare. He placed his valise at his feet to look back with a sigh at the treatment center.

The woman by the bungalow door made a half turn, her gaze fixed upon the floor. "Have you traveled far? May I give you a cup of water?" He strained to catch her voice as the rustle of leaves moving in the breeze covered her words.

"That would be most welcome." He took out his handkerchief to wipe his hands. "It has been a long journey. I have recently come from Vellore and I am hoping Laine Harkness can help me find my friend."

"You came all the way from Amritsar...in search of a missing friend? Your friend is indeed blessed by your compassion, Dr. Kaur." She turned her face fully to him.

As though he were a kite, floating on the wind, the string that bound him to earth jerked. He did not move, but felt as though he lurched and spiraled on the current of air. The ground lay far below. Eshana's voice. But how could this poor, frail shell be Eshana?

"Yes, it is me, Jai." She met his eyes. "Do you wish me to take you to see Laine now?"

He let out a wisp of breath. "It is you I am searching for."

Her hands quickened and she gestured for him to sit. "I will bring you water. The road has taken your strength."

His strength had indeed left him, for he could not find the words to stop her from serving him when it was she who clearly had suffered, and perhaps still did. When she returned he accepted the cup she offered. The cold water quelled the parching that had overtaken his throat.

Eshana swept a glance at the woman sitting in the swing who did nothing to hide her curiosity. Eshana still did not look at him directly but spoke in English. "Are you fatigued, doctor, or do you have the strength to walk with me?"

At his nod she stepped down from the porch, and he followed her. Midway across the drive in front of the bungalow he stopped her from going toward the treatment tents. "I would enjoy seeing this doctor's work later. For now, Eshana, it is your story I must hear."

"Of course."

Her simple acquiescence brought him that lurching feeling again. He fought for his equilibrium as they strolled from the compound down the drive. To ward off the desire to assist her in her fragile condition, he clasped his hands behind his back.

"Had you been ill with the cholera?" he asked her.

She did not speak for many minutes, and he seemed to hear each different birdsong, the squabbling of monkeys, the whir of a hummingbird's wings. At last she began to talk, and all sense of the world narrowed and darkened to her experience in the house of her cousins. His fury gathered to a blazing pyre of outrage. How foolish many of his countrymen were to treat their womenfolk in such deplorable ways.

The telling of such an account deserved the reverence of a quiet listener, and with each step he took her story in. Truth be known, her narrative cut off his ability to form words. They reached the end of the drive and stood at the main road.

Still, he was unable to loosen his tongue, and his vision swam with tears.

She comforted him with a gentle hand on his arm. "I am well, Jai. Do not be misled by my—" Her voice caught. "—do not be misled by my appearance. My Savior, Yeshu, has endowed me with greater strength and greater vision than before. That is the way it is with Yeshu, when all seems darkest and lost, he brings life where there was death."

He smiled, and his vision cleared. "It is a joy...to see you. I can only praise Almighty God."

They turned to retrace their steps, and he noticed the sweetness of the back of her neck for the first time. He had never before seen it as her heavy plait used to hang down to her waist. He grew warm at the vulnerable sight.

"Many times, Jai, in my loneliness within my cell, I thought of your blessing, the one you gave me at the train station in Amritsar. Do you not remember?"

"May your devotion to the Lord be perpetual. May grace be showered upon you...and your sustenance be the perpetual divine singing of the Glories of the Lord."

Her smile lit her face like the light of a hundred small lamps. "Your prayer became my truth. My praises to Almighty God and His son were my food. Though I felt the pangs, I did not truly hunger."

She stopped, and lines furrowed between her brows. How was it possible that she seemed more beautiful in her sad and abused condition than when he had last seen her strong and proficiently directing the mission in Amritsar? The mission? Did she know yet of the new administrator?

"I have explained the change in my appearance, Jai. Now you must explain to me why you are not carrying yourself as a Sikh. Why have you cut your hair and shaved your beard? Where is the steel *kara* that you used to wear on your arm?"

With the toe of his English brogues, he disturbed the dust on the road. Before he had left Vellore he had put on his British clothing. He had thought he would be more comfortable in them to search Madras. For many months he had not felt at ease in his own skin—not knowing what God he sought—so that even his Indian clothing felt alien.

"As I waited for the train in Vellore a great heaviness came over me. For some time I have been asking Almighty God to show me if what Sundar Singh has been writing is true. Is Yeshu the true master? I have been praying for a vision of the truth."

She waited for him to continue.

"Before the Madras Mail had come to a stop to take on passengers, I asked Yeshu to show me, should I go to Madras or go first to Laine in this obscure place. I received no vision, Eshana."

"Then why did you come here?"

"A small pull on my heart said to go to your nurse friend, and start there. It was at that moment that I saw my reflection in a glass and I felt ashamed. How could I as a Sikh be calling on the name of Yeshu as if he were God? Until I know if I am still truly a Sikh, I will not dishonor the outward appearance that unites all Sikhs. It was in the train station that I had my hair cut and beard shaved."

Her frown puzzled him. He had thought she would be pleased that he looked more like a Christian. He touched his jaw and winced.

She began to walk again. "Your study of Yeshu must have offended your father. For this I am sad, but I cannot be sad that you are thinking of the Messiah. But, Jai, whether your hair is long or shorn does not make Yeshu love you any less. And the wearing of your turban and the combing of your full beard, as well as the *kara* around your wrist, would bless your father and mother."

Her words halted him in the middle of the road. "Do you not understand, Eshana, it is not only for the study of Yeshu that I have severed my allegiance to my people. I did this for you. I had hoped...that if I found you...you and I could find a way to worship the Almighty in our different ways if I met you on common ground."

She turned to face him.

"Eshana, I have long held you in great esteem. It is your face that I see at night when I try to sleep, and the memory of your voice that stirs me in the morning. I would strive to bring joy to your heart with every one of my breaths for the rest of my life if you would honor me as my wife."

The tears that fell from her face were not the tears of joy he had hoped and prayed for. "You honor me, Jai, as you have honored me before. But I cannot...I cannot meet you halfway. You and I both long to worship the true God with all our being. You have been seeking the Almighty through your Sikh ways. I rejected my Hindu religion many years ago when I put my life—earthly and eternal—into the hands of Yeshu." She clutched her fist to her heart. "I believe as Sundar Singh does, that Yeshu is not another road to God the Father, but that He is the only road."

Wind rattled the palm fronds. A group of women coming from rice paddies nearby walked past them. The kite string that held him to earth yanked upon his soul.

"Jai..." A pleading note entered her voice. "I will not allow you to turn against your Sikh ways because of your esteem for me." Her voice broke. "I will continue to pray that the deepest desire of your heart will be given you—that you discover the true master and join with Him because you are responding to His love."

In the growing twilight more villagers had taken to the road with the settling coolness. A moment ago each leaf, each stone, had been outlined in molten gold with the setting sun, now everything disappeared in a wash of purple and gray. He and Eshana walked back to the compound, but now an extra space had wedged between them.

"I will retrieve my valise and hire a conveyance to take me to the train station."

Her sigh came out low. "It would sadden me to lose the joy of your company so soon. Can you not stay and help with the patients? There are still many."

His sigh echoed hers. A small delight—her presence for a while only—but he reached for it like a hungry man for a *chapatti*. "This would please me greatly. There is still much for us to discuss." Soon he would have to tell her about the new administrator. And Dr. Ida Scudder's hospital. This thought brought a salve to his aching heart. Though she could not marry him, she could go for the schooling she had long desired.

Women holding earthenware jars at their hips walked past. Villagers herded goats and cows home from grazing lots as he trudged beside Eshana to the compound. The tang of wood smoke from cooking fires teased his nose. Though the cholera had hit this area hard, life was returning.

Darkness fell with the swiftness of a curtain dropping. Lamps burning in the bungalow windows sent out a welcoming glow as they passed a banyan tree with its many convoluted roots. Eshana went by the banyan without a glance.

But he caught a smell, coming from within the tree's darkened enclosure. A presence he could not account for. The deep breaths of a living being.

Jai's footsteps faltered, but a tingle at the back of his neck urged him to take Eshana's elbow to hasten her steps. He gave no explanation to her questioning glance. Someone—or was it an animal?—stood within the dark created by the roots of the banyan.

They had almost reached the bungalow, and as Eshana climbed to the veranda he glanced back. In the day the world was defined by textures and colors. At night all had flattened to patterns of light and dark.

As he watched, a silhouette against the wan moon partially emerged from the darkened banyan tree. Not enough of a shape to tell—a large animal? A man crouching?

31

By the festival of *Pongal* a week later, their hopes for the outbreak had been fulfilled. There had been no new cases in the last six days. Laine sat beside Eshana on the veranda swing as they both read their letters that had come in the post. The entire compound lay as quiet as a dance hall after the band had packed up. From the veranda they could hear tom-toms beating in the closest village, but they were too far away to hear the harmoniums and flutes that must be playing, the singing and revelry that would be in full swing.

Only those few patients laboring with cholera remained. Every other patient—as long as they weren't contagious and Rory stopped them—stumbled from their cots, hobbled down the road, or clambered into a cart to join the festivities in their villages.

Seeing Jai Kaur turn up last week had knocked Laine off her pins. He'd stayed, taking up residence at the plantation and rendering his services as a physician at the dispensary. It was wonderful to see him again. And Adam had issued the invitation to stay at his place quickly enough as soon as he'd heard of Jai's arrival.

Since she and Adam had returned to the compound almost two weeks ago, she'd not been invited to the big house. Rory had been up, several times of course, but the only other inhabitant issued an invite had been Ruchi. Adam had driven down in his black Daimler and taken the little girl up to visit Hector almost daily. Which was entirely unfair since Laine was still clearly banned. She chided herself for the green tint that corroded her heart. How could she be jealous of the child getting to see the tiger cub?

She set down Violet's letter and reached for a glass of lemonade on the small bamboo table. Violet was a deplorable correspondent, telling her nothing about the other nurses back in Amritsar military hospital. She glanced at Eshana. Her letters engrossed her far more than Laine's had.

Kicking off the canvas plimsolls, she sat deeper in the swing and let the sun warm her bare feet and shins. With so few patients now, and with Jai helping Rory, she and Eshana could take the luxury of a few days off. Adam stayed up at his plantation, where he'd been most of the time since coming home, but he'd sent a small contingent of men to dismantle the tents that Rory no longer needed.

Ruchi and her mother had gone for a walk to pick flowers. Laine craned her neck to see them down the road. They seemed safe enough, but Nandi had mentioned seeing that nasty little *sadhu* loitering about this past week. They'd heard rumors he'd been stirring up the villagers in the hopes of causing trouble. She didn't trust that old ash-smeared scoundrel one inch.

Finally, Eshana put down her letter, and her gaze also went out to where Lala and Ruchi collected armloads of bell-shaped thunbergia and sweet-smelling spider lilies.

Laine stretched her arms over her head. "Well, what's the news from Amritsar?"

Eshana gave her a wry smile. "What you are really wanting to know is how the new administrator is doing at Miriam's mission."

"Yes, well, quite. It was good of Jai to let you know ahead of time. Otherwise you'd have been terribly disappointed."

"Not as disappointed as you might be thinking. When the cholera outbreak is fully at an end, I will go to Madras. However, not for many weeks. I would like to remain here. If your hosts will allow me to stay longer. Jai has told me of the teaching hospital in Vellore. I am going to apply, and if I am accepted as a student...I will have a new place to call my home."

She couldn't resist clapping her hands. "Eshana, this is absolutely marvelous. Jai has been right all along. You were meant to be a doctor."

"A medical practitioner," Eshana corrected like a prim schoolteacher, but her smile gave her away.

"For now, but you'll be a doctor one day. Well I'll be blown down with a feather. And I'm so pleased you're planning on going to Madras to see your parents at long last. Really, Eshana, I don't know why you haven't written them yet."

The faint smile vanished. Eshana bowed her head and ran the palm of her hand over the soft dark fuzz of hair. "I wanted to wait..." Her hand fell to her lap. "I wanted to look a little more like my old self before I presented myself to my mother and father."

The fragile-looking neck and bowed head plucked at Laine's heartstrings, and she laid her hand on Eshana's. "Your father seemed genuinely concerned about you."

"I am believing what you say," came the answer on a husk of air.

"Then what is it?"

"It is the many years keeping us apart, like a great wall of stones. There was much hurt after my father and uncle left me at the *ashram*. For a long time I held anger in my heart."

"Eshana, your father told me he regrets that bitterly."

"That may be. But so many years...without the embrace of my mother... and of my father. I was but a child when he left me." Eshana looked up at the umbrella trees surrounding the compound, her eyes swimming with tears that refused to fall. "Even with all forgiven, my circumstances have made me a different person...a different daughter. For all my years in Amritsar, it was Miriam who was my mother. How can my parents and I begin again?"

Her gaze lifted to the same leafy boughs that captured Eshana's eyes. "If I know anything of Miriam, she's probably up in Heaven right now, giving you a sound dressing down, saying, 'Stop acting the limp lily and get to work. Mend those broken walls and build anew.' That's what Miriam would say, I'd bet my best pair of working shoes on that."

A chuckle erupted from Eshana. "Laine, your wit is a gift from God. Not only does your training as a nurse bring healing to others, but the joy that bubbles from you."

"I don't know about that, old bean, but you're changing the subject as usual. You're still in a blue funk when things are starting to look up. Is it your uncle that concerns you?"

"Most assuredly not. I will not allow him to take charge of me ever again."

"It's not just your parents. It's got to be Jai. Because he's stayed on? You're in two minds about him, aren't you?"

Eshana's pause put truth to Laine's words. "He will be leaving tomorrow."

"Blast! So soon? It's been like old times with you two working side by side with the patients. You handing him the instruments before he's had a chance to finish his sentences. It's obvious he wants to marry you."

"I have told you why I cannot." Eshana's gentle gaze pierced her.

Laine fingered a loose button on her blouse. "Yes, and I don't know whether to applaud you for putting your faith first, or give you a cuff on the back of your delightfully fuzzy head."

Eshana released a heavy exhale. A woman with a gaze of fire replaced the somber girl of moments ago. "Oh Laine, now is not the time for joking. Do you not realize? It would be much easier for me to say there are many roads to God. The idea of many roads sounds so charitable. But is it loving of me to encourage others in something that I believe will not save them? Or is it more charitable to risk offending people by telling them of the One whom I know has the power and authority to save them?"

The passion in her young Indian friend sent a shiver down her back. "You've never spoken so outright before. I've taken your gentleness for acceptance of other ways to God."

"You have mistaken the gentleness of Christ, thinking that He does not care whether you follow Him or not. Believe me, Laine, His heart breaks for you to follow Him to life. But He will not force this upon you. It is because I love Jai that I have left him—and you—to the freedom of making your own decision to follow Yeshu...or not."

The stillness of the afternoon cloaked the veranda. The industry of Adam's men taking down the tents mingled with that of the sounds of the jungle, the whir of insects, the usual din the birds made, a steady drumbeat from the village. And a sweet closeness to the air. Memories gently crowded in of old Sunday school lessons, and the sense of another...who listened intently to the words that hovered on her tongue before she spoke them. The tender, persistent, but oh-so-quiet presence of the God-man she used to worship as a child.

"All right, Eshana." Her voice came out in soft submission. "I've been sitting on the fence a long time. I'll think about what you've said. I promise."

The engine of a vehicle disturbed the peace of the afternoon. She and Eshana looked up to see who could be coming down the road, as both Adam's vehicles were at the plantation.

Lala screeched, and she and Ruchi dropped the blossoms they'd been picking. She swung Ruchi into her arms and ran shrieking all the way to the veranda. "Eshana, it is our relatives. And Uncle is with them. Do not let him take me. Do not let him do to me what he had done to you." She raced into the bungalow with a wide-eyed Ruchi on her hip, slammed the door and slid the bolt closed.

Laine felt Eshana stiffen at her side as they both stared at the road where Lala and Ruchi had been only minutes ago. The blossoms they had dropped cast a white and purple carpet on the road until a dusty black coupe turned the bend in the drive. Behind that car came the huge gray Rolls Royce belonging to Prince Udee.

She put her arm around Eshana's shoulders. "It'll be all right. The cavalry's arrived in perfect timing in that enormous gray car."

Eshana seemed unaware of her as the vehicles motored up to the bungalow. A man in a high-collared jodhpur coat of white silk sat in the back of the first car, while in the front sat a smartly dressed driver in Indian livery as well as a few servants. From his unsmiling face, the man in the back had to be Eshana and Lala's infamous uncle. And a right nasty-looking specimen he was.

In the gray Rolls that followed, Laine could make out Prince Udee sitting with two others, one of them a woman in a red sari. As the car came closer she recognized Ganan and Sumitra, and red, the color of joy that Sumitra wore—surely this had to be a good sign. She squeezed Eshana's shoulder. *Oh dear Lord, we need you now to smooth things out. Make it a happy reunion.*

Eshana clapped a hand to her mouth to hold back a whimper. "*Amma*," she whispered but remained stock still. "*Appa*."

The Rolls came to a stop, and Udee hurried to open the door for Eshana's mother, but Sumitra, in her red silk and gem-encrusted gauze that covered her head, opened her own door and ran to the bungalow while the man in the back jumped out behind her. Udee smiled up at Laine on the veranda and held out his hands in a helpless gesture.

But Eshana hung back as Sumitra approached.

Sumitra slowed as if she came upon a deer in the forest, afraid the deer would bound off with any sudden movement. She slowly opened her arms. "Eshana..." Her voice broke. "Heart of my heart..." She clasped her hands in supplication. Her tears fell unheeded as she whispered and fell to her knees. "Heart of my heart..." Her hands opened like lotus blossoms.

With one cry, Eshana fled down the steps and helped her mother to stand. Laine's heart beat in rapid staccato as Eshana and her mother embraced and clung to each other, both weeping. Her father stood at a distance, his face wet with tears, while Harish waited with bowed head and watched them from the car. Eshana couldn't speak with the sobs that had overtaken her. But at something her mother said, she moved her arm to include her father in their embrace, and Ganan's weeping matched the two women's in strength.

Laine wiped the wetness from her own face.

Harish got out of the vehicle and stood awkwardly, a man awaiting his doom. At first his expression resembled that of a sour lime, but then tears began to stream down his face. Maybe there was hope for the old blighter after all.

A lace curtain inside the bungalow twitched and Lala, apparently unconvinced that it was safe outside, kept a wary watch on Harish.

Udee strolled toward Harish and bowed over his hands. "It is as Gandhi has said, 'It is good to swim in the waters of tradition, but to sink in them is suicide.' A new day is dawning for India. So let us rejoice with your brother and his wife that they have their daughter returned to them. Let us rejoice, for the festival of *Pongal* is a time to celebrate new beginnings."

Harish nodded through his tears.

Udee joined Laine on the veranda and offered her a clean handkerchief. "Nothing quite like a family reunion, is there?" His Eton accent brought a strangled giggle out of her as she attempted to control her own blubbering. Now if only she could find some peace in her own life.

For the entire day the steady beat of the village tom-toms synchronized with Adam's pulse. The sound of Indian *murasu* drums that he'd heard all his life, for some reason today left him restless. He'd fought to focus on the task at hand, throwing his weight into pruning a section of mango trees with a vengeance until Udee showed up this afternoon.

Good old Udee had brought Eshana's parents as soon as he'd received Adam's letter.

For an hour he and Udee had quietly sat on the veranda drinking lime and soda until Udee went upstairs to visit John. First time in over a year since those two had talked, but Udee had left now, on his way to his father's bastion tucked into the low ranges of the Western Ghats.

Since Udee's car had driven off, the cricket oval held Adam's gaze. He picked up the blue lapis pen Laine had given him years ago. The sun began to set, turning the sky to liquid rose and gold. The remembered strains of music rippled through his mind with an increasing crescendo of piano keys.

As Nandi approached the veranda, Adam's vision pulled back from the memories that continually drew him like bees to nectar. He silenced the pounding piano keys in his mind by setting the pen down with care on the Empire desk.

"We are being watched, Adam, as you suspected."

"The swami?"

"That old fox is rummaging around. But I am puzzled. When I speak with the elders in the villages I am told that they prefer to listen to their temple priests. The villagers want none of the trouble this swami wishes to stir up. Too many of their family members had been saved through the outbreak thanks to the doctor, and our own men kept the village safe from flooding during the cyclone by setting out the sandbags you had prepared. The villagers have sent the *sadhu* away to wander once more. Only a few of the younger, hot-blooded men have followed him."

Adam ran a hand along his jaw. "Right then, since it's getting dark take Motti and Satish, and a few others to keep the perimeter safe. I don't want any incidents stirred up by the festival."

Nandi flashed a white smile. "Do not concern yourself. A few of the men are already armed."

John's voice cut in, "Armed fff...for what?" Though Adam was unable to see his expression, John's tone held a smile.

Adam swiveled in his chair as John came through the den out to the veranda. His cousin hadn't demurred one iota at the male houseguest they'd had all week. He'd stayed out of the way as he did whenever outsiders came onto the property, but Jai Kaur and Udee this afternoon could not disturb John's world at the top of the house. In his room with his books and his gramophone, he'd got on with his daily existence of trying to put his own memories behind him.

"That *sadhu* is slinking about the shadows, John. Nothing more worrying than that. I'm sure he'll be off in a day or two as soon as the festival excitement dies down."

"So that's all it is. Thought another war'd been d...declared?" He rolled back his shoulders. "Well count me in."

Adam motioned with a nod for Nandi to carry on, but directed his words to his cousin. "It's covered, old chap. No need for you to go out in the dark. If you want a spot of shooting we can go out early tomorrow for snipe."

"Quite right. I'm happy to do my bit, but it's sensible ttt...to not have me out in the jungle with a gun at nnn...night. I'm liable to miss the enemy and...shoot me old comrades in arms." John's right eye glistened with laughter while the other eye, permanently shut, stayed hidden behind the mask. The flat painted face looked more like an advertisement on the side of a biscuit tin than flesh and blood.

"It's your vision at night—"

"Nnn...need to explain, old chap. I could always...remove the mask, but my sight is pretty bbb...bunged up. Still though, don't you get ttt...tired of ccc...coddling me?" came the slurred consonants. John took a handkerchief from his pocket and raised it behind the tin mask.

Adam reached for the cajoling voice he'd been using with John these past few years. "Coddle you, old man? Ridiculous. It was you who saved my life. If it weren't for you acting the hero, you'd not have been...hurt the way you were."

"It was war, Adam. Ch...chances of you...making it out with only a few scars was a rrr...ruddy miracle. There's more Tommies...look like me than you."

Adam's jaw turned to stone. John had no idea how that truth hurt. If only he had taken the bullet. "Correct as usual. All the same, what do you say to a spot of shooting tomorrow morning?"

"Righto. Even with one eye I can almost match you for bagging birds."

"You always were the best shot."

"Not ggg...good enough to have stopped that sniper trained on us though. I sss...should have got him before he got us."

There had been no *us* about it. John had thrust him down into the trenches when the shooting had started.

But somehow he was tiring of constantly being beholden to John. He measured his next question with care. "How was your visit with Udee upstairs?" As long as their life at the compound held few visitors, and ran along similar lines day after day after day, his cousin remained his old cheery self. But he watched John's stillness now, often the forerunner of emotions that ran the gamut after the recent disturbances.

"Ruddy cheek he has!" John's voice shook, a different sound altogether from his usual slurring. While the mask hid every expression, he had to be as red as a beet under it. His tone took on a playful pitch. "Udee may be...a prince in this country, but I remember him as only a fff...fair-to-midland cricketer at Oxford. Says I have to join the human race again, and let you rejoin it too." The rueful tone was belied by John's white-knuckled grip on the veranda railing. "We're quite happy, we men, to not have to leap to the ccc...capricious whims of women, aren't we, Adam? Why all of us live a full life here, what with sport... good hard days of work."

A cloud blotted out what had been the beginnings of a new moon. The sickle of white that had hung in a green sky a moment ago disappeared. Adam couldn't find his voice. What was there to say anyway? He did fill his days with work and exercise until he dropped into bed from sheer exhaustion, anything to stop himself from thinking when the breezes blew in like the touch of a woman.

John must have read something in his face. "Are you all right, Adam? You're looking a bit shattered. In my opinion you've been doing too much lately. Let's hope this outbreak is over at last and life can get back to status quo." He slanted a look at Adam. "Any chance that...girl will leave now the emergency is over? Bella's all right...stays out of the way."

"I'm not..." Adam cleared his throat. "I'm not sure what Laine's plans are. It's possible she and Rory may make a twosome. Get married."

"Laine and Rory?" John went still. "Is there to be no peace? I mean it's bad enough for me just having her around, but for you, Adam...it's got to be bleedin' torture. I know what she used to mean to you. Can't you do something?" His voice rose in pitch. "I can't abide...I can't abide... an English girl so close. You've got to do something, for both our sakes. Keep her away."

He strode to his cousin, gripped him by the shoulders, and fought his growing resentment of mollycoddling John. "Calm down. Laine is not Clarice. And haven't I kept Laine out of your usual spots? Haven't I looked out for you? Like you looked after me in the war, and I...looked after you since the war ended?"

John's white-knuckled fists hung at his sides as his teeth chattered. "Yes. Yes. I'm sorry, Adam. You and me are in this together. Like old times. Like old times. Just us."

He dropped his hands from John's shoulders, his voice frayed. "Nothing to worry about. I'll see you through to the last. I'll keep my promise."

"And no flaming fff...female will come between us. We don't need 'em. Right, Adam?"

Still, what answer could he give? Adam sucked back a breath and turned to his desk. He reached for the blue lapis pen and set it back in its nook. A life of peace he'd vowed to John. No females. And most especially not Laine's comforting, scented presence and lilting laughter.

32

Night fell as the village drums continued to send their rhythmic call through the jungle. Laine pulled on trousers and a fresh blouse. From beyond the banana groves a roar broke the silence in the bungalow. She wasn't sure what large cat made that noise, but it had to be several miles away. A moment later from outside her screened window came the chuffing of a leopard nearby. Sounds from the forest were no different than they were any other night, but something had set her teeth on edge.

Eshana's family took care of themselves and their Hindu food regulations. Off to the side of the house their servants lit a fire and prepared a meal. They sat around the fire on cushions, talking and laughing, and Laine couldn't get over the change in Eshana, who giggled and teased like a teenager along with Lala and Sumitra. The little girl danced and played, flitting like a butterfly from relative to relative.

Bella and Rory had done the polite thing and prepared a quiet dinner for the three of them inside the bungalow. But the aroma of cardamom, cumin, and cloves from the family meal outside wafted its way to them. Laine listened to their happiness as if that intangible element lay for her a thousand miles off. She stole a glimpse at Rory across the table as they finished their rice pudding. He was a good man. Attractive in a mature way. Charming to a fault, and she liked him so very much. They could make a go of it, like she'd almost made a go of it with Reese Campbell two years ago.

But she couldn't do that to Rory. He deserved a woman who would love him wholeheartedly. Better to be single than live a lie.

Bella served the tea, and Laine stirred milk into hers. When Eshana went to Madras, she'd go with her, obtain a position in the general hospital. Soon—but not tonight—she'd have to tell Rory.

Their threesome pulled away from the table. Rory sent her a puzzled look and kissed her on the cheek. "I've got paperwork to do, but if you'd like we can take a stroll instead."

"Of course, do your paperwork." She hoped her relief didn't show.

Lines of hurt grew between his brows, and a shade pulled down behind his eyes. He was no fool. And she wanted to kick herself. Why couldn't she take this wonderful man and be happy?

Bella nodded a little sadly and helped Devaram clear the table, urging Laine with a smile to take her tea and relax.

Relax? She rubbed her temple. How could she relax with those drums pounding? With the knowledge that she was going to wound a man who shouldn't be wounded? That when she settled in Madras she would be the length of India away from Abby and Geoff and the children when they eventually returned from Singapore? And once she left this plantation and compound, there would be no reason for her to return, ever.

Outside, a sliver of a moon glimmered through a film of cloud. The conversation of Eshana and her adult relatives around the fire had lowered to a hum. Even the uncle seemed to have loosened up and chatted with Lala as if they had never conspired to imprison Eshana, though they all grieved the loss of Lala's husband. But the little one wasn't there. Probably dancing somewhere in a corner of the veranda that ran around the bungalow.

Laine took her tea to stand at the end of the veranda, giving Eshana and her family privacy. Only the night birds sang. Frogs and crickets raised a ruckus. Snuffles and grunts came from various corners of the jungle. And the drums.

She set her teacup on a table. Where had the child gone? Her family seemed unconcerned. Either they knew where she played, or were too absorbed in one another to notice. Eshana's face reflected the light as she sat around the fire, unable to remove her gaze from her mother's smiling countenance. The way Eshana and her mother leaned together, their hands clasped, warmed Laine's sore heart, but she cocked her ear to listen for the child.

Still no sound.

She strolled the perimeter of the bungalow. No sign of Ruchi.

The time had come to barge in and ask. She marched over to the group around the fire. "Where's Ruchi? I haven't seen her these past twenty minutes."

Everyone jumped up as if she'd thrown a bomb and began to talk at once between calling out for the child. "Ruchi!"

Lala went squealing, "Ruchi," onto the veranda Laine had already searched, which brought out Rory and Bella. Harish started up the car and decided to drive the length of the track and out to the main road. Ganan and Rory began to beat the bushes and garden along with Eshana and Sumitra, all crying out, "Ruchi! Come to us, Ruchi!"

Laine stood in the middle of the drive, her hands planted on her hips. What she'd seen of Ruchi these past few weeks had proven that the little Indian girl was a minx, as precocious as Laine had been as a child. And if she were six years old, and would be leaving soon to return to her home, and a tiger cub lived just a ways up the road...

She grabbed hold of Eshana's arm as she went running to the edge of the jungle, Rory close behind her. "Eshana, you all search this area. I'll take the bicycle and go up to the plantation. I'll alert Adam and his men, and they'll start looking too. She may be up there."

"Yes, of course, she must have gone to visit the tiger cub. Oh do hurry, Laine. We will stay here to look."

In two shakes she found the bicycle. She tore up the road as dark as pitch, guiding herself by looking up at the sky between the flanking trees and calling out for Ruchi. Soon the lights of Adam's house greeted her as they had the first night she'd come. This time no one waited in the garden pavilion. The veranda stood empty as well. No other music filled the night but that of the village drums. They seemed louder in this direction.

"Ruchi?" she called out.

Silence. Only the blasted frogs, crickets, birds. Not a one of Adam's men. Where on God's green earth had everyone gone? But nothing in the house would have interested Ruchi. Only Hector in the barn. It had to be. Laine thrust the bicycle down and cut across the grass. "Ruchi!"

Adam's few horses nickered. The elephants made a few grunts in their stalls next door. She tore down to the end to Hector's stall. Empty. *Dear Lord, where's the child?*

She whirled to view the dark corners of the barn and raced out again into the night. Then her ear caught the tiniest tinkling sound. Like that of bangles. She ran toward the noise. Up the road past Adam's house, deeper on his plantation than she had ever been before. And there at last...Ruchi, leading Hector with his leather lead. The tiger, though still small, had grown. He ambled at Ruchi's side, as tall as the little girl's hip while she chattered to him some childish nonsense. Laine had never heard anything so wonderful. And the tiger cub released a rusty yowl in response. Still though, he was a tiger.

Heaving for breath she stopped and bent to clasp her knees, and let out a croak, "Ruchi, you rascal."

Both the child and the cub turned. Hector padded to her on paws that were still too big for his body, greeting her with his squeaky door hinge of a rumble. The scant moonlight lit his tawny fur to a smoky gray and reflected from his topaz eyes. He'd lost his baby blues.

Laine stood, still working to control her breath. "You might have let on to one of us that you wanted to visit Hector. It's a bit dark out here for a little girl alone."

"I am not afraid. Hector is a tiger, and he can protect me."

She strolled toward the child. "Yes darling, but, even he has a bit yet to grow. You can't expect him to fend off...a hyena for example."

Ruchi let out a small huff. "That is very silly. I know he cannot fight a hyena. But if we run into something ferocious then Yeshu will protect us both."

"Well I can't argue with that. Sounds entirely reasonable. All the same, your mother is off her head with worry. Shall we take Hector to the big house and have Adam drive us back to the bungalow? Eshana and your auntie Sumitra are worried too."

Ruchi ducked her head, and Hector strained at the lead to butt his head against Laine's knees. "I did not mean to worry Eshana and my auntie."

"Of course not, darling." She worked to hold in her laugh at the serious little face. "But let's get a move on, shall we?"

She took the cub's lead from Ruchi and held her tiny hand as they started back to Adam's house. Hector padded beside them, the softness of his fur rubbing against Laine's leg. They could see the lights from the big house through the trees when Hector yanked on his lead.

He stood waiting on the track, his head cocked, ears twitching, and his mouth open to take in whatever scent he'd caught on the breeze.

Laine strained to see into the mango grove to find what held Hector's fascination. She could see nothing. But something was there. Or someone. Was it her imagination, or did she hear someone breathing?

Probably that nuisance of a *sadhu* skulked in the jungle like he'd been doing all week. She nudged Ruchi onward and pulled on Hector's lead. The cub came unwillingly and let out a yowl.

Footsteps disturbed the grass beneath the mango trees, and Hector froze.

"Who's there?" Laine pelted out. "I'll not stand for any nonsense. Show yourself, or better still, get a move on."

No answer, no sound but the village drums, and the hairs on her arm and at the back of her neck stood on end. What ruddy lunacy was this? She pulled both the child and the tiger cub along with her toward the lights but then stopped.

Movement of black on black between the trees. Perhaps she only felt the movement of whoever crept closer to the track where they stood.

But it wasn't a man.

A filament of light from the crescent moon caught the movement of an animal's whiskers as it sniffed the air. Then the silver light set in silhouette a huge head with rounded ears, turning the lighter color of its fur between the black stripes on its face to gray. The scruff of white around the head eased completely out of the darkness.

A tiger emerged to face them on the track not ten yards away. Between them and the house, even if they could have moved.

Ruchi gripped her hand and glued herself to Laine's side. Laine's own heart had turned to water. Yet still it beat, a hollow thumping that covered up all sound. Only Hector's mewling penetrated the air.

Hector? His mother? The tigress Adam had been hunting? The tigress opened its mouth to take in the scent of them and the small cub. Her round eyes caught the trace of moonlight and glittered like ambers.

Laine's hand toyed with the lead, ready to let it drop. If the cub went to his mother, this might distract the predator. Let her and Ruchi run to safety. But if they ran, this would only set the tigress to chase them. She opened her hand. But she'd waited too long. The tigress let out a roar that burst over them, flaying them and stripping them of all courage.

The animal sprang, its feet eating up the short space between them.

Ruchi screamed, and she threw the child behind her.

Only feet away, the tiger's face, its eyes lit from within. Mere feet away. And she stood as frozen as an ice sculpture.

Another sound, an incongruous crack from the house startled her. And another.

The tigress carried on its arcing leap, falling with a thud to the ground at her feet. Laine staggered backward, numb, her heart lodged in her throat. It took a long moment to realize the amber eyes were vacant. Lifeless. The tiger's talons could do them no harm.

She reached for Ruchi and hitched the child up to her hip, her own teeth chattering. But she couldn't move. Couldn't take a step away from the beautiful yet terrifying creature on the ground. But it was dead, and they were not. She glanced up. A man stood on the track, down the road from where the tiger had sprang. He lowered a rifle from his shoulder. She could smell the burnt cordite as he stared at her and Ruchi.

Voices shouted, ricocheting from all directions. Her hand stroked the back of Ruchi's hair, her brain only able to comprehend and hold on to the softness and life in the child's trembling body...the scent of roses and lilies and spices that clung to the little girl's sari. She focused on what she could make sense of—the tinkle and jingle of the child's silver anklets and bangles—as she returned the shooter's steady gaze, noting his English clothes, gray flannels and white shirt.

Someone shouted her name. Adam? Then Eshana and Rory called out. She kissed Ruchi's temple, her mind searching for and clinging to the remembered feel of little Miri and Cam, the way their small arms used to return her hugs. Tears leaked out and dribbled down her cheeks. *Dear Lord, we're alive. Like the child said, you protected us. It was always you, all along, Yeshu.*

People were coming closer. Jai. A whole group of Adam's men. She felt Adam's hand on her shoulder, but kept her eyes on the man down the road. He still stood there, in the darkness beneath a mango tree. Light from a torch reflected off his face. Did he wear glasses? It appeared he did. Perhaps her vision was still blurred. A strange face. A flattish face. The face she'd seen once before in the barn.

Someone...Eshana...reached her and took Ruchi, and Laine wiped her eyes.

"Laine..." Adam took her by the shoulders. "You're all right. Not a scratch." His voice wavered.

"I know." The strength and calm of her own voice surprised her. "I know."

The crowd grew around her, the child, and the dead tiger. The coupe arrived with Harish, Ganan and Sumitra, along with Bella. Rory was somewhere in the hubbub. Their talk tumbled over one another's, and she couldn't make it out.

"She is in shock." Jai's voice rose above the chatter like that of a yard full of ducks.

Adam dropped his hands from her shoulders, and she moved past him.

The tiger cub trailing his loose lead came with her.

"Laine," Adam called out to her. "Don't. Please let him be."

She strode toward the man who had shot the tigress. He turned away and hurried in the direction of the house. "Stop." She softened her tone to a breath. "Stop, please."

With the commotion still going on behind her, she shut out all sound and raced to follow the man. Tall, slender of hip and wide, lean shoulders, she knew that frame. So much like Adam's.

The closer they got to the lights of the house she could make out the dark hair, the way it curled just overlong as it reached his collar. But it wasn't Adam. Adam was behind her. She could hear his step.

"John?" She tested the name. Her voice lowered. "John. You're alive." She clapped her hand to her mouth and swung back to Adam. He must recognize that her silence accused him. He stared back at her bleakly, the truth in his eyes. He had let her believe a lie. What else had he been unable to trust her with?

She ran to catch up with John who had almost reached the veranda. "John, please, we were friends once. Let me talk to you for a moment."

Every muscle in his lean back seemed to twitch, but he halted in his steps still holding the rifle in his hand. He turned to face her. She expected to see the sensitive smile, so much like Adam's, that family resemblance in his brow. But the features before her struck her dumb. The village drums beat to the cadence of a heartbeat. She knew this type of mask well, the tin features so many men wore to cover faces that had been destroyed in the war. Faces that resembled more the mud-churned pits of the trenches than the human visage of nose, mouth and eyes.

"What do you want, Laine?"

She took a tentative step. "To thank you."

"Nnno...need."

"You saved my life, you deserve proper recognition."

"No," came his garbled cry, but he remained rooted where he was, as frozen at her approach as she had been with the tigress.

She gauged her steps closer and touched his arm, strong and viral, sprinkled with soft dark hairs. A bright eye shone from behind the painted face that hooked with a pair of spectacles around his ears. He backed a step away as she reached up to touch the mask. He hissed a breath.

"Laine, no." Adam spoke behind her. He took hold of her arm but she shook him off.

With two hands she gently lifted the mask from John and brought it down to hold before her as she looked.

She bit the inside of her cheek to hold back her cry. If he'd been simply a patient and not someone she knew, she could have acknowledged that Dr. Gillis back in England had done a fair job. The skin grafting had healed. A sort of mouth had been reshaped, a semblance of a nose. But gone was the beautiful face that had been. What pain John must have suffered with operation after operation to create this final façade that he would live with for the rest of his life. His pain weighted her down.

"So there you are at long last." She smiled, handed the mask to Adam and took John's hand.

He shuddered but remained within her touch, his gaze begging her to leave him. But no, that wasn't what his eyes begged. He wanted what everyone wanted.

Inching upward, she lifted her lips to press them against his scarred check. "I missed you, John. I grieved for you when I thought you'd died."

He slumped in her arms and began to sob. She wrapped her arms around him and led him to the veranda steps where they sat, and she rocked with him. "It's all right, old friend. It's all right."

33

Jai waited in the entrance hall of Adam's house with his valise. Last night's ordeal had simmered down. The festivities in nearby villages had ended peacefully. A *sadhu* that Adam's men had been keeping an eye on had disappeared, and the men of the plantation had burned the body of the tigress early this morning.

Last night after Laine and the little girl had been saved, he had briefly spoken to Eshana. Though they had smiled, their short discourse had not revealed the wringing of his heart. She would never be his. As she had explained, a married couple needed to be as two bullocks harnessed by the same yoke. If they were to marry, their different theologies would pull them in separate directions and cause great pain.

Nor had he received the vision of God like the one Sundar Singh had been given. He could not believe in Yeshu without a vision.

In moments Adam would drive him to the train station, and the everyday noise of men working the plantation surrounded him. A few rode elephants on their way out to the forests. He waited for Adam on the veranda, when the shock of pink cloth against the backdrop of green lawn drew him from his thoughts.

The little girl pranced toward the barn. He shook his head. Could no one keep a watch on this highly spirited child? Leaving his valise on the veranda, he strode to follow Ruchi. She made it to the barn before him and had skipped past the stalls to the one at the end. She cuddled the tiger cub as he approached.

Her thickly fringed and kohl-outlined eyes swept him a glance. "I told Eshana that I wanted to visit Hector, but she was taking too long. We will be leaving tomorrow, and I have only one more day with him."

He had no desire to scold her. "You are a lady of great heart to be traveling the road by yourself."

"Last night I told Laine the same thing. I am not afraid." She petted the small predator as it lay sleeping in a corner of the pen.

He leaned his arms on the gate and fought to control the twitching of his lips. "And why are you so full of courage?"

"Yeshu protects me and Hector."

"You are a follower of Yeshu? I thought you were Hindu?"

Her brow wrinkled. "I do not know of these things. But Yeshu made sure we had food for my wedding. And he took me to Eshana when the household was sick." She set her mouth in rigid rebuke.

A chuckle escaped him. This child had an abundance of imagination. "How did Yeshu lead you to Eshana?"

She found Hector's lead and proceeded to attach it to the cub's collar. "I was afraid when I saw the servants being sick." She trembled. "Then *amma* and *appa* too." She looked up at him. "Then I saw Yeshu. He was standing by the window in the sunlight. He told me to come. So I took His hand."

His heart quickened. "*You* saw Yeshu?"

"He took me to the room where Eshana stayed." She turned to Hector who was taking too long to leave his bed of straw, and she pulled on the lead. The cub came sleepily as she opened the halfdoor to the pen.

Footsteps rang on the floor of the barn, but Jai paid no heed to who had entered. He shook his head at Ruchi, and turned to mutter under his breath, "A child cannot see Yeshu."

"Yes I did." She stamped one small foot. "I know his voice, and I know what his face is like. Now I must take Hector for his walk. He has been sleeping too long."

"Yeshu's face?"

"The sun shines through Yeshu's eyes. And he pats me on the head." She pushed past him.

The quickening of his heart increased. This was the foolishness of a child. How could one believe in such simplicity? Yet, he had searched India for a vision, and God had not granted his request. His heart turned hard. Why would God withhold a vision from him, but bestow it to a mere babe?

"You are a very silly man not to believe me. I am not telling lies."

His gaze fell to the child's neatly plaited hair. Could it be possible that God had given the vision he sought to this little girl? Sundar Singh had been only fifteen when he received his vision. And something Sundar said in his writings pulled at his mind. He had quoted his master, about becoming as a little child and believing as simply as a child in Yeshu as the Son of God.

A small noise rustled behind him, and Jai whirled to see who made it.

Eshana had come upon them silently and waited at the side of the pen. A shaft of sunlight pierced the barn roof and touched her new growth of hair, bringing an ache to his chest. He longed to touch her. Protect her. Share his deepest thoughts with her.

She chucked Ruchi under the chin and winked at her. How much of his conversation with Ruchi had she heard? Together they followed the little girl as she led the tiger cub from the barn.

He wanted to broach the subject of this vision with Eshana, but the words would not be loosened. "I am leaving momentarily for the train station with Adam. I am returning to Amritsar."

They reached the lawn, the plantation house on their left, the gardens and lemon trees before them. He walked at her side, so that if he dared he could reach out to her. But she walked, her head bent as if she studied their steps.

Minutes. Less than minutes were all he had. The pressure to speak... to ask...built within him. "Theology is most complex, is it not?" he asked at last.

He kept walking though Eshana had stopped. She hurried to catch up, and he did not explain why he asked such a question. He was not clear in his own mind why he thrust the question out like a flag.

She found her gait at his side again. "Theology can be complex, and yet I have found the words of my master to be so simple a child can grasp its truth before an adult."

This time he stopped short.

She looked up into his face, searching. The fragrance of the lemon trees saturated the warm air around them and mingled with her sandalwood perfume. More of Sundar's words came to him—that a true Christian is like sandalwood, which imparts its fragrances to the axe which cuts it, without doing any harm in return.

Like Eshana.

Like Yeshu, the only god he had ever heard of who allowed himself to suffer and die for those he came to save.

The little girl thrust the cub's lead into his hand. His fingers curled around it, while she ran to play among rows of flowerbeds, and the cub sat at his feet to watch her. "When I was a child, Eshana, I tried to understand spiritual truths. My father told me that I would understand these things when I grew older. Sundar Singh had been told the same as a boy, which set him on his quest for the true master."

"All that I can tell you, Jai, is what my master says from the Holy Bible, 'Verily I say unto you, except ye be converted, and become as little children, ye shall not enter into the kingdom of heaven.'"

"Can it be so simple? Just believe in Him. Change my heart in an instant?" His throat grew raw. "Turn my back on my Sikh heritage?"

She gripped his arm. "You have been studying the ways of Sundar, yet you fail to realize that as he followed Christ, he took on the robes and ways of an Indian holy man, a *sadhu*, and kept his hair long and covered with a turban, his beard uncut and tidy. Like a Sikh." She touched his hair that had been cut. "I say to you, Christ looks upon the heart, not on the outside. Jai, I would like to see you wear your royal blue turban once more."

He took Eshana's hand and looked up into the sun to let the warmth radiate into his soul. *Like a little child. Take Christ. Take the salvation He freely offers.* He saw no vision, only the red of the sun through his eyelids, and heard the song the child sang as she skipped among the flowers, and smelled the sandalwood fragrance of Eshana. Yeshu had sent this little girl and this woman to be his vision to point the way. A wild, unreasonable joy filled his heart. A sudden lifting of his soul.

He opened his eyes to look down into Eshana's. "Yeshu sent you to point the way."

She smiled through tears. "Yes, I know."

"It is the way, is it not?" He looked around dazed. "I am on the same road now as you, Eshana."

She choked on a sob. "I am knowing this too. It takes but a heartbeat to change eternity."

He shook his head. Could his life change so suddenly? But Yeshu *was* the way, and he could only follow the true way.

Adam came out of his house and called to him that he was ready to leave for the train station.

Jai raised his hand in response to Adam, but kept his gaze on Eshana, unwilling to lose the connection to this new elation that flowed in his bloodstream. "The current of my life has suddenly switched. I cannot be returning to Amritsar." He swept a hand through his hair. "I cannot speak with my parents about this new awareness of Christ until I have had time to fully understand it myself."

"Where will you go?"

"I do not know... I must find a place where I can study the scriptures that speak of Yeshu. I will return to Vellore." He looked past her at the treetops. "Perhaps I can obtain a position in the government hospital there. Dr. Ida may know of someone who can teach me in the ways of Yeshu."

He lowered his gaze. "But I fear to leave you now."

Her brow wrinkled. "Why are you fearful?"

"What if this new joy leaves me when I am away from you?"

"If you have truly seen Christ as the savior, then He will capture your heart and secure it. So go to Vellore, and find the truth you are seeking."

He looked over his shoulder at Adam patiently waiting, and back at her. "I must go. But I will wait for you there...to be your friend."

Her eyes shone.

"I will wait for you to finish your studies, Eshana."

She took his hands in hers. "We are on the same road, Jai. There are no barriers between us. And I will go first to Madras, but will write to gain entrance to the college you speak of."

He released her hands with great reluctance. "It is only time then, and I will be seeing you again."

Laughter rippled from her. "It is but time alone that separates us."

He ran toward the black car where Adam had placed his valises. As he opened the door he turned to wave to Eshana standing against the lemon trees and waving. At her feet a tiger cub lolled, and the child in the pink sari had spent herself twirling in rapture and fallen on the grass like an untidy blossom. And the joy in his heart surged.

Sitting beside Adam on the road driving to the train station, that ecstasy continued to build. It was not only for the woman he loved, but for the true Master who spurred him on to love and laughter and feeling truly alive.

Perhaps it was looking into the eyes of a predator that could have killed her with one swipe of his claws that changed everything. Laine sat on the bed in her room, working up the courage to enter the dining room. The early morning sounds of the bungalow that had been such a comfort these past few months no longer brought her the same peace. Or maybe it was holding a shaking John in her arms the other night, and feeling his pain at the loss of all his dreams of love. Or was it the slight accusation she'd seen in Eshana's eyes when she'd told her about marrying Rory that peeled away the last of her lies to herself?

Bella had already left the breakfast table as Laine joined Rory in the dining room. With a smile he set the journal down that he'd been reading, and lifting her cup, filled it from the teapot.

His smile hung suspended as she took the teacup from him and reached across to take hold of his hand, not able to return his smile. The clock on the sideboard ticked. Bella's and Devarum's voices hummed in the back kitchen as they discussed that day's menu. Laine couldn't touch her tea.

Rory placed his hand over hers. "What is it, Laine?"

She shook her head, tears brimming. "It's not going to work, Rory."

Stillness came over him. Bless him, he didn't need more than that to understand. But the cost to him showed in his swiftly lowered head and the catch to his breath. He looked up at her, and cleared his throat of roughness. "I think I've known all along that we wouldn't marry."

She felt tears trickle down her cheeks. "I don't know what to say."

"Don't say anything, Laine. I don't think I could bear to hear why you don't want to marry me—"

"It's not a matter of not wanting—"

"No my darling girl, it's more of you trying to convince yourself that you want to marry me."

She could no longer look into his eyes, but a moment later felt his fingertips lift her chin, drawing her gaze to his.

"Laine, this has less to do with me and everything to do with Adam—"

"No, Rory. Don't." She stood from the table. "Eshana is leaving today. I...I thought it best I go with her. It's not because I feel I need to run away from you or Bella. You understand."

He stood with her. "Of course, dear. We would never think that of you." With his mouth set in a sad line and his eyes dark with disappointment he brought her hand up to his lips. "Thinking of you as my future wife was a bright shining dream for a time. I thank you for that, my darling Laine."

Blinded by tears she turned from him to run to her room. If she couldn't marry a man as good as Rory, there was no hope at all. She had to resign herself to that, and stop tormenting herself with what could never be.

An hour later Laine squashed the last of her belongings into her cases and trunk. Yesterday Adam had taken Jai to the train station, and today he was driving Lala and Ruchi to their home along the River Palar. Harish had gone with them to take charge of Kadhir's ashes and see to the rest of that household. These arrangements had been made to allow Ganan and Sumitra as well as his big black coupe and driver to return to Madras, and take Eshana with them. They had agreed with pleasure to include Laine in their party.

Laine closed the lid on her case and blew out a huff. Adam would be gone for hours, eliminating the chance of him coming upon her final good-byes to Rory and Bella. She squared a straw-brimmed hat on her head, yanking off a trail of silk blossoms that dangled in her eyes. She'd already said her good-byes to Bella, and Eshana waited outside with her parents.

Only Rory waited in the cool, dim parlor. He looked up now as she came into the parlor. "All set, then?"

The beginnings of fresh tears stung her eyes.

He leaned toward her and placed his lips against her forehead. "Don't cry, my dear. We'll always be friends. Dear, dear friends."

"I don't deserve your friendship—"

He laughed. "What utter rot all this talk you and Adam have been dishing out lately—deserving this love or that. Love isn't about deserving. It's simply love. And a deep and abiding friendship is another form of love." His tone grew serious. "Sometimes, as it says in the Good Book, the love of friends can be greater than the passion between a man and a woman."

He gripped her upper arms and his smile returned. "Just give me a few weeks, Laine, to adjust to the idea of what we are not, and what we are, and Bella and I will hop down to Madras and visit you at the first opportunity. You may even drag me onto the dance floor if you insist."

She sniffled. "That makes me so happy."

"What, dancing?"

Her laughter chased the last of the tears away. "No you fool, that we're still friends."

"Always. And we'll work together again one day. You'll see. Now come on." He took her arm, led her to the waiting vehicle and tucked her into the back seat with Sumitra and Eshana. Ganan sat in front with the driver, and their servants sat in the rumble seat.

She turned back when the car reached the bend in the road. Not only Bella and Rory waved to her from the bungalow porch, but several of Adam's men who were finishing the removal of the treatment tents.

Adam would return to his plantation later today, and John still hid himself in Adam's house. But she could not be the one to release them from their self-imposed tomb.

34

Adam pinched the crown of his slouch hat into shape and placed it on his head. The livable temperatures of December and January had left along with Laine. February and March had dragged by, but had left now as well as the blossoms off the mango trees. As the temperature increased each day, the fruits ripened and would soon be ready for picking. The heat in the Madras Presidency became hotter. By May it would be broiling. Everything had returned to the status quo, as John put it, to what it had been before Laine had showed up last November. Had she really been gone now two months?

The only differences were that since the night the tigress had been shot, John had retreated to his room and rarely came down, even for meals.

As for himself, he had the plantation. He had work. And the men, those who remained.

Ranjit had been good as his word. As soon as the cholera outbreak ended he took himself off by train to the Punjab. He'd sent a letter last week, stating how happy he was to have returned to the bosom of his family. Soon after, Vishnu began to talk about returning to his village. Nandi and Motti started making noises in that direction too. Still though, there were enough to remain who needed the seclusion of the plantation.

He strode to the veranda and sank into a cane chair, extending his legs the length of the lounger. Later on as the sun set, the men would come out of their private quarters for a cricket match. Perhaps they'd play soccer or croquet if it was too warm. John would probably watch from his room.

Adam jerked the brim of his hat down to shade his eyes and opened the George MacDonald book he'd been reading, but after catching himself reading the same page three times, he snapped it closed.

If he had to live like a monk for John's sake, the least John could do was stop sulking like a child. Not once since Laine had left had John wanted to discuss her astonishing actions the night of the shooting when she'd brazenly removed the mask from his face. But each time Adam thought back on it, he'd wanted to applaud and yell, "Bravo, good for you, Laine. Best medicine you could give him."

He propped an elbow on the arm of the chair, squeezed his eyes shut and leaned his mouth against his fist. *Dear Lord, she always did have pluck. What am I to do without her? I can't bear it.* But even if he were free, she wouldn't give him the time of day. And rightly so.

"Adam?"

His eyes shot open to see John standing in front of him.

"Are you all…right, Adam?"

"I'll live. Glad to see you made it downstairs."

His cousin went to lean against the Empire desk. Now that all guests had gone, and the chance of a stray female wandering onto the grounds had been eliminated, John removed his mask. He set it on the blotter, and his fingers traced the painted features, the tin nose. "You're not all right th…though, are you?"

"I told you I'm fine."

John looked off to the tops of the mango trees. "Well it's been shown to me that I've been a bit…unfair to you. First Udee, then Rory butt… butting their noses in. For in all honesty, Adam, I believe you and I have been unfair to each other."

Adam's booted feet landed on the floor. "What are you talking about? I've done everything possible—"

"You shouldn't have made that promise to me back when I was in the Queen Mary Hossss…pital. I was too vulnerable. How was I to possibly say no to your…grand offer? Nnn…naturally I took you up on it."

He stood and strode to the railing, overlooking the plantation, the private huts he'd built to give each man a sense of his own home and belongings. "You're my cousin, my friend. I couldn't…I simply couldn't leave you to face the world alone."

"Greater love hath no man…" John's voice rose a notch. "But at what ex…pense? You've denied yourself the love of a wife, a lover. And I'm not facc…cing the world at all, am I?"

Neither of them had to say the name that hovered in the thickening silence.

John went on as if he had spoken. "I didn't realize how you were suffering. Not until...she came. Then I knew. Ttt...tried to ignore it. But then...when I saw her, and she had the boldness to..." His voice grew ragged. "I felt her lips on what's left of my cheek. And I thought, dear God, this is what I'm robbing Adam of...because I'm ttt...too afraid."

A shiver ran down Adam's back.

His cousin came to stand behind him. "I saved you once...when bullets were flying. You saved me from kkk...killing myself after Clarice ran off at the sight of me. And now it's my turn again...to save you. I'm leaving, Adam."

John's tone turned jocular. "Time I went home to old...Blighty, don't you think?" He took hold of the banister and stared out at the cricket green. "Sure it's been grand, but India's not my home like...it's yours. Had a letter from my old mam—"

"What?" He swiveled to face John.

"Appears she and the old ppp...pater want me home. I've told them that me 'andsome mug ain't what it used to be. But you know the manor. Big as a barn. I can live out my days in peace and...quiet with them. So what do you say, old man, shall we call it quits, and I go home to England?"

"Call it quits? Leave what we've built together?"

"Pish posh. This was your dream. I bbb...barely know...difference between a banana and a...mmmango. And Udee was telling me of other chaps back home. With faces like mine. Or lack of. They watch out for one another, even got a few prrr...ivate communities for us to live in. But truth is, Adam, I wanttt...to go home. At least there I can get a decent cuppa. None of this Indian *chai* stuff with spices and butter...you prefer."

The wind had gone out of Adam. He gripped the veranda railing for support.

John placed a hand on Adam's shoulder. "Rory put in his two cents as well. Said it was time to start acting like Lazarus and let the Lord raise us from the dead."

Adam couldn't stop the chuckle that came out of him. "Since when did you start discussing doctrine with our revered doctor?"

"Oh cccc...come now, as a boy...went to church faithful as a lamb. I've had plenty of time to ponder the meaning of life and ettt...ternity." He pulled back from Adam and put out his hand. "So what do you say...shall I quit India?"

Adam took his hand and squeezed it. "I'll miss you, John."

"Of course you will, old chap. Bbbb...but I'm rather hoping...you won't be lonely for long."

The headline splashed across all the newspapers. Gandhi had been arrested.

Laine reclined in the claw-footed tub in the nurses' quarters, propped her feet on the edge, and blew a frothy mound of bubbles away from the newspaper. With any luck she'd have the bathroom to herself for five blessed minutes without some other nurse banging on the door.

Since she'd returned to Madras, the first thing she'd run into was the general strike in opposition to the Prince of Wales's visit. No matter how Gandhi pleaded for non-violence, violence had indeed escalated in the town of Chauri Chaura. A gang of men attacked the police station there, killing twenty-one policemen. But arresting Gandhi was a rotten shame, really. Locking him away for a few years would not endear the British government to the Indian people. Only rub salt in the wound, in her opinion.

She threw the newspaper onto the floor, and wiggled down into the bubbles to wash her hair with the peony-scented shampoo she'd become so fond of back at the compound. The fragrance only made her miss Rory and Bella, but it washed away today's weariness from the surgical wards. She was under the water rinsing suds from her hair when sure enough someone hammered on the door that there was a message left for her.

If she weren't the peace-loving individual she was, for tuppence she'd happily throw a wet sponge at the offender. But in a syrup-drenched tone she requested that the blighter of a nurse slip the message under the door.

She got out of the tub, dripping. Wrapped in a towel, she bent to read the note and gasped.

Prince Udee and his wife, Innila, requested her presence for dinner this evening at their palace by the sea. They were sending a car for her at seven. She put a hand to her wet hair. Great leaping elephants, it was six-thirty now. When had this message arrived, or did Udee think it a lark to give her only half an hour to prepare for a visit to his palatial home?

In this heat, dashing around her room dried her hair quickly enough while she applied rouge to her lips and cheeks, and added kohl to her eyes, Indian-style. She pulled on a pair of sheer stockings and garters, and slipped the close-fitting slip over her head as a knock came to the door.

It was one of the nurses. "A great boat of a Rolls Royce has arrived downstairs. So what's up, Laine? Got a bleedin' maharajah taking you to tea?"

Laine threw a pillow at the girl's head, and pulled on the sheer voile overdress. Strange that Udee hadn't given her the opportunity to accept or decline. Still, it didn't matter. This was the first social event she'd accepted since coming back to Madras, not counting her visit to Eshana's family home last week, the Jasmine Palace. It was absolutely glorious to see Eshana so happy, planning her studies, and her reunion soon with Jai in Vellore.

Darkness landed with the softness of an egret on water as the Rolls entered the palace grounds. Torches lit the drive along splashing fountains and the canal that linked them to the front of the palace. Udee dashed down the steps that ran the width of the mansion when his driver pulled up with her in the back.

The usual mob of servants came with the prince as he personally assisted her from the vehicle. "So good of you to come on such short notice, Laine."

"I'm assuming you've invited an odd number to your table and thought of me to even the numbers. I'm delighted to see you as always, Your Highness."

"Nonsense, as our special guest this evening, it is you who honors us. And you must stop calling me your highness. The family's been deposed, remember?"

Udee was his charming, mischievous self, but the kindness of this good man frayed a nerve she didn't know had shredded quite so much. Her throat swelled with the desire to cry.

"My goodness, Udee, you're good for a person's sore heart."

"Has your heart been sore?"

She clutched his proffered arm. "Not any longer. I'm so happy to see you and Innila."

He gave her an odd look, but kept his thoughts to himself and escorted her into the vast, echoing foyer. Innila waited by the base of the curving staircase.

The chandelier suspended above cast glittering light on Persian carpets, gold inlays on the walls, and the sheer drapery in rose, vermillion, and scarlet. It all brought a flutter of sensuality to the base of Laine's spine. Perhaps it was the exquisite midnight blue and silver sari draped around Innila, or Udee's fingers cupping his wife's bare waist. Or memories of the last time she'd visited, but of course not. She was all past Adam.

"It is most lovely on the beach this evening," Innila said with a smile. "The air is as warm silk tonight."

Udee extended his hand to show Laine the hall that would take her through the house to the beach, and to the covered walkway that led to the pavilion overlooking the surf. "Dinner will be served out there. Won't you go on, and we will join you...shortly."

She crinkled her face in confusion at them. They both seemed to suppress an excitement. Perhaps they were expecting a baby at long last, they were beaming so proudly. But if they wished her to proceed to the pavilion first, then so be it.

The sound of surf pounding the shore met her halfway down the wide gilded hall, growing louder as she went through the French doors. Her heels clicked on the marble pathway that led to the pavilion at the end, where the surf sprayed as a backdrop at frequent intervals. A small circular table had been laid. On the tablecloth that fluttered in the breeze, a crystal globe had been filled with flickering candles. A spray of scarlet hibiscus spread over half the table. But only two places had been set with velvet chairs and gold fittings.

She strolled to the pavilion's railing. The beach below lay like a strand of white sugar in the moonlight. Its surf frothed and glowed phosphorescent in the dark as it crept upwards and dissolved with a hiss into the hard-packed sand. The breeze scented by frangipani rustled the palm leaves.

Still no one came, except for a servant who offered her a glass of mango juice from a golden tray.

She smiled wryly at the beverage. She'd never be able to look a mango in the face again and not think of Adam. With his sharp mind, his care for the villagers, and those blue eyes that skewered her—he'd ruined all other men for her. Listening to the surf overtake the beach and recede with perfect rhythm back into the depths only to push forward again and again, filled her senses with longing. For him.

As if she'd conjured up the sound with her thoughts, a gramophone began to play from inside the pavilion. Another silent servant had started up the recording of Rachmaninoff's *Second*, only increasing the longing that held her in a vise. Rachmaninoff? Truly? Would the entire evening drown her in memories?

Then over the surf she caught the sound of a squeaky yowl. Down the beach, beneath a sky of black velvet dotted with diamonds, a man in a white evening jacket and black trousers walked with an animal on a lead padding beside him. The moonlight captured the animal, turning the tawny spaces between the black stripes to a pearly gray.

Of its own volition her hand clapped to her mouth. What cruel joke was this? She was as amiable as the next person to take a joke, but this was too much.

She turned to hurry back into the house and seek Innila's company. She'd almost made it the full length of the walkway when Adam called out, "Wait, Laine, wait. Please."

He was running now, Hector bounding easily beside him along the surf. A wave caught them and drenched Adam's shoes and the lower half of his trousers. He paid no heed but hurried up the steps to the pavilion, tying Hector to a marble urn.

A strand of hair fell over, almost into his eyes as he turned to her. He breathed heavily, but surely not from running when he had such stamina.

"What's going on, Adam? Is this little rendezvous something Udee cooked up?"

"I arranged this. Udee and Innila were only too happy to help."

"You?"

He glanced at the table. "I wanted a private place to have dinner...with you. A chance to talk."

"To talk? What is there left to talk about? You practically shoved me into another man's arms. You didn't trust me enough to tell me what had happened to John. But in all truth, you really don't owe me an explanation. You ended things between us civilly three years ago, not kindly but civilly. So pay no mind to my emotions that seem to be running away with me."

"Are they, Laine?"

"What?"

"Why are your emotions running away with you?"

"Well now it's your turn to wonder, isn't it?"

She rushed past him to the steps leading down to the beach. Her heels dug into the deep sand, making it impossible to walk, and she bent down to wrench off her shoes. She stalked off, following along the surf. The sound of the waves drowned out the noise of Rachmaninoff's building concerto. But before she'd gone far, a hand reached for her elbow. She swung round to Adam and gasped at the despair lining his face. But his misery could only be mirroring her own.

"Stop, Laine. I do not mean to hurt you ever again." He inched closer and took her by the upper arms.

She shirked off his hands. "You certainly have your nerve. Never hurt me again? Nothing you could say would make me believe that, considering what happened the last time we were here."

"I deserve that. But it's true. For the life of me, I can't bear to see you hurt. But I have no way to convey...all the poets, all the poetry in the world, they're but dry...empty words—"

"Poetry!" She dropped her shoes that she'd been carrying into the creeping waves. "You're absolutely right about that. A sentence or two of no-nonsense words would be refreshing for a change."

"I don't deserve...a second chance with you is more than I—"

"You're spot on there." Rory's words rang in her head. What did deserving have to do with love? But she hardened herself against the etching of pain on Adam's face, the way he let his hands drop to his sides in defeat. Still the words were wrung out of her, "Why, Adam? Why?"

"I was wounded. Not physically. But Laine, I *was* wounded."

She bit down on her lip.

"It wasn't just my men...and John. When I saw my men wounded. When I held them. It hurt terribly, Laine. The only thing that helped me was to take care of them. Give them a refuge."

"You don't have to explain, Adam. But you seemed to have forgotten. I also held the dying in the trenches, and felt that pain. I dream of them at night, those young men, those boys."

He winced as the shadow of a nightmare passed behind his eyes. "That's what shames me the most. How utterly foolish of me to try caring for them on my own. To take on John's anguish as my own. As if I could heal them all, and myself. Alone. I thought I had to do it alone. It sounds so infantile when I think of it now." His arms hung at his sides.

She stood transfixed.

"Wounds, Laine, they take time to heal, don't they?"

With her eyes closed she could almost hear the barrage of artillery, the cries of men she'd treated at the bottom of mud-filled trenches. No one but Adam could have mended her heart. He'd always been a part of her.

He searched for words. "It took you to come uninvited to the plantation. To heal, I needed you. And my men's wisdom—they're showing me the way, as one by one they make their plans to leave." He raked his hair off his forehead. "Oh dear Lord, give me the words to say. But Laine, so few words are needed. I love you. That's all. I never stopped loving you. It's been torture to try and exist without you in my life. I can't explain how much..."

"If you'd only had the gumption to trust me." She closed the space between them. "I could have helped. I would have joined the two of you anywhere in the world and been John's friend as well as your... I would have willingly come to the plantation and helped with all your men."

He looked so broken. She couldn't bear to let him suffer a second longer and took his hands. "You hurt me deeply, Adam, but as you say, wounds do heal. I've had enough time. Three years too much. All I need is the truth between us."

A quiver ran through him, and he squeezed her hands that were holding his, not knowing how hard he gripped her. Her fingers throbbed, but it didn't matter. Neither she nor Adam removed their gaze from each other. This was Adam. The fool may have broken her heart, but he was the man who had held her heart from the time she was twelve. How could she let the poor man stand there in his misery?

She reached out to take his face in her hands, and pulled his mouth down to hers.

He gasped and didn't move at first. And then he placed a hand around to the small of her back to pull her close. His lips brushed hers, and when the waves reached her ankles he returned her kiss in full.

She wound her hands up across his shoulders and touched the collar of his shirt and the hair that touched the back of his neck as he pulled her closer yet. She moaned against his mouth. His hand moving along her back and up her spine drove her mad with yearning. Dear Lord, she didn't have the strength to let him go again. What if his kiss meant nothing more than just the physical attraction they'd always had for each other?

With that thought the soft night turned cold, the waves that moments ago were warm and swirling around her ankles turned frigid, and she backed away.

He let her go, a flinch forming around his eyes. "What is it, Laine?"

"What does this kiss mean exactly?" She heard the plaintiveness in her voice. Felt the emptiness within her if he were to leave her again.

"It means I'm laying my heart on the line. I want to marry you. Dear God, Laine, put me out of my wretchedness. Let me try to make you happy."

"What about John?"

"He's going home to England."

Far off the tiger cub yowled as the news about John sank in.

"The future is just you and me, Laine, and what God wants to do with that." A strain of desperation thickened his voice.

The breeze rattled the palms. A hint of jasmine mingled with frangipani. Waves that eddied around her ankles and then her knees turned warm again as renewed hope wound its way up to her heart. That new tingling warmth worked its way up her thighs to the center of her body to her arms and fingertips caressing the back of his neck.

A moment later she released a shallow breath. Loneliness drifted away with the receding wave while another rushed in moments later with her growing desire to give love and receive love. They'd both seen too much suffering. Suffered too much in their own right. It was time to grasp joy with both hands.

She wrapped her arms around his shoulders as he pulled her closer, and their lips exchanged a sweet, deep growing hunger that would take a lifetime of marriage to fill.

"All right, Adam Brand." She said against his lips, and took a step from him. "You've made some mighty blunders in your life, but the answer's a resounding yes."

Another yowl from Hector on the pavilion drew a shaky chuckle from her.

Adam's eyes lit, but he didn't get a chance to speak as Hector emitted a heart-rending growl, and hauled with his might, pulling the marble urn off the balustrade where it crashed to the floor. The tiger cub bounded toward them and splashed in the waves. When he reached them he wound his soaking wet and sand-encrusted body around their legs.

She stooped to rub Hector's head and ears with hands that still shook with desire for Adam. "You know, darling, he really is getting big. When are you going to release him?"

"When he's ready to fend for himself," Adam answered in a whisper as quaking as hers. "I can't just shove him out without preparing him for a life on his own." Laughter lay just below Adam's words as he stroked the valley at the small of her back.

She stood to face him. "I see. But I don't quite understand why you brought him to dinner at the palace in the first place. I can't imagine social events like this are really the training he requires for taking care of his own matters."

Adam's laughter sputtered out of him. "I see your point. But I'm afraid I had other reasons for bringing him this evening."

"Well I was wondering. While I'm thrilled you brought Hector along, I'm not sure how he can help if your purpose was to woo me."

Adam slanted a lop-sided grin. "I thought if I flopped in the romance department—which was highly likely—then Hector would soften you up."

She let out a belabored sigh and leaned against him, placing her lips against the base of his neck. "And a good thing you did. That proposal of yours...all I can say is for a man with a First in literature from Oxford, you were sadly lacking in eloquence."

He lifted her face to his and touched his smiling lips to hers, muttered softly. "I know, shameful, isn't it? I'm sorry, Laine, I'll work on doing better in the future. I promise after we're married to quote poetry in your ear while we dance slowly every evening. Will that suit?"

The tiger cub leapt in the waves, and the moonlight shone over the Bay of Bengal as she wrapped her arms around Adam's neck. "Darling, your proposal was perfect. Couldn't have proposed better myself. I recognize the signs of the old flame, of old desire too, you know. But I give you fair warning, poetry, slow dancing, and kissing will do only for a start."

Acknowledgments

No man is an island entire of itself. No book is written by solely one heart and mind. In the acknowledgments for *Shadowed in Silk*, Book 1 of this series, there was a terrible oversight on my part. I had always meant to correct that oversight with the release of Book 2, but sadly publication came a little too late for the person I wanted to honor.

John Affleck, husband to my dear friend, Marlene Affleck, passed away just before Christmas 2012. John and Marlene had spent many years serving in Pakistan as missionaries with their children. Before the Indian independence in 1947, Pakistan used to belong to India. It was John who inspired me with his sadness over the birthing pains of the new country, Pakistan, as it was wrenched away from India. I still have several of John's books on the history of India. Books he never seemed to be in a hurry to retrieve, because that was John's way. I'd also like to thank John and Marlene's kids for their memories of Pakistan, and especially of their childhood camel rides which make up a big part of *Shadowed in Silk*. And to Marlene, whose sweet spirit has always been such an encouragement to me.

The other two I'd like to thank are my birth-daughter, Sarah, and her husband, Mark Blaney, for their dedication to Christ. When I relinquished my first child to adoption when she was three days old, I trusted that God would redeem a special relationship for Sarah and me. Twenty years after her adoption, Sarah and I were reunited. But as the years have passed, my breath is taken away by God's tender goodness to me as a birth-mom. Sarah is a nurse and currently serving the Lord in full-time missionary work with Global Aid Network: http://globalaid.net

As I was writing *Shadowed in Silk* and then *Captured by Moonlight*, I had not shared with Sarah that the true-life heroine behind my Indian Christian characters was Pandita Ramabai. Months later, my heart swelled with awe as I listened to Sarah and Mark share that they felt called to serve in full-time missions, and that within their sphere of interest would be the Ramabai Mukti Mission in India. Only a very tender-hearted heavenly Father could entwine our hearts and callings in such a special way.

The rest of my thanks goes to my critique partner, Rachel Phifer, an inspirational author whose insights bless my writing and life. Thank you also to Roseanna White and Dina Sleiman of WhiteFire Publishing for your wonderful hand in editing *Captured by Moonlight* and in designing the cover. And to Eric Svendson for your lovely photographs of the front cover model.

A huge thanks to my beloved family—my mother Sarah Lindsay, my brother Steve Lindsay, for your constant assistance in research and brainstorming. To my sons Kyle and Rob, and a very special thanks to my beautiful daughter Lana who is the model for the front cover for *Captured by Moonlight*.

Lastly, but absolutely not the least, to my husband, David—you are still the inspiration behind every hero I write. And to our sweet doggy, Zeke, who kept my feet warm when he lay at them when I wrote. Zeke baby, you gave us ten wonderful years.

Author's Note about Ramabai

My Love of India came from so many sources, but I'd like to name three of the true-life heroes who did so much for the suffering in India—Pandita Ramabai, Dr. Ida Scudder, and Sundar Singh. Being so inspired by these giants of the Christian faith in India, I could not write my series, Twilight of the British Raj, without placing these real persons between the scenes. It is my prayer that my fictional story around these persons will honor their memory and their continued work today.

When I was a girl I read a book about a young woman in India who desired to become a doctor to help her fellow women. This young woman received her education from the Vellore Hospital built by the great American missionary, Dr. Ida Scudder. Dr. Ida's teaching hospital is still one of the largest private hospitals in Southeast Asia. You can learn more about Dr. Ida from this website http://www.cmch-vellore.edu.

What I have written about Sundar Singh in *Captured by Moonlight* is taken from his biography and his various writings. This former Sikh who became a Christian did travel over all of India and parts of the world as the yellow *sadhu* in his desire to share the message about the true Master, Jesus Christ. I am always inspired when I read of how another person from such a diametrically different culture as India sees the Lord Jesus Christ, the God of all.

Lastly, my very favorite Christian Indian heroine, Pandita Ramabai. http://www.mukti-mission.org/default.htm. This beautiful woman, a former Hindu widow, found Christ while reading some of her husband's books. When she realized that Christ fulfilled all of her desires for God, she devoted her life to His service. Her compound, giving a home and education to young girls that had been cast off for being Hindu widows or abused children, is still in existence today.

Discussion Questions

1.) A line of poetry runs through Laine's mind at the beginning of the book...*little, nameless, unremembered acts of kindness and of love...* The Lord often speaks to me through nature, especially my garden. Aside from God's Word, has He ever used other things to speak to you?

2.) Jai gives Eshana the following Sikh blessing. "May your devotion to the Lord be perpetual. May grace be showered upon you...and your sustenance be the perpetual divine singing of the Glories of the Lord." This is obviously not a Christian blessing, but Eshana receives it in a spirit of understanding and acceptance even though she is totally devoted to Christ. Why do you think she does this?

3.) "Wounded men still lived. Though they may not want to." In that line running through Adam's head, he gives a strong hint about what has captured him. I've had loved ones in my life—including myself a long time ago—who had no desire to continue living. Suicide or hiding away seems an easy way out for some people. But neither of these actions please God. Why does God not want people to give up?

4.) Eshana raised her hands palm upward, beseeching. "I have much work to do. Why do you lock me away when I could be working for your Kingdom?" Have you ever felt this way—that God has locked you away from the good work you want to do for Him, by giving you a painful illness, or a boring day job just to pay the bills when your heart desires to do something of greater value for His kingdom?

5.) Uma reminds Jai what Sundar Singh wrote in his book, that a true Christian is like sandalwood, which imparts its fragrance to the axe which cuts it, without doing any harm in return. This Christian truth is written in beautiful Indian sentiment. How do you compare this to what our Lord did for us on the cross? How does this metaphor relate to how Christ wants you to react when others hurt you?

6.) Adam says, "There are many beautiful elements to the various faiths. But during the war one element about Christ stood out for me in the trenches as I saw men dying...getting terribly wounded...in their attempt to save one another, as if they were imitating something holy. 'Greater love hath no man than this, that a man lay down his life for his friends.' These words stop me in my tracks from turning to other beliefs. No other god but Jesus laid down His life for others. And that speaks truth to me."

Again, this fact that we come up against—what will you do with this God who died for you?

1Cor 15:1-4 "*The gospel is that Jesus Christ died for our sins according to the Scriptures, that He was buried, and then He was resurrected on the third day.*"

7.) *Beloved, are you ready to die, as I died? Are you ready to cease striving, cease fretting? Are you ready to say as I had said, "Not my will, but Thine, heavenly Father"?Come, light of my eyes, be one with the Father and with me. You have believed. You have been buried with me. Now walk with me in newness of life, for I am the resurrection.*

This is the whole reason for this book. Christ saves us not only for our salvation, but for His purposes. Eshana wanted to do what she thought would serve God well, but He had other plans. Are you starting to understand the metaphor of Eshana's funeral clothes? Have you fully "died" to yourself so that Christ may live His life through you?

8.) Throughout the book, Jai had been looking for a vision, for God to talk to him in some stupendous manner. But as Jai opened the car door he turned to wave to Eshana standing against the lemon trees and waving. At her feet a tiger cub lolled, and the child in the pink sari had spent herself twirling in rapture and fallen on the grass like an untidy blossom. And the joy in his heart surged.

In my opinion as the writer, this is Jai's vision from the Lord. What metaphors do you see in the child twirling and playing in complete trust, and the tiger cub beside her? What scriptural truths to you find in these images?

Don't miss the final installment of
Twilight of the British Raj

Veiled at Midnight

Coming February 2014!

Twilight of the British Raj
~ Book 1~

Shadowed in Silk

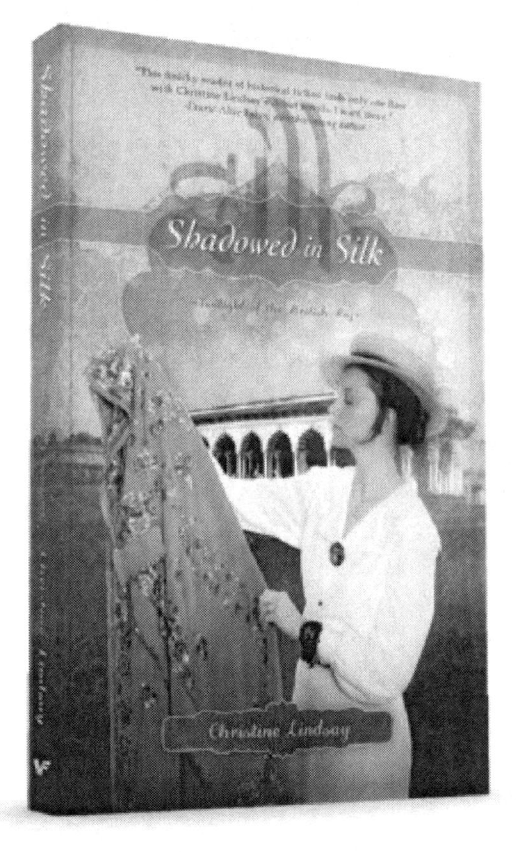

Available now!

Other Titles from WhiteFire Publishing

Dance of the Dandelion
by Dina L. Sleiman

Love's quest leads her the world over.

Jewel of Persia
by Roseanna M. White

How can she love the king of kings
without forsaking her Lord of lord?

A Stray Drop of Blood
by Roseanna M. White

One little drop to soil her garment.
One little drop to cleanse her soul.

Walks Alone
by Sandi Rog

A Cheyenne warrior bent on vengeance.
A pioneer woman bent on fulfilling a dream.
Until their paths collide.

Trapped: The Adulterous Woman
by Golden Keyes Parsons

A trap has been set...by her own foolish heart.

CPSIA information can be obtained at www.ICGtesting.com
Printed in the USA
LVOW13s0758300813